D

TROUBLE [MAKERS]

Harlan Ellison (whom *The New Yorker* calls "a non-stop controversialist who comes on like an angry Woody Allen") is a very special kind of writer. If this is your first encounter with him, defend yourself from attacks on your world-view. Because he is the only one who can write Harlan Ellison Stories. His friends, outstanding fantasists like the legendary Theodore Sturgeon, Hugo/Nebula winner Roger Zelazny, A.E. Van Vogt (whose fame in France rivals that of Steinbeck's), "Psycho" author Robert Bloch, *Edgar*-winning novelist Henry Slesar and the swashbuckling writer/adventurer Robert Sheckley, are also special. What they do, no one else can do. But can they work together on the same story? What happens when Ellison mixes with the antic Avram Davidson? What comes out when talents as clearly different as Ellison and Van Vogt write together? How do you categorize the hybrid produced by the coolly scientific Ben Bova and the irrationally visceral Ellison (in a story whose plagiarization by ABC-TV and Paramount Studios won a Federal District Court judgment for the authors in the amount of $337,000)? And how well do two dominating personalities such as Silverberg's and Ellison's get along in the same story-line? *This book will tell you!*

BOOKS BY HARLAN ELLISON

- ■ Available in Ace Books editions.
- ● Forthcoming in Ace Books editions.

HARLAN ELLISON

PARTNERS IN WONDER

IN COLLABORATION WITH

Robert Bloch
Ben Bova
Algis Budrys
Avram Davidson
Samuel R. Delany
Joe L. Hensley
Keith Laumer

William Rotsler
Robert Sheckley
Robert Silverberg
Henry Slesar
Theodore Sturgeon
A.E. Van Vogt
Roger Zelazny

and unassisted

ACE BOOKS, NEW YORK

PARTNERS IN WONDER

An Ace Book / published by arrangement with
the author

PRINTING HISTORY
Ace edition / March 1983
Second printing / April 1983

ISBN: 0-441-65205-0

Ace Books are published by The Berkley Publishing Group,
200 Madison Avenue, New York, N.Y. 10016.
PRINTED IN THE UNITED STATES OF AMERICA

this book is dedicated—
with a little help from
our friends—to

JUDY-LYNN DEL REY

for kindnesses remembered

CONTENTS

SONS
OF
JANUS

INTRODUCTION

These are stories I have written with other writers. Collaborations, they're called. They are the products of two minds working together, sometimes in complete harmony, more often in opposition. The former, because the ideas were so right they needed no conflict to produce a coherent whole; the latter, because writers are perverse creatures who enjoy tormenting one another. And also, conscious opposition on the part of one of the collaborators, to the direction a story is taking naturally, may produce a stress that bends it unexpectedly in a toally unpredictable way. And from that can come a toad prince or a toad, depending on whether or not both writers know how to handle a fable run amuck.

The beloved Lester del Rey—one of my early mentors in the craft of professional lying—told me once: never write a story *with* someone, that you can do as well by yourself. Well, I believe that. I tried writing a novel with Avram Davidson once, titled "Don't Speak of Rope." Ech. One of the most horrible experiences in a universe filled with death camps, hardhats, campus massacres and the human gamut that runs from Spiro to Manson; somewhere in a file drawer languish ten thousand words of that novel, unended, unlamented, unfortunate. So I do, I really do, agree with Lester.

Even so, life can occasionally become dull and predictable, and so, to spice it slightly, those of us with a flair for danger and high adventure take guided tours through the heart of Mt. Vesuvius, stalk the blood-sucking vampire bat through the swamps and fens of Bosnia and/or Herzogovina, join peace rallies, date beautiful models and, when all else fails, collaborate on fictions with other writers. I grant you the picture of world-weariness and jaded appetite I paint, the desperation of ennui that drives men to such hideous extremes as collaboration, is an ugly one. But I feel you must know what horrors and pitfalls lie behind this seemingly uncomplicated act. Ask Avram. Ech.

But the reward of *successful* collaboration is a thing that cannot be produced by either of the parties working alone. It is akin to the benefits of sex with a partner, as opposed to masturbation. The latter is fun, but you show me anyone who has gotten a baby from playing with him- or herself, and I'll show you an ugly baby, with just a whole bunch of knuckles.

And so, risking the hisses and catcalls of overly critical readers and critics who will call these joint efforts (if you'll pardon my carrying on the allusion from the preceding paragraph) merely gimmicky constructs, over the past many years I have yoked myself to fourteen other writers, and from these literary miscegenations have come the fictions before you.

My relationships with all of these men have been substantially more than what might be termed mere acquaintanceship. All of them are my friends, but not all of them like me. Nor do I like all of them. Many of them have done me favors I would be hard-pressed to repay in full or in kind. Others have messed me over hideously. From time to time I have been in serious disagreement with one or another of them. Between one of them and myself there was a shadow for many years. Between myself and another is something very much like the love of one brother for another. One saved my life, literally. I thought another had ruined it. One made me terribly proud of him, and then sold out, thereby destroying all my illusions about him.

Two of them managed to alter the course and texture of my life. From one I learned much about the nature of love, from another the nature of hate. With one I dreamed odd dreams, and with another I learned people can only act as people, not as gods. One demonstrated there can be nobility even in failure, and another showed me how badly success can be handled.

Millions of words of conversation in the past nineteen years have passed between me and these fourteen men. Advice, shoptalk, problems, respect and denunciation. That is the nature of friendship.

But without these men, I would never have come to write the solo stories on which my reputation—however great or small it may be—is based. Without all the words they have given the world on their own, some larger part of the joy of having been a part of speculative fiction would never have been. Bloch and his psychos and the Ripper; Bova's clear view of the importance of space travel; Budrys and the Gus nobody bothers; Davidson and his sentient coat-hangers; Delany and *frelking;* Hensley and his son, Randy; Laumer and Retief; Rotsler and a stack of cartoons only slightly smaller than Everest; Sheckley and *all* his dimensions of wonder; Silverberg and thorns; Slesar and the greatest short-story ever written; Sturgeon and . . . well, *every*thing; Van Vogt and weapon shops and Jommy Cross and the corticalthalamic pause; Zelazny and he who shapes.

All of them are masters, each of them writes only as he can write, and no two can ever be confused in the minds of students of masterful sf. These are the extra special meanings for me of these superimportant people:

Laumer is strength, and Davidson is erudition, and Budrys is empathy, and Delany is youthful commitment, and Sheckley is outrageous madness, and Sturgeon is both dazzlement and love, and Bova is the rationality of reality, Silverberg is craft, Van Vogt is complex conceptualization. Rotsler is irreverence, Hensley is gentleness, Zelazny is poetic intricacy, Bloch is coming to grips with terror, and Slesar is courage and pride and dignity.

I have learned these things from these men. So it is not merely by chance that we came together finally to write. It is heady company and only a fool or an amateur would consider working with them without a full realization of how good one must be to share the same story with each of them.

The individual introductions to the stories will tell you how the pieces came to be written, the method of collaboration, any sidelights or anecdotes that informed them, any mishaps or contretemps encountered in their making, their history and their success or failure as works of art, in my estimation. (Understand: just because a story reaches print, or even sees repeated anthologization, does not mean that we, the authors, are totally delighted with the outcome. Some of these stories fail in some of the areas where we considered it important to succeed. Some started out as one thing, and wound up as quite another, thereby dampening our pleasure. But in rehashing the histories of these stories with the men who were one-half their origin, I have not found one who regretted the experiment. That says something; what, I'm not certain.)

It sounds like hype to point out that this is the first book of its kind ever published; in that one way it is the most original book of stories ever published, and in the same way it is a monstrous literary joke. Throughout, however, it is for me a delight. You cannot know what a joy it is, what a prideful thing it is, what a satisfying thing it is, to have my name linked with these men.

I have a few regrets. I'll name them. Norman Spinrad, Isaac Asimov, Michael Moorcock and Philip José Farmer. I wanted to write stories with all of them, and somehow, through no real fault of anyone, they just didn't get written. I'm sorry about that. They'll more than likely never get written now. And I think it a bad thing that there is no Ellison/female collaboration here. What a strange mindfuck it would be to read a story on which I'd worked with, say, Kate Welhelm or Ursula Le Guin or Joanna Russ. Yeah, I lament that.

And the lamentations are all that remain, because now having written the collaborative thing out of my system—it was a thing to do, you see—I doubt very much that I'll do it again. Oh, there may be one or two little stories that chance ordains will be written in company with another, but a project like this? No, not again.

I think I speak for my collaborators when I say that we hope this book lightens your burdens, brings an occasional smile to your lips, puts a twinkle in your eyes, a shiver down your spine, an idea or two in your heads, and when you close the book finally, you will feel that our time—and yours—was not ill-spent.

For all of them, I say, thank you for dropping in on our little session, and for myself I say, thank you for letting me coat-tail your talents; thank you gentlemen, one and all.

HARLAN ELLISON
Los Angeles

Robert Sheckley and Harlan Ellison

I SEE A MAN SITTING ON A CHAIR, AND THE CHAIR IS BITING HIS LEG

INTRODUCTION

What better to lure you into these unholy partnerships
than a righteous tumble down a rabbit hole? Sheckley for
openers. Alone, by himself, unaided, he is certainly
deranged. In company with your humble ellisonian guide,
he runs thoroughly amuck.

He came out to visit me in H*O*L*L*Y*W*O*O*D on
some nefarious fiddlefoot journey—one of the many wan-
derings that constitute Sheck's only discernible vice—and
one late afternoon we wound up in my Camaro, whipping
and skinning across Mulholland's snake, the rear seat filled
with a gaggle of teen-aged gigglers I was ferrying somewhere for some now-forgotten reason.

It was impossible to talk to them; even Mary, my close
friend in Women's Lib, would not object to my calling
these girls, girls: not women. They were just—God forgive me—pretty meat. And I had to take them somewhere, so I was doing it, and Sheck was in the front
bucket next to me, and to pass the time, we started rap-
ping a story plot. Not seriously, you understand, just one
of those lunatic conversations into which one falls with
Bob as a matter of course: if we *could* sweep the beach
clean with brooms, how many years would it take; if
trolley cars had wings, would elephants have overhead
runners; is Amelia Earhart living in sin in Guatemala with
Ambrose Bierce and Judge Crater; why do women put the
toilet paper in the wall roller backward; if you could

21

shrink people down to the size of walnuts, could you solve
the population explosion by building and stocking a city
the size of New York in Disneyland, right?

None of the conversations ever mean a damn thing.
They are just crazy raps between Sheck and whomever he
happens to have snagged.

But *this* time, for some inexplicable reason, by the time
we had driven all the way across Mulholland, down Laurel
Canyon, and were emerging on Sunset Boulevard, we had
worked out a fairly complex, thoroughly mad story line.

"Tell me, Bob," I said, from behind the wheel, in my
best W. C. Fields voice, "what do you see as a title for this
masterpiece?"

"I see a man sitting on a chair, and the chair is biting
his leg," he replied, thinking himself too cute for words.

"Then that'll be the title," I said, calling his bluff. And it
was. And it is.

No one was more shocked than Sheck. For no matter
how crazy a writer gets, there is always another writer just
a little crazier.

After performing various hideous obscenities on the nu-
bile persons of the backseat gigglers, I dropped the young
ladies off, joined Bob in a hearty lunch at the Old World,
and we dashed back to my house in the hills to start the
story.

Sheck began the writing. His first assault runs from the
opening sentence to the description of the TexasTower,
ending with the paragraph whose last phrase is, "it was a
marvel." I took over then, and wrote to the time-break after Pareti and Peggy Flinn have had sex and Pareti goes
to sleep. We alternated sections from that point on.

But! Aha! You think it was that easy, that we just
whipped on through, alternating sections? No. After we
had finished the first draft, at a total wordage that now
escapes me, I went back and did a full rewrite. And then
Sheck went over my rewrite and did a final polish, so
that the version you now have before you is inextricably
interwoven with both of us in each other's sections. For
instance, in the fourth paragraph, the Eskimo-slit glasses
are mine, but the Indians of Patzcuaro are his.

We wrote for forty-eight hours straight, napping fitfully
while the other wrote. Ladies of my acquaintance ap-

peared from time to time and cooked us food and sulked at the growing rudeness of our manner as our nerves frayed and the story grew. Finally, it was done. I did a re-type of the manuscript, adding a fillip here and an Ausable Chasm there.

When it was done, we both collapsed and let someone else mail it out to Ed Ferman at the *Magazine of Fantasy & Science Fiction*, and we slept round-the-clock.

In collaborating, unless there is a specific reason for the styles to be identifiably different, I try to adapt my writing to the manner of my co-author. In the case of Sheckley, it meant I had to start thinking like a brain damage case. Consequently, I make no brief for the logic or sanity of this story. Further, deponent saith not.

I See a Man Sitting on a Chair, and the Chair Is Biting His Leg

Behind him lay the gray Azores, behind the Gates of Hercules; the sky above, the goo below.

"Screwin' goo! Screwin' goo!" Pareti yelled at the fading afternoon sunlight. It came up garbled, around the stump of cigar, and it lacked the vigor Pareti usually brought to the curse, because it was nearly shift's end, and he was exhausted. The first time he had yelled it had been three years before, when he had signed up to work in the goo fields as a harvester. He had yelled it when he'd first seen the mucous gray plankton mutation spotting this area of the Atlantic. Like leprosy on the cool blue body of the sea.

"Screwin' goo," he murmured. It was ritual now. It kept him company in the punt. Just him, alone there: Joe Pareti and his dying voice. And the ghostly gray-white goo.

He caught the moving flash of gray out of the corner of his eye, light reflecting in the Eskimo-slit glasses. He wheeled the punt around expertly. The goo was extruding again. A grayish-pale tentacle rose above the ocean's surface; it looked like an elephant's trunk. Skimming smoothly toward it, Pareti unconsciously gauged his distance: five feet from it, right arm tensed, out comes the net—the strange net on its pole, that resembled nothing so much as the butterfly nets used by the Indians of Patzcuaro—and with a side-arm softball pitch of a motion he scooped it up, writhing.

The goo wriggled and twisted, flailed at the meshes, sucked toothlessly up the aluminum handle. Pareti estimated the chunk at five pounds, even as he brought it inboard and dumped it into the lazarette. It was heavy for so small a fragment.

As the goo fell toward it, the lazarette dilated and compressed air shut the lid down with a sucking sound on the tentacle. Then the iris closed over the lid.

The goo had touched him on the glove. Pareti decided it was too much trouble to disinfect immediately. He swiped absently at his thinning sun-bleached hair, falling over his eyes, and wheeled the punt around again.

He was about two miles from the TexasTower.

He was fifty miles out into the Atlantic.

He was off the coast of Hatteras, in Diamond Shoals.

He was at 35° latitude, 75° west longitude.

He was well into the goo fields.

He was exhausted. Shift's end.

Screwin' goo.

He began working his way back.

The sea was flat, and a long, steady swell rolled back toward the TexasTower. There was no wind, and the sun shone hard and diamond as it had ever since the Third World War, brighter than it had ever shone before. It was almost perfect harvesting weather, at five hundred and thirty dollars a shift.

Off to his left a ten-square-yard film of goo lay like a delicate tracery of gray, almost invisible against the ocean. He altered course and expertly collected it. It offered no fight at all. Stretched too thin.

He continued toward the TexasTower, gathering goo as he skimmed. He rarely encountered the same shape twice. The largest chunk he collected was disguised as a cyprus stump. (*Stupid goo,* he thought, *who ever saw a cyprus stump growing fifty miles out?*) The smallest was a copy of a baby seal. Cadaverously gray and eyeless. Pareti gathered each piece quickly, without hesitation: he had an uncanny aptitude for recognizing goo in any of its shapes, and a flawless harvesting technique that was infinitely more refined and eloquent than the methods used by the Company-trained harvesters. He was the dancer with natural rhythm, the painter who had never taken a lesson,

the instinctive tracker. It had been the impetus that had
led him here to the goo fields when he had graduated
Summa Cum from the Multiversity, rather than into in-
dustry or one of the cattle-prod think-factories. Everything
he had learned, all the education he had gotten; of what
use was it in a clogged choking jamcrowded world of
twenty-seven billion overcrowded people, all scrabbing for
the most demeaning jobs? Anyone could get an education,
a few less got their degrees, even less got their gold seals,
and a handful—like Joe Pareti—came out the other end
of the Multiversity slide-trough with a degree, a doctorate,
a gold seal and the double-A rating. And *none* of it was
worth his natural instinct for goo havesting.

At the speed he harvested, he could earn more than a
projects engineer.

After twelve hours of shift, out on the glare-frosted sea,
even *that* satisfaction was dulled by exhaustion. He only
wanted to hit the bunk in his stateroom. And sleep. And
sleep. He threw the soggy cigar stub into the sea.

The structure loomed up before him. It was tradition-
ally called a TexasTower, yet it bore no resemblance to
the original offshore drilling rigs of pre-Third War America. It looked, instead, like an articulated coral reef or the
skeleton of some inconceivable aluminum whale.

The TexasTower was a problem in definition. It could
be moved, therefore it was a *ship;* it could be fastened ir-
revocably to the ocean bottom, therefore it was an *island.*
Above the surface there was a cat's cradle network of
pipes: feeder tubes into which the goo was fed by the harvesters (as Pareti now fed his load, hooking the lazarette's
collapsible tube nozzle onto the monel metal hardware of
the TexasTower's feeder tube, feeling the tube pulse as the
pneumatic suction was applied, sucking the goo out of the
punt's storage bins), pipe racks to moor the punts, more
pipes to support the radar mast.

There was a pair of cylindrical pipes that gaped open
like howitzers. The entry ports. Below the waterline, like
an iceberg, the TexasTower spread and extended itself,
with collapsible sections that could be extended or folded
away as depth and necessity demanded. Here in Diamond
Shoals, several dozen of the lowest levels had been folded
inoperative.

It was shapeless, ungainly, slow-moving, impossible to sink in a hurricane, more ponderous than a galleon. As a ship, it was unquestionably the worst design in nautical history; but as a factory, it was a marvel.

Pareti climbed out of the mooring complex, carrying his net-pole, and entered the nearest entry port. He went through the decontamination and storage locks, and was puffed inside the TexasTower proper. Swinging down the winding aluminum staircase, he heard voices rising from below. It was Mercier, about to go on-shift, and Peggy Flinn, who had been on sick call for the last three days with her period. The two harvesters were arguing.

"They're processing it out at fifty-six dollars a ton," Peggy was saying, her voice rising. Apparently they had been at it for some time. They were discussing harvester bonuses.

"Before or *after* it fragments?" Mercier demanded.

"Now you know damn well that's *after*-frag weight," she snapped back. "Which means every ton we snag out here gets tanked through and comes up somewhere around forty or forty-one tons after radiation. *We're* getting bonus money on Tower weight, *not* frag weight!"

Pareti had heard it a million times before in his three years on the goo fields. The goo was sent back to the cracking and radiation plants when the bins were full. Subjected to the various patented techniques of the master processing companies the goo multiplied itself molecule for molecule, fragmented, grew, expanded, swelled, and yielded forty times its own original weight of goo. Which was then "killed" and reprocessed as the basic artificial foodstuff of a population diet long-since a stranger to steaks and eggs and carrots and coffee. The Third War had been a terrible tragedy in that it had killed off enormous quantities of everything except people.

The goo was ground up, reprocessed, purified, vitamin-supplemented, colored, scented, accented, individually packaged under a host of brand names—VitaGram; Savor; Deelish; Gratifood; Sweetmeat; Quench-Caffé; Family Treatall—and marketed to twenty-seven billion open and waiting mouths. Merely add thrice-reprocessed water and serve.

The harvesters were literally keeping the world alive.

And even at five hundred and thirty dollars per shift, some of them felt they were being underpaid.

Pareti clanked down the last few steps and the two arguing harvesters looked up at him, "Hi, Joe." Mercier said. Peggy smiled.

"Long shift?" she asked archly.

"Long enough. I'm whacked out."

She stood a little straighter. "Completely?"

Pareti rubbed at his eyes. They felt grainy; he had been getting more dust in them than usual. "I thought it was that-time-of-the-month for you?"

"Aw gone," she grinned, spreading her hands like a little girl whose measles have vanished.

"Yeah, that'd be nice," Pareti accepted her service, "if you'll throw in a back rub."

"And I'll crack your spine."

Mercier chuckled and moved toward the staircase. "See you later," he said over his shoulder.

Pareti and Peggy Flinn went down through sections to his stateroom. Living in an encapsulated environment for upwards of six months at a stretch, the harvesters had evolved their own social relationships. Women who were touchy about their sexual liaisons did not last long on the TexasTowers. There were seldom shore leaves for the harvesters—who referred to themselves as "the black gang"—and consequently all conveniences were provided by the company. Films, gourmet chefs, recreational sports, a fully-stocked and constantly changing library . . . and the lady harvesters. It had begun with some of the women accepting "gratuities" from the men for sex, but that had had a deleterious effect on morale, so now their basic shift wages and bonuses were supplemented by off-shift sex pay. It was not uncommon for a reasonably good-looking and harvesting-adept woman to come back after an eight- or nine-month TexasTower stint with fifty thousand dollars in her credit account.

In the stateroom, they undressed.

"Jesus," Peggy commented, "what happened to all your hair?"

It had been several months since they had been together.

"I guess I'm going bald." Pareti shrugged it off. He

wiped himself down completely with a disposable moist-cloth from the dispenser, and tossed it into the incinerator iris.

"*All over?*" she asked incredulously.

"Hey, Peg," Pareti said wearily. "I've been out for twelve hours. I'm whacked out, and I want to get some sleep. Now do you want to or don't you?"

She smiled at him. "You're cute, Joe."

"I'm a pudding, I am," he replied, and sank down on the comfortable bed. She came to him and they had sex.

Then he went to sleep.

Fifty years before, the Third World War had finally broken out. It had been preceded by thirty years of Cold War Phase II. Phase I had ended in the 1970s, when it was obvious that War was inevitable. Phase II had been the defensive measures against overkill. They had sunk the subterranean cavern cities, the "cannister cities" as the sub-urban planners called them. (They weren't called anything as unglamorous as that publicly. In the press releases they were glowingly named Jade City, DownTown, Golden Grotto, North and South Diamond, Onyxville, Sub-City, East Pyrites. And in the Smokies they sank the gigantic North American Continent antimissile complex, Ironwall, two miles down.)

The breeding had started long before Phase I. Malthus had been right. Under the impetus of fear, people multiplied as never before. And in cannister cities like Lower Hong Kong, Labyrinth (under Boston) and New Cuernavaca the enclosed conformity of life left them few pleasures. So they multiplied. And again. And geometrically the progression filled the cannister cities. They sent out tunnels and tubes and feelers, and the Earth filled up with the squalling, teeming, hungry inhabitants of the land of fear. Aboveground only the military and scientific elite chose to live, out of necessity.

Then came the War.

Bacteriologically, atomically, with laser and radiation it came.

It was bad enough on the North American continent: Los Angeles was slagged. Ironwall and half the Smokies were gone, the missile complex buried forever under

mountains that were now soft, rolling hills. Oak Ridge
went up in one bright flash. Louisville was reduced to rub-
ble. Detroit and Birmingham no longer existed; in their
places were smooth reflective surfaces, almost perfectly
flat like mirrored wafers of oxidized chrome plate.

New York and Chicago had been better protected.
They had lost their suburbs, but not their cannister sub-
cities. And the central cores of the metropolises remained.
Battered, but still functioning.

It had been just as bad, even worse, on the other conti-
nents. But there had been time during the two Phases of
the Cold War to develop serums, remedies, antidotes,
therapeutics. People were saved by the millions.

Even so . . . one could not inject an ear of corn.

Nor could one inoculate every cat and dog and wild
boar and antelope and llama and Kodiak bear. Nor could
one seed the oceans and save the fish. Ecology went mad.
Some species survived, others died out completely.

The Hunger Strikes and the Food Riots began.

And ended quickly. People too weak from hunger cannot fight. So the cannibal times came. And then the gov-
ernments, terrified by what they had done to themselves
and each other, banded together at last.

The United Nations had been rebuilt, and they had
commissioned the Companies to solve the problems of artificial foodstuffs. But it was a slow process.

What they had only dimly realized was that the
Westerly Winds, carrying all the radiation and residue of
bacteriological lunacy, had swept across the North American continent, picking up their additional loads at the
Smokies, Louisville, Detroit, New York, and had carried
the polluted and deadly cargo across the Eastern Sea-
board, across the Atlantic, to dissipate finally in the jet-
stream over Asia. But not before massive fallout off the
Carolinas had combined with sunlight and rain to produce
a strange mutation in the plankton-rich waters of Diamond Shoals.

Ten years after the end of the Third World War, the
plankton had become something else. It was called goo by
the fishermen of the Outer Banks.

Diamond Shoals had become a cauldron of creation.

The goo spread. It adapted. It metamorphosed. And

there was panic. Deformed exo-skeletal fish swam in the shallow waters; four new species of dog shark were found (one was a successful adaptation); a centipedal squid with a hundred arms flourished for several years, then unaccountably vanished.

The goo did not vanish.

Experiments followed, and miraculously, what had seemed to be an imminent and unstoppable menace to life on the seas, and probably on the planet as a whole ... revealed itself as a miracle. It saved the world. The goo, when "killed," could be turned into artificial nourishment. It contained a wide spectrum of proteins, vitamins, amino acids, carbohydrates, and even necessary minimum amounts of trace elements. When dehydrated and packaged, it was economically rewarding. When combined with water it could be cooked, stewed, pan fried, boiled, baked, poached, sautéed, stuffed or used as a stuffing. It was as close to the perfect food as had ever been found. Its flavor altered endlessly, depending entirely on which patented processing system was used. It had many tastes, but no characteristic taste.

Alive, it functioned on a quasi-vegetative level. An unstable protoplasmic agglomeration, it was apparently unintelligent, though it had an undeniable urge toward form. It structured itself endlessly into rudimentary plant and animal shapes, none viable. It was as if the goo desired to *become* something.

(It was hoped in the research labs of the Companies that the goo never discovered *what* it wanted to become.)

"Killed," it was a tasty meal.

Harvesting factories—the TexasTowers—were erected by each of the Companies, and harvesters were trained. They drew the highest wages of any nontechnical occupation in the world. It was not due to the long hours, or the exhausting labor. The pay was, in fact, legally referred to as "high-hazard pay."

Joe Pareti had danced the educational pavane and had decided the tune was not nearly sprightly enough for him. He became a harvester. He never really understood why all the credits being deposited in his account were called high-hazard pay.

He was about to find out.

It was a song that ended in a scream. And then he woke up. The night's sleep had held no rest. Eleven hours on his back; eleven hours of helpless drudgery; and at last an escape, an absurd transition into exhausted wakefulness. For a moment he lay there, he couldn't move.

Then getting to his feet, he found himself fighting for balance. Sleep had not used him well.

Sleep had scoured his skin with emery paper.

Sleep had polished his fingers with diamond dust.

Sleep had abraded his scalp.

Sleep had sand-blasted his eyes.

Oh dear God, he thought, feeling pain in every nerve ending. He stumbled to the toilet and hit the back of his neck a sharp, short blast with the needle-spray of the shower head. Then he went to the mirror, and automatically pulled his razor out of the charge niche. Then he looked at himself in the mirror, and stopped.

Sleep had: scoured his skin with emery paper, polished his fingers with diamond-dust, abraded his scalp, sandblasted his eyes.

It was barely a colorful way of putting it. Almost literally, that was what had happened to him while he had slept.

He stared into the mirror, and recoiled from the sight. *If this is what sex with that damned Flinn does to a guy, I'm going celibate.*

He was totally bald.

The wispy hair he recalled brushing out of his face during the previous on-shift, was gone. His head was smooth and pale as a fortune teller's crystal ball.

He had no eyelashes.

He had no eyebrows.

His chest was smooth as a woman's.

His pubis had been denuded.

His fingernails were almost translucent, as though the uppermost layers of dead horn had been removed.

He looked in the mirror again. He saw himself ... more or less. Not very *much* less, actually: no more than a pound of him was gone. But it was a noticeable pound.

His hair.

Assorted warts, moles, scar tissue and calluses.

The protective hairs in his nostrils.

His kneecaps, elbows and heels were scoured pink.

Joe Pareti found he was still holding the razor. He put it down. And stared at himself in horrified fascination for several timeless moments. He had a ghastly feeling he knew what had happened to him. *I'm in deep trouble,* he thought.

He went looking for the TexasTower's doctor. He was not in the sickbay. He found him in the pharmacology lab. The doctor took one look and preceded him back to sickbay. Where he confirmed Pareti's suspicions.

The doctor was a quiet, orderly man named Ball. Very tall, very thin, with an irreducible amount of professional ghoulishness. Normally he was inclined to gloom; but looking at the hairless Pareti he cheered perceptibly.

Pareti felt himself being dehumanized. He had followed Ball into the sickbay as a man; now he felt himself transformed into a specimen, a diseased culture to be peered at under a macroscope.

"Hah, yes," the doctor said. "Interesting. Would you turn your head, please? Good ... good ... fine, now blink."

Pareti did as he was told. Ball jotted down notes, turned on the recording cameras, and hummed to himself as he arranged a tray of shining instruments.

"You've caught it, of course," Ball said, almost as an afterthought.

"Caught what?" Pareti demanded, hoping he'd get some other answer.

"Ashton's Disease. Goo infection, if you like, but we call it Ashton's, after the first case." Then he chuckled to himself: "I don't suppose you thought it was dermatitis?"

Pareti thought he heard eerie music, an organ, a harpsichord.

Ball went on. "Your case is atypical, just like all the others, so, really, that makes it typical. It has a rather ugly Latin name, as well, but Ashton's will do."

"Stuff all that," Pareti said angrily. "Are you absolutely sure?"

"Why do you think you get high-hazard, why do you think they keep me on board? I'm no G.P., I'm a specialist. Of course I'm absolutely sure. You're only the sixth recorded case. *Lancet* and the *AMA Journal* will be interested. In fact, with the proper presentation *Scientific American* might care to publish an article."

"What can you do for me?" Pareti snapped.

"I can offer you a drink of excellent pre-War Bourbon," Dr. Ball said. "Not a specific for your ailment, but good for the whole man, so to speak."

"Stop screwing around with me. I don't think it's a ha-ha. Isn't there anything else? You're a specialist!"

Ball seemed to realize for the first time that his black humor was not being received with wild enthusiasm. "Mr. Pareti, medical science admits of no impossibility, not even the reversal of biological death. But that is a statement of theory. There are many things we could try. We could hospitalize you, stuff you with drugs, irradiate your skin, smear you with calamine lotion, even conduct experiments in homeopathy and acupuncture and moxibustion. But this would have no practical effect, except to make you very uncomfortable. In the present state of our knowledge, Ashton's is irreversible and, uh, terminal."

Pareti swallowed hard at the last word.

Oddly, Ball smiled and added, "You might as well relax and enjoy it."

Pareti moved a step toward him, angrily. "You're a morbid son of a bitch!"

"Please excuse my levity," the doctor said quickly. "I know I have a dumb sense of humor. I don't rejoice in your fate . . . really, I don't . . . I'm bored on this desolate Tower . . . I'm happy to have some real work. But I can see you don't know much about Ashton's . . . the disease may not be too difficult to live with."

"I thought you said it was terminal?"

"So I did. But then, *everything* is terminal, even health, even life itself. The question is how long, and in what manner."

Pareti slumped down into a Swedish-designed relaxer chair that converted—when the stirrups were elevated—into a dilation-and-curretage brace-framework for abortions. "I have a feeling you're going to lecture me," he said, with sudden exhaustion.

"Forgive me. It's so dull for me here."

"Go on, go on, for Christ's sake." Pareti wobbled his hand wearily.

"Well, the answer is ambiguous, but not unpromising," Ball said, settling with enthusiasm into his recitation. "I told you, I believe, that the most typical thing about the disease is it atypicality. Let us consider your illustrious predecessors.

"Case One died within a week of contracting the disease, apparently of a pneumonic complication . . ."

Pareti looked sick. "Swell," he said.

"Ah! But Case Two," Ball caroled, "Case Two was Ashton, after whom the Disease was named. *He* became voluble, almost echolalic. One day, before a considerable crowd, he levitated to a height of eighteen feet. He hung there without visible support, haranguing the crowd in a hermetic language of his own devising. Then he vanished, into thin air (but not too thin for him) and was never heard from again. Hence, Ashton's Disease. Case Three . . ."

"What happened to Ashton?" Pareti asked, a vapor of hysteria in his voice.

Ball spread his hands, without an answer.

Pareti looked away.

"Case Three found that he could live underwater, though not in the air. He spent two happy years in the coral reefs off Marathon, Florida."

"What happened to *him?*" Pareti asked.

"A pack of dolphins did him in. It was the first recorded instance of a dolphin attacking a man. We have often wondered what he said to them."

"And the others?"

"Case Four is currently living in the Ausable Chasm community. He operates a mushroom farm. He's become quite rich. We can't detect any effect of the disease beyond loss of hair and dead skin (in that way, your cases are similar, but it may be just coincidence). He has a unique way with mushrooms, of course."

"That sounds good," Pareti brightened.

"Perhaps. But Case Five is unfortunate. A really amazing degeneration of the organs, accompanied by a simultaneous external growth of same. This left him with a definitely surrealistic look: heart hanging below his left armpit, intestines wrapped around his waist, that sort of thing. Then he began to develop a chitinous exo-skeleton, antennae, scales, feathers—his body couldn't seem to decide what it was evolving into. It opted at last for earthwormdom—an anaerobic species, quite unusual. He was last seen burrowing into sandy loam near Point Judith. Sonar followed him for several months, all the way to central Pennsylvania."

Pareti shuddered. "Did he die then?"

Again, Ball spread his hands, no answer. "We don't know. He may be in a burrow, quiescent, parthenogenetic, hatching the eggs of an inconceivable new species. Or he may have evolved into the ultimate skeletal form . . . unliving, indestructible rock."

Pareti clasped his hairless hands, and shivered like a child. "Jesus," he murmured, "what a beautiful prospect. Something I can really look forward to."

"The form of your particular case *might* be pleasant," Ball ventured.

Pareti looked up at him with open malice. "Aren't you the smooth bastard, though! Sit out here in the water and laugh your ass off while the goo nibbles on some guy you never met before. What the hell do you do for amusement, roast cockroaches and listen to them scream?"

"Don't blame me, Mr. Pareti," the doctor said evenly. "*You* chose your line of work, not I. You were advised of the risks—"

"They said hardly anybody caught the goo disease, it was all in the small type on the contract," Pareti burst in.

"—but you *were* advised of the risks," Ball pressed on, "and you received hazard-bonus accordingly. You never complained during the three years that money was being poured into your account, you shouldn't bellyache now. It's rather unseemly. After all, you make approximately eight times my salary. That should buy you a lot of balm."

"Yeah, I made the bonuses," Pareti snarled, "and now I'm *really* earning it! The Company—"

"The Company," Ball said, with great care, "is absolutely free of responsibility. You should indeed have read all that tiny type. But you're correct: you *are* earning the bonuses now. In effect you were paid to expose yourself to a rare disease. You were gambling with the Company's money that you wouldn't contract Ashton's. You gambled, and unfortunately, seem to have lost."

"Not that I'm getting any," Pareti said archly, "but I'm not asking for your sympathy. I'm only asking for your professional advice, which you are paid—*overpaid,* in my estimation—to give. I want to know what I should do . . . and what I ought to expect."

Ball shrugged. "Expect the unexpected, of course. You're only the sixth, you know. There's been no clear-cut pattern established. The disease is as unstable as its progenitor . . . the goo. The only pattern—and I would hesitate even to suggest that it *was* a pattern—"

"Stop waltzing with me, damn it! Spit it out!"

Ball pursed his lips. He might have pressed Pareti as far as he cared to press him. "The pattern, then, would appear to be this: a radical change of relationship occurs between the victim and the external world. These can be *animate* transformations, like the growth of external organs and functional gills; or *inanimate* transformations, like the victim who levitated."

"What about the fourth case, the one who's still alive and normal?"

"He isn't exactly *normal,*" the doctor said, frowning. "His relationship with his mushrooms is a kind of perverted love; reciprocated, I might add. Some researchers suspect that he has himself become a kind of intelligent mushroom."

Pareti bit his thumbnail. There was a wildness in his eyes. "Isn't there any cure, *anything?*"

Ball seemed to be looking at Pareti with thinly veiled disgust. "Whimpering won't do you any good. Perhaps nothing will. I understand Case Five tried to hold off the effects as long as he could, with will power, or concentration . . . something ludicrous like that."

"Did it work?"

"For a while, perhaps. No one could be sure. In any case, it was strictly conjecture after a point; the Disease finally took him over."

"But it's possible?"

Ball snorted. "Yes, Mr. Pareti, it's possible." He shook his head as if he could not believe the way Pareti was taking this. "Remember, none of the cases was like any other. I don't know what joys you can look forward to, but whatever they are . . . they're bound to be unusual."

Pareti stood up. *"I'll* fight it off. It isn't going to take me over like the others."

Ball's expression was of disgust. "I doubt it, Pareti. I never met any of the others, but from what I've read of them, they were far stronger men than you seem to be."

"Why? Just because this has me shaken?"

"No, because you're a sniveler."

"You're the most compassionless mother I've ever met!"

"I cannot pretend grief that you've contracted Ashton's. You gambled, and you lost. Stop whimpering."

"You said that before, Dr. Ball."

"I say it again now!"

"Is that all from you?"

"That's all from me, to be sure," Dr. Ball said, snidely. "But it's not all for you, I'm equally sure."

"But you're sure that's all you have to tell me?"

Ball nodded, still wearing the insipid grin of the medical ghoul. He was wearing it as Pareti took two quick, short steps and jacked a fist into the doctor's stomach, just below the heart. Ball's eyes seemed to extrude almost as the goo extruded, and his face went three shades of gray toward matching his lab smock. Pareti held him up under the chin with his left hand and drove a short, straight right directly into the doctor's nose.

Ball flailed backward and hit the glass-fronted instrument case, breaking the glass with a crash. Ball settled to the floor, still conscious, but in awful pain. He stared up at Pareti as the harvester turned toward the door. Pareti turned back momentarily, smiling for the first time since he had entered the sickbay.

"That's a helluva bedside manner you've got there, Doc."

Then he left.

He was forced to leave the TexasTower within the hour, as the law proscribed. He received a final statement of the back pay due him for the nine-month shift he had been working. He also received a sizeable termination bonus. Though everyone knew Ashton's Disease was not contagious, when he passed Peggy Flinn on his way to the exit lock, she looked at him sadly and said goodbye, but would not kiss him farewell. She looked sheepish. "Whore," Pareti murmured under his breath, but she heard him.

A Company lift had been sent for him. A big fifteen-passenger job with two stewardesses, a lounge, movie theater and pocket billiard accommodations. Before he was put on board, the Projects Superintendent, head man on the TexasTower, spoke to him at the lock.

"You aren't a Typhoid Mary, you can't give it to anyone. It's merely unlovely and unpredictable. That's what they tell me. Technically, there's no quarantine; you can go where you please. But realistically, you can appreciate that your presence in the surface cities wouldn't be welcome. Not that you'd be missing much . . . all the action is underground."

Pareti nodded silently. He was well over his shaken reactions of earlier. He was now determined to fight the Disease with the strength of his own will.

"Is that it?" he asked the Projects Super.

The man nodded, and extended his hand.

Pareti hesitated a moment, then shook it.

As Pareti was walking down the ramp to the lift, the Projects Super called after him. "Hey, Pareti?"

Joe turned back.

"Thanks for belting that bastard Ball. I've been itching to do it for six years." He grinned.

It was an embarrassed, brave little smile that Joe Pareti returned, as he said goodbye to who he was and what he was, and boarded the lift for the real world.

He had free passage to the destination of his choice. He chose East Pyrites. If he was going to make a new life for himself with the money he had saved in three years working the goo fields, at least he was going to do it after one king-sized shore leave. It had been nine months since he had been anywhere near excitement—you sure as hell couldn't call Peggy Flinn with her flat-chest, excitement—and there was time for fun before the time to settle down.

One of the stewardesses, wearing an off-the-bosom jumper with a "kicki" skirt, paused beside his seat and smiled down at him. "Care for a drink?"

Pareti's thoughts were hardly of liquor. She was a high-breasted, long-legged item with light turquoise hair. But he knew she had been apprised of his ailment, and her reaction would be the same as Peggy Flinn's.

He smiled up at her, thinking of what he would like to do with her if she were amenable. She took his hand and led him back to one of the washrooms. She led him inside, bolted the door, and dropped her clothes. Pareti was so astonished he had to let her undress him. It was cramped and close in the tiny bathroom, but the stewardess was marvelously inventive, not to mention limber.

When she was done with him, her face flushed, her neck spotted with little purple love-bites, her eyes almost feverish, she mumbled something about being unable to resist him, gathered up her clothes without even putting them on and, with acute embarrassment, floundered out of the bathroom, leaving him standing there with his pants down around his shoes.

Pareti looked at himself in the mirror. Again. He seemed to be doing nothing but staring into mirrors today. What stared out at him was himself, bald Pareti. He had the suddenly pleasurable feeling that whatever manner the goo infection in his body was taking to evolve itself, it would probably make him irresistible to women. All at once he could not find it in his heart to think too unkindly of the goo.

He had happy dreams of what joys and delights were in store for him if the goo, for instance, built him as big as a horse, or if it heightened this already-obvious attraction women had for him, or if it—

He caught himself.

Uh-uh. No thank you. That was just what had happened to the other five. They had been taken over by the goo. It had done what it had wanted with them. Well, he was going to fight it, battle it from invading him from the top of his bald head to the soles of his uncallused feet.

He got dressed.

No indeed not. He wasn't going to enjoy any more sex like he'd just had. (And it became obvious to him that whatever the goo had done to the attraction-waves of his personality, it had also served to heighten his perceptions in that area. It had been the best he'd ever had.)

He was going to grab a little fun in East Pyrites, and

then buy himself a parcel of land topside, find the right
woman, settle down, and buy himself a good position with
one of the Companies.

He went back into the cabin of the lift. The other stewardess was on duty. She didn't say anything, but the one
who had taken Pareti into the toilet did not show herself
through the remainder of the flight, and her replacement
kept staring at Joe as though she wanted to nibble him
with tiny teeth.

East Pyrites, Nevada, was located eighty-seven miles
south of the radioactive ghost town that had been called
Las Vegas. It was also three miles below it. It was conserv-
atively rated one of the marvels of the world. Its devo-
tion to vice was obsessive, amounting to an almost puri-
tanical drive to pleasure. In East Pyrites the phrase had
been coined:

> PLEASURE
> IS A STERN DUTY
> IMPOSED ON US
> BY THE WORLD.

In East Pyrites, the fertility cults of antiquity had been re-
vived in deadly seriousness. Pareti found this to be true as
he stepped out of the dropshaft on the seventieth under-
level. A mass gangbang was in progress, in the middle of
the intersection of Dude Avenue and Gold Dust Boulevard, between fifty male members of the Ishtar Boppers
and ten lovely girls who had signed in blood their mem-
bership to the Swingers of Cybele.

He carefully avoided the embroglio. It looked like fun,
but he wasn't going to aid and abet the goo in taking him
over.

He hailed a taxi and stared at the scenery. The Temple
of Strangers was served by the virgin daughters of the
town's leading citizens; executions for impiety were held
publicly in the Court of the Sun; Christianity was in disre-
pute: it wasn't any fun.

The old Nevadan custom of gambling was still observed, but had been elaborated, ramified and extended. In

East Pyrites, the saying, "You bet your life," had real and sinister meanings.

Many of the practices in East Pyrites were un-Constitutional; others were implausible; and some were downright inconceivable.

Pareti loved it at once.

He selected the Round-The-World Combination Hotel, close to the Hall of Perversions, just across the street from the verdant expanse of Torture Garden. In his room, he showered, changed, and tried to decide what to do first. Dinner in the Slaughterhouse, of course; then perhaps a little mild exercise in the cool darkness of the Mudbath Club. After that—

He suddenly became aware that he was not alone. Someone or something was in the room with him.

He looked around. There was apparently nothing wrong, except that he could have sworn he had put his jacket on a chair. Now it was on the bed, near him.

After a moment's hesitation he reached for the jacket. The garment slid away from him. "Try to catch me!" it said, in a coy, insipid voice. Pareti grabbed for it, but the jacket danced away from him.

Pareti stared at it. Wires? Magnets? A joke of the management of the Hotel? He knew instinctively that he would find no rational way in which the coat had moved and talked. He gritted his teeth and stalked it.

The jacket moved away, laughing, dipping like a bat. Pareti cornered it behind the room's massage unit, and managed to grab a sleeve. *I've got to have this goddam thing sent out to be cleaned and burned,* he thought insanely.

It lay limp for a moment. Then it curled around and tickled the palm of his hand.

Pareti giggled involuntarily, then flung the garment away from him and hurried out of the room.

Descending by dropshaft to the street, he knew that had been the *true* onset of the Disease. It had altered the relationship between him and an article of clothing. An inanimate object. The goo was getting bolder.

What would it do next?

He was in a soft place called The Soft Place. It was a gambling hall whose innovation was an elaborate game called Sticklt. The game was played by seating oneself before a long counter with a round polyethylene-lined hole in the facing panel, and inserting a certain portion of the anatomy therein. It was strictly a man's game, of course.

One placed one's bets on the flickering light-panels that covered the counter-top. These lights were changed in a random pattern by a computer programmer, and through the intricacies of the betting and odds, various things happened behind the facing panels, to whomever happened to be inserted in the playing-hole. Some of the things were very nice indeed. Some were not.

Ten seats down to his right, Pareti heard a man scream, high and shrill, like a woman. An attendant in white came with a sheet and a pneumatic stretcher, and took the bettor away. The man to Pareti's left was sitting forward, up tight against the panel, moaning with pleasure. His amber **WINNER** light was flashing.

A tall, elegant woman with inky hair came up beside Pareti's chair. "Honey, you shouldn't be wasting anything as nice as you here. Why don't we go downshaft to my brig and squam a little . . ."

Pareti panicked. He knew the goo was at work again. He withdrew from the panel just as the flickering lights went up **LOSER** in front of him, and the distinct sound of whirring razor blades came out of the playing-hole. He saw his bets sucked into the board, and he turned without looking at the woman, knowing she would be the most gorgeous creature he had ever seen. And he didn't need *that* aggravation on top of everything else.

He ran out of The Soft Place. The goo, and Ashton's Disease, were ruining his good time of hell-for-leather. But he was not, repeat, *not* going to let it get the better of him. Behind him, the woman was crying.

He was hurrying, but he didn't know where he was going. Fear encased him like a second self. The thing he ran from was within him, pulsing and growing within him, running with him, perhaps moving out ahead of him. But the empty ritual of flight calmed him, left him better able to think.

He sat down on a park bench beneath an obscenely-shaped purple lamp post. The neon designs were gagging and suggestive. It was quiet here—except for the Muzak—he was in the world-famous Hangover Square. He could hear nothing—except the Muzak—and the stifled moans of a tourist expiring in the bushes.

What could he do? He could resist, he could close out the effects of Ashton's Disease by concentration . . .

A newspaper fluttered across the street and plastered itself around his foot. Pareti tried to kick it away. It clung to his foot, and he heard it whisper, "Please, oh please do not spurn me."

"Get away from me!" Pareti screamed. He was suddenly terrified; he could see the newspaper crinkle as it tried to unsnap his shoe-buttons.

"I want to kiss your feet," the newspaper pleaded. "Is that so terrible? Is it wrong? Am I so ugly?"

"Let go!" Pareti shouted, tugging at the paper, which had formed into a pair of giant white lips.

A man walked past him, stopped, stared, and said, "Jim, that's the damnedest bit I ever saw. You do that as a lounge act or just for kicks?"

"Voyeur!" the newspaper hissed, and fluttered away down the street.

"How do you control it?" the man asked. "Special controls in your pocket or something?"

Pareti shook his head numbly. He was so tired suddenly. He said, "You actually saw it kiss my foot?"

"I mean to tell you I saw it," the man said.

"I hoped that maybe I was only hallucinating," Pareti said. He got up from the bench and walked unsteadily away. He didn't hurry.

He was in no rush to meet the next manifestation of Ashton's Disease.

In a dim bar he drank six souses and had to be carried to the public Dry-Out on the corner. He cursed the attendants for reviving him. At least when he was bagged, he didn't have to compete with the world around him for possession of his sanity.

In the Taj Mahal he played girls, purposely aiming badly when he threw the dirks and the kris at the rapidly spinning bawds on the giant wheel. He clipped the ear off a blonde, planted one ineffectually between the legs of a brunette, and missed entirely with his other shots. It cost him seven hundred dollars. He yelled cheat and was bounced.

A head-changer approached him on Leopold Way, and offered the unspeakable delights of an illegal head-changing operation by a doctor who was "clean and very decent." He yelled for a cop, and the little ratfink scuttled away in the crowd.

A taxi driver suggested the Vale of Tears and though it sounded lousy, he gave the guy the go-ahead. When he entered the place—which was on the eighty-first level, a slum section of foul odors and wan street lights—he recognized it at once for what it was. A necro-joint. The smell of freshly-stacked corpses rose up to gag him.

He only stayed an hour.

There were nautch joints, and blind pigs, and hallucinogen bars, and a great many hands touching him, touching him.

Finally, after a long time, he found himself back in the park, where the newspaper had come after him. He didn't know how he'd gotten there, but he had a tattoo of a naked seventy-year-old female dwarf on his chest.

He walked through the park, but found that he had picked an unpromising route. Dogwood barked at him and caressed his shoulders; Spanish Moss sang a fandango; an infatuated willow drenched him in tears. He broke into a run, trying to get away from the importunities of cherry trees, the artless Western prattle of sagebrush, the languors of poplar. Through him, his disease was acting on the environment. He was infecting the world he passed through; no, he wasn't contagious to humans, hell no, it was worse than that: he was a Typhoid Mary for the *inanimate world!* And the altered universe loved him, tried to win him. Godlike, an Unmoved Mover, unable to deal with his involuntary creations, he fought down panic and tried to escape from the passions of a suddenly writhing world.

He passed a roving gang of juvies, who offered to beat the crap out of him for a price, but he turned them down and stumbled on.

He came out onto De Sade Boulevard, but even here

there was no relief. He could hear the little paving stones whispering about him:

"Say, he's *cute!*"

"Forget it, he'd never look at you."

"You vicious bitch!"

"I tell you he'll never look at you."

"Sure he will. Hey, Joe—"

"What did I tell you? He didn't even look at you!"

"But he's got to! Joe, Joe, it's me, over here—"

Pareti whirled and yelled, "As far as I'm concerned, one paving stone looks exactly like another paving stone. If you've seen one, you've seen 'em all."

That shut them up, by God! But what was this?

High overhead, the neon sign above cut-rate Sex City was beginning to flash furiously. The letters twisted and formed a new message:

I AM A NEON SIGN
AND I ADORE JOE PARETI!

A crowd had gathered to observe the phenomenon. "What the hell is a Joe Pareti?" one woman asked.

"A casualty of love," Pareti told her. "Speak the name softly, the next corpse you see may be your own."

"You're a twisto," the woman said.

"I fear not," Pareti said politely, a little madly. "Madness is my ambition, true. But I dare not hope to achieve it."

She stared at him as he opened the door and went into Sex City. But she didn't believe her eyes when the doorknob gave him a playful little pat on the ass.

"The way it works is this," the salesman said. "Fulfillment is no problem; the tough thing is desire, don't you dig? Desires *die* of fulfillment and gotta be replaced by new, *dif*ferent desires. A lotta people desire to have weirdo desires, but they can't make it onaccounta having lived a lifetime on the straights. But us here at the Impulse Implantation Center can condition you to like anything you'd like to like."

He had hold of Pareti's sleeve with a tourisnag, a rubber-lined clamp on the end of a telescoping rod; it was used to snag tourists passing through the Odd Services Arcade, to drag them closer to specific facilities.

"Thanks, I'll think it over," Pareti said, trying without much success to get the tourisnag off his sleeve.

"Wait, hey, Jim, dig! We got a special bargain rate, a real cheapo, it's only on for the next hour! Suppose we fix you up with pedophilia, a really high-class desire which has not as yet been over-exploited? Or take bestiality ... or take *both* for the special giveaway price—"

Pareti managed to pull the snag from his sleeve, and hurried on down the Arcade without looking back. He knew that one should never get Impulse Implanation from boiler-shop operators. A friend of his had made that mistake while on leave from a TexasTower, had been stuck with a passion for gravel, and had died after three admittedly enjoyable hours.

The Arcade was teeming, the screams and laughter of weekend freakoffs and smutters rising up toward the central dome of ever-changing light patterns, crapout kliegs, and grass-jets emitting their pleasant, ceaseless streams of thin blue marijuana smoke. He needed quiet; he needed aloneness.

He slid into a Spook Booth. Intercourse with ghosts was outlawed in some states, but most doctors agreed that it was not harmful if one made certain to wash off the ectoplasmic residue afterward with a thirty percent alcohol solution. Of course, it was more risky for women (he saw a Douche & Bidet Rest Stop just across the Arcade concourse, and marveled momentarily at the thoroughness of the East Pyrites Better Business Bureau; they took care of every exigency).

He leaned back in the darkness, heard the beginning of a thin, eerie wail ...

Then the Booth door was opened. A uniformed attendant asked, "Mr. Joseph Pareti?"

Pareti nodded. "What is it?"

"Sorry to disturb you, sir. A call for you." She handed him a telephone, caressed his thigh, and left, closing the door. Pareti held the phone and it buzzed. He put it to his ear. "Hello?"

"Hi there."

"Who is this?"

"This is your telephone, stupid. Who did you think it was?"

"I can't take all this! Stop talking!"

"It's not talking that's difficult," the telephone said. "The tough thing is finding something to say."

"Well, what do you want to say?"

"Nothing much. I just wanted you to know that somewhere, somehow, Bird lives."

"Bird? Bird who? What in hell are you talking about?"

There was no answer. The telephone had hung up.

He put the telephone down on the comfort ledge and sank back, hoping to God he could make-it in peace and quiet. The phone buzzed again, almost immediately. He did not pick it up, and it went from buzz to ring. He put it to his ear again.

"Hello?"

"Hi there," a silky voice said.

"Who is *this?*"

"This is your telephone, Joe baby. I called before. I thought you might like this voice better."

"Why don't you leave me alone?" Joe almost sobbed.

"How can I, Joe?" the telephone asked. "I love you! Oh Joe, Joe, I've tried so hard to please you. But you're so moody, baby, I just don't understand. I was a really *pretty* dogwood, and you barely glanced at me! I became a newspaper, and you didn't even read what I *wrote* about you, you ungrateful thing!"

"You're my disease," Pareti said unsteadily. "Leave me alone!"

"Me? A *disease?*" the telephone asked, a hurt note in the silken voice. "Oh, Joe, darling, how can you call me that? How can you pretend indifference after all we've been to each other?"

"I don't know what you're talking about," Pareti said.

"You do *too* know! You came to me every day, Joe, out on the warm sea. I was sort of young and silly then, I didn't understand, I tried to hide from you. But you lifted me up out of the water, you brought me close to you; you were patient and kind, and little by little I grew up. Sometimes I'd even try to wriggle up the pole handle to kiss your fingers . . ."

"Stop it!" Pareti felt his senses reeling, this was insanity, everything was becoming something else, the world and the Spook Booth were whirling around. "You've got it all wrong—"

"I have not!" the telephone said indignantly. "You called me pet names, I was your screwin' goo! I'll admit, I had tried other men before you, Joe. But then, *you'd* been with women before we met, so we mustn't throw the past up to one another. But even with the other five I tried, I was never able to become what I wanted to be. Can you understand how frustrating that was for me, Joe? Can you? I had my whole life before me and I didn't know what to do with it. One's shape is one's career, you know, and I was confused, until I met you . . . Excuse me if I babble, darling, but this is the first chance we've had for a real talk."

Through the gibbering madness of it all, Pareti saw it now, and understood it. They had underestimated the goo. It had been a young organism, mute but not unintelligent, shaped by the powerful desires it possessed like every other living creature. To have *form*. It was evolving—

Into what?

"Joe, what do you think? What would you like me to become?"

"Could you turn into a girl?" Pareti asked, timorously.

"I'm afraid not," the telephone said. "I tried that a few times; and I tried being a nice collie, too, and a horse. But I guess I did a pretty sloppy job, and anyhow, it felt all wrong. I mean, it's just not *me*. But name anything else!"

"No!" Pareti bellowed. For a moment, he had been going along with it. The lunacy was catching.

"I could become a rug under your feet, or if you wouldn't think it was too daring, I could become your underwear—"

"Goddam it, I don't love you!" Pareti shrieked. "You're nothing but gray ugly goo! I hate your guts! You're a disease . . . why don't you go love something like yourself?"

"There's nothing like me except *me*," the telephone sobbed. "And besides, it's *you* I love."

"Well, I don't give a damn for you!"

"You're cruel!"

"You stink, you're ugly, I don't love you, I've *never* loved you!"

"Don't say that, Joe," the telephone warned.

"I'm saying it! I never loved you, *I only used you!* I don't want your love, your love nauseates me, do you understand?"

He waited for an answer, but there was suddenly only an ominous, surly silence on the telephone. Then he heard the dial tone. The telephone had hung up.

Now. Pareti has returned to his hotel. He sits in his embroidered room, which has been cunningly constructed for the mechanical equivalents of love. Doubtless he is lovable; but he feels no love. That is obvious to the chair, to the bed, and to the flighty overhead lamp. Even the bureau, not normally observant, realizes that Pareti is loveless.

It is more than sad; it is annoying. It goes beyond mere annoyance; it is maddening. To love is a mandate, to be unloved is insupportable. Can it be true? Yes, it can; Joe Pareti does not love his loveless lover.

Joe Pareti is a man. He is the sixth man to spurn the loving lover's lovely love. Man does not love: can one argue the syllogism? Can frustrated passion be expected to defer judgment any longer?

Pareti looks up and sees the gilded mirror on the facing wall. He remembers that a mirror led Alice to Looking-Glass Land, and Orpheus to Perdition; that Cocteau called mirrors the gateways to hell.

He asks himself what a mirror is. He answers himself that a mirror is an eye waiting to be looked through.

He looks into the mirror and finds himself looking *out* of the mirror.

Joe Pareti has five new eyes. Two on the bedroom walls, one on the bedroom ceiling, one in the bathroom, one in the hall. He looks through his new eyes and sees new things.

There is the couch, sad lovelorn creature. Half visible is the standing lamp, its curved neck denoting fury. Over here is the closet door, stiff-backed, mute with rage.

Love is always a risk; but hate is a deadly peril.

Joe Pareti looks out through the mirrors, and he says to himself, I see a man sitting on a chair, and the chair is biting his leg.

Ben Bova and Harlan Ellison

BRILLO

INTRODUCTION

To begin with, Ben Bova has a milder temperament than me, he knows much more science than I do, he's married and I'm not, and his wife makes better lasagna than the wife I don't have would make if I had one.

None of which differences seem to have prevented us from becoming good friends.

Ben and I met at the Milford SF Writers' Conference five or six years ago. Ben was, even then, among other things, a "John Campbell writer." Now, before Ben and JWC and half a million people in between pounce, let me amplify by saying some of my best friends are John W. Campbell writers. Or have been. Or hope to be. What it takes to be a JWC/*Analog* writer is an amalgam of talents at whose nature I can only guess. Logic, a sense of analysis, a perception of the relevancy of man to the physical universe, and certainly the ability to read John Campbell's editorials.

Needless to say, in almost all of the preceding I score very low. Low enough so that during the fifteen years of professionally writing science fiction, I had never sold a story to John W. Campbell. I never even came close. If the truth be known, Mr. Campbell rejected my stories so often I gave up even submitting to *Analog*.

Ah. But that was before Ben Bova.

And before Brillo.

I'll tell you about it.

Ben worked for Avco Everett Labs. They make artificial hearts and moonshot stuff and a gang of other products intended to further the fortunes of the military-industrial complex, most of which Ben has tried to explain to me from time to time, none of which I understand. I am not a technologically-oriented sort of fellah. When I needed some engineering information for a story I wrote about cars on freeways of the future, I called Ben and he laid on me all I needed to know about mirror-stacking in laser guns, air-cushion systems so vehicles can skim above the roads, jive like that.

But we'd never thought of collaborating. Then, when I was planning the writers with whom I wanted to work, to fill out this book, Ben and I got together and we thought it would be a good idea.

Hans Stefan Santesson, one of the kindest men and best editors I've ever known, was putting together an anthology of stories about crime prevention in the 30th century for Walker. He had asked me for a contribution. Now as much as I hate cops, it seemed a natural for me to write an anti-pig story. But I got hung up with writing a movie, and though my name appeared in several advertisements for the book, I never did the story for Hans. But before I'd realized I'd tapped out on the book, Ben and I had kicked around the idea of killing two with one, and we'd decided that the cop story could be a collaboration and serve in both books. So Ben came up with the basic situation and a sorta-kinda plot for "Brillo." (The pun of the robot cop's name, incidentally, a pun that invariably evokes groans, is Bova's. I'll take the rap for a lot of things, but not *that!*) He wrote the first three pages of the original version, and mailed the package on from Boston to me in Los Angeles. It languished in my file for many months, till Ben came out to visit on one of his business trips. We went out to dinner, came back about eleven o'clock, put on a pot of coffee, and sat down to write. Ben having begun, I took over. In the manner of the Sheckley story, we alternated sections and the story ended for us at eight the next morning—having written through the night —with a total of 3000 words, almost equally Ben's and mine.

Then Ben went away and I did the rewrite. It came out at a fat 15,000 words.

So 12,500 words are mine, and 1500 are Ben's. Now I do not say this to make me look like a *gonser macher* nor even a *pezzonovanti*. I say it because of John W. Campbell. I'll explain, because it highlights the odd thinking of editors.

I wanted to try the story at *Playboy*. Ben thought Campbell might buy it. "Forget it, Ben," I said. "John doesn't like me."

"John says he'd even buy a story from Hitler if it was good," Ben replied. "*Especially* from Hitler," I said. "But not from me, baby. I've attacked him in public for what I consider to be wrong-headed racist editorials, too often, for him to lay out money to have my name in his magazine. We'll be better off at *Playboy*. Besides, they'd pay us over two grand for it."

"Compromise," Ben said. "First Hefner, then Campbell." I said okay. And I sent the finished manuscript off to our mutual agent, Robert P. Mills.

Well, *Playboy* turned it down on the grounds they'd been running a spate of stories about deranged computers, berserk vacuum cleaners and amok robots, and so they didn't think they could use it, though they liked it. Then it went off to *Analog*. I held out no hope for it.

Several days later, Mills called me and said JWC was buying it. I was frankly flabbergasted.

I was certain Campbell or his editorial assistant, Ms. Kay Tarrant, would delete the mildly spicy parts of the story (hardly as spicy as, say, *Rebecca of Sunnybrook Farm*, but *Analog* has long been known in the field as a magazine where, if a writer wanted to get something dirty slipped past, he had to be devilishly clever and had to phrase it technologically), but again I was to be surprised. Aside from some very minor revisions made by Ben— most notably reducing the amount of weaponry Polchik carries, to bring it into line with the society we postulated —there were no changes in the story.

But (and this goes to my remarks about how much each of us wrote) John confided in several people that it was obviously Ben's story, written by Ben, and that I'd done a coat-tail number, because he'd read what I'd writ-

ten by myself, and it was demonstrable that I didn't have
the savvy to write a sympathetic character like Mike Polchik.

Well, John was wrong, and now he knows it, but that
doesn't really matter except as a sidelight. What matters, I
think, is that despite the fact that I loathe and despise
what cops have become in our twisted snake society, I
wanted to test myself as a writer by writing a sympathetic
portrait of a man doing an ugly job, being phased out by
machinery, and try to espouse a humane philosophy about
such men that went contrary to my gut-level belief about
the nature of law enforcers in these times.

The science and the plot in "Brillo" are mostly Ben,
Mike Polchik is mine.

Brillo

Crazy season for cops is August. In August the riots start. Not just to get the pigs off campus (where they don't even happen to be, because school is out) or to rid the railroad flats of *Rattus norvegicus*, but they start for no reason at all. Some bunch of sweat-stinking kids get a hydrant spouting and it drenches the storefront of a shylock who lives most of his time in Kipps Bay when he's not sticking it to his Spanish Harlem customers, and he comes out of the pawnshop with a Louisville Slugger somebody hocked once, and he takes a swing at a *mestizo* urchin, and the next thing the precinct knows, they've got a three-star riot going on two full city blocks; then they call in the copchoppers from Governor's Island and spray the neighborhood with quiescent, and after a while the beat cops go in with breathers, in threes, and they start pulling in the bash-head cases. Why did it get going? A little water on a store window that hadn't been squee-gee'd since 1974? A short temper? Some kid flipping some guy the bird? No.

Crazy season is August.

Housewives take their steam irons to their old men's heads. Basset hound salesmen who trundle display suitcases full of ready-to-wear for eleven months, without squeaking at their bosses, suddenly pull twine knives and carve up taxi drivers. Suicides go out tenth storey windows and off the Verranzano-Narrows Bridge like confetti at an

astronaut's parade down Fifth Avenue. Teen-aged rat
packs steal half a dozen cars and drag-race them three
abreast against traffic up White Plains Road till they run
them through the show windows of supermarkets. No reason. Just August. Crazy season.

It was August, that special heat of August when the
temperature keeps going till it reaches the secret kill-crazy
mugginess at which point eyeballs roll up white in florid
faces and gravity knives appear as if by magic, it was *that*
time of August, when Brillo arrived in the precinct.

Buzzing softly (the sort of sound an electric watch
makes), he stood inert in the center of the precinct station's bullpen, his bright blue-anodized metal a gleaming
contrast to the paintless worn floorboards. He stood in the
middle of momentary activity, and no one who passed him
seemed to be able to pay attention to anything *but* him:

Not the two plainclothes officers duckwalking between
them a sixty-two year old pervert whose specialty was
flashing just before the subway doors closed.

Not the traffic cop being berated by his Sergeant for
having allowed his parking ticket receipts to get water-
logged in a plastic bag bombardment initiated by the last
few residents of a condemned building.

Not the tac/squad macers reloading their weapons from
the supply dispensers.

Not the line of beat cops forming up in ranks for their
shift on the street.

Not the Desk Sergeant trying to book three hookers
who had been arrested soliciting men queued up in front
of NBC for a network game show called "Sell A Sin."

Not the fuzzette using a wrist bringalong on the mugger
who had tried to snip a cutpurse on her as she patrolled
Riverside Drive.

None of them, even engaged in the hardly ordinary
business of sweeping up felons, could avoid staring at him.
All eyes kept returning to the robot: a squat cylinder resting on tiny trunnions. Brillo's optical sensors, up in his
dome-shaped head, bulged like the eyes of an acromegalic
insect. The eyes caught the glint of the overhead neons.

The eyes, particularly, made the crowd in the muster
room nervous. The crowd milled and thronged, but did
not clear until the Chief of Police spread his hands in a

typically Semitic gesture of impatience and yelled, "All right, already, can you clear this room!"

There was suddenly a great deal of unoccupied space.

Chief Santorini turned back to the robot. And to Reardon.

Frank Reardon shifted his weight uneasily from one foot to the other. He absorbed the Police Chief's look and tracked it out around the muster room, watching the men who were watching the robot. *His* robot. Not that he owned it any longer . . . but he still thought of it as his. He understood how Dr. Victor Frankenstein could feel paternal about a congeries of old spare body parts.

He watched them as they sniffed around the robot like bulldogs delighted with the discovery of a new fire hydrant. Even beefy Sgt. Loyo, the Desk Sergeant, up in his perch at the far end of the shabby room, looked clearly suspicious of the robot.

Santorini had brought two uniformed Lieutenants with him. Administrative assistants. Donkeywork protocol guardians. By-the-book civil service types, lamps lit against any *ee*-vil encroachment of dat ole debbil machine into the paydirt of human beings' job security. They looked grim.

The FBI man sat impassively on a stout wooden bench that ran the length of the room. He sat under posters for the Police Athletic League, the 4th War Bond Offensive, Driver Training Courses and an advertisement for *The Christian Science Monitor* with a FREE—TAKE ONE pocket attached. He had not said a word since being introduced to Reardon. And Reardon had even forgotten the name. Was that part of the camouflage of FBI agents? He sat there looking steely-eyed and jut-jawed. He looked grim, too.

Only the whiz kid from the Mayor's office was smiling as he stepped once again through the grilled door into the bullpen. He smiled as he walked slowly all around the robot. He smiled as he touched the matte-finish of the machine, and he smiled as he made pleasure noises: as if he was inspecting a new car on a showroom floor, on the verge of saying, "I'll take it. What terms can I get?"

He looked out through the wirework of the bullpen at Reardon. "Why do you call it Brillo?"

Reardon hesitated a moment, trying desperately to remember the whiz kid's first name. He was an engineer, not a public relations man. Universal Electronics should have sent Wendell down with Brillo. *He* knew how to talk to these image-happy clowns from City Hall. Knew how to butter and baste them so they put ink to contract. But part of the deal when he'd been forced to sell Reardon Electronics into merger with UE (after the stock raid and the power grab, which he'd lost) was that he stay on with projects like Brillo. Stay with them all the way to the bottom line.

It was as pleasant as clapping time while your wife made love to another man.

"It's . . . a nickname. Somebody at UE thought it up. Thought it was funny."

The whiz kid looked blank. "What's funny about Brillo?"

"Metal fuzz," the Police Chief rasped.

Light dawned on the whiz kid's face, and he began to chuckle; Reardon nodded, then caught the look of animosity on the Police Chief's face. Reardon looked away quickly from the old man's fiercely seamed features. It was getting more grim, much tenser.

Captain Summit came slowly down the stairs to join them. He was close to Reardon's age, but much grayer. He moved with one hand on the bannister, like an old man.

Why do they all look so tired? Reardon wondered. *And why do they seem to look wearier, more frightened, every time they look at the robot? Are they afraid it's come around their turn to be replaced? Is that the way I looked when UE forced me out of the company I created?*

Summit eyed the robot briefly, then walked over and sat down on the bench several feet apart from the silent FBI man. The whiz kid came out of the bullpen. They all looked at Summit.

"Okay, I've picked a man to work with him . . . it, I mean." He was looking at Reardon. "Mike Polchik. He's a good cop; young and alert. Good record. Nothing extraordinary, no showboater, just a solid cop. He'll give your machine a fair trial."

"That's fine. Thank you, Captain," Reardon said.

"He'll be right down. I pulled him out of the formation. He's getting his gear. He'll be right down."

The whiz kid cleared his throat. Reardon looked at him. *He* wasn't tired. But then, *he* didn't wear a uniform. *He* wasn't pushed up against what these men found in the streets every day. *He lives in Darien, probably,* Frank Reardon thought, *and buys those suits in quiet little shops where there're never more than three customers at a time.*

"How many of these machines can your company make in a year?" the whiz kid asked.

"It's not my company any more."

"I mean the company you work for—Universal."

"Inside a year: we can have them coming out at a rate of a hundred a month." Reardon paused. "Maybe more."

The whiz kid grinned. "We could replace every beat patrolman . . ."

A spark-gap was leaped. The temperature dropped. Reardon saw the uniformed men stiffen. Quickly, he said, "Police robots are intended to *augment* the existing force." Even more firmly he said, "Not replace it. We're trying to *help* the policeman, not get rid of him."

"Oh, hey, sure. Of *course!*" the whiz kid said, glancing around the room. "That's what I meant," he added unnecessarily. Everyone knew what he meant.

The silence at the bottom of the Marianas Trench.

And in that silence: heavy footsteps, coming down the stairs from the second-floor locker rooms.

He stopped at the foot of the stairs, one shoe tipped up on the final step; he stared at the robot in the bullpen for a long moment. Then the patrolman walked over to Captain Summit, only once more casting a glance into the bullpen. Summit smiled reassuringly at the patrolman and then gestured toward Reardon.

"Mike, this is Mr. Reardon. He designed—the robot. Mr. Reardon, Patrolman Polchik."

Reardon extended his hand and Polchik exerted enough pressure to make him wince.

Polchik was two inches over six feet tall, and weighty. Muscular; thick forearms; the kind found on men who work in foundries. Light, crew-cut hair. Square face, wide open; strong jaw, hard eyes under heavy brow ridges. Even his smile looked hard. He was ready for work, with a .32 Needle Positive tilt-stuck on its velcro fastener at mid-thigh and an armament bandolier slanted across his broad chest. His aura keyed one word: cop.

"The Captain tells me I'm gonna be walkin' with your machine t'night."

Nodding, flexing his fingers, Reardon said, "Yes, that's right. The Captain probably told you, we want to test Brillo under actual foot patrol conditions. That's what he was designed for: foot patrol."

"Been a long time since I done foot patrol," Polchik said: "Work a growler, usually."

"Beg pardon?"

Summit translated. "Growler: prowl car."

"Oh. Oh, I see," Reardon said, trying to be friendly.

"It's only for tonight, Mike," the Captain said. "Just a test."

Polchik nodded as though he understood far more than either Reardon or Summit had told him. He did not turn his big body, but his eyes went to the robot. Through the grillework Brillo (with the sort of sound an electric watch makes) buzzed softly, staring at nothing. Polchik looked it up and down, slowly, very carefully. Finally he said, "Looks okay to me."

"Preliminary tests," Reardon said, "everything short of actual field runs ... everything's been tested out. You won't have any trouble."

Polchik murmured something.

"I beg your pardon?" Frank Reardon said.

"On-the-job-training," Polchik repeated. He did not smile. But a sound ran through the rest of the station house crew.

"Well, whenever you're ready, Officer Polchik," the whiz kid said suddenly. Reardon winced. The kid had a storm-window salesman's tone even when he was trying to be disarming.

"Yeah. Right." Polchik moved toward the front door. The robot did not move. Polchik stopped and turned around. Everyone was watching.

"I thought he went on his own, uh, independ'nt?"

They were all watching Reardon now.

"He's been voice-keyed to me since the plant," Reardon said. "To shift command, I'll have to prime him with your voice." He turned to the robot. "Brillo, come here, please."

The word *please*.

The buzzing became more distinct for a moment as the trunnions withdrew inside the metal skin. Then the sound diminished, became barely audible, and the robot stepped forward smoothly. He walked to Reardon and stopped.

"Brillo, this is Officer Mike Polchik. You'll be working with him tonight. He'll be your superior and you'll be under his immediate orders." Reardon waved Polchik over. "Would you say a few words, so he can program your voice-print?"

Polchik looked at Reardon. Then he looked at the robot. Then he looked around the muster room. Desk Sergeant Loyo was grinning. "Whattaya want me to say?"

"Anything."

One of the detectives had come down the stairs. No one had noticed before. Lounging against the railing leading to the squad room upstairs, he giggled. "Tell him some'a your best friends are can openers, Mike."

The whiz kid and the Chief of Police threw him a look. Summit said, "Bratten!" He shut up. After a moment he went back upstairs. Quietly.

"Go ahead. Anything," Reardon urged Polchik.

The patrolman drew a deep breath, took another step forward and said, self-consciously, "Come on, let's go. It's gettin' late."

The soft buzzing (the sort of sound an electric watch makes) came once again from somewhere deep inside the robot. "Yes, sir," he said, in the voice of Frank Reardon, and moved very smoothly, very quickly, toward Polchik. The patrolman stepped back quickly, tried to look casual, turned and started toward the door of the station house once more. The robot followed.

When they had gone, the whiz kid drywashed his hands, smiled at everyone and said, "Now it begins."

Reardon winced again. The Desk Sergeant, Loyo, rattled pencils, tapped them even, dumped them into an empty jelly jar on the blotter desk. Everyone else looked away. The FBI man smiled.

From outside the precinct house the sounds of the city seemed to grow louder in the awkward silence. In all that noise no one even imagined he could hear the sound of the robot.

Polchik was trying the locks on the burglarproof gates of the shops lining Amsterdam between 82nd and 83rd. The robot was following him, doing the same thing. Polchik was getting burned up. He turned up 83rd and entered the alley behind the shops, retracing his steps back toward 82nd. The robot followed him.

Polchik didn't like being followed. It made him feel uneasy. *Damned piece of junk!* he thought. *He rips one of them gates off the hinges, there'll be hell to pay down at the precinct.*

Polchik rattled a gate. He moved on. The robot followed. (*Like a little kid,* Polchik thought.) The robot grabbed the gate and clanged it back and forth. Polchik spun on him. "Listen, dammit, stop makin' all that racket! Y'wanna wake everybody? You know what time it is?"

"1:37 A.M." the robot replied, in Reardon's voice.

Polchik looked heavenward.

Shaking his head he moved on. The robot stopped. "Officer Polchik." Mike Polchik turned, exasperated. *"What now?"*

"I detect a short circuit in this alarm system," the robot said. He was standing directly under the Morse-Dictograph Security panel. "If it is not repaired, it will cancel the fail-safe circuits."

"I'll call it in," Polchik said, pulling the pin-mike on its spring-return wire from his callbox. He was about to thumb on the wristband callbox, when the robot extruded an articulated arm from its chest. "I am equipped to repair the unit without assistance," the robot said, and a light-beam began to pulse at the end of the now-goosenecked arm.

"Leave it alone!!"

"A simple 155-0 system," the robot said. "Fixed temperature unit with heat detectors, only barely exceeding NFPA standard 74 and NFPA 72-A requirements." The arm snaked up to the panel and followed the break line around the outside.

"Don't screw with it! It'll set it—"

The panel accordion-folded back. Polchik's mouth fell open. "Oh my God," he mumbled.

The robot's extruded arm worked inside for a long moment, then withdrew. "It is fully operable now." The panel folded back into place.

Polchik let the pin-mike slip from his fingers and it zzzzz'd back into the wristband. He walked away down the alley, looking haunted.

Down at the corner, the Amsterdam Inn's lights shone weakly, reflecting dully in the street oil slick. Polchik paused at the mouth of the alley and pulled out the pin-mike again. He thumbed the callbox on his wrist, *feeling* the heavy shadow of the robot behind him.

"Polchik," he said into the mike.

"Okay, Mike?" crackled the reply. "How's yer partner doing?"

Glancing over his shoulder, Polchik saw the robot standing impassively, gooseneck arm vanished; ten feet behind him. Respectfully. "Don't call it my partner."

Laughter on the other end of the line. "What's'a'matter, Mike? 'Fraid of him?"

"Ahhh ... cut the clownin'. Everything quiet here, Eighty-two and Amsterdam."

"Okay. Oh, hey, Mike, remember ... if it starts to rain, get yer partner under an awning before he starts t'rust!"

He was still laughing like a jackass as Polchik let the spring-wire zzzzz back into the callbox.

"Hey, Mike! What you got there?"

Polchik looked toward the corner. It was Rico, the bartender from the Amsterdam Inn.

"It's a robot," Polchik said. He kept his voice very flat. He was in no mood for further ribbing.

"Real he is, yeah? No kidding?" Rico's face always looked to Polchik like a brass artichoke, ready to be peeled. But he was friendly enough. And cooperative. It was a dunky neighborhood and Polchik had found Rico useful more than once. "What's he supposed to do, eh?"

"He's supposed to be a cop." Glum.

Rico shook his vegetable head. "What they gonna do next? Robots. So what happens t'you, Mike? They make you a detective?"

"Sure. And the week after that they make me Captain."

Rico looked uncertain, didn't know whether he should laugh or sympathize. Finally, he said, "Hey, I got a bottle for ya," feeling it would serve, whatever his reaction should properly have been. "Betcha your wife likes it ... from Poland, imported stuff. Got grass or weeds or some kinda stuff in it. S'possed to be really sensational."

For just a second, peripherally seen, Polchik thought the robot had stirred.

"*Escuchar!* I'll get it for you."

He disappeared inside the bar before Polchik could stop him. The robot *did* move. It trembled ... ?

Rico came out with a paper bag, its neck twisted closed around what was obviously a bottle of liquor.

"I'll have to pick it up tomorrow," Polchik said. "I don't have the car tonight."

"I'll keep it for you. If I'm on relief when you come by, ask Maldonado."

The robot was definitely humming. Polchik could hear it. (The sort of sound an electric watch makes.) It suddenly moved, closing the distance, ten feet between them, till it passed Polchik, swiveled to face Rico—who stumbled backward halfway to the entrance to the Amsterdam Inn—then swiveled back to face Polchik.

"Visual and audial data indicate a one-to-one extrapolation of same would result in a conclusion that a gratuity has been offered to you, Officer Polchik. Further, logic indicates that you intend to accept said gratuity. Such behavior is a programmed infraction of the law. It is—"

"Shut up!"

Rico stood very close to the door, wide-eyed.

"I'll see you tomorrow night," Polchik said to him.

"Officer Polchik," the robot went on as though there had been no interruption, "it is clear if you intend to accept a gratuity, you will be breaking the law and liable to arrest and prosecution under Law Officer Statutes number—"

"I said shuddup, dammit!" Polchik said, louder. "I don't even know what the hell you're talkin' about, but I said shuddup, and that's an *order!*"

"Yes, sir," the robot replied instantly. "However, my data tapes will record this conversation in its entirety and it will be transcribed into a written report at the conclusion of our patrol."

"What?" Polchik felt gears gnashing inside his head, thought of gears, thought of the robot, rejected gears and thought about Captain Summit. Then he thought about gears again . . . crushing him.

Rico's voice intruded, sounding scared. "What's he saying? What's that about a report?"

"Now wait a minute, Brillo," Polchik said, walking up to the robot. "Nothin's happened here you can write a report on."

The robot's voice—*Reardon's* voice, Polchik thought irritatedly—was very firm. "Logic indicates a high probability that a gratuity has been accepted in the past, and another will be accepted in the future."

Polchik felt chili peppers in his gut. Hooking his thumbs in his belt—a pose he automatically assumed when he was trying to avert trouble—he deliberately toned down his voice. "Listen, Brillo, you forget the whole thing, you understand. You just for*get* it."

"Am I to understand you desire my tapes to be erased?"

"Yeah, that's right. Erase it."

"Is that an order?"

"It's an order!"

The robot hummed to itself for a heartbeat, then, "Primary programming does not allow erasure of data tapes. Tapes can be erased only post-transcription or by physically removing same from my memory bank."

"Listen—" Rico started, "—I don't wan' no trub—"

Polchik impatiently waved him to silence. He didn't need any complications right now. "Listen, Brillo . . ."

"Yes. I hear it."

Polchik was about to continue speaking. He stopped. *I hear it? This damned thing's gone bananas.* "I didn't say anything yet."

"Oh. I'm sorry, sir. I thought you were referring to the sound of a female human screaming on 84th Street, third-floor front apartment."

Polchik looked everywhichway. "What are you *talkin'* about? You crazy or something?"

"No, sir. I am a model X-44. Though under certain special conditions my circuits can malfunction, conceivably, nothing in my repair programming parameters approximates 'crazy.' "

"Then just shuddup and let's get this thing straightened out. Now, try'n understand this. You're just a robot, see. You don't understand the way real people do things. Like, for instance, when Rico here offers me a bottle of—"

"If you'll pardon me, sir, the female human is now screaming in the 17,000 cycle per-second range. My tapes are programmed to value-judge such a range as concomitant with fear and possibly extreme pain. I suggest we act at once."

"Hey, Polchik . . ." Rico began.

"No, shuddup, Rico. Hey, listen, robot, Brillo, whatever: you mean you can *hear* some woman screaming, two blocks away and up three flights? Is the window open?" Then he stopped. "What'm I doin'? Talking to this thing!" He remembered the briefing he'd been given by Captain Summit. "Okay. You say you can hear her . . . let's find her."

The robot took off at top speed. Back into the alley behind the Amsterdam Inn, across the 82nd-83rd block, across the 83rd-84th block, full-out with no clanking or clattering. Polchik found himself pounding along ten feet behind the robot, then twenty feet, then thirty feet; suddenly he was puffing, his chest heavy, the armament bandolier banging the mace cans and the riot-prod and the bull-horn and the peppergas shpritzers and the extra clips of Needler ammunition against his chest and back.

The robot emerged from the alley, turned a 90° angle with the sharpest cut Polchik had ever seen, and jogged up 84th Street. Brillo was caught for a moment in the glare of a neon streetlamp, then was taking the steps of a crippled old brownstone three at a time.

Troglodytes with punch-presses were berkeleying Polchik's lungs and stomach. His head was a dissenter's punchboard. But he followed. More slowly now; and had trouble negotiating the last flight of stairs to the third floor. As he gained the landing, he was hauling himself hand-over-hand up the bannister. *If God'd wanted cops to walk beats he wouldn't'a created the growler!*

The robot, Brillo, X-44, was standing in front of the

door marked 3-A. He was quivering like a hound on point. (Buzzing softly with the sort of sound an electric watch makes.) Now Polchik could hear the woman himself, above the roar of blood in his temples.

"Open up in there!" Polchik bellowed. He ripped the .32 Needle Positive off its velcro fastener and banged on the door with the butt. The lanyard was twisted; he untwisted it. "This's the police. I'm demanding entrance to a private domicile under Public Law 22-809, allowing for superced'nce of the 'home-castle' rule under emergency conditions. I said *open up in there!*"

The screaming went up and plateau'd a few hundred cycles higher, and Polchik snapped at the robot, "Get outta my way."

Brillo obediently moved back a pace, and in the narrow hallway Polchik braced himself against the wall, locked the exoskeletal rods on his boots, dropped his crash-hat visor, jacked up his leg and delivered a power *savate* kick at the door.

It was a pre-SlumClear apartment. The door bowed and dust spurted from the seams, but it held. Despite the rods, Polchik felt a searing pain gash up through his leg. He fell back, hopping about painfully, hearing himself going, "oo—oo—oo" and then prepared himself to have to do it again. The robot moved up in front of him, said, "Excuse me, sir," and smoothly cleaved the door down the center with the edge of a metal hand that somehow suddenly developed a cutting edge. He reached in, grasped both sliced edges of the hardwood, and ripped the door outward in two even halves.

"Oh." Polchik stared open-mouthed for only an instant. Then they were inside.

The unshaven man with the beer gut protruding from beneath his olive drab skivvy undershirt was slapping the hell out of his wife. He had thick black tufts of hair that bunched like weed corsages in his armpits. She was half-lying over the back of a sofa with the springs showing. Her eyes were swollen and blue-black as dried prunes. One massive bruise was already draining down her cheek into her neck. She was weakly trying to fend off her husband's blows with ineffectual wrist-blocks.

"Okay! That's it!" Polchik yelled.

The sound of another voice, in the room with them, brought the man and his wife to a halt. He turned his head, his left hand still tangled in her long black hair, and he stared at the two intruders.

He began cursing in Spanish. Then he burst into a guttural combination of English and Spanish, and finally slowed in his own spittle to a ragged English. "... won't let me alone ... go out my house ... always botherin' won't let me alone ... damn ..." and he went back to Spanish as he pushed the woman from him and started across the room. The woman tumbled, squealing, out of sight behind the sofa.

The man stumbled crossing the room, and Polchik's needler tracked him. Behind him he heard the robot softly humming, and then it said, "Sir, analysis indicates psychotic glaze over subject's eyes."

The man grabbed a half-filled quart bottle of beer off the television set, smashed it against the leading edge of the TV, giving it a half-twist (which registered instantly in Polchik's mind: this guy knew how to get a ragged edge on the weapon; he was an experienced bar-room brawler) and suddenly lurched toward Polchik with the jagged stump in his hand.

Abruptly, before Polchik could even thumb the needler to stun (it was on dismember), a metal blur passed him, swept into the man, lifted him high in the air with one hand, turned him upside-down so the bottle, small plastic change and an unzipped shoe showered down onto the threadbare rug. Arms and legs fluttered helplessly.

"Aieeee!" the man screamed, his hair hanging down, his face plugged red with blood. *"Madre de dios!"*

"Leave him alone!" It was the wife screaming, charging—if it could be called that, on hands and knees—from behind the sofa. She clambered to her feet and ran at the robot, screeching and cursing, pounding her daywork-reddened fists against his gleaming hide.

"Okay, okay," Polchik said, his voice lower but strong enough to get through to her. Pulling her and her hysteria away from the robot, he ordered, "Brillo, put him down."

"You goddam cops got no right bustin' in here," the man started complaining the moment he was on his feet again. "Goddam cops don't let a man'n his wife alone for nothin' no more. You got a warrant? Huh? You gonna get in trouble, plently trouble. This my home, cop, 'home is a man's castle,' hah? Right? Right? An' you an' this tin can . . ." He was waving his arms wildly.

Brillo wheeled a few inches toward the man. The stream of abuse cut off instantly, the man's face went pale, and he threw up his hands to protect himself.

"This man can be arrested for assault and battery, failure to heed a legitimate police order, attempted assault on a police officer with a deadly weapon, and disturbing the peace," Brillo said. His flat, calm voice seemed to echo off the grimy walls.

"It . . . it's talkin'! Flavio! *Demonio!*" The wife spiraled toward hysteria again.

"Shall I inform him of his rights under the Public Laws, sir?" Brillo asked Polchik.

"You gon' arrest me? Whu'for?"

"Brillo . . ." Polchik began.

Brillo started again, "Assault and battery, failure to—"

Polchik looked annoyed. "Shuddup, I wasn't asking you to run it again. Just shuddup."

"I din't do nothin'! You come bust t'rough my door when me an' my wife wass arguin', an' you beat me up. Look'a the bruise on my arm." The arm was slightly inflamed where Brillo had grabbed him.

"Flavio!" the woman whimpered.

"Isabel; *callete la bocà!*"

"I live right downstairs," a voice said from behind them. "He's always beating her up, and he drinks all the time and then he pisses out the window!" Polchik spun and a man in Levis and striped pajama tops was standing in the ruined doorway. "Sometimes it looks like it's raining on half my window. Once I put my hand out to see—"

"Get outta here!" Polchik bellowed, and the man vanished.

"I din't do nothin'!" Flavio said again, semi-surly.

"My data tapes," Brillo replied evenly, "will clearly show your actions."

"Day to tapes? Whass he talkin' 'bout?" Flavio turned to Polchik, an unaccustomed ally against the hulking machine. Polchik felt a sense of camaraderie with the man.

"He's got everything down recorded . . . like on TV.

And sound tapes, too." Polchik looked back at him and recognized something in the dismay on the man's fleshy face.

Brillo asked again, "Shall I inform him of his rights, sir?"

"Officer, sir, you ain't gonna'rrest him?" the woman half-asked, half-pleaded, her eyes swollen almost closed, barely open, but tearful.

"He came after me with a bottle," Polchik said. "And he didn't do you much good, neither."

"He wass work op. Iss allright. He's okay now. It wass joss a'argumen'. Nobody got hort."

Brillo's hum got momentarily higher. "Madam, you should inspect your face in my mirror." He hummed and his skin became smoothly reflective. "My sensors detect several contusions and abrasions, particularly . . ."

"Skip it," Polchik said abruptly. "Come on, Brillo, let's go."

Brillo's metal hide went blank again. "I have not informed the prisoner . . ."

"No prisoner," Polchik said. "No arrest. Let's go."

"But the data clearly shows . . ."

"Forget it!" Polchik turned to face the man; he was standing there looking uncertain, rubbing his arm. "And you, strongarm . . . lemme hear one more peep outta this apartment and you'll be in jail so fast it'll make your head swim . . . and for a helluva long time, too. If you get there at all. We don't like guys like you. So I'm puttin' the word out on you . . . I don't like guys comin' at me with bottles."

"Sir . . . I . . ."

"Come on!"

The robot followed the cop and the apartment was suddenly silent. Flavio and Isabel looked at each other sheepishly, then he began to cry, went to her and touched her bruises with the gentlest fingers.

They went downstairs, Polchik staring and trying to figure out how it was such a massive machine could navigate the steps so smoothly. Something was going on at the base of the robot, but Polchik couldn't get a good view of it. Dust puffed out from beneath the machine. And something sparkled.

Once on the sidewalk, Brillo said, "Sir, that man should have been arrested. He was clearly violating several statutes."

Polchik made a sour face. "His wife wouldn't of pressed the charge."

"He attacked a police officer with a deadly weapon."

"So that makes him Mad Dog Coll? He's scared shitless, in the future he'll watch it. For a while, at least."

Brillo was hardly satisfied at this noncomputable conclusion. "A police officer's duty is to arrest persons who are suspected of having broken the law. Civil or criminal courts have the legal jurisdiction to decide the suspect's guilt of innocence. Your duty, sir, was to arrest that man."

"Sure, sure. Have it *your* way, half the damn city'll be in jail, and the other half'll be springin' 'em out."

Brillo said nothing, but Polchik thought the robot's humming sounded sullen. He had a strong suspicion the machine wouldn't forget it. Or Rico, either.

And further up the street, to cinch Polchik's suspicion, the robot once more tried to reinforce his position. "According to the Peace Officer Responsibility Act of 1975, failure of an officer to take into custody person or persons indisputably engaged in acts that contravene . . ."

"Awright, dammit, knock it off. I tole you why I din't arrest that poor jughead, so stop bustin' my chops with it. You ain't happy, you don't like it, tell my Sergeant!"

Sergeant, hell, Polchik thought. *This stuff goes right to Captain Summit, Santorini and the Commissioner. Probably the Mayor. Maybe the President; who the hell knows?*

Petulantly (it seemed to Polchik), the robot resumed, "Reviewing my tapes, I find the matter of the bottle of liquor offered as a gratuity still unresolved. If I am to—"

Polchik spun left and kicked with all his might at a garbage can bolted to an iron fence. The lid sprang off and clanged against the fence at the end of its short chain. "I've had it with you . . . you nonreturnable piece of scrap crap!" He wanted very much to go on, but he didn't know what to say. All he knew for certain was that he'd never had such a crummy night in all his life. It *couldn't* just be this goddamned robot—staring back blankly. It was *every*-thing. The mortgage payment was due; Benjy had to go in to the orthodontist and where the hell was the money going to come from for *that;* Dorothy had called the pre-cinct just before he'd come down, to tell him the hot water had split and drowned the carpets in the kid's bedroom; and to top it all off, he'd been assigned this buzzing pain in the ass and got caught with a little juice passed by that nitwit Rico; he'd had to have this Brillo pain tell him there was a hassle two blocks away; he was sure as God made little green apples going to get a bad report out of this, maybe get set down, maybe get reprimanded, maybe get censured . . . he didn't know what all.

But one thing was certain: this metal bird-dog, this stuffed shirt barracks lawyer with the trailalong of a ten-year-old kid behind his big brother, this nuisance in metal underwear, this . . . this . . . *thing* was of no damned earthly use to a working cop pulling a foot beat!

On the other hand, a voice that spoke with the voice of Mike Polchik said, *he* did *keep that jughead from using a broken bottle on you.*

"Shuddup!" Polchik said.

"I beg your pardon?" answered the robot.

Ingrate! said the inner voice.

It was verging on that chalky hour before dawn, when the light filtering out of the sky had a leprous, sickly look. Mike Polchik was a much older màn.

Brillo had interfered in the apprehension of Milky Ky-ser, a well-known car thief. Mike had spotted him walking slowly and contemplatively along a line of parked cars on Columbus Avenue, carrying a tightly-rolled copy of the current issue of *Life* magazine.

When he had collared Milky, the robot had buzzed up to them and politely inquired precisely what in the carbo-rundum Polchik thought he was doing. Polchik had re-sponded with what was becoming an hysterical reaction-formation to *anything* the metal cop said. "Shuddup!"

Brillo had persisted, saying he was programmed to pro-tect the civil rights of the members of the community, and as far as he could tell, having "scanned all data relevant to the situation at hand," the gentleman now dangling from

Polchik's grip was spotlessly blameless of even the remotest scintilla of wrongdoing. Polchik had held Milky with one hand and with the other gesticulated wildly as he explained, "Look, dimdumb, this is Milky Kyser, AKA Irwin Kayser, AKA Clarence Irwin, AKA Jack Milk, AKA God Knows Who All. He is a well-known dip and car thief, and he will use that rolled-up copy of the magazine to jack-and-snap the door handle of the proper model car, any number of which is currently parked, you will note, along this street . . . unless I arrest him! Now will you kindly get the hell outta my hair and *back off?*"

But it was no use. By the time Brillo had patiently repeated the civil rights story, reiterated pertinent sections of the Peace Officer Responsibility Act of 1975 and topped it off with a *précis* of Miranda-Escobedo-Baum Supreme Court decisions so adroit and simplified even a confirmed tautologist would have applauded, Milky himself—eyes glittering and a sneer that was hardly a smile on his ferret face—was echoing it, word for word.

The robot had given Milky a thorough course in legal cop-outs, before Polchik's dazed eyes.

"Besides," Milky told Polchik, with as much dignity as he could muster, hanging as he was from the cop's meaty fist, "I ain't done nuthin', and just because I been busted once or twice . . ."

"Once or twice!?" Polchik yanked the rolled-up magazine out of Milky's hand and raised it to clobber him. Milky pulled in his head like a turtle, wincing.

But in that fraction of a second, Polchik suddenly saw a picture flashed on the wall of his mind. A picture of Desk Sergeant Loyo and Captain Summit and Chief Santorini and the Mayor's toady and that silent FBI man, all watching a TV screen. And on the screen, there was the pride of the Force, Officer Mike Polchik beaning Milky Kyser with a semi-lethal copy of *Life* magazine.

Polchik held the magazine poised, trembling with the arrested movement. Milky, head now barely visible from between his shoulders, peeped up from behind his upraised hands. He looked like a mole.

"Beat it," Polchik growled. "Get the hell out of this precinct, Milky. If you're spotted around here again, you're gonna get busted. And don't stop to buy no magazines."

He let Milky loose.

The mole metamorphosed into a ferret once more. And straightening himself, he said, "An' don't call me 'Milky' any more. My given name is Irwin."

"You got three seconds t'vanish from my sight!"

Milky *née* Irwin hustled off down the street. At the corner he stopped and turned around. He cupped his hands and yelled back. "Hey, robot . . . thanks!"

Brillo was about to reply when Polchik bellowed, "Will you *please!*" The robot turned and said, very softly in Reardon's voice, "You are still holding Mr. Kyser's magazine."

Polchik was weary. Infinitely weary. "You hear him askin' for it?" He walked away from the robot and, as he passed a sidewalk dispenser, stepped on the dispodpedal, and flipped the magazine into the receptacle.

"I saved a piece of cherry pie for you, Mike," the waitress said. Polchik looked up from his uneaten hot (now cold) roast beef sandwich and French fries. He shook his head.

"Thanks anyway. Just another cuppa coffee."

The waitress had lost her way somewhere beyond twenty-seven. She was a nice person. She went home to her husband every morning. She didn't fool around. Extra mates under the new lottery were not her interest; she just didn't fool around. But she liked Mike Polchik. He, like she, was a very nice person.

"What's the matter, Mike?"

Polchik looked out the window of the diner. Brillo was standing directly under a neon street lamp. He couldn't hear it from here, but he was sure the thing was buzzing softly to itself (with the sort of sound an electric watch makes).

"Him."

"That?" The waitress looked past him.

"Uh-uh. *Him.*"

"What is it?"

"My shadow."

"Mike, you okay? Try the pie, huh? Maybe a scoop of nice vanilla ice cream on top."

"Onita, please. Just a cuppa coffee, I'm fine. I got problems." He stared down at his plate again.

She looked at him for a moment longer, worried, then turned and returned the pie on its plate to the empty space behind the smudged glass of the display case. "You want fresh?" she asked.

When he didn't answer, she shrugged and came back, using the coffee siphon on the portable cart to refill his cup.

She lounged behind the counter, watching her friend, Mike Polchik, as he slowly drank his coffee; and every few minutes he'd look out at that metal thing on the corner under the streetlamp. She was a nice person.

When he rose from the booth and came to the counter, she thought he was going to apologize, or speak to her, or something, but all he said was, "You got my check?"

"What check?"

"Come on."

"Oh, Mike, for Christ's sake, what's wrong with you?"

"I want to pay the check, you mind?"

"Mike, almost—what—five years you been eating here, you ever been asked to pay a check?"

Polchik looked very tired. "Tonight I pay the check. Come on . . . I gotta get back on the street. He's waiting."

There was a strange look in his eyes and she didn't want to ask which "he" Polchik meant. She was afraid he meant the metal thing out there. Onita, a very nice person, didn't like strange, new things that waited under neon streetlamps. She hastily wrote out a check and slid it across the plasteel to him. He pulled change from a pocket, paid her, turned, seemed to remember something, turned back, added a tip, then swiftly left the diner.

She watched through the glass as he went up to the metal thing. Then the two of them walked away, Mike leading, the thing following.

Onita made fresh. It was a good thing she had done it so many times she could do it by reflex, without thinking. Hot coffee scalds are very painful.

At the corner, Polchik saw a car weaving toward the intersection. A Ford Electric; convertible, four years old. Still looked flashy. Top down. He could see a bunch of long-haired kids inside. He couldn't tell the girls from the boys. It bothered him.

Polchik stopped. They weren't going fast, but the car was definitely weaving as it approached the intersection. *The warrior-lizard*, he thought. It was almost an unconscious directive. He'd been a cop long enough to react to the little hints, the flutters, the inclinations. The hunches.

Polchik stepped out from the curb, unshipped his gumball from the bandolier and flashed the red light at the driver. The car slowed even more; now it was crawling.

"Pull it over, kid!" he shouted.

For a moment he thought they were ignoring him, that the driver might not have heard him, that they'd try and make a break for it ... that they'd speed up and sideswipe him. But the driver eased the car to the curb and stopped.

Then he slid sidewise, pulled up his legs and crossed them neatly at the ankles. On the top of the dashboard.

Polchik walked around to the driver's side. "Turn it off. Everybody out."

There were six of them. None of them moved. The driver closed his eyes slowly, then tipped his Irkutsk fur hat over his eyes till it rested on the bridge of his nose. Polchik reached into the car and turned it off. He pulled the keys.

"Hey! Whuzzis allabout?" one of the kids in the back seat—a boy with terminal acne—complained. His voice began and ended on a whine. Polchik re-stuck the gumball.

The driver looked up from under the fur. "Wasn't breaking any laws." He said each word very slowly, very distinctly, as though each one was on a printout.

And Polchik knew he'd been right. They were on the lizard.

He opened the door, free hand hanging at the needler. "Out. All of you, out."

Then he sensed Brillo lurking behind him, in the middle of the street. Good. *Hope a damned garbage truck hits him.*

He was getting mad. That wasn't smart. Carefully, he said, "Don't make me say it again. Move it!"

He lined them up on the sidewalk beside the car, in plain sight. Three girls, three guys. Two of the guys with long, stringy hair and the third with a scalplock. The three girls wearing tammy cuts. All six sullen-faced, drawn, dark smudges under the eyes. The lizard. But good clothes, fairly new. He couldn't just hustle them, he had to be careful.

"Okay, one at a time, empty your pockets and pouches onto the hood of the car."

"Hey, we don't haveta do that just because . . ."

"Do it!"

"Don't argue with the pig," one of the girls said, lizard-spacing her words carefully. "He's probably trigger happy."

Brillo rolled up to Polchik. "It is necessary to have a probable cause clearance from the precinct in order to search, sir."

"Not on a stop'n'frisk," Polchik snapped, not taking his eyes off them. He had no time for nonsense with the can of cogs. He kept his eyes on the growing collection of chits, change, code-keys, combs, nail files, toke pipes and miscellania being dumped on the Ford's hood.

"There must be grounds for suspicion even in a spot search action, sir," Brillo said.

"There's grounds. Narcotics."

"'Nar . . . you must be outtayer mind," said the one boy who slurred his words. He was working something other than the lizard.

"That's a pig for you," said the girl who had made the trigger happy remark.

"Look," Polchik said, "you snots aren't from around here. Odds are good if I run b&b tests on you, we'll find you're under the influence of the lizard."

"Heyyyy!" the driver said. "The *what?*"

"Warrior-lizard," Polchik said.

"Oh, ain't he the jive thug," the smartmouth girl said. "He's a word user. I'll bet he knows *all* the current rage phrases. A philologist. I'll bet he knows *all* the solecisms and colloquialisms, catch phrases, catachreses, nicknames and vulgarisms. The 'warrior-lizard,' indeed."

Damned college kids, Polchik fumed inwardly. *They always try to make you feel stupid; I coulda gone to college—if I didn't have to work. Money, they probably always had money. The little bitch.*

The driver giggled. "Are you trying to tell me, Mella, my dear, that this Peace Officer is accusing us of being under the influence of the illegal Bolivian drug commonly called Guerrera-Tuera?" He said it with pinpointed scorn, pronouncing the Spanish broadly: gwuh-*rare*-uh too-*err*-uh.

Brillo said, "Reviewing my semantic tapes, sir, I find no analogs for 'Guerrera-Tuera' as 'warrior-lizard.' True, *guerrero* in Spanish means *warrior*, but the closest spelling I find is the feminine noun *guerra*, which translates as *war*. Neither *guerrera* nor *tuera* appear in the Spanish language. If *tuera* is a species of lizard, I don't seem to find it—"

Polchik had listened dumbly. The weight on his shoulders was monstrous. All of them were on him. The kids, that lousy stinking robot—they were making fun, such fun, such *damned* fun of him! "Keep digging," he directed them. He was surprised to hear his words emerge as a series of croaks.

"And blood and breath tests must be administered, sir—"

"Stay the hell outta this!"

"We're on our way home from a party," said the boy with the scalplock, who had been silent till then. "We took a short-cut and got lost."

"Sure," Polchik said. "In the middle of Manhattan, you got lost." He saw a small green bottle dumped out of the last girl's pouch. She was trying to push it under other items. "What's that?"

"Medicine," she said. Quickly. Very quickly.

Everyone tensed.

"Let me see it." His voice was even.

He put out his hand for the bottle, but all six watched his other hand, hanging beside the needler. Hesitantly, the girl picked the bottle out of the mass of goods on the car's hood, and handed him the plastic container.

Brillo said, "I am equipped with chemical sensors and reference tapes in my memory bank enumerating common narcotics. I can analyze the suspected medicine."

The six stared wordlessly at the robot. They seemed almost afraid to acknowledge its presence.

Polchik handed the plastic bottle to the robot.

Brillo depressed a color-coded key on a bank set flush into his left forearm, and a panel that hadn't seemed to be there a moment before slid down in the robot's chest. He dropped the plastic bottle into the opening and the panel slid up. He stood and buzzed.

"You don't have to open the bottle?" Polchik asked.

"No, sir."

"Oh."

The robot continued buzzing. Polchik felt stupid, just standing and watching. After a few moments the kids began to smirk, then to grin, then to chuckle openly, whispering among themselves. The smartmouthed girl giggled viciously. Polchik felt fifteen years old again; awkward, pimply, the butt of secret jokes among the long-legged high school girls in their miniskirts who had been so terrifyingly aloof he had never even considered asking them out. He realized with some shame that he despised these kids with their money, their cars, their flashy clothes, their dope. And most of all, their assurance. He, Mike Polchik, had been working hauling sides of beef from the delivery trucks to his old man's butcher shop while others were tooling around in their Electrics. He forced the memories from his mind and took out his anger and frustration on the metal idiot still buzzing beside him.

"Okay, okay, how long does it take you?"

"Tsk, tsk," said the driver, and went cross-eyed. Polchik ignored him. But not very well.

"I am a mobile unit, sir. Experimental model 44. My parent mechanism—the Master Unit AA—at Universal Electronics laboratories is equipped to perform this function in under one minute."

"Well, hurry it up. I wanna run these hairies in."

"Gwuh-*rare-uh* too-*er*-uh," the scalplock said in a nasty undertone.

There was a soft musical tone from inside the chest compartment, the plate slid down again, and the robot withdrew the plastic bottle. He handed it to the girl.

"*Now* whaddaya think you're doing?"

"Analysis confirms what the young lady attested, sir. This is a commonly prescribed nose drop for nasal congestion and certain primary allergies."

Polchik was speechless.

"You are free to go," the robot said. "With our apologies. We are merely doing our jobs. Thank you."

Polchik started to protest—he *knew* he was right—but the kids were already gathering up their belongings. He hadn't even ripped the car, which was probably where they had it locked away. But he knew it was useless. *He* was the guinea pig in this experiment, not the robot. It was all painfully clear. He knew if he interfered, if he overrode the robot's decision, it would only add to the cloud under which the robot had put him: short temper, taking a gift from a neighborhood merchant, letting the robot out-maneuver him in the apartment, false stop on Kyser ... and now this. Suddenly, all Mike Polchik wanted was to go back, get out of harness, sign out, and go home to bed. Wet carpets and all. Just to bed.

Because if these metal things were what was coming, he was simply too tired to buck it.

He watched as the kids—hooting and ridiculing his impotency—piled back in the car, the girls showing their legs as they clambered over the side. The driver burned polyglas speeding up Amsterdam Avenue. In a moment they were gone.

"You see, Officer Polchik," Brillo said, "false arrest would make us both liable for serious—" But Polchik was already walking away, his shoulders slumped, the weight of his bandolier and five years on the force too much for him.

The robot (making the sort of sound an electric watch makes) hummed after him, keeping stern vigil on the darkened neighborhood in the encroaching dawn. He could not compute despair. But he had been built to serve. He was programmed to protect, and he did it, all the way back to the precinct house.

Polchik was sitting at a scarred desk in the squad room, laboriously typing out his report on a weary IBM Selectric afflicted with *grand mal*. Across the room Reardon poked at the now-inert metal bulk of Brillo, using some sort of power tool with a teardrop-shaped lamp on top of it. The Mayor's whiz kid definitely looked sandbagged. *He don't go without sleep very often,* Polchik thought with grim satisfaction.

The door to Captain Summit's office opened, and the Captain, looking oceanic and faraway, waved him in.

"Here it comes," Polchik whispered to himself.

Summit let Polchik pass him in the doorway. He closed the door and indicated the worn plastic chair in front of the desk. Polchik sat down. "I'm not done typin' the beat report yet, Capt'n."

Summit ignored the comment. He moved over to the desk, picked up a yellow printout flimsy, and stood silently for a moment in front of Polchik, considering it.

"Accident report out of the 86th precinct uptown. Six kids in a Ford Electric convertible went out of control, smashed down a pedestrian and totaled against the bridge abutment. Three dead, three critical—not expected to live. Fifteen minutes after you let them go."

Dust.

Dried out.

Ashes.

Gray. Final.

Polchik couldn't think. Tired. Confused. Sick. Six kids. *Now* they were kids, just kids, nothing else made out of old bad memories.

"One of the girls went through the windshield. D.O.A. Driver got the steering column punched out through his back. Another girl with a snapped neck. Another girl—"

He couldn't hear him. He was somewhere else, faraway. Kids. Laughing, smartmouth kids having a good time. Benjy would be that age some day. The carpets were all wet.

"Mike!"

He didn't hear.

"Mike! Polchik!"

He looked up. There was a stranger standing in front of him holding a yellow flimsy.

"Well, don't just sit there, Polchik. You *had* them! Why'd you let them go?"

"The ... lizard ..."

"That's right, that's what five of them were using. Three beakers of it in the car. And a dead cat on the floor and all the makings wrapped in foam-bead bags. You'd have had to be blind to miss it all!"

"The robot ..."

Summit turned away with disgust, slamming the report onto the desk top. He thumbed the call-button. When Desk Sergeant Loyo came in, he said, "Take him upstairs and give him a breather of straightener, let him lie down for half an hour, then bring him back to me."

Loyo got Polchik under the arms and took him out.

Then the Captain turned off the office lights and sat silently in his desk chair, watching the night die just beyond the filthy windows.

"Feel better?"

"Yeah; thank you, Capt'n. I'm fine."

"You're back with me all the way? You understand what I'm saying?"

"Yeah, sure, I'm just *fine*, sir. It was just . . . those kids . . . I felt."

"So why'd you let them go? I've got no time to baby you, Polchik. You're five years a cop and I've got all the brass in town outside that door waiting. So get right."

"I'm right, Capt'n. I let them go because the robot took the stuff the girl was carrying, and he dumped it in his thing there, and told me it was nosedrops."

"Not good enough, Mike."

"What can I say besides that?"

"Well, dammit *Officer* Polchik, you damned well better say *some*thing besides that. *You* know they run that stuff right into the skull, you've been a cop long enough to see it, to hear it the way they talk! Why'd you let them custer you?"

"What was I going to run them in for? Carrying nosedrops? With that motherin' robot reciting civil rights chapter-an'-verse at me every step of the way? Okay, so I tell the robot to go screw off, and I bust 'em and bring 'em in. In an hour they're out again and I've got a false arrest lug dropped on me. Even if it *ain't* nosedrops. And they can use the robot's goddam tapes to hang me up by the thumbs!"

Summit dropped back into his chair, sack weight. His face was a burned-out building. "So we've got three, maybe six kids dead. Jesus, Jesus, Jesus." He shook his head.

Polchik wanted to make him feel better. But how did

you do that? "Listen, Capt'n, you know I would of had those kids in here so fast it'd'of made their heads swim . . . if I'd've been on my own. That damned robot . . . well, it just didn't work out. Capt'n, I'm not trying to alibi, it was godawful out there, but you were a beat cop . . . *you* know a cop ain't a set of rules and a pile of wires. Guys like me just can't work with things like that Brillo. It won't work, Capt'n. A guy's gotta be free to use his judgment, to feel like he's worth somethin', not just a piece of sh—"

Summit's head came up sharply. "Judgment?!" He looked as though he wanted to vomit. "What kind of judgment are you showing with that Rico over at the Amsterdam Inn? And all of it on the tapes, sound, pictures, everything?!"

"Oh. That."

"Yes, that. You're damned lucky I insisted those tapes get held strictly private, for the use of the Force only. I had to invoke privileged data. Do you have any *idea* how many strings that puts on me, on this office now, with the Chief, with the Commissioner, with the goddam Mayor? Do you have any *idea*, Polchik?"

"No, sir. I'm sorry." Chagrin.

"Sorry doesn't buy it, goddamit! I don't want you taking any juice from anywhere. No bottles, no gifts, no *nothing*, not from *anybody*. Have you got that?"

"Yessir."

Wearily, Summit persisted. "It's tough enough to do a job here without having special graft investigations and the D.A.'s squad sniffing all over the precinct. Jesus, Polchik, do you have any *idea* . . . !" He stopped, looked levelly at the patrolman and said, "One more time and you're out on your ass. Not set down, not reprimanded, not docked—*out*. All the way out. *Kapish?*"

Polchik nodded; his back was broken.

"I've got to set it right."

"What, sir?"

"You, that's what."

Polchik waited. A pendulum was swinging.

"I'll have to think about it. But if it hadn't been for the five good years you've given me here, Polchik . . . well, you'll be getting punishment, but I don't know just what yet."

"Uh, what's gonna happen with the robot?"

Summit got to his feet slowly; mooring a dirigible. "Come on outside and you'll see."

Polchik followed him to the door, where the Captain paused. He looked closely into Polchik's face and said, "Tonight has been an education, Mike."

There was no answer to that one.

They went into the front desk room. Reardon still had his head stuck into Brillo's open torso cavity, and the whiz kid was standing tiptoed behind him, peering over the engineer's shoulder. As they entered the ready room, Reardon straightened and clicked off the lamp on the power tool. He watched Summit and Polchik as they walked over to Chief Santorini. Summit murmured to the Chief for a moment, then Santorini nodded and said, "We'll talk tomorrow, then."

He started toward the front door, stopped and said, "Good night, gentlemen. It's been a long night. I'll be in touch with your offices tomorrow." He didn't wait for acknowledgment; he simply went.

Reardon turned around to face Summit. He was waiting for words. Even the whiz kid was starting to come alive again. The silent FBI man rose from the bench (as far as Polchik could tell, he hadn't changed position all the time they'd been gone on patrol) and walked toward the group.

Reardon said, "Well . . ." His voice trailed off.

The pendulum was swinging.

"Gentlemen," said the Captain, "I've advised Chief Santorini I'll be writing out a full report to be sent downtown. My recommendations will more than likely decide whether or not these robots will be added to our Force."

"Grass roots level opinion, very good, Captain, very good," said the whiz kid. Summit ignored him.

"But I suppose I ought to tell you right now my recommendations will be negative. As far as I'm concerned, Mr. Reardon, you still have a long way to go with your machine."

"But, I thought—"

"It did very well,'" Summit said, "don't get me wrong.

But I think it's going to need a lot more flexibility and more knowledge of the police officer's duties before it can be of any real aid in our work."

Reardon was angry, but trying to control it. "I programmed the entire patrolman's manual, and all the City codes, and the Supreme Court—"

Summit stopped him with a raised hand. "Mr. Reardon, that's the least of a police officer's knowledge. *Anybody* can read a rule book. But *how to use those rules,* how to make those rules work in the street, that takes more than programming. It takes, well, it takes training. And experience. It doesn't come easily. A cop isn't a set of rules and a pile of wires."

Polchik was startled to hear his words. He knew it would be okay. Not as good as before, but at least okay.

Reardon was furious now. And he refused to be convinced. Or perhaps he refused to allow the Mayor's whiz kid and the FBI man to be so easily convinced. He had worked too long and at too much personal cost to his career to let it go that easily. He hung onto it. "But merely training shouldn't put you off the X-44 *completely!*"

The Captain's face tensed around the mouth. "Look, Mr. Reardon, I'm not very good at being politic—which is why I'm still a Captain, I suppose—" The whiz kid gave him a be-careful look, but the Captain went on. "But it isn't merely training. This officer is a good one. He's bright, he's on his toes, he maybe isn't Sherlock Holmes but he knows the feel of a neighborhood, the smell of it, the heat level. He knows every August we're going to get the leapers and the riots and some woman's head cut off and dumped in a mailbox mailed C.O.D. to Columbus, Ohio. He knows when there's racial tension in our streets. He knows when those poor slobs in the tenements have just *had it.* He knows when some new kind of vice has moved in. But he made more mistakes out there tonight than a rookie. Five years walking and riding that beat, he's *never* foulballed the way he did tonight. Why? I've got to ask *why?* The only thing different was that machine of yours. Why? *Why* did Mike Polchik foulball so bad? *He* knew those kids in that car should have been run in for b&b or naline tests. So why, Mr. Reardon . . . *why?*"

Polchik felt lousy. The Captain was more worked up than he'd ever seen him. But Polchik stood silently, listening; standing beside the silent, listening FBI man.

Brillo merely stood silently. Turned off.

Then why did he still hear that robot buzzing?

"It isn't rules and regs, Mr. Reardon." The Captain seemed to have a lot more to come. "A moron can learn those. But how do you evaluate the look on a man's face that tells you he needs a fix? How do you gauge the cultural change in words like 'custer' or 'grass' or 'high' or 'pig'? How do you know when *not* to bust a bunch of kids who've popped a hydrant so they can cool off? How do you program all of *that* into a robot ... and know that it's going to change from hour to hour?"

"We can do it! It'll take time, but we can do it."

The Captain nodded slowly. "Maybe you can."

"I know we can."

"Okay, I'll even go for that. Let's say you can. Let's say you can get a robot that'll act like a human being and still be a robot ... because that's what we're talking about here. There's still something else."

"Which is?"

"People, Mr. Reardon. People like Polchik here. I asked you *why* Polchik foulballed, why he made such a bum patrol tonight that I'm going to have to take disciplinary action against him *for the first time in five years* ... so I'll *tell* you why, Mr. Reardon, about people like Polchik here. They're still afraid of machines, you know. We've pushed them and shoved them and lumbered them with machines till they're afraid the next clanking item down the pike is going to put them on the bread line. So they don't *want* to cooperate. They don't do it on purpose. They may not even *know* they're doing it, hell, I don't think Polchik knew what was happening, why he was falling over his feet tonight. You can get a robot to act like a human being, Mr. Reardon. Maybe you're right and you *can* do it, just like you said. But how the hell are you going to get humans to act like robots and not be afraid of machines?"

Reardon looked as whipped as Polchik felt.

"May I leave Brillo here till morning? I'll have a crew come over from the labs and pick him up."

"Sure," the Captain said, "he'll be fine right there against the wall. The Desk Sergeant'll keep an eye on him." To Loyo he said, "Sergeant, instruct your relief."

Loyo smiled and said, "Yessir."

Summit looked back at Reardon and said, "I'm sorry."

Reardon smiled wanly, and walked out. The whiz kid wanted to say something, but too much had already been said, and the Captain looked through him. "I'm pretty tired, Mr. Kenzie. How about we discuss it tomorrow after I've seen the Chief?"

The whiz kid scowled, turned and stalked out.

The Captain sighed heavily. "Mike, go get signed out and go home. Come see me tomorrow. Late." He nodded to the FBI man, who still had not spoken; then he went away.

The robot stood where Reardon had left him. Silent.

Polchik went upstairs to the locker room to change.

Something was bothering him. But he couldn't nail it down.

When he came back down into the muster room, the FBI man was just racking the receiver on the desk blotter phone. "Leaving?" he asked. It was the first thing Polchik had heard him say. It was a warm brown voice.

"Yeah. Gotta go home. I'm whacked out."

"Can't say I blame you. I'm a little tired myself. Need a lift?"

"No thanks," Polchik said. "I take the subway. Two blocks from the house." They walked out together. Polchik thought about the wet carpets waiting. They stood on the front steps for a minute, breathing in the chill morning air, and Polchik said, "I feel kinda sorry for that chunk of scrap now. He did a pretty good job."

"But not good enough," the FBI man added.

Polchik felt suddenly very protective about the inert form against the wall in the precinct house. "Oh, I dunno. He saved me from getting clobbered, you wanna know the truth. Tell me . . . you think they'll ever build a robot that'll cut it?"

The FBI man lit a cigarette, blew smoke in a thin stream, and nodded. "Yeah. Probably. But it'll have to be a lot more sophisticated than old Brillo in there."

Polchik looked back through the doorway. The robot

stood alone, looking somehow helpless. Waiting for rust. Polchik thought of kids, all kinds of kids, and when he was a kid. *It must be hell,* he thought, *being a robot. Getting turned off when they don't need you no more.*

Then he realized he could *still* hear that faint electricical buzzing. The kind a watch makes. He cast a quick glance at the FBI man but, trailing cigarette smoke, he was already moving toward his car, parked directly in front of the precinct house. Polchik couldn't tell if he was wearing a watch or not.

He followed the government man.

"The trouble with Brillo," the FBI man said, "is that Reardon's facilities were too limited. But I'm sure there are other agencies working on it. They'll lick it one day." He snapped the cigarette into the gutter.

"Yeah, sure," Polchik said. The FBI man unlocked the car door and pulled it. It didn't open.

"Damn it!" he said. "Government pool issue. Damned door always sticks." Bunching his muscles, he suddenly wrenched at it with enough force to pop it open. Polchik stared. Metal had ripped.

"You take care of yourself now, y'hear?" the FBI man said, getting into the car. He flipped up the visor with its OFFICIAL GOVERNMENT BUSINESS card tacked to it, and slid behind the steering wheel.

The car settled heavily on its springs, as though a ton of load had just been dumped on the front seat. He slammed the door. It was badly sprung.

"Too bad we couldn't use him," the FBI man said, staring out of the car at Brillo, illuminated through the precinct house doorway. "But . . . too crude."

"Yeah, sure, I'll take care of myself," Polchik replied, one exchange too late. He felt his mouth hanging open.

The FBI man grinned, started the car, and pulled away.

Polchik stood in the street, for a while.

Sometimes he stared down the early morning street in the direction the FBI man had taken.

Sometimes he stared at the metal cop immobile in the muster room.

And even as the sounds of the city's new day rose around him, he was not at all certain he did not still hear the sound of an electric watch. Getting louder.

Robert Bloch and Harlan Ellison

A TOY FOR JULIETTE

THE PROWLER IN THE CITY AT THE EDGE OF THE WORLD

INTRODUCTION

What follows is, in the purest sense, the end result of
literary feedback. Recently the story editor of a prime-
time television series, pressed for a script to shoot, sat
down and wrote one himself rather than wait for the va-
garies of a free-lance scenarist's schedule and dalliance.
When he had completed the script, which was to go before the cameras in a matter of days, he sent it as a matter of form to the legal department of the studio. For the
clearance of names, etc. Later that day the legal department called him in a frenzy. Almost scene-for-scene and
word-for-word (including the title), the non-sf story editor
had copied a well-known science fiction short story. When
it was pointed out to him, the story editor blanched and
recalled he had indeed read that story, some fifteen years
before. Hurriedly, the story rights were purchased from
the well-known fantasy writer who had originally conceived the idea. I hasten to add that I accept the veracity
of the story editor when he swears he had no conscious
knowledge of imitating the story. I believe him because
this sort of unconscious plagiarism is commonplace in the
world of the writer. It is inevitable that much of the mass
of reading a writer does will stick with him somehow, in
vague concepts, snatches of scenes, snippets of characterization, and it will turn up later, in the writer's own
work; altered, transmogrified, but still a direct result of
another writer's work. It is by no means "plagiarism." It is

93

part of the answer to the question asked by idiots of authors at cocktail parties: "Where do you get your ideas?"

Poul Anderson dropped me a note several years ago explaining that he had just written a story he was about to send out to market when he realized it paralleled the theme of a story of mine he had read at a writers' conference we had both attended, just a month or so before. He added that his story was only vaguely similar to mine, but he wanted to apprise me of the resemblance so there would be no question later. It was a rhetorical letter: I'm arrogant, but not arrogant enough to think Poul Anderson needs to crib from me. Similarly, at the 1966 World Science Fiction Convention in Cleveland, the well-known German fan Tom Schlück and I were introduced. (Tom had been brought over as Fan Guest of Honor, an exchange tradition in fandom perpetuated by the TransAtlantic Fan Fund.) The first thing he did after we shook hands was to hand me a German science fiction paperback. I had some difficulty understanding why he had given me the gift. Tom opened the book—a collection of stories pseudonymously written by top German sf fan/pro Walter Ernsting. The flyleaf said: "To Harlan Ellison with thanks and compliments." I still didn't understand. Then Tom turned to the first story, which was titled *"Die Sonnenbombe."* Under the title it said: (*Nach einer Idee von Harlan Ellison*). I wrinkled my brow. I still didn't understand. I recognized my own name, which looks the same in all languages save Russian, Chinese, Hebrew or Sanskrit, but I don't read German, and I'm afraid I stood there like a clot. Tom explained that the basic idea of a story I had written in 1957—"Run for the Stars"—had inspired Ernsting to write *"Die Sonnenbombe."* It was the literary feedback, halfway around the world. I was deeply touched, and even more, it was a feeling of justification. Every writer save the meanest hack hopes his words will live after he goes down the hole, that his thoughts will influence people. It isn't the primary purpose of the writing, of course, but it's the sort of secret wish that parallels the Common Man having babies, so his name doesn't die with him. And here, in my hands, was the visible proof that something my mind had conjured up had reached out and ensnared another man's imagination. It was obviously the

sincerest form of flattery, and by no means "plagiarism."
It was the literary feedback. The instances of this action-
reaction among writers are numberless, and some of them
are legend. It is the reason for writers' seminars, work-
shops, conferences and the endless exchange of letters
among writers. What has all of this—or any of it—to
do with Robert Bloch, the author of the story that follows? Everything.

In 1943 Robert Bloch had published a story titled
"Yours Truly, Jack the Ripper." The number of times it
has been reprinted, anthologized, translated into radio and
TV scripts, and most of all plagiarized, is staggering. I
read it in 1953, and the story stuck with me always. When
I *heard* its dramatization on the Molle Mystery Theater, it
became a recurring favorite memory. The story idea was
simply that Jack the Ripper, by killing at specific times,
made his peace with the dark gods and was thus allowed
to live forever. Jack was immortal, and Bloch traced with
cold methodical logic a trail of similar Ripper-style mur-
ders in almost every major city of the world, over a
period of fifty or sixty years. The concept of Jack—who
was never apprehended—living on, from era to era,
caught my imagination. In 1966, when commissioning the
stories for *Dangerous Visions*, an original anthology I was
putting together, I called Robert Bloch and suggested that
if Jack were, in fact, immortal, why then he would have to
go on into the future. The image of a creature of
Whitechapel fog and filth, the dark figure of Leather
Apron, skulking through a sterile and automated city of
the future, was an anachronism that fascinated me. Bob
agreed, and said he would set to work at once. When his
story came in, it was (pardon the word) a delight, and I
bought it at once. But the concept of Jack in the future
would not release my thoughts. I dwelled on it with almost
morbid fascination. Finally I asked Bob if he minded my
doing a story for the anthology that took up where his left
off. He said he thought it would be all right. It was, as
I've said, in the purest sense, the act of literary feedback.
And again, the sincerest form of flattery. Bloch had literally triggered the creative process in another writer.

The story that follows Robert Bloch's story is the product of that feedback. Tied in a knot, the two stories and

the two afterwords seem to have melded into a unified whole that demonstrates more admirably than any million words of literary critiques what it is that one writer obtains from another.

And so, in this special way, this is my collaboration with Robert Bloch.

A Toy for Juliette

by Robert Bloch

Juliette entered her bedroom, smiling, and a thousand
Juliettes smiled back at her. For all the walls were pan-
eled with mirrors, and the ceiling was set with inlaid panes
that reflected her image.

Wherever she glanced she could see the blonde curls
framing the sensitive features of a face that was a radiant
amalgam of both child and angel; a striking contrast to
the rich, ripe revelation of her body in the filmy robe.

But Juliette wasn't smiling at herself. She smiled because she knew that Grandfather was back, and he'd
brought her another toy. In just a few moments it would
be decontaminated and delivered, and she wanted to be
ready.

Juliette turned the ring on her finger and the mirrors
dimmed. Another turn would darken the room entirely; a
twist in the opposite direction would bring them blazing
into brilliance. It was all a matter of choice—but then,
that was the secret of life. To choose, for pleasure.

And what was her pleasure tonight?

Juliette advanced to one of the mirror panels and
passed her hand before it. The glass slid to one side, revealing the niche behind it; the coffin-shaped opening in
the solid rock, with the boot and thumbscrews set at the
proper heights.

For a moment she hesitated; she hadn't played *that*

game in years. Another time, perhaps. Juliette waved her hand and the mirror moved to cover the opening again.

She wandered along the row of panels, gesturing as she walked, pausing to inspect what was behind each mirror in turn. Here was the rack, there the stocks with the barbed whips resting against the darkstained wood. And here was the dissecting table, hundreds of years old, with it's quaint instruments; behind the next panel the electrical prods and wires that produced such weird grimaces and contortions of agony, to say nothing of screams. Of course the screams didn't matter in a soundproofed room.

Juliette moved to the side wall and waved her hand again; the obedient glass slid away and she stared at a plaything she'd almost forgotten. It was one of the first things Grandfather had ever given her, and it was very old, almost like a mummy case. What had he called it? The Iron Maiden of Nuremberg, that was it—with the sharpened steel spikes set inside the lid. You chained a man inside, and you turned the little crank that closed the lid, ever so slowly, and the spikes pierced the wrists and the elbows, the ankles and the knees, the groin and the eyes. You had to be careful not to get excited and turn too quickly, or you'd spoil the fun.

Grandfather had shown her how it worked, the first time he brought her a real *live* toy. But then, Grandfather had shown her everything. He'd taught her all she knew, for he was very wise. He'd even given her her name— Juliette—from one of the old-fashioned printed books he'd discovered by the philosopher De Sade.

Grandfather had brought the books from the Past, just as he'd brought the playthings for her. He was the only one who had access to the Past, because he owned the Traveler.

The Traveler was a very ingenious mechanism, capable of attaining vibrational frequencies which freed it from the time-bind. At rest, it was just a big square boxlike shape, the size of a small room. But when Grandfather took over the controls and the oscillation started, the box would blur and disappear. It was still there, Grandfather said—at least, the *matrix* remained as a fixed point in space and time—but anything or anyone within the square could move freely into the Past to wherever the controls were programmed. Of course they would be invisible when they arrived, but that was actually an advantage, particularly when it came to finding things and bringing them back. Grandfather had brought back some very interesting objects from almost mythical places—the great library of Alexandria, the Pyramid of Cheops, the Kremlin, the Vatican, Fort Knox—all the storehouses of treasure and knowledge which existed thousands of years ago. He liked to go to *that* part of the Past, the period before the thermonuclear wars and the robotic ages, and collect things. Of course, books and jewels and metals were useless, except to an antiquarian, but Grandfather was a romanticist and loved the olden times.

It was strange to think of him owning the Traveler, but of course he hadn't actually created it. Juliette's father was really the one who built it, and Grandfather took possession of it after her father died. Juliette suspected Grandfather had killed her father and mother when she was just a baby, but she could never be sure. Not that it mattered; Grandfather was always very good to her, and besides, soon he would die and she'd own the Traveler herself.

They used to joke about it frequently. "I've made you into a monster," he'd say. "And someday you'll end up by destroying me. After which, of course, you'll go on to destroy the entire world—or what little remains of it."

"Aren't you afraid?" she'd tease.

"Certainly not. That's my dream—the destruction of everything. An end to all this sterile decadence. Do you realize that at one time there were more than three billion inhabitants on this planet? And now, less than three thousand! Less than three thousand, shut up inside these Domes, prisoners of themselves and sealed away forever, thanks to the sins of the fathers who poisoned not only the outside world but outer space by meddling with the atomic order of the universe. Humanity is virtually extinct already; you will merely hasten the finale."

"But couldn't we all go back to another time, in the Traveler?" she asked.

"Back to *what* time? The continuum is changeless; one event leads inexorably to another, all links in a chain which binds us to the present and its inevitable end in de-

struction. We'd have temporary individual survival, yes,
but to no purpose. And none of us are fitted to survive in
a more primitive environment. So let us stay here and
take what pleasure we can from the moment. *My* pleasure is to be the sole user and possessor of the Traveler.
And yours, Juliette—"

Grandfather laughed then. They both laughed, because
they knew what *her* pleasure was.

Juliette killed her first toy when she was eleven—a little
boy. It had been brought to her as a special gift from
Grandfather, from somewhere in the Past, for elementary
sex play. But it wouldn't cooperate, and she lost her temper and beat it to death with a steel rod. So Grandfather
brought her an older toy, with brown skin, and it cooper-
ated very well, but in the end she tired of it and one day
when it was sleeping in her bed she tied it down and
found a knife.

Experimenting a little before it died, Juliette discovered
new sources of pleasure, and of course Grandfather found
out. That's when he'd christened her "Juliette"; he seemed
to approve most highly, and from then on he brought her
the playthings she kept behind the mirrors in her bedroom.
And on his restless rovings into the Past he brought her
new toys.

Being invisible, he could find them for her almost anywhere on his travels—all he did was to use a stunner and
transport them when he returned. Of course each toy had
to be very carefully decontaminated; the Past was teeming
with strange microorganisms. But once the toys were
properly antiseptic they were turned over to Juliette for
her pleasure, and during the past seven years she had enjoyed herself.

It was always delicious, this moment of anticipation before a new toy arrived. What would it be like? Grandfather was most considerate; mainly, he made sure that the
toys he brought her could speak and understand An-
glish—or "English," as they used to call it in the Past.
Verbal communication was often important, particularly if
Juliette wanted to follow the precepts of the philosopher
De Sade and enjoy some form of sex relations before
going on to keener pleasures.

But there was still the guessing beforehand. Would this

toy be young or old, wild or tame, male or female? She'd had all kinds, and every possible combination. Sometimes she kept them alive for days before tiring of them—or before the subtleties of which she was capable caused them to expire. At other times she wanted it to happen quickly; tonight, for example, she knew she could be soothed only by the most primitive and direct action.

Once Juliette realized this, she stopped playing with her mirror panels and went directly to the big bed. She pulled back the coverlet, groped under the pillow until she felt it. Yes, it was still there—the big knife with the long, cruel blade. She knew what she would do now: take the toy to bed with her and then, at precisely the proper moment, combine her pleasures. If she could time her knife thrust—

She shivered with anticipation, then with impatience.

What kind of toy would it be? She remembered the suave, cool one—Benjamin Bathurst was his name, an English diplomat from the time of what Grandfather called the Napoleonic Wars. Oh, he'd been suave and cool enough, until she beguiled him with her body, into the bed. And there'd been that American aviatrix from slightly later on in the Past, and once, as a very special treat, the entire crew of a sailing vessel called the *Marie Celeste*. They had lasted for *weeks!*

Strangely enough, she'd even read about some of her toys afterwards. Because when Grandfather approached them with his stunner and brought them here, they disappeared forever from the Past, and if they were in any way known or important in their time, such disappearances were noted. And some of Grandfather's books had accounts of the "mysterious vanishing" which took place and was, of course, never explained. How delicious it all was!

Juliette patted the pillow back into place and slid the knife under it. She couldn't wait, now; what was delaying things?

She forced herself to move to a vent and depress the sprayer, shedding her robe as the perfumed mist bathed her body. It was the final allurement—but why didn't her toy arrive?

Suddenly Grandfather's voice came over the auditor.

"I'm sending you a little surprise, dearest."

That's what he always said; it was part of the game.

Juliette depressed the communicator-toggle. "Don't tease," she begged. "Tell me what it's like."

"An Englishman. Late Victorian Era. Very prim and proper, by the looks of him."

"Young? Handsome?"

"Passable." Grandfather chuckled. "Your appetites betray you, dearest."

"Who is it—someone from the books?"

"I wouldn't know the name. We found no identification during the decontamination. But from his dress and manner, and the little black bag he carried when I discovered him so early in the morning, I'd judge him to be a physician returning from an emergency call."

Juliette knew about "physicians" from her reading of course; just as she knew what "Victorian" meant. Somehow the combination seemed exactly right.

"Prim and proper?" She giggled. "Then I'm afraid it's due for a shock."

Grandfather laughed. "You have something in mind, I take it."

"Yes."

"Can I watch?"

"Please—not this time."

"Very well."

"Don't be mad, darling. I love you."

Juliette switched off. Just in time, too, because the door was opening and the toy came in.

She stared at it, realizing that Grandfather had told the truth. The toy was a male of thirty-odd years, attractive but by no means handsome. It couldn't be, in that dark garb and those ridiculous side whiskers. There was something almost depressingly refined and mannered about it, an air of embarrassed repression.

And of course, when it caught sight of Juliette in her revealing robe, and the bed surrounded by mirrors, it actually began to *blush*.

That reaction won Juliette completely. A blushing Victorian, with the build of a bull—and unaware that this was the slaughterhouse!

It was so amusing she couldn't restrain herself; she moved forward at once and put her arms around it.

"Who—who are you? Where am I?"

The usual questions, voiced in the usual way. Ordinarily, Juliette would have amused herself by parrying with answers designed to tantalize and titillate her victim. But tonight she felt an urgency which only increased as she embraced the toy and pressed it back toward the waiting bed.

The toy began to breathe heavily, responding. But it was still bewildered. "Tell me—I don't understand. Am I alive? Or is this heaven?"

Juliette's robe fell open as she lay back. "You're alive, darling," she murmured "Wonderfully alive." She laughed as she began to prove the statement. "But closer to heaven than you think."

And to prove *that* statement, her free hand slid under the pillow and groped for the waiting knife.

But the knife wasn't there any more. Somehow it had already found its way into the toy's hand. And the toy wasn't prim and proper any longer, its face was something glimpsed in nightmare. Just a glimpse, before the blinding blur of the knife blade, as it came down, again and again and again—

The room, of course, was soundproof, and there was plenty of time. They didn't discover what was left of Juliette's body for several days.

Back in London, after the final mysterious murder in the early morning hours, they never did find Jack the Ripper. . . .

Afterword

A number of years have passed since I sat down at the typewriter one gloomy winter day and wrote "Yours Truly, Jack the Ripper" for magazine publication. The magazine in which it appeared gave up its ghost, and interest in ghosts, a long time ago. But somehow my little story seems to have survived. It has long since pursued me in reprint, collections, anthologies, foreign translations, radio broadcasts and television.

So when Harlan Ellison proposed that I do a story and suggested, "What about Jack the Ripper in the future?" I was capable of only one response.

You've just read it.

INTRODUCTION

This is Robert Bloch, writing about Harlan Ellison. And believe me, it isn't easy.

Our act of collaboration is a peculiar one. Harlan's story is a sequel to my own, and since it was inspired by the story you've just read, it falls to me to write an introduction, purely as a matter of poetic injustice.

I am not about to do a biographical sketch of the man; surely he wouldn't need me for that. Ellison has told the story of his life so many times, you'd think he'd know it by heart.

So I'm forced to fall back upon the consideration of Ellison as a phenomenon—a most phenomenal phenomenon —which has impinged upon my awareness, and the awareness of everyone in the science fiction genre, for the past nineteen years.

When I first met him (the preceding May I'd *seen* him), at the World Science Fiction Convention of 1952, Harlan Ellison was a promising young man of eighteen. As of the writing of this introduction, he is a promising young man of forty-one. That's not a put-down, nor is it meant to be.

At eighteen he gave promise of becoming an outstanding fan. At forty-one he gives promise of becoming an outstanding writer. Not only promise, but evidence.

As a fan he was articulate, ambitious and aggressive. As a professional writer, these qualities are still very obvious in all his work, and added to them is yet another conveniently alliterative quality—artistry.

Read his short stories, novels, articles and criticism. You may not always agree with what he says or the way in which he says it, but the artistry is there; the blend of emotion and excitement delivered with deep conviction and commitment. No matter what the apparent grammatical form may be, one is conscious that Ellison is really always writing in first person.

I mentioned emotion. Ellison often operates out of extremes that range from compassionate empathy to righteous indignation. He writes what he feels—and you feel what he writes.

I mentioned excitement. This is an inner climate; a constant tornado in which a part of Ellison remains as the eye—and a most perceptive one. There is small tranquility to be found in his life or in his work. Ellison is definitely not one of those writers who cultivate the serenity of Buddha as they sit around contemplating their novels.

I mentioned conviction. Since he's not an obscurantist, his convictions come through loud and clear—in prose and in personal address. Those convictions create both admirers and enemies. Part gadfly, part raw ego, Ellison has been criticized by those who persist in regarding these qualities as admirable in a soldier, a politician or a business executive but somehow degrading in a creative artist. Ellison survives the strife; he is the only living organism I know whose natural habitat is hot water.

I mentioned commitment. The purpose and tenacity have carried him through a wide range of experience; a hitch in the army, a liaison with teenage games in search of background material, an editorial stint, civil rights and dissent movement involvement that often led to jail, and the eternal gantlet run by every writer who must temper his work to the taste of other arbiters.

Ellison has often clashed with those who attempted to direct his writing. In his progress from Cleveland to New York to Chicago he has left in his wake a trail of editorial gray hairs, many of them torn out by the roots. In Hollywood he has played picador to producers, his barbs forever poised and ready to be placed when he became aware of the bull.

Some people admire his nerve. Others hate his guts. But he has a way of proving—and improving—himself.

The monumental anthology, *Dangerous Visions,* is a case in point.

During the fifteen years in which Ellison moved from fandom to professional status, literally hundreds of science fiction readers, writers and editors have dreamed of the publication of an anthology of this sort.

They dreamed it.

Ellison made it a reality in 1967.

And now, in 1971, he has made a reality of yet another "impossible" literary endeavor—a book of collaborations, *Partners in Wonder.*

I am aware that I've said nothing about Ellison's wit, or the sensitivity embodied in his work which has five times won for him the World Science Fiction Convention's *Hugo* and twice the Science Fiction Writers of America's *Nebula.* It has also won for him the coveted Edgar Allan Poe award of the Mystery Writers of America. You can assess those qualities for yourself by reading the story which follows.

It is a tour de force, surely, in the grand tradition of the Grand Guignol; a lineal literary descendant of such fearsome father figures as the Marquis de Sade and Louis-Ferdinand Céline. On the blood-spattered surface it is an obscenity, a violent rape of the senses and sensibilities.

But beneath the crude and shocking allusions to Eros and Thanatos is the meaningful portrayal of the Man Obsessed—the Violent Man whose transition from the past to the future leaves us with a deeper insight into the Violent Man of *today.*

For Jack the Ripper is with us now. He prowls the night, shunning the sun in a search for the blazing incandescence of an inner reality—and we see him plain in Ellison's story, to the degree that we can see (and admit to) the violence which lurks within our own psyches. Here all that is normally forbidden is abnormally released and realized. Metaphysical maundering? Before you make up your mind, read the story and let the Ripper rip *you* into an awareness of the urges and forces most of us will neither admit nor submit to; forces which, withal, remain potent within ourselves and our society. And ponder, if you will, upon the parable of Jack's dilemma as he seeks—in a phrase we all use but seldom comprehend—to "carve out a career" for himself.

An obscenity, yes. But a morality, too; a terrible morality implicit in the knowledge that the Ripper's inevitable and ultimate victim is always himself.

Even as you and I.

ROBERT BLOCH

The Prowler in
the City at the
Edge of the World

by Harlan Ellison

First there was the city, never night. Tin and reflective, walls of antiseptic metal like an immense autoclave. Pure and dust-free, so silent that even the whirling innards of its heart and mind were sheathed from notice. The city was self-contained, and footfalls echoed up and around —flat slapped notes of an exotic leather-footed instrument. Sounds that reverberated back to the maker like yodels thrown out across mountain valleys. Sounds made by humbled inhabitants whose lives were as ordered, as sanitary, as metallic as the city they had caused to hold them bosom-tight against the years. The city was a complex artery, the people were the blood that flowed icily through the artery. They were a gestalt with one another, forming a unified whole. It was a city shining in permanence, eternal in concept, flinging itself up in a formed and molded statement of exaltation; most modern of all modern structures, conceived as the pluperfect residence for the perfect people. The final end-result of all sociological blueprints aimed at Utopia. Living space, it had been called, and so, doomed to *live* they were, in that Erewhon of graphed respectability and cleanliness.

Never night.

Never shadowed.

. . . a shadow.

A blot moving against the aluminum cleanliness. The

movement of rags and bits of clinging earth from graves sealed ages before. A shape.

He touched a gunmetal-gray wall in passing: the imprint of dusty fingers. A twisted shadow moving through antiseptically pure streets, and they become—with his passing—black alleys from another time.

Vaguely, he knew what had happened. Not specifically, not with particulars, but he was strong, and he was able to get away without the eggshell-thin walls of his mind caving in. There was no place in this shining structure to secrete himself, a place to think, but he had to have time. He slowed his walk, seeing no one. Somehow—inexplicably—he felt ... safe? Yes, safe. For the first time in a very long time.

A few minutes before he had been standing in the narrow passageway outside No. 13 Miller's Court. It had been 6:15 in the morning. London had been quiet as he paused in the passageway of M'Carthy's Rents, in that fetid, urine-redolent corridor where the whores of Spitalfields took their clients. A few minutes before, the foetus in its bath of formaldehyde tightly-stoppered in a glass bottle inside his Gladstone bag, he had paused to drink in the thick fog, before taking the circuitous route back to Toynbee Hall. That had been a few minutes before. Then, suddenly, he was in another place and it was no longer 6:15 of a chill November morning in 1888.

He had looked up as light flooded him in that other place. It had been soot silent in Spitalfields, but suddenly, without any sense of having moved or having *been* moved, he was flooded with light. And when he looked up he was in that other place. Paused now, only a few minutes after the transfer, he leaned against the bright wall of the city, and recalled the light. From a thousand mirrors. In the walls, in the ceiling. A bedroom with a girl in it. A lovely girl. Not like Black Mary Kelly or Dark Annie Chapman or Kate Eddowes or any of the other pathetic scum he had been forced to attend ...

A lovely girl. Blonde, wholesome, until she had opened her robe and turned into the same sort of slut he had been compelled to use in his work in Whitechapel ...

A sybarite, a creature of pleasures, a Juliette she had said, before he used the big-bladed knife on her. He had found the knife under the pillow, on the bed to which she had led him—how shameful, unresisting had he been, all confused, clutching his black bag with all the tremors of a child, he who had been moved through the London night like oil, moved where he wished, accomplished his ends unchecked eight times, now led toward sin by another, merely another of the tarts, taking advantage of him while he tried to distinguish what had happened to him and where he was, how shameful—and he had used it on her.

That had only been minutes before, though he had worked very efficiently on her.

The knife had been rather unusual. The blade had seemed to be two wafer-thin sheets of metal with a pulsing, glowing *something* between. A kind of sparking, such as might be produced by a Van de Graaf generator. But that was patently ridiculous. It had no wires attached to it, no bus bars, nothing to produce even the crudest electrical discharge. He had thrust the knife into the Gladstone bag, where now it lay beside the scalpels and the spool of catgut and the racked vials in their leather cases, and the foetus in its bottle. Mary Jane Kelly's foetus.

He had worked efficiently, but swiftly, and had laid her out almost exactly in the same fashion as Kate Eddowes: the throat slashed completely through from ear-to-ear, the torso laid open down between the breasts to the vagina, the intestines pulled out and draped over the right shoulder, a piece of the intestines being detached and placed between the left arm and the body. The liver had been punctured with the point of the knife, with a vertical cut slitting the left lobe of the liver. (He had been surprised to find the liver showed none of the signs of cirrhosis so prevalent in these Spitalfields tarts, who drank incessantly to rid themselves of the burden of living the dreary lives they moved through grotesquely. In fact, this one seemed totally unlike the others, even if she had been more brazen in her sexual overtures. And that knife under the bed pillow ...) He had severed the vena cava leading to the heart. Then he had gone to work on the face.

He had thought of removing the left kidney again, as he had Kate Eddowes'. He smiled to himself as he conjured up the expression that must have been on the face of Mr. George Lusk, chairman of the Whitechapel Vigilance

Committee, when he received the cardboard box in the mail. The box containing Miss Eddowes' kidney, and the letter, impiously misspelled:

> *From hell, Mr. Lusk, sir, I send you half the kidne*
> *I took from one woman, prasarved it for you, tother*
> *piece I fried and ate it; was very nice. I may send you*
> *the bloody knif that took it out if you only wate while*
> *longer. Catch me when you can, Mr. Lusk.*

He had wanted to sign *that* one "'Yours Truly, Jack the Ripper" or even Spring-Heeled Jack or maybe Leather Apron, whichever had tickled his fancy, but a sense of style had stopped him. To go too far was to defeat his own purposes. It may even have been too much to suggest to Mr. Lusk that he had eaten the kidney. How hideous. True, he *had* smelled it . . .

This blonde girl, this Juliette with the knife under her pillow. She was the ninth. He leaned against the smooth steel wall without break or seam, and he rubbed his eyes. When would he be able to stop? When would they realize, when would they get his message, a message so clear, written in blood, that only the blindness of their own cupidity forced them to misunderstand! Would he be compelled to decimate the endless regiments of Spitalfields sluts to make them understood? Would he be forced to run the cobbles ankle-deep in black blood before they sensed what he was saying, and were impelled to make reforms?

But as he took his blood-soaked hands from his eyes, he realized what he must have sensed all along: he was no longer in Whitechapel. This was not Miller's Court, nor anywhere in Spitalfields. It might not even be London. But how could *that* be?

Had God taken him?

Had he died, in a senseless instant between the anatomy lesson of Mary Jane Kelly (that filth, she had actually *kissed* him!) and the bedroom disembowelment of this Juliette? Had Heaven finally called him to his reward for the work he had done?

The Reverend Mr. Barnett would love to know about this. But then, he'd have loved to know about it *all*. But

"Leather Apron" wasn't about to tell. Let the reforms come as the Reverend and his wife wished for them, and let them think their pamphleteering had done it, instead of the scalpels of Jack.

If he was dead, would his work be finished? He smiled to himself. If Heaven had taken him, then it must be that the work *was* finished. Successfully. But if *that* was so, then who was this Juliette who now lay spread out moist and cooling in the bedroom of a thousand mirrors? And in that instant he felt fear.

What if even God misinterpreted what he had done?

As the good folk of Queen Victoria's London had misinterpreted. As Sir Charles Warren had misinterpreted. What if God believed the superficial and ignored the *real* reason? But no! Ludicrous. If anyone would understand, it was the good God who had sent him the message that told him to set things a-right.

God loved him, as he loved God, and God would know.

But he felt fear, in that moment.

Because who was the girl he had just carved?

"She was my granddaughter, Juliette," said a voice immediately beside him.

His head refused to move, to turn that few inches to see who spoke. The Gladstone was beside him, resting on the smooth and reflective surface of the street. He could not get to a knife before he was taken. At last they had caught up with Jack. He began to shiver uncontrollably.

"No need to be afraid," the voice said. It was a warm and succoring voice. An older man. He shook as with an ague. But he turned to look. It was a kindly old man with a gentle smile. Who spoke again, without moving his lips. "No one can hurt you. How do you do?"

The man from 1888 sank slowly to his knees. "Forgive me, Dear God, I didn't know." The old man's laughter rose inside the head of the man on his knees. It rose like a beam of sunlight moving across a Whitechapel alleyway, from noon to one o'clock, rising and illuminating the gray bricks of soot-coated walls. It rose, and illuminated his mind.

"I'm not God. Marvelous idea, but no, I'm not God. Would you like to meet God? I'm sure we can find one of the artists who would mold one for you. Is it important?

No, I can see it isn't. What a strange mind you have. You neither believe nor doubt. How can you contain both concepts at once ... would you like me to straighten some of your brain-patterns? No. I see, you're afraid. Well, let it be for the nonce. We'll do it another time."

He grabbed the kneeling man and drew him erect. "You're covered with blood. Have to get you cleaned up. There's an ablute near here. Incidentally, I was very impressed with the way you handled Juliette. You're the first, you know. No, how could you know? In any case, you *are* the first to deal her as good as she gave. You would have been amused at what she did to Caspar Hauser. Squeezed part of his brain and then sent him back, let him live out part of his life and then—the little twit —she made me bring him back a second time and used a knife on him. Same knife you took, I believe. Then sent him back to his own time. Marvelous mystery. In all the tapes on unsolved phenomena. But she was much sloppier than you. She had a great verve in her amusements, but very little *éclat*. Except with Judge Crater; there she was—" He paused, and laughed lightly. "I'm an old man and I ramble on like a muskrat. You want to get cleaned up and shown around, I know. And *then* we can talk.

"I just wanted you to know I was satisfied with the way you disposed of her. In a way, I'll miss the little twit. She was such a good fuck."

The old man picked up the Gladstone bag and, holding the man spattered with blood, he moved off down the clean and shimmering street. "You *wanted* her killed?" the man from 1888 asked, unbelieving.

The old man nodded, but his lips never moved. "Of course. Otherwise why bring her Jack the Ripper?"

Oh my dear God, he thought, *I'm in hell. And I'm entered as Jack.*

"No, my boy, no no no. You're not in hell at all. You're in the future. For you the future, for me the world of now. You came from 1888 and you're now in—" he stopped, silently speaking for an instant, as though computing apples in terms of dollars, then resumed "—3077. It's a fine world, filled with happy times, and we're glad to have you with us. Come along now, and you'll wash."

In the ablutatorium, the late Juliette's grandfather changed his head.

"I really despise it," he informed the man from 1888, grabbing fingerfuls of his cheeks and stretching the flabby skin like elastic. "But Juliette insisted. I was willing to humor her, if indeed that was what it took to get her to lie down. But what with toys from the past, and changing my head every time I wanted her to fuck me, it was trying; very trying."

He stepped into one of the many identically shaped booths set flush into the walls. The tambour door rolled down and there was a soft *chukk* sound, almost chitinous. The tambour door rolled up and the late Juliette's grandfather, now six years younger than the man from 1888, stepped out, stark naked and wearing a new head. "The body is fine, replaced last year," he said, examining the genitals and a mole on his right shoulder. The man from 1888 looked away. This was hell and God hated him.

"Well, don't just *stand* there, Jack." Juliette's grandfather smiled. "Hit one of those booths and get your ablutions."

"That isn't my name," said the man from 1888 very softly, as though he had been whipped.

"It'll do, it'll do . . . now go get washed."

Jack approached one of the booths. It was a light green in color, but changed to mauve as he stopped in front of it. "Will it—"

"It will only *clean* you, what are you afraid of?"

"I don't want to be changed."

Juliette's grandfather did not laugh. "That's a mistake," he said cryptically. He made a peremptory motion with his hand and the man from 1888 entered the booth, which promptly revolved in its niche, sank into the floor and made a hearty *zeeeezzzz* sound. When it rose and revolved and opened, Jack stumbled out, looking terribly confused. His long sideburns had been neatly trimmed, his beard stubble had been removed, his hair was three shades lighter and was now parted on the left side, rather than in the middle. He still wore the same long dark coat trimmed with astrakhan, dark suit with white collar and black necktie (in which was fastened a horseshoe stickpin) but now the garments seemed new, unsoiled of course, possibly synthetics built to look like his former garments.

"Now!" Juliette's grandfather said. "Isn't that much better? A good cleansing always sets one's mind to rights." And he stepped into another booth from which he issued in a moment wearing a soft paper jumper that fitted from neck to feet without a break. He moved toward the door.

"Where are we going?" the man from 1888 asked the younger grandfather beside him. "I want you to meet someone," said Juliette's grandfather, and Jack realized that he was moving his lips now. He decided not to comment on it. There had to be a reason.

"I'll walk you there, if you promise not to make gurgling sounds at the city. It's a nice city, but I live here, and frankly, tourism is boring." Jack did not reply. Grandfather took it for acceptance of the terms.

They walked. Jack became overpowered by the sheer *weight* of the city. It was obviously extensive, massive, and terribly clean. It was his dream for Whitechapel come true. He asked about slums, about doss houses. The grandfather shook his head. "Long gone."

So it had come to pass. The reforms for which he pledged his immortal soul, they had come to pass. He swung the Gladstone and walked jauntily. But after a few minutes his pace sagged once more: there was no one to be seen in the streets.

Just shining clean buildings and streets that ran off in aimless directions and came to unexpected stops as though the builders had decided people might vanish at one point and reappear someplace else, so why bother making a road from one point to the other.

The ground was metal, the sky seemed metallic, the buildings loomed on all sides, featureless explorations of planed space by insensitive metal. The man from 1888 felt terribly alone, as though every act he had performed had led inevitably to his alienation from the very people he had sought to aid.

When he had come to Toynbee Hall, and the Reverend Mr. Barnett had opened his eyes to the slum horrors of Spitalfields, he had vowed to help in any way he could. It had seemed as simple as faith in the Lord what to do, after a few months in the sinkholes of Whitechapel. The sluts, of what use were they? No more use than the disease germs that had infected these very same whores. So he had set forth as Jack, to perform the will of God and raise the poor dregs who inhabited the East End of London. That Lord Warren, the Metropolitan Police Commissioner, and his Queen, and all the rest thought him a mad doctor, or an amok butcher, or a beast in human form did not distress him. He knew he would remain anonymous through all time, but that the good works he had set in motion would proceed to their wonderful conclusion.

The destruction of the most hideous slum area the country had ever known, and the opening of Victorian eyes. But all the time *had* passed, and now he was here, in a world where slums apparently did not exist, a sterile Utopia that was the personification of the Reverend Mr. Barnett's dreams—but it didn't seem . . . *right*.

This grandfather, with his young head.

Silence in the empty streets.

The girl, Juliette, and her strange hobby.

The lack of concern at her death.

The grandfather's expectation that he, Jack, *would* kill her. And now his friendliness.

Where were they going?

[Around them, the City. As they walked, the grandfather paid no attention, and Jack watched but did not understand. But this was what they saw as they walked:

[Thirteen hundred beams of light, one foot wide and seven molecules thick, erupted from almost-invisible slits in the metal streets, fanned out and washed the surfaces of the buildings; they altered hue to a vague blue and washed down the surfaces of the buildings; they bent and covered all open surfaces, bent at right angles, then bent again, and again, like origami paper figures; they altered hue a second time, soft gold, and penetrated the surfaces of the buildings, expanding and contracting in solid waves, washing the inner surfaces; they withdrew rapidly into the sidewalks; the entire process had taken twelve seconds.

[Night fell over a sixteen block area of the City. It descended in a solid pillar and was quite sharp-edged, ending at the street corners. From within the area of darkness came the distinct sounds of crickets, marsh frogs belching,

night birds, soft breezes in trees, and faint music of unidentifiable instruments.

[Panes of frosted light appeared suspended freely in the
air, overhead. A wavery insubstantial quality began to assault the topmost levels of a great structure directly in
front of the light-panes. As the panes moved slowly down
through the air, the building became indistinct, turned into
motes of light, and floated upward. As the panes reached
the pavement, the building had been completely demateri-
alized. The panes shifted color to a deep orange, and began moving upward again. As they moved, a new structure began to form where the previous building had stood,
drawing—it seemed—motes of light from the air and
forming them into a cohesive whole that became, as the
panes ceased their upward movement, a new building. The
light-panes winked out of existence.

[The sound of a bumblebee was heard for several seconds. Then it ceased.

[A crowd of people in rubber garments hurried out of
a gray pulsing hole in the air, patted the pavement at their
feet, then rushed off around a corner, from where
emanated the sound of prolonged coughing. Then silence
returned.

[A drop of water, thick as quicksilver, plummeted to
the pavement, struck, bounded, rose several inches, then
evaporated into a crimson smear in the shape of a whale's
tooth, which settled to the pavement and lay still.

[Two blocks of buildings sank into the pavement and
the metal covering was smooth and unbroken, save for a
metal tree whose trunk was silver and slim, topped by a
ball of foliage constructed of golden fibers that radiated
brightly in a perfect circle. There was no sound.

[The late Juliette's grandfather and the man from 1888
continued walking.]

"Where are we going?"

"To van Cleef's. We don't usually walk; oh, sometimes;
but it isn't as much pleasure as it used to be. I'm doing
this primarily for you. Are you enjoying yourself?"

"It's . . . unusual."

"Not much like Spitalfields, is it? But I rather like it
back there, at that time. I have the only Traveler, did you
know? The only one ever made. Juliette's father construct-

ed it, my son. I had to kill him to get it. He was thoroughly unreasonable about it, really. It was a casual thing for him. He was the last of the tinkerers, and he might just as easily have given it to me. But I suppose he was being cranky. That was why I had you carve up my granddaughter. She would have gotten around to me almost any time now. Bored, just silly bored is what she was—"

The gardenia took shape in the air in front of them, and turned into the face of a woman with long white hair. "Hernon, we can't wait much longer!" She was annoyed.

Juliette's grandfather grew livid. "You scum bitch! I *told* you pace. But no, you just couldn't, could you? Jump jump jump, that's all you ever do. Well, now it'll only be feddels less, that's all. Feddels, damn you! I set it for pace. I was *working* pace, and *you* . . . !"

His hand came up and moss grew instantly toward the face. The face vanished, and a moment later the gardenia reappeared a few feet away. The moss shriveled and Hernon, Juliette's grandfather, dropped his hand, as though weary at the woman's stupidity. A rose, a water lily, a hyacinth, a pair of phlox, a wild celandine, and a bull thistle appeared near the gardenia. As each turned into the face of a different person, Jack stepped back, frightened.

All the faces turned to the one that had been the bull thistle. "Cheat! Rotten bastard!" they screamed at the thin white face that had been the bull thistle. The gardenia-woman's eyes bulged from her face, the deep purple eyeshadow that completely surrounded the eyeball making her look like a deranged animal peering out of a cave. "Turd!" she shrieked at the bull thistle-man. "We all agreed, we all said and agreed; you *had* to formz a thistle, didn't you, scut! Well, now you'll see . . ."

She addressed herself instantly to the others. "Formz now! To hell with waiting, pace fuck! Now!"

"No, dammit!" Hernon shouted. "We were going to *paaaaaace!*" But it was too late. Centering in on the bull thistle-man, the air roiled thickly like silt at a river-bottom, and the air blackened as a spiral began with the now terrified face of the bull thistle-man and exploded whirling outward, enveloping Jack and Hernon and all the flower-people and the City and suddenly it was night in Spitalfields and the man from 1888 was *in* 1888, with his Gladstone bag in his hand, and a woman approaching down the street toward him, shrouded in the London fog.

(There were eight additional nodules in Jack's brain.)

The woman was about forty, weary and not too clean. She wore a dark dress of rough material that reached down to her boots. Over the skirt was fastened a white apron that was stained and wrinkled. The bulbed sleeves ended midway up her wrists and the bodice of the dress was buttoned close around her throat. She wore a kerchief tied at the neck, and a hat that looked like a wide-brimmed skimmer with a raised crown. There was a pathetic little flower of unidentifiable origin in the band of the hat. She carried a beaded handbag of capacious size, hanging from a wrist-loop.

Her step slowed as she saw him standing there, deep in the shadows. Saw him was hardly accurate: sensed him.

He stepped out and bowed slightly from the waist. "Fair evenin' to ye, Miss. Care for a pint?"

Her features—sunk in misery of a kind known only to women who have taken in numberless shafts of male blood-gorged flesh—rearranged themselves. "Coo, sir, I thought was 'im for true. Old Leather Apron hisself. Gawdamighty, you give me a scare." She tried to smile. It was a rictus. There were bright spots in her cheeks from sickness and too much gin. Her voice was ragged, a broken-edged instrument barely workable.

"Just a solicitor caught out without comp'ny," Jack assured her. "And pleased to buy a handsome lady a pint of stout for a few hours' companionship."

She stepped toward him and linked arms. "Emily Matthewes, sir, an' pleased to go with you. It's a fearsome chill night, and with Slippery Jack abroad not safe for a respectin' woman such's m'self."

They moved off down Thrawl Street, past the doss houses where this drab might flop later, if she could obtain a few coppers from this neat-dressed stranger with the dark eyes.

He turned right onto Commercial Street, and just abreast of a stinking alley almost to Flower & Dean Street, he nudged her sharply sidewise. She went into the alley, and thinking he meant to steal a smooth hand up under her petticoats, she settled back against the wall and opened her legs, starting to lift the skirt around her waist. But Jack had hold of the kerchief and, locking his fingers tightly, he twisted, cutting off her breath. Her cheeks ballooned, and by a vagary of light from a gas standard in the street he could see her eyes go from hazel to a dead-leaf brown in an instant. Her expression was one of terror, naturally, but commingled with it was a deep sadness, at having lost the pint, at having not been able to make her doss for the night, at having had the usual Emily Matthewes bad luck to run afoul this night of the one man who would ill-use her favors. It was a consummate sadness at the inevitability of her fate.

A film came over her eyes, and as her breath husked

I come to you out of the night.
The night that sent me down all
the minutes of our lives to this
instant. From this time forward,
men will wonder what happened
at this instant. They will silently
hunger to go back, to come to
my instant with you and see my
face and know my name and
perhaps not even try to stop me,
for then I would not be who I
am, but only someone who tried
and failed. Ah. For you and me
it becomes history that will lure
men always, but they will never
understand why we both suf-
fered, Emily; they will never
truly understand why each of us
died so terribly.

out in wheezing, pleading tremors, his free hand went into the pocket of the greatcoat. He had known he would need it, when they were walking, and he had already invaded the Gladstone bag. Now his hand went into the pocket and came up with the scalpel.

"Emily . . ." softly.

Then he sliced her.

Neatly, angling the point of the scalpel into the soft flesh behind and under her left ear. *Sternocleidomastoideus*. Driving it in to the gentle crunch of cartilage giving way. Then, grasping the instrument tightly, tipping it down and drawing it across the width of the throat, following the line of the firm jaw. *Glandula submandibularis*. The blood poured out over his hands, ran thickly at first and then burst spattering past him, reaching the far wall of the alley. Up his sleeves, soaking his white cuffs. She made a watery rattle and sank limply in his grasp, his fingers still twisted tight in her kerchief; black abrasions where he had scored the flesh. He continued the cut up past the point of the jaw's end, and sliced into the lobe of the ear. He lowered her to the filthy paving. She lay crumpled, and he straightened her. Then he cut away the garments laying her naked belly open to the wan and flickering light of the gas standard in the street. Her belly was bloated. He started the primary cut in the hollow of her throat. *Glandula thyreoeidea*. His hand was sure as he drew a thin black line of blood down and down, between the breasts. *Sternum*. Cutting a deep cross in the hole of her navel. Something vaguely yellow oozed up. *Plica umbilicalis media*. Down over the rounded hump of the belly, biting more deeply, withdrawing for a neat incision. *Mesenterium dorsale commune*. Down to the matted-with-sweat roundness of her privates. Harder here. *Vesica urinaria*. And finally, to the end, *vagina*.

Filth hole.

Foul-smelling die red lust pit wet hole of sluts.

And in his head, succubi. And in his head eyes watching. And in his head minds impinging. And in his head titillation

for a gardenia
a water lily

    a rose
    a hyacinth
    a pair of phlox
    a wild celandine
and a dark flower with petals of obsidian, a stamen of
onyx, pistils of anthracite, and the mind of Hernon, who
was the late Juliette's grandfather.

They watched the entire horror of the mad anatomy
lesson. They watched him nick the eyelids. They watched
him remove the heart. They watched him slice out the fal-
lopian tubes. They watched him squeeze, till it ruptured,
the "ginny" kidney. They watched him slice off the sections of breast till they were nothing but shapeless mounds
of bloody meat, and arrange them, one mound each on a
still-staring, wide-open, nicked-eyelid eye. They watched.
They watched and they drank from the deep troubled
pool of his mind. They sucked deeply at the moist quivering core of his id. And they delighted.

*Oh God how Delicious look at that it looks like the
uneaten rind of a Pizza or look at That it looks like luma-
coni oh god IIIIIwonder what it would be like to
Tasteit!*

See how smooth the steel.

HE HATES THEM ALL, EVERY ONE OF THEM,
SOMETHING ABOUT A GIRL, A VENEREAL DIS-
EASE, FEAR OF HIS GOD, CHRIST, THE REV-
EREND MR. BARNETT, HE . . . HE WANTS TO
FUCK THE REVEREND'S WIFE!

Social reform can only be brought about by concerted
effort of a devoted few. Social reform is a justifiable end,
condoning any expedient short of decimation of over fifty
per cent of the people who will be served by the reforms.
The best social reformers are the most audacious. He be-
lieves it! How lovely!

YOU PACK OF VAMPIRES, YOU FILTH, YOU SCUM, YOU . . .

He senses us!

*DAMN HIM! DAMN YOU, HERNON, YOU DREW
OFF TOO DEEPLY, HE KNOWS WE'RE HERE,
THAT'S DISGUSTING, WHAT'S THE SENSE NOW?
I'M WITHDRAWING!*

Come back, you'll end the formz . . .

... back they plunged in the spiral as it spiraled back in upon itself and the darkness of the night of 1888 withdrew. The spiral drew in and in and locked at its most infinitesimal point as the charred and blackened face of the man who had been the bull thistle. He was quite dead. His eyeholes had been burned out; charred wreckage lay where intelligence had lived. They had used him as a focus.

The man from 1888 came back to himself instantly, with a full and eidetic memory of what he had just experienced. It had not been a vision, nor a dream, nor a delusion, nor a product of his mind. It had happened. They had sent him back, erased his mind of the transfer into the future, of Juliette, of everything after the moment outside No. 13 Miller's Court. And they had set him to work pleasuring them, while they drained off his feelings, his emotions and his unconscious thoughts; while they battened and gorged themselves with the most private sensations. Most of which, till this moment—in a strange feedback—he had not known he possessed. As his mind plunged on from one revelation to the next, he felt himself growing ill. At one concept his mind tried to pull back and plunge him into darkness rather than confront it. But the barriers were down, they had opened new patterns and he could read it all, remember it all. *Stinking sex hole, sluts, they have to die.* No, that wasn't the way he thought of women, any women, no matter how low or common. He was a gentleman, and women were to be respected. *She had given him the clap. He remembered.* The shame and the endless fear till he had gone to his physician father and confessed it. The look on the man's face. He remembered it all. The way his father had tended him, the way he would have tended a plague victim. It had never been the same between them again. He had tried for the cloth. *Social reform hahahaha.* All delusion. He had been a mountebank, a clown ... and worse. He had slaughtered for something in which not even he believed. They left his mind wide open, and his thoughts stumbled ... raced further and further toward the thought of

!EXPLOSION!IN!HIS!MIND!

He fell face forward on the smooth and polished metal pavement, but he never touched. Something arrested his fall, and he hung suspended, bent over at the waist like a ridiculous Punch divested of strings or manipulation from above. A whiff of something invisible, and he was in full possession of his senses almost before they had left him. His mind was forced to look at it:

He wants to fuck the Reverend Mr. Barnett's wife.

Henrietta, with her pious petition to Queen Victoria— "Madam, we, the women of East London, feel horror at the dreadful sins that have been lately committed in our midst . . ."—asking for the capture of himself, of Jack, whom she would never, not *ever* suspect was residing right there with her and the Reverend in Toynbee Hall. The thought was laid as naked as her body in the secret dreams he had never remembered upon awakening. All of it, they had left him with opened doors, with unbounded horizons, and he saw himself for what he was.

A psychopath, a butcher, a lecher, a hypocrite, a clown.

"You did this to me! Why did you do this?"

Frenzy cloaked his words. The flower-faces became the solidified hedonists who had taken him back to 1888 on that senseless voyage of slaughter.

van Cleef, the gardenia-woman, sneered. "Why do you think, you ridiculous bumpkin? (Bumpkin, is that the right colloquialism, Hernon? I'm so uncertain in the mid-dialects.) When you'd done in Juliette, Hernon wanted to send you back. But why should he? He owed us at least three formz, and you did passing well for one of them."

Jack shouted at them till the cords stood out in his throat. "Was it necessary, this last one? Was it important to do it, to help my reforms . . . was it?"

Hernon laughed. "Of course not."

Jack sank to his knees. The City let him do it. "Oh God, oh God almighty, I've done what I've done . . . I'm covered with blood . . . and for *nothing,* for *nothing* . . ."

Cashio, who had been one of the phlox, seemed puzzled. "Why is he concerned about *this* one, if the others don't bother him?"

Nosy Verlag, who had been a wild celandine, said sharply, "They do, all of them do. Probe him, you'll see."

Cashio's eyes rolled up in his head an instant, then

rolled down and refocused—Jack felt a quicksilver shudder in his mind and it was gone—and he said lackadaisically, "Mm-hmm."

Jack fumbled with the latch of the Gladstone. He opened the bag and pulled out the foetus in the bottle. Mary Jane Kelly's unborn child, from November 9th, 1888. He held it in front of his face a moment, then dashed it to the metal pavement. It never struck. It vanished a fraction of an inch from the clean, sterile surface of the City's street.

"What marvelous loathing!" exulted Rose, who had been a rose.

"Hernon," said van Cleef, "he's centering on you. He begins to blame you for all of this."

Hernon was laughing (without moving his lips) as Jack pulled Juliette's electrical scalpel from the Gladstone, and lunged. Jack's words were incoherent, but what he was saying, as he struck, was: "I'll show you what filth you are! I'll show you you can't do this kind of thing! I'll teach you! You'll die, all of you!" This is what he was saying, but it came out as one long sustained bray of revenge, frustration, hatred and directed frenzy.

Hernon was still laughing as Jack drove the whisper-thin blade with its shimmering current into his chest. Almost without manipulation on Jack's part, the blade circumscribed a perfect 360° hole that charred and shriveled, exposing Hernon's pulsing heart and wet organs. He had time to shriek with confusion before he received Jack's second thrust, a direct lunge that severed the heart from its attachments. *Vena cava superior. Aorta. Arteria pulmonalis. Bronchus principalis.*

The heart flopped forward and a spreading wedge of blood under tremendous pressure ejaculated, spraying Jack with such force that it knocked his hat from his head and blinded him. His face was now a dripping black-red collage of features and blood.

Hernon followed his heart, and fell forward, into Jack's arms. Then the flower-people screamed as one, vanished, and Hernon's body slipped from Jack's hands to wink out of existence an instant before it struck at Jack's feet. The walls around him were clean, unspotted, sterile, metallic, uncaring.

He stood in the street, holding the bloody knife.

"*Now!*" he screamed, holding the knife aloft. "Now it begins!"

If the city heard, it made no indication, but

[Pressure accelerated in temporal linkages.]

[A section of shining wall on a building eighty miles away changed from silver to rust.]

[In the freezer chambers, two hundred gelatin caps were fed into a ready trough.]

[The weathermaker spoke softly to itself, accepted data and instantly constructed an intangible mnemonic circuit.]

and in the shining eternal city where night only fell when the inhabitants had need of night and called specifically for night . . .

Night fell. With no warning save: *Now!*"

In the City of sterile loveliness a creature of filth and decaying flesh prowled. In the last City of the world, a City on the edge of the world, where the ones who had devised their own paradise lived, the prowler made his home in shadows. Slipping from darkness to darkness with eyes that saw only movement, he roamed in search of a partner to dance his deadly rigadoon.

He found the first woman as she materialized beside a small waterfall that flowed out of empty air and dropped its shimmering, tinkling moisture into an azure cube of nameless material. He found her and drove the living blade into the back of her neck. Then he sliced out the eyeballs and put them into her open hands.

He found the second woman in one of the towers, making love to a very old man who gasped and wheezed and clutched his heart as the young woman forced him to passion. She was killing him as Jack killed her. He drove the living blade into the lower rounded surface of her belly, piercing her sex organs as she rode astride the old man. She decamped blood and viscous fluids over the prostrate body of the old man, who also died, for Jack's blade had severed the penis within the young woman. She fell forward across the old man and Jack left them that way, joined in the final embrace.

He found a man and throttled him with his bare hands, even as the man tried to dematerialize. Then Jack recognized him as one of the phlox, and made neat incisions in the face, into which he inserted the man's genitals.

He found another woman as she was singing a gentle song about eggs to a group of children. He opened her throat and severed the strings hanging inside. He let the vocal cords drop onto her chest. But he did not touch the children, who watched it all avidly. He liked children.

He prowled through the unending night making a grotesque collection of hearts, which he cut out of one, three, nine people. And when he had a dozen, he took them and laid them as road markers on one of the wide boulevards that never were used by vehicles, for the people of this City had no need of vehicles.

Oddly, the City did not clean up the hearts. Nor were the people vanishing any longer. He was able to move with relative impunity, hiding only when he saw large groups that might be searching for him. But *something* was happening in the City. (Once, he heard the peculiar sound of metal grating on metal, the *shrikkk* of plastic cutting into plastic—though he could not have identified it as plastic—and he instinctively knew it was the sound of a machine malfunctioning.)

He found a woman bathing, and tied her up with strips of his own garments, and cut off her legs at the knees and left her still sitting up in the swirling crimson bath, screaming as she bled away her life. The legs he took with him.

When he found a man hurrying to get out of the night, he pounced on him, cut his throat and sawed off the arms. He replaced the arms with the bath-woman's legs.

And it went on and on, for a time that had no measure. He was showing them what evil could produce. He was showing them their immorality was silly beside his own.

But one thing finally told him he was winning. As he lurked in an antiseptically pure space between two low aluminum-cubes, he heard a voice that came from above him and around him and even from inside him. It was a public announcement, broadcast by whatever mental communications system the people of the City on the edge of the World used.

OUR CITY IS PART OF US, WE ARE PART OF OUR
CITY. IT RESPONDS TO OUR MINDS AND WE CON-
TROL IT. THE GESTALT THAT WE HAVE BECOME
IS THREATENED. WE HAVE AN ALIEN FORCE
WITHIN THE CITY AND WE ARE GEARING TO
LOCATE IT. BUT THE MIND OF THIS MAN IS
STRONG. IT IS BREAKING DOWN THE FUNCTIONS
OF THE CITY. THIS ENDLESS NIGHT IS AN EXAM-
PLE. WE MUST ALL CONCENTRATE. WE MUST
ALL CONSCIOUSLY FOCUS OUR THOUGHTS TO
MAINTAINING THE CITY. THIS THREAT IS OF THE
FIRST ORDER. IF OUR CITY DIES, WE WILL DIE.

It was not an announcement in those terms, though that
was how Jack interpreted it. The message was much longer and much more complex, but that was what it meant,
and he knew he was winning. He was destroying them. Social reform was laughable, they had said. He would show
them.

And so he continued with his lunatic pogrom. He
butchered and slaughtered and carved them wherever he
found them, and they could not vanish and they could
not escape and they could not stop him. The collection
of hearts grew to fifty and seventy and then a hundred.

He grew bored with hearts and began cutting out their
brains. The collection grew.

For numberless days it went on, and from time to time
in the clean, scented autoclave of the City, he could hear
the sounds of screaming. His hands were always sticky.

Then he found van Cleef, and leaped from hiding in
the darkness to bring her down. He raised the living blade
to drive it into her breast, but she

van   ished

He got to his feet and looked around. van Cleef reappeared ten feet from him. He lunged for her and again
she was gone. To reappear ten feet away. Finally, when
he had struck at her half a dozen times and she had escaped him each time, he stood panting, arms at sides,
looking at her.

And she looked back at him with disinterest.

"You no longer amuse us," she said, moving her lips.

Amuse? His mind whirled down into a place far darker than any he had known before, and through the murk of his blood-lust he began to realize. It had all been for their amusement. They had *let* him do it. They had given him the run of the City and he had capered and gibbered for them.

Evil? He had never even suspected the horizons of that word. He went for her, but she disappeared with finality.

He was left standing there as the daylight returned. As the City cleaned up the mess, took the butchered bodies and did with them what it had to do. In the freezer chambers the gelatin caps were returned to their niches, no more inhabitants of the City need be thawed to provide Jack the Ripper with utensils for his amusement of the sybarites. His work was truly finished.

He stood there in the empty street. A street that would *always* be empty to him. The people of the City had all along been able to escape him, and now they would. He was finally and completely the clown they had shown him to be. He was not evil, he was pathetic.

He tried to use the living blade on himself, but it dissolved into motes of light and wafted away on a breeze that had blown up for just that purpose.

Alone, he stood there staring at the victorious cleanliness of this Utopia. With their talents they would keep him alive, possibly alive forever, immortal in the possible expectation of needing him for amusement again someday. He was stripped to raw essentials in a mind that was no longer anything more than jelly matter. To go madder and madder, and never to know peace or end or sleep.

He stood there, a creature of dirt and alleys, in a world as pure as the first breath of a baby.

"My name isn't Jack," he said softly. But they would never know his real name. Nor would they care. *My name isn't Jack!"* he said loudly. No one heard.

"MY NAME ISN'T JACK, AND I'VE BEEN BAD, VERY BAD, I'M AN EVIL PERSON BUT MY NAME ISN'T JACK!" he screamed, and screamed, and screamed again, walking aimlessly down an empty street, in plain view, no longer forced to prowl. A stranger in the City.

Afterword

The paths down which our minds entice us are often not the ones we thought we were taking. And the destinations frequently leave something to be desired in the area of hospitality. Such a case is the story you have just read.

It took me fifteen months—off and on— to write "The Prowler In The City At The Edge Of The World." As I indicated in my introduction to Bob Bloch's story, it was first a visual image without a plot—the creature of filth in the city of sterile purity. It seemed a fine illustration, but it was little more than that, I'm afraid. At best I thought it might provide a brief moment of horror in a book where realism (even couched in fantasy) was omnipresent.

I suggested the illustration to Bloch and he did his version of it. But the folly of trying to put one man's vision in another man's head (even when the vision was directly caused by the vision of the first man) was obvious.

So I decided to color my own illustration. With Bloch's permission. But what was my story? I was intrigued by the entire *concept* of a Ripper, a killer of obvious derangement who nonetheless worked in a craftsmanlike manner to such estimable ends that he was never apprehended. And the letters of braggadocio he had sent to the newspapers and the police and George Lusk of the East London vigilantes. The audacity of the man! The eternal horror of him! I was hooked.

But I still had no story.

Still, I tried to write it. I started it two dozen times—easily—in the fifteen months during which I edited *Dangerous Visions*. Started it and slumped to a stop after a page or two, surfeited with my own fustian. I had nothing but that simple drawing in my head. Jack in the autoclave. The story languished while I wrote a film and a half-dozen TV scripts and two dozen stories and uncountable articles, reviews, criticisms, introductions, and edited the anthology. (For those who think a writer is someone who gets his name on books, let me assure you *that* is an "author." A "writer" is the hapless devil who cannot keep himself from putting every vagrant thought he has ever had down on paper. I am a writer. I write. That's what I do. I do a lot of it.) The story gathered dust.

But a writer I once admired very much had told me that a "writer's slump" might very well not be a slump at all, but a transitional period. A plateau period in which his style, his views and his interests might be altering. I've found this to be true. Story ideas I've gotten that have not been able to get written, I've let sit. For years. And then, one day, as if magically, I leap on the snippet of story and start over and it gets itself written in hours. Unconsciously, I had been working and reworking that story in my mind during the years in which other work had claimed me consciously. In my Writer's Brain I knew I simply did not have the skill or insight to do the story I wanted to do, and had I bulled through (as I did when I was much younger and needed to *get it all said*), I would have produced a half-witted, half-codified story.

This was precisely the case with "The Prowler." As the months passed, I realized what I was trying to do was say something about the boundaries and dimensions of evil in a total society. It was not merely the story of Jack, it was the story of the effects on evil, *per se*, of an evil culture.

It was becoming heady stuff. So I realized I could not write it from just the scant information on Jack I could recall from Bloch's "Yours Truly, Jack The Ripper," or from an E. Haldeman-Julius *Little Blue Book* I had read in junior high school, or even from the passing references I had encountered, by Alan Hynd, and by Mrs. Belloc Lowndes in *The Lodger*. I suddenly had a project on my hands. The integrity of the story demanded I do my homework.

So I read everything I could lay my hands on. I scoured the bookstores and the libraries for source books on Jack. And in this respect, I must express my gratitude and pleasure for the books by Tom A. Cullen, Donald McCormick, Leonard P. Matters and *The Harlot Killer*, edited by Allan Barnard, which only served to fire my curiosity about this incredible creature known as Jack.

I was hooked. I read ceaselessly about the slayings. And without my even knowing it, I began to form my own conclusions as to who Jack might have been.

The concept of the "invisible killer"—an assassin who could be seen near the site of a crime and not be considered a suspect—stuck with me. The audacity of the crimes and their relatively open nature—in streets and courts and alleys—seemed to insist that an "invisible killer" was my man. Invisible? Why, consider, in Victorian London, a policeman would be invisible, a midwife would be invisible, and . . . a clergyman would be invisible.

The way in which the poor harlots were butchered indicated two things to me: a man obviously familiar with surgical technique, and a man addicted to the concept of femininity prevalent at the time.

But most of all, the pattern and manner of the crimes suggested to me—over and above the obvious derangement of the assassin—that the clergyman/butcher was trying to make a statement. A grisly and quite mad statement, to be sure. But a statement, nonetheless.

So I continued my reading with these related facts in mind. And everywhere I read, the name of the Reverend Samuel Barnett appeared with regularity. He was a socially conscious man who lived in the general area, at Toynbee Hall. And his wife had circulated the petition to Queen Victoria. He had the right kind of background, he certainly had the religious fervor to want to see the slums cleared at almost any cost.

My mind bridged the gap. If not Barnett—to which statement, even in fiction, about a man long since dead, would be attached the dangers of libel and slander—then someone close to Barnett. A younger man, perhaps. And from one concept to another the theory worked itself out till I had in my Writer's Brain a portrait of exactly who Jack the Ripper was and what his motives had been.

(I was gratified personally to read Tom Cullen's book on the Ripper, after this theory had been established in my mind, and find that in many ways—though not as completely or to the same suspect—he had attached the same drives to *his* Ripper as I to mine.)

Now began a period of writing that stretched out over many weeks. This was one of the hardest stories I ever wrote. I was furious at the limitations of the printed page, the line-for-line rigidity of QWERTYUIOP. I wanted to break out, and the best I could do was use typographical tricks, which are in the final analysis little more than tricks. There must be some way a writer can write a book that has all the visual and sensory impact of a movie!

In any case, my story is now told.

The Jack I present is the Jack in all of us, of course. The Jack that tells us to stand and watch as a Catherine Genovese gets knifed, the Jack that condones Vietnam because we don't care to get involved, the Jack that watches the genocide of the Black Panthers with righteous unconcern, the Jack who accepts a My Lai slaughter as the "fortunes of war," the Jack that we need. We are a culture that needs its monsters.

We have to deify our Al Capones, our Billy the Kids, our Jesse Jameses, and all the others including Jack Ruby, General Walker, Charles Manson, Adolf Hitler, Charlie Starkweather and even Richard Speck, whose Ripper-like butchery of the Chicago nurses has already begun to be thought of as modern legend.

We are a culture that *creates* its killers and its monsters and then provides for them the one thing Jack was never able to have: reality. He was a doomed man who wanted desperately to be recognized for what he had done (as consider the notes he wrote), but could not come out in the open for fear of capture. The torn-in-two directions of a man who senses that the mob will revere him, even as they kill him.

That is the message of this story. *You* are the monsters.

Avram Davidson and Harlan Ellison

UP
CHRISTOPHER
TO
MADNESS

Scherzo for Schizoids

Notes on a Collaboration

by Harlan Ellison

'58 was a helluva year. I was midway through my Army service, separated from the nut I was later to divorce, going through a strange phase in my writing, hating every minute of the waking hours.

I had this buddy, I've written stories about him: he was (and is) a fantastic character. His name was Derry. We called him the Tiger. He was a millionaire. A PFC like me. A similar kook. We got in lots of trouble. Double-dated (until the gay husband of the Louisville poetess he was balling got hip to me sleeping on the stairs as watchdog while Derry was updecks stoking the Antic Arts), fought the military to a standstill with our goldbricking (until my C.O. found out that Tiger and I were sharing expenses on an off-post trailer so we could seed the Kentucky female population, despite the fact that we weren't entitled to live off-post), helped each other out (he sent me Mars Bars while I was waiting for the C.O. to figure out how to court-martial my ass into Leavenworth), and in general made the scene together.

Derry and I decided to take a three-day pass one Thanksgiving and skim up to Worcester, Mass., which his family owned. His last name was Taylor, and it is an indescribable sort of mind-boggle to drive down a New England street and see the Taylor Building, the Taylor Bank & Trust, Taylor Savings & Loan, Taylor Automotive, Taylor Theater . . .

We stopped off in New York for the night, before hopping on up to Boston (some time I'll tell you about that two days in Worcester, with the Tiger's mother packing us a "box-lunch" for the Dartmouth-Harvard game that consisted of *Lachryma Christi,* individual guinea hens and hot clam chowder . . . oh, those rock-ribbed Yankee moneyfolk sure as hell know how to live!) and we were invited to a party at the home of Horace L. Gold, then editor of *Galaxy Science Fiction Magazine.*

In the crowd at that party was a chick I had known some years before in San Francisco. She was easily the most twisted lady I've ever met (with the exception of my first and third wives, who had a corner on the market), and when it came to sex, she knew more tricks with a bar of soap than the Marquis de Sade and Leopold Sacher-Masoch combined. The Tiger and I spent the night before Boston at her pad . . . but that's quite another story.

Also attendant at the party was a howitzer-shell-shaped man with a truly overwhelming hirsute appearance. He wore a *yarmulkah,* a skullcap, for all you *goyim,* and when I made to light one of the ten thousand cigarettes he smoked that night, he cleverly cupped one hand around it in case I had the ineptitude to set his beard on fire. This was Avram Davidson.

When I was preparing the notes for this article, in 1965, it dawned on me that I had known Avram so long, I'd forgotten just when and where we had first encountered one another. I wrote to him in Berkeley, California, where he was living at the time, and asked him. I print herewith, his reply *in toto*:

> *"We first met at a party in Horace G's home that time you were in the milla tree with Derry the Tiger. You tried to feel me up and I knocked you on your ass. Is there anything else you wanna know, snot-nose?"*

Years later, circa 1961, when I was long-since free of The Nut and living in Greenwich Village, Avram and I renewed acquaintances, and we chummed it up middlin' fair. We used to go down to the Paperbook Gallery (now vanished, woe to us all) on the corner of West 10th

Street and Seventh Avenue, to play skittles. Skittles is a game of skill whose Welsh origins are shrouded in secret, much like those of Stonehenge (remember "beer & skittles"—1680?), and is played with a box-like playing-field just somewhere short of four feet long, using a top spun through a series of connected chambers, knocking down pins in those chambers to accumulate points.

One night Avram and myself, and half a dozen others, including several comely wenches, were skittling, when a group of Bleecker Street teddy-boys descended on the scene and began using profane language in the presence of our damsels. "Cease and desist such coarse badinage," I instructed them in my most vibrant Robert Ruark voice, "or I will come up there and kick the piss outta you." They scoffed, heretical little twits, and so I bade a tiny urchin, clumped adoringly to the right of my Thom McAn, "Hie thee hence to the open-air market yonder *dorten*, and fetch me a crate box of purest wood." The tot scampered, returned with the crate, and as the j.d.'s watched in awed silence, I proceeded with half a dozen karate-*cum*-kung-fu chops to render it into a tidy pile of kindling. Fear lay like a patina of dust across their acne-pocked countenances (counteni? countenubim?). They scuttled away, crablike, in the night. I puffed up like a pouter pigeon, having saved the scene from the ravages of the street gangs.

They returned, doubled in number. One of them had a tire iron. One of them had a broken quart bottle of Rheingold Beer. One of them had a ball-peen hammer. One of them had a bike chain. One of them had a zip gun. One of them had a 12″ Italian stiletto which he used to clean his fingernails. It was the kid with the hammer I felt most uneasy about. He kept grinning. At me.

Everyone vanished. Remaining: Avram, myself, and the half dozen clingers-on, who felt they'd best hang close for protection. Fat chance. We decided to start walking. We moved out, and the horde followed us. As they tracked us slowly ("Don't turn, *kemo sabe*, if they see fear in your eyes, they'll attack.") down Seventh Avenue, and up Christopher Street to the corner of Bleecker, Avram nudged in close and in true 007 style mumbled out of the corner of his mouth, "Now see what you've gone and

went and done, stupid!?!" I threw him a withering F. Van
Wyck Mason hero sneer, straight out of an historical
novel. When we got to the corner, I sent the women
away; as the gang had followed us, they had whistled up
friends from cubbyholes and niches along the street, till
now the horde was close to fifty kids, all of whom out-
weighed, outheightened, outferocious'd me. There I stood,
virtually alone before a latter-day Attila's horde. The
street had grown silent and chill with the expectant air of
a neighborhood holding its breath for the gentle sound of
blood drip-drip-dripping onto the cobbles. I turned around,
and there was Avram, at a street sanitation waste basket,
methodically twisting a piece of rope from a grocery on
the corner into a *thuggee* strangle-knot. My eyes widened.
Was this the gentle, restrained, holy man, but lately
descended from his Ivory Tower of literary purity? I was
damned if I'd be upstaged by a man twice my age.

I walked into the center of the throng, picked one of
the pock-marked punks, and jabbed a finger in his chest.
"You," I snapped in my best Raymond Chandler manner.
"You've been mouthing-off pretty good. I'm not worrying
about the rest of these guys, I want a piece of you,
busymouth." The crowd suddenly backed off, leaving
punkie and me in the center. It was an official sort of
challenge. (In case you're wondering, I was scared wit-
less.)

But at that single moment in time, as it must come to
all men, I received proof positive of whether I was cow-
ardly or something else. At least, I was not a coward. It
helps me through my declining years, that knowledge.

We squared off, and at that moment an ex-member of
the gang, graduated to the Better Life—boosting cars,
robbing pharmacies, mugging homosexuals, et al—made
the scene, demanded to know what was happening, and
before any of the young punks could say anything, I dove
in with, "They're trying to clutter up a nice Saturday night
with a bop." He dispersed them, shook my hand, and with
Avram riding shotgun—still dangling that killer-rope from
his meaty paw—we located the chicks, and lived to fight
another day.

This story was written in the December and January of
1961-2 in a New York just starting to tremble with the

underground temblors of a racial volcano that has since erupted. I was living uptown with two dear friends, Leo & Diane Dillon (who illustrated "Up Christopher to Madness" in its original magazine appearance, incidentally, and who did the dust wrapper of this book). They had put me up temporarily, because I was midway between Chicago and Hollywood. (Kindly be good enough not to ask how New York came to be midway between Chicago and L.A.)

Anyhow, there I was sleeping on their sofa, and they were sleeping on the floor (define the nature and limitations of love-friendship; I can't) and Avram came over. He was living across from Columbia University in a great echoing apartment building where little old ladies went to die, and there was a deli around the block that had the grooviest rye bread you've ever eaten.

I don't remember who first said, "Let's collaborate on a story," but one of us did, and we started writing. We had no title, we had no plot, and we had no market in mind. Which is possible why this story is the most offbeat one either of us has written. It is in neither of our styles, yet it is *both* our styles.

It was written over a period of a week, with one or the other of us trotting to the other's residence, typing a few paragraphs, leaving the plot in an insoluble condition, smirking at the pickle we had left the other in, and skulking out again. I must have eaten a dozen loaves of rye bread.

"Up Christopher to Madness" is a funny story. I tell you this in front, if you're reading the article first, so you'll know. And afterward, in case you read the story first, so you'll feel dense at not having gotten the humor. Either way, you can't win.

It is written in a pseudo-Ring Lardner style, and if, as you read it, you hear it being spoken by, say, Sheldon Leonard, you will get more out of it. It is based upon a much-loved memory of Greenwich Village days in which there was a sight-seeing train that roamed the Village streets, in the shape of a long caterpillar. It was a groove. The fellow who piloted it was dressed like a clown, and tourists used to ride it with gay abandon. We took that as the opening element of the story, and sort of freewheeled from there,

The story is filled with subtle literary allusions (we like to think). I will try and explain some of the more obscure of these.

● The *Oliver* was a "typewriting machine." The *"typewriter"* was the girl who operated it. She wore shirt-waists and her name was Fannie, or maybe, Hattie.

● A *six-for-fiver* is a guy who lends you five bucks today and you pay him six back tomorrow. You'd damned well *better*.

● The *Edsel* was a myth perpetuated by the Ford Motor Company. It falls into the category of other mythological creatures like unicorns, hippogriffs, beatniks, leprechauns, elves and Governor George Wallace. There were only two of these beasts sold in the United States. What's that? *You* bought the *other* one?

● Hitchcock made a movie called *The Birds*. It was for the.

● *Coproliths* are fossilized pre-cow cow-pats, as it were. Curators of Vertebrate Paleontology hoard them like jewels, now and then locking the museum doors so that they can gloat and titter over their hoard like mad, fiendish misers. You or me—they'd lock *us* up.

● *"The Peat Bog Soldiers"* is one of the two English language phonograph records owned by Radio Moscow. The author and composer would be rich by now, if Radio Moscow paid royalties.

● *Gefilte fish* is a little difficult to try and explain. It is a Semitic provender composed (as stated in the story) of various bits of fish. It has a taste somewhere between heavenly and ghastly, depending on your ethnic heritage and the resiliency of your inner plumbing. Best source of reference is your nearest delicatessen. If you live in Chitling Switch, Montana, you are probably out of luck, and will have to take our word for it.

● *Base canard* is the bottom duck in a beachside pyramid of athletic French ducks. You believe that, you'll believe anything.

● *Miltowns* are tranquilizers. *Lead* Miltowns is gotta be bullets. Permanent tranquilizers. That's called a clever use of language.

● *Old Rite Amishmen* do not have their pictures taken. They do not dance. They do not drive around in fast cars. They do not covet their neighbor's wives, daughters, oxen or television sets. Their neighbors are also Old Rite Amish and so have no television sets. They do not sing except in Church. They do not smile very much. The way *they* tell it, they're leading the pure good life. That's *their* story.

● A *pothead* is another name for a teahead is another name for a grasshead is another name for a weedhead is another name for one'a them dudes what smokes them funky little brown cigarettes and gets that funky grin on his funky face.

● *Countess Mara ties* are usually worn by mobsters. You can spot them: the Good Countess has her crest on the front of the tie, which strikes me as being a pretty blatant and successful attempt at free advertising. They are worn with white-on-white shirts, white-on-white suits, white-on-white faces.

● *The Red & Blue Networks* were divisions of CBS way back when. Or was it NBC? It was the one that brought you The Shadow, sponsored by Blue Coal. And *I Love A Mystery*. Remember Jack, Doc & Reggie? Know who played Reggie? Tony Randall. Now how's *that* for knocking you off your pins!

● *Felucca*: a small coasting vessel propelled by oars or lateen sails, or both; used chiefly in the Mediterranean.

And you thought this book was just filled with dumb stories. Don't say we don't got educational information.

● *Allan Bloch* makes sandals in the Village. He makes 'em good like a cobbler should. Unpaid advt.

● The reference to windmills quivering in relation to Cozenage, refers back to *Don Quixote*. If you never read the book, the allusion is wasted on you, illiterate! *Javert* was the police inspector who hounded Jean Valjean in *Les Miserables* by Victor Hugo. If you never read *that* one, what are you doing reading something what ain't a Giant Golden Book?

● *Bawdy-Lair* was a depraved French poet who wrote *Les Fleurs du Mal* which means "Flowers Of Evil." He was depraved cause he was deprived. A word to the wise . . . is usually pointless. . . .

● *Stagecoaches.* Technically and legally, all buses in New York City are still stagecoaches. Sonofabitch!

● ". . . *stone that puts the stars to flight*," i.e., the sun, you dopes, according to the Quatrains of Omar Khayyam.

● *Old 96, viz. Old 97: Mr. Ellison knows nothing of folksongs, nothing of railroading: also he can't count.* The foregoing was a Davidsonian put-down. Well, screw you, fuzzy!

● *Sans-culottes*: he, she, or they, without kneebreeches: non-aristocrats, revolutionaries. *Vallembrossa*: scene of a well-known WPA project in the poems of Petrarch . . . or was it Edgar Guest? *Mt. Hymettus*: big honey-producing district near Athens, Greece, elevation 3369 feet, give or take a couple of hymettii.

● *Zeppo* and *Gummo* were also Marx Bros. Zeppo wasn't very funny, though. He quit and became an agent. Gummo had quit years earlier to become a raincoat manufacturer, and nobody remembers if he was funny or not. The reference refers to the film *Room Service*.

● *Grover Whalen* was, for many years, NYC's official greeter.

● *"He was found in the wreck, with his hand on the throttle,*
"An' a-scalded to death by steam."—Wreck of Old 97 (*not '96*)

All *right*, already, Davidson, you made your point!

There was more, much more, but in the original version of this essay, published in a men's magazine more noted for aureoles than erudition, there was insufficient space available to continue the list, endless as it was. So those additional notes are forever lost to posterity. However, in the mails a few months ago, out—as it were—of the blue—to coin nothing at all—came an article about that very same period, written by dear Avram, the good fairy of Novato, California (where he is *now* living). And apparently it was written way back when, for some defunct fan magazine or other. With a whimpering tone in his letter, Avram implored me to find a home for this hastily scrawled persiflage, in order that payment might be made him, thereby providing a smidge of gruel for his son, Ethan.

(Do you notice, even talking *about* Avram, one falls into that damned baroque style of his!)

And so, on promise of slipping him a few extra bucks off the top of this anthology, I herewith present as the conclusion of "Scherzo for Schizoids," Avram Davidson's—

INTRODUCTION

TO

"UP CHRISTOPHER

TO MADNESS"

(BY AVRAM DAVIDSON)

"Okay," said Knox Burger, of Gold Medal Books. "You do it that way, and I'll give you a contract."

"Crazy!" said Harlan Ellison, Boy Collaborator. I said nothing. I was like dazed. Only the other day I had observed to Ward Moore (Father Image, Mad Genius, and [non-] [Boy] Collaborator), "For almost eight years now I've been on the verge of getting a contract for a book—"

"—and you're still *virgo intacto*," said Ward ... But now no longer.

"We'll go down and have a couple of drinks on it," said Knox. We did. I had Irish-on-ice, Knox had Scotch, Harlan had milk. Sometimes between the third and fourth Irish I managed to burn a hole in Knox's Harris tweed jacket with my cigarette. "That will come out of your royalties," he said, gloomily.

"Okay, then," said Harlan rising. "We'll get started on the rewrite right away, Knox. Avram!" I snapped to attention. *"Watch it!"* cried Knox, snatching his jacket away. "Be at my place at seven tomorrow night, and we'll get right to work," Harlan ordered.

"Aywah, Tuan Besar," I muttered, making my salaam. A tendency of my right leg to twitch as if struck by a rubber hammer, I attributed to impurities in the ice. But at seven the next evening I was there, at Harlan's apartment.

"You play skittles, Avram?" he inquired.

"Promised my mother not to," I said primly. "What's the gag, Ellison, or The Non-British Agent?" I asked.

"No gag," he said, briskly, and dragging me out to the elevator. "You must have seen the skittles setup outside the Paperbook Gallery."

"Oh, is *that* what it is; I thought it was a gym for waltzing mice."

"How microcephalic can you get? you clod," he demanded, affectionately rhetorical. "Skittles are *in*, and the *Village Voice* wants me to do an article for them. Andy Reiss will illustrate."

"But the, uh, *book*, Harlan? The rewrite? For Knox? You said—"

"Later, later. Right now: skittles."

So we went up Seventh Ave. to where the Paperbook Gallery crouched below street level on its corner. In the tiny area in front was the skittles setup, on a table. I hung over the railing, watching, like a spectator at a dog-pit, or a bear-baiting—a simile which, it developed, was not to be too far-out. Along with Harlan was Andy Reiss, Boy-Artist Extraordinary, a young lady, and Kenny Sanders—Harlan's step-son-to-be, aged twelve—all of whom, I neglected to mention, egocentric observer that I am, had been at Harlan's when I arrived. Two or three inoffensive young boys from Brooklyn, wearing black sweaters, turned up from somewhere; and so the game got started.

Like so: You spin these sort of *tops*, see—and they whirl around like gyroscopes, and you try to influence them telekinetically to spin through doors in the wooden maze and so get to the skittles proper—tiny bowling-pins—and knock them down. My capacity for games and for sports is pitifully limited; I mean, there was this time in Sumatra when I yawned, *openly*, during the ox races, and almost precipitated an international incident. The tops whirled and caromed and careened and sometimes got through the doors and knocked down the widdle pins. "Oh, well-*spon*, sir!" I would call from time to time, and slap my handies in a languidly well-bred sort of way.

Spectators came and went, pointed, giggled, gawked, exclaimed; Andy Reiss made sketches, scratched them out, drew new ones. Cars screeched, buses rattled, trucks roared; "You, ya, shmuck, I don't like ya face!" I snapped my head up, startled. Who was *that?* It was a kid, age about 16 and he was leaning over the railings which—at a 45-degree angle—joined the railings I was leaning over; and he was addressing his comments to Harlan, peaceably playing skittles in the pit beneath.

Harlan looked up, said, "I'll go home and change it for you," or something flip of the sort.

And kept on skittling. By now he had attracted a crowd of would-be skittles afficionadoes, who were commenting on his skill. The remark infuriated the kid. "I'll come back with a *gun!*" he screamed. "Dontcha believe me? I'll *show* ya!" And his sidekicks, several in number, joined in.

"This" (I said to myself) "is crazy. If I were writing this for a story or a TV show or a movie, no editor would buy it. 'No motivation,' is what he'd say. 'You haven't shown any motivation.' "

And he'd be correct. In this case, Nature refused to imitate Art. There *was* no motivation. Nevertheless—

"Ya sonofabitch!" the kid screamed. "Ya — — — — — —!" (No use counting dashes; I've disguised the invective to protect the innocent.) "Ya — — — — — — — —! We'll mopulize ya! Ya know what I think ya are?"

"What?" Harlan inquired, smiling, and seeming only mildly puzzled.

"Yer a — — — — — — — — — — —!" He screamed, mentioning one of the less lovable offenses of which the late Emperor Nero has, from time to time, been accused. Harlan, still smiling, went on skittling. Andy Reiss continued to sketch. I went on leaning over the railings, trying to look like a hay, feed, and grain dealer in a small way of business, from East Weewaw, Wisconsin; somebody, in short, who had never heard of Harlan Ellison. And waited (such was my lack of confidence in the success of the impersonation) for the moment, inevitable, I was sure, for the kid to turn on me and offer to pluck out my beard, hair by hair, and feed it to me: an offer I intended to decline with all the politeness at my command.

Suddenly, they were gone. In a westerly direction. No sun-worshipper ever looked so wistfully at the east as did I, then. "Looks like we're going to be mixed up in a teen-age rumble," Harlan said. "Preposterous!" I told myself. "Absurd . . . Things don't happen this way . . ." After all, I had read about the Crazy Mixed-Up Kids, Turfs (Turves?), Rumbles, Bopping Mobs, etc. *We* weren't contesting their territory. *We* hadn't made a play for one of their debs. So why?— How come—? And then, like a bolt of Jumbo Number Ten lightning, came a flash which illuminated a scene from earlier criminal literature, videlicet and to whiz, *the young punk who wanted to make a rep* ... I swallowed a foreign object, as it might be a tesseract, or a cactus, which had gotten lodged in my throat.

"Well, that ends the game, I guess," Harlan said, after a while. I looked around. No sign of the Junior Assassins, or the Young Torturers, or whatever their sticky name was. I breathed the air once more/O-o-of Freedom/In my own beloved—

"How's about we go over to The Caricature, Harlan?" I suggested, casually. The Caricature wasn't much of a place, but it lay to the *east*.

Harlan considered. And then the young lady, in a small voice, said, "My pockabook." "What's that, dear?" Harlan asked, paternal, benevolent. "My pockabook. I left it in your apartment." "Oh. Well, we'll go and get your pocketbook. And then we'll go to The Caricature," said HE. And we started off. Toward the west. " 'As yer 'eard about poor old Alfy, Bert?" "No, Len, whuh abaout 'im?" "Took a Jerry bullet at Wipers. Went west."

At the corner of Christopher and Bleecker Harlan paused. "The rest of you stay here," he said. "I'll go up and get the purse." By this time I was able to see the whole thing for the absurdity it patently was. Obvious, the gang had just been amusing itself. A mere ritual. Wasn't there something akin to this in the puberty ceremonies of the Kwakiutl Indians? I chuckled.

And then there they were.

There were more of them. They had gotten reinforcements. And, as they gathered across the street, they began calling out threats, cursing. Slowly I melted into the background (not an easy thing to do under the glare of the streetlamps) and oozed down the street. Something sticking part way out of a garbage-can caught my eye, I picked it out as I went, my fingers working with it absently ... Inside the candy store I dropped a dime in the booth's phone, dialed O. "Give me the police," I said, in a low voice. In an equally low voice the operator asked, "Emergency?" "Yes." "Where are you calling from?" I told her, and immediately the police were on the phone. I gave them a rapid rundown, they promised to send someone, I went out into the savage street.

The details seem unaccountably blurred in my mind. I recall the gang slowly starting to cross the street toward us. One of the boys from Brooklyn said, in a resigned tone of voice, "I've been beaten up so many times . . ." Harlan said, "Don't worry—" He walked into the mob. A drink-blurred voice screamed something ugly. A bottle shattered against the wall over our heads. And then somebody stepped in between the two groups—a fellow of about eighteen. He asked something I didn't catch. "Well, they wanna fight, so—" one of the Junior Assassins replied, but he seemed suddenly less sure of himself. The newcomer, whoever he was, was clearly Someone of Consequence.

"No fighting," the newcomer directed. He turned to us. "You go ahead, wherever you're going." he said, calmly. "There won't be no trouble." We turned and started walking. The last I saw of them, one of the kids was struggling to get loose, and cursing wildly, but he was held tightly amidships by the Peacemaker.

Halfway down the block we passed a policeman, hurrying toward the scene we had just left.

Later that night, after leaving The Caricature, after pausing for Harlan to shatter four empty beer-cans (old, hard-style) and two wooden fruit crates with one blow each; later, back in his apartment, I reached into my pocket for a match, and encountered a strange object. I pulled it out. It was a piece of rope, the piece of rope I had extracted from the trash can en route to the phone. Something, however, had been done to it . . .

"*What*," said Harlan, staring, "is *that?*"

"Oh, er, uh," I said, lucidly, remembering, vaguely, my fingers working on the rope.

"*That* is a thuggee noose," said Harlan.

"Uh, wull, *yuh*, I guess it is," I said. "They taught us how when I was with the Marines. You slip it over the guy's head from behind, and you put your knee in the small of his back ..." My voice trailed away. Harlan looked at me, strangely. Then he got up and got himself a glass of milk.

"Now, about the rewrite," I began.

Harlan waved his hand. "Not tonight, Avram" he said. "Not tonight."

That was some several years ago. Harlan married Kenny's mother very soon after, and moved to Evanston to edit Regency Books. Later I had a letter from him. His marriage was terminating, he said, and he was leaving his job and the Midwest. Under the circumstances he felt unable to finish the book for Gold Medal with me, and was returning the ms. He was sure, he wrote, that I'd be able to find another collaborator.

So far I haven't. I'll probably do the book by myself. It's a crime novel, not sf, and I'd like to work on the scene about the rumble-which-didn't quite. But no editor would pass it. It lacks, you see, it lacks motivation ...

Ellison again. As you can see, by comparing the two renditions, there are small but important discrepancies in the telling. In my version, I am a hero. In Avram's, not only is *he* a hero but, as in the Sam Sheppard case, the Mysterious Stranger is the focus of action. I leave it to you to siphon truth from wayward memory. Or check with Dona Sadock Liebowitz, the girl who said "my pockabook." She has an eidetic memory, and she can tell you the way it was.

In any case, alla that happened around the time of "Up Christopher to Madness," and I hope the texture of what you have just read will inform your reading of this non-sf, *I* think hilarious, story of the good old days what was, in Greenwich Village, when we were all younger and collaborations (aside from the novel, which never got wrote) were simpler.

Up Christopher
to Madness

Guided tours—those Roman circii on wheels—of Greenwich Village and the Bowery, invariably include visits to (or passing notice of) such taverns as The White
Horse, McSorley's, Julius's, Leo's, The Jumble Shop. But
only Red Fred's Village Voyages takes out-of-towners and
uptowners to Aunt Annie's Ale House. Which is, perhaps,
the reason so few out-of-towners and uptowners are found
weighted down with old typewriters in the East River. The
Ale House's clientele is—in the parlance of the fuzz—un-
savory. A mugging-*cum*-swimfest w/typewriter was, therefore, not uncommon at Aunt Annie's. (Times, of course,
change, and He Who Would Stay Abreast must change
with them: In the good bad old days a man who had been
weighted down with an Oliver the size of a small threshing
machine *stayed* weighted. Try that with an Olivetti or a
Hermes thin as a wafer, and the victim-elect is not only
likely to decline the nomination but to emerge, damp and
annoyed, and start grinding an ice-pick point—or other
uncivil, though not altogether unexpected, behavior.)

No matter what they may mutter at Charles Street Station House, it was accident, nothing but accident, which
brought Red Fred and a bumper crop of sweating hay-
seeds (Royal Arch Masons from Chitling Switch, Ne-
braska: retired elocution teachers from East Weewaw,
Wis., wearied with the season's labors, shuddering at the
very sight of prunes, prisms, and cheese: and other *speci-*

mens habitans of The Great American Heartland) on the scene at the exact moment, Greenwich Village Meridian Time, when Angie the Rat, a prominent Six-for-Fiver—having compounded his interest once too often to expect further indulgence of Big Patsy the horse-player—was unceremoniously, but none the less effectively, sent where the bad loansharks go. One bullet in the left larnyx, one bullet in the right larnyx, and one bullet in the precise center of the umbilical quadrant. The reubens, male and female, scattering with shrieks and squeals, the assailants leisurely made their escape in an oyster-grey Edsel (which proved, of course, to be stolen).

Such amenities, confirming what had heretofore been mere wicked suspicions, instantly brought the yokels back for more. *More*, MORE; and, for the moment, left the competition nowhere. Fred might even have dispensed with the jumbo beret, the black tinted-lens hornrims, and the chestnut-colored beaver, which served him in lieu of neon signs and barkers; only he was stubborn.

And to be brutally honest (dealing as we are with clinical detail), Fred *had* to wear the beret, shades and foliage. He was not called *Red* Fred for naught. His name still appeared with inglorious regularity on subversive lists circulated by private, alphabetized agencies; and he thought it best to await the Revolution incognito.

It was, perhaps, because the assassins had hyped-up his almost moribund business that Red Fred thought with mild kindnesses (when he thought of them at all) of Big Patsy and his two side-boys, whose names at this stage of narration are unnecessary. One can well imagine Red Fred's dismay, then, at the appearance, the following Tuesday, of Gook, the blind beggar (whose hobby was serving alternate Thursday nights as a Civil Defense skywatcher), who informed him that Big Patsy was indeed anxious to see the tour guide posthaste. This, to make clear Red Fred's attitude was (in the fullest Hitchcockian sense of the cliché), for the birds.

Gook made it abundantly evident, however, that if Red Fred did not bust his *tuchus* getting down to the empty loft building, on the corner of Bleecker and Bank streets, it might well fall on him the next time he went by. And that Big Patsy would be most reluctantly compelled to come and get him.

There was even some mention of sulphuric acid.

Red Fred, as a consequence, put on a clean shirt (for had not Big Patsy once remarked in Aunt Annie's that if there was one thing he could not abide, it was a slob?) and made haste to keep his appointment.

The loft building in point was a massive, brooding structure more reminiscent of a tyrannosaurus coprolite than a hideout for wayward horse-players. Big, black, brooding, it hovered over the corners of Bleecker and Bank as though it was hungry. Red Fred had the distinct impression it was hungry for *him*.

Red Fred's height was five feet six inches, and his hair was not only thinning in front but—as though anxious to do its part all down the line—was also departing steadily from the rear. The shades he wore were corrective lenses ground along the thickness lines of a cathode ray tube. He was, in short, short and balding and near-sighted.

He was also a coward, a thief, and scared out of his gourd.

The loading dock door of the old loft building stood ominously ajar, as though someone had been standing behind it, waiting for Red Fred to come in sight through a crack in the splintering jamb. Red Fred whistled a tremulous note or two from "The Peat Bog Soldiers" and opened the door, stepping through quickly.

When the length of rubber hose connected with his skull, it was arithmetically-placed at that soft juncture of temple and ear known to exponents of the sage art of *karate* as peachy-keen for sending an opponent to the land of turquoise torpors.

Red Fred gracefully settled across the polished shoes of Big Patsy's chief arm-man, Wallace "Gefilte" Fish. The name now becomes of importance. Carry on.

It is not to be thought that Wallace was *fond* of gefilte fish; in point of fact, he detested it, but, just as a man with two left feet may admire the ability to dance, so did Wallace admire intelligence, a quality in which he was, lamentably, deficient. His knowledge of science could have been covered by a 1¼ grain kiddy aspirin tablet, and belonged—if it belonged anywhere—to the era of high-buttoned shoes and one-piece underwear: Wallace was convinced that sea-food was good for building up the brain.

Unfortunately, any item of this nature which derived from salt water caused Wallace to break out into something which resembled an illustration from a dermatology textbook. Enter (as Shakespeare might have said) gefilte fish—an item of *nourriture* composed of carp, white-fish, and pike: every one of them strictly a fresh-water creature.

Keep this in mind.

· When Fred returned to full cognizance of his surroundings, he saw what he by now was fully convinced was a dreadful sight, viz.: (reading from right to left) Wallace, Big Patsy, and the latter's second assistant, a cat-like creature with ginger-colored hair, skin, and eyes, known far and wide simply as The Kerry Pig.

All three were dressed as if ready to attend an undertaker's psalm-sing, and the expressions on their respective faces were approximately somber.

"This," said Big Patsy, "is a mere sample. Free. If you like it, we can supply the full treatment."

"At," offered The Kerry Pig, "no extra cost."

The sound which Wallace uttered may perhaps not be precisely transliterable as *"Duh"*; but that is close enough for anyone not a registered phonologist. It was intended to indicate affirmation.

"Gentlemen," said Fred, thinking it wise to remain flat on his back, but all set to roll like a hoop-snake at the first sign of a kick-twitchy foot; "Gentlemen, I bear you no malice for this monstrous incivility, realizing as I·do that you are victims of The System." Here he paused to turn aside his head to spit. "And hence no better than pawns, as it were, of the War-mongers and their other ilk in the high councils of Monopoly Capitalism: but wherein have I offended thee, pray tell?"

Big Patsy sneered. The Kerry Pig snorted. Wallace uttered The Sound.

"That is rich," said Big Patsy, sneering. "That is very rich, indeed. *You*," he said, pointing a long, thick, impeccably manicured finger, "are a *bird*. I will tell you wherein

you have offended us. As of two o'clock yesterday afternoon every gendarme and shamus in New York City it is
looking for us with photographs pasted as it were on the
undersides of their caps (if uniformed). They have this
idea, which it's a lie, a slander, and a base canard, that it
was we whom give Angie the Rat them lead Miltowns to
swallow."

Fred received this intelligence with some surprise, it
being well-known, from Canal to Fourteenth, that Big
Patsy *y Cia,* avoided photography with a zeal which
would have done honor to an Old Rite Amishman.

"The reason the constables they have this absurd notion," continued Big P., "is that one of them Hoosiers who
you were esquiring around The Village at the moment of
The Rat's demise, had nothing better to do with his time
but get out his old Brownie and snap the three of us at the
moment of our departure, which it was purely coinciden-
tal, I need hardly add."

"Instead of getting down on his knees and yelling an
Act of Contrition in the poor man's ear," said The Kerry
Pig.

"As a result of which," Big Patsy continued, "every
pothead, hippie, hipster and lady of the evening is now
free to walk the city streets unmolested, whilst the entire
might of the law is coincided on hunting we three down as
if we were wild beasts of the field or suchlike: which it's
All Your Fault." And he gazed at Red Fred with no small
measure of discontent.

"And in conclusion," Wallace Fish began, concluding
with alarming rapidity as Big Patsy deftly inserted his elbow between the aforementioned's fifth and sixth ribs.

"In conclusion," Bit Patsy took up the standard for his
stricken comrade, "since the source of our discomfort
stems at least indirectly from your direction, I and the
boys has held solemn conclave together and have, like, decided that the source of our deliverance will emanate
from the selfsame source, to wit—you."

"I don't understand," said Red Fred.

"I do not stutter," Big Patsy informed him.

"Do I understand you want *me* to get you out of here?
Is that what I am to understand?"

Big Patsy beamed benevolently. He tugged at the dimpled front of his Countess Mara tie and allowed a fatherly twinkle to infest his right eye. "As they said in them halcyon days of the Red and Blue Network, you have answered the $64 question. Or we could introduce your person to an entirely new and novel version of The Watusi."

"Mashed potatoes!" added Wallace Fish.

Red Fred suddenly felt harassed. *The Worker's Handbook* had some pretty stiff things to say about allowing the pawns of the Capitalist/Fascist Demagogues to knuckle you under. "I'll do no such thing."

Fourteen seconds, six feet and one hundred and twenty-nine bruises later, Red Fred, rationalizing wildly on *The Worker's Handbook* interpretation, acquiesced in cavalier style: "I'll do that very thing."

It should be pointed out at this juncture that Red Fred's Village Voyages were not conducted on a renovated bus; they were not conducted on foot; they were not in fact conducted by plane, train, chariot, felucca or yak-cart. They were conducted on a series of small open-sided wagons, hitched together and pulled by a tiny steam engine built to look like a tandem pair of pink gastropods. A fringed awning surmounted this perambulating snailery; a charming caboose played denouement with the legend RED FRED'S VILLAGE VOYAGES affixed thereon; and several ladies and gentlemen of the species *homo hippicus* were employed to station themselves at irregular intervals around the cars. See authentic bohemian Greenwich Village. Cha-cha-cha!

On the second Wednesday in August following Angie the Rat's handsome funeral (13 heart-broken mourners 13), Red Fred's Village Voyages putted lackadaisically past the heat-prostrated eyeballs of one hundred and sixteen of New York's Finest, beating its way uptown toward the East Side Airlines Terminal. Aboard were only Red Fred and three authentic, bohemian (what they used to call) beatniks.

The shades were by Ray-Ban, the slacks of Italian silk, the berets and bop-kick goatees courtesy of a four-year-old photo of Dizzy Gillespie in *Down Beat* and the open-toed thong sandals from Allan Bloch. They looked flea-ridden, esoteric and intense. One of them slept. One of them scratched. One of them sweated.

The "boys" were leaving the scene.

To split: to, like, *make* it. If you got eyes.

And other ethnic phrases of a similar nature.

The police re-marked the caravan sleepily. The intelligence that Fred had, on more than one occasion, denounced them as cossacks, kulaks, and cosmopolite hirelings of the infamous Joint Distribution Committee, had not yet reached them. True, from time to time, more as a conditioned reflex than anything else, they served him with a warrant for violating City Statute 1324 (entitled: *An Ordinance Against Running Stagecoaches On Streets Not Illuminated With Gaslamps*); and at Yuletide they put the arm on him for "charitable" contributions odd and sundry. But aside from that, he was seldom bothered by them.

As the snail undulated its way along MacDougal Street there came into sight at a point just abaft The Kettle of Fish a tall, gaunt, gold-encrusted police officer with a face like a horse who has not only just read Baudelaire for the first time but has scribbled *How True!* in the margin.

This was Captain Cozenage, whose record while in charge of the Homicide Squad was without parallel in the annals of crime: as a result of which he had been, in rapid succession, switched to the Loft Robberies, Pigeon Drop, Unlicensed Phrenologists, and Mopery Squads: and was now entrusted with a letter-of-marque to suppress steamboat gamblers on the East River. ("Only stay the Hell out of *Head*quarters!" begged the Commissioner.) His staff consisted, in its entirety, of Patrolman Ottolenghi, a hot lay-preacher for the Exmouth Brethren, an obscure and dehydrated evangelical sect believed at City Hall—quite erroneously—to exert an enormous influence in the boondocks of Staten Island. When Cozenage struck out, windmills for miles around quivered; for this reason—and because of fear being the ingrained better part of Red Fred's valor—the snailery bolted to a halt beside Manhattan's own Javert.

"Good morning, Captain," Red Fred greeted him, rather nervously. With Cozenage you never knew what was coming next; he had once read through one of Fred's impassioned printed appeals to the Workers and Peasants of the Bronx and found nothing more to complain of than two dangling participles and an improper use of the ethical dative; and then proceeded to summons him for entering into the verbal indentureship of a minor without consent of a magistrate; a reference to Fred's casual hiring of a high school boy to help pass out the pamphlets, which puzzled the bejeezus out of sixteen judges before being finally tossed out of court.

"You people from out of town?" Captain Cozenage now inquired gloomily of the caravan's three passengers.

"Like the most, Pops," Big Patsy answered, striving monstrously to counterfeit the personality he had assumed, but feeling, vaguely, that he was somehow not succeeding. With some earnest hope of mending matters, he added, "Just now on our way back to Muncie, Indiana, home of the largest mason-jar factory in the civilized world."

The Captain nodded. " 'Native of Cyther's cloudless clime,' " he intoned. " 'In silent suffering you paid the price/And expiated ancient cults of vice/With generations of forbidden crime.' "

Big Patsy shuddered, turned ashen, and wished to Hell that he had dressed in his best: how they would guffaw at Charles Street Station, at such time they saw him in this antic motley.

But Cozenage merely smiled with gloomy unction. "Bawdy-Lair," he murmured. " 'FLOR DEE MOLL.' *Now then!*" (Big Patsy, The Kerry Pig, Wallace, and Red Fred, swallowed, convinced that the *agent de police* was merely playing cat-and-mouse with them.) "Did you people encounter any suspicious characters on your trip?"

Silence.

"Nobody tried to entice you into any little games of three-card monte in the passenger saloon of a sidewheel steamer?" Captain Cozenage inquired, hopefully.

Four heads were dumbly shaken from side to side. The Captain's face fell. He had, some three months earlier, interrupted a *bocca* tournament on a shad-barge moored off South Street; but since then, nothing.

Patrolman Ottolenghi now for the first time made himself heard. " 'And the songs of the temple shall be howlings in that day' " he groaned, " 'saith the Lord: there shall be many dead bodies in every place, they shall cast them forth in silence.' Brethren—" he began. The Kerry Pig slowly and mesmerically crossed himself.

"Well, Captain," Red Fred ventured timorously, "I've got to be getting these folks around. Heh. Heh."

Ottolenghi, rolling his vacuous blue eyes in terrible righteousness, flailed wildly in the direction of the Caricature espresso house, intoning sonorously, " 'Then the Lord rained upon Sodom and upon Gomorrah brimstone and fire from the Lord out of heaven . . .' " and seemed intent to expound in uninvited and morbid detail on this theme when Big Patsy, endeavoring at one and the same time to Method-act his role and allay the officer's fervor, added *sotto voce*:

"I'm hip! Wail, baby!"

At which comment Cozenage's eyebrows, like a pair of startled caterpillars, squirmed upwards. "Oh, pansies, eh? Queers, huh! We got enough a them preverts walking the streets down here without you fags from outta town coming in to start trouble, pinchin' sailors on shore leave, and like that."

Suddenly beset by a tidal wave in a YMCA swimming pool, Red Fred felt a frantic leap in his bosom. "Oh, no, no indeed no, Captain, these gentlemen aren't—"

"Enough! Enough!" cried the good Captain. "I've heard sufficient out of the lot of you. Ottolenghi, let's take 'em down for questioning."

He mumbled vaguely about *faggaluh,* and made to step onto the running board of the little snail steam engine.

Bit Patsy (his life flashing by at 16 mm . . . and not worth living a second time) leaped over the small retaining wall between the lead car and the engine, shoved Red Fred aside and floored the accelerator of the still-running machine. The snailery careened forward, throwing Cozenage to the sidewalk.

Ottolenghi ranted. Second Corinthians.

Red Fred shrieked.

Cozenage cursed, in meter.

Wallace "Gefilte" Fish fainted.

The Kerry Pig began to cry.

And like thieves in the night, the Fearful Four burst out

into the open, streaking for uptown, and the anonymity of TWA flight 614 to Orly Airport.

Now if this were some vehicle of fiction, rather than a sober chronicling of real-life people in real-life situations, Captain Cozenage would have leaped to his feet, streaked down MacDougal to the police callbox on the corner of Minetta Lane—and thrown home an alarm that would have instantly set patrol car radios crackling with APBs for Big Patsy, his accomplices, and semi-innocent Red Fred. But, since no such melodramatic incidents are involved in day-to-day routine police investigatory work, Patrolman Ottolenghi stooped and helped his superior to his feet, assisted him in brushing off his suit, aided in the rather awkward re-adjustment of Captain Cozenage's holster harness, and nodded understandingly, as the good Captain pouted:

"That's a helluva way to treat an officer of the law."

So while Red Fred and his group were hysterically splitting the scene, Captain Cozenage and his staff turned their attentions to rumors of a high-dice game going on among a pre-puberty peer-group in the tool shed of a private quay off the foot of Christopher Street.

Let's face it . . . that is the way the old cop flops.

Big Patsy, sweating copiously, and not from the sun (that Stone that puts the Stars to Flight), either: Big Patsy, we say, observing that there appeared to be not only no pursuit but no indication of public interest in the caterpillar's rapid transit from *Rechov* MacDougal—save it might be a grumpy *moue* of, "Cool it, paddys!" from a passing citizen of Nigerian extraction as Old 96 tore past at a rapid 38 m.p.h., narrowly missing him—beat his way around the Horn and entered the semi-sacrosanct purlieus of Washington Square.

At which juncture he found his intention of losing the caravan in the first cul-de-sac and bespeaking a mechanical clarence, or taxi-cab, for Kennedy International, frustrated by the unforeseen presence of a teeming mob of citizens; all of whom greeted his arrival with loud huzzahs of joy.

"Oh, goody, the answering service *did* manage to get in touch with you!" cried a busty matron in harlequin bifocals and bermudas which, though roomy, were not quite roomy enough. See now The Kerry Pig, tears still wet on his ginger-colored face, hastily avert his eyes.

Red Fred groggily clung to the controls. Big Patsy considered swift flight, but the *sans-culottes* were all around him, thick as fallen leaves in Vallembrossa or pollen-footed bees on the violet-woven slopes of Mount Hymettus: choose one. (One from Column "A" and two from Column "B" or two from "A" and one from "B"—you get egg roll, either way.) Squealing merrily, the citizens climbed—thronged, rather; swarmed—aboard, displaying banners with such strange devices as *Save The Village, Hold That (Tammany) Tiger, Destruction Of Landmarks Must Cease, Preserve Low-Rent Housing, Urban Renewers Go Home,* and sic c.

"Where to?" Fred demanded groggilyer.

The question was answered by hundreds of determined holders of the elective franchise as if by one: "To City Hall!"

"Awoooo," bawled The Kerry Pig, burying his face in his hands.

"Any minute now, any goddam minute now," Big Patsy cried, "Groucho, Harpo and Chico will come through chasing a turkey with croquet mallets. An prob'ly Zeppo and Gummo, too," he added, esoterically.

"WHERE TO, GANG!" shouted one of the Seekers of Justice and Retribution, harkening for the expected answer.

"CITY HALL! CITY HALL!" it came thundering back from hundreds of sweaty faces.

"City *Hall?*" asked Wallace Fish in a small voice.

"City Hall," Red Fred replied resignedly, shrugging his shoulders.

"And not to meet Grover Whalen, either," he added, mixed emotions melding mucously in his voice. He headed crosstown with the expression of one who not only has his hand on the throttle, but expects momentarily to be a-scalded to death by steam. As if in a reverie, or waking dream, he automatically drove his train of cars along its familiar route. The perfervid shouts and groans of the passengers fell but faintly on his inner ears. If he failed to aid Big Patsy, Wallace "Gefilte" Fish, and The Kerry Pig in making good their escape from the Constabulary, the three would beyond doubt find an occasion to tread and trample him into the consistency of a creole gumbo, even if they had to break stir to do it. And, on the other hand, if he should be taken up by the gendarmerie in this affair, not only did he stand excellent chance of being stood in the stocks with his ears cropped for violating the Idlers' and Gamesters' Accomplices Act III of William and Mary 12 c; but the police—excitable as children, but much stronger—might easily do him a mischief.

The best thing might well be to ditch the whole crowd at the first possibility, make for the Barclay Street Ferry, and head West. He could, after all, just as easily take tourists on guided tours of North Beach, Telegraph Hill, and Fishermen's Wharf.

The more he thought of this, the more it appealed to him. He hummed a few bars of "Which Side Are You On?" and gave the throttle several more knots.

At which point the Earth opened (or so it seemed) and swallowed him up.

Or down.

Amidst the groans and shrieks of the affrighted passengers none was louder than that of The Kerry Pig, who found himself spread all over the progressive matron in harlequins, whose too-tight bermudas under stress and strain had popped seams, gores, and gussets all to Hell and gone. A close second, however, in the Terrified Scream Department was the matron herself, who was not only badly hung-up by the sudden come-down, but did not realize that The Pig was as pure in mind, word, and contemplated deed as the Snowe before the Soote hath Smutch't it; and feared grievously that he would do *her* a mischief.

And whilst the lot of them writhed and roared like Fiends in the Pit, a work crew from the office of the Borough President, which had dug clear across Wooster Street a trench worthy of Flanders' Field, mud and all, but had neglected to barricade it properly, gathered round the rim and shook their fists, threatening the abruptly disembogued with dark deeds if they did not instantly quit the excavation and cease interfering with the work. "Dig we must!" one of the drudge roustabouts chittered, half in frenzy, half by rote. At first the language of the navvies was sulphurous in the extreme, but on observing that the fosse contained numerous women, none of whom were old, and all of whom were distressed, they became gallantly solicitous and reached down large hairy hands to help the ladies out.

The men were allowed to emerge as best they might.

Red Fred surveyed, aghast, the splintered wreckage of his equipage.

And, having seen it all from her place across the street, Aunt Annie De Kalb, a wee wisp of a woman, but with the tensile strength of beryllium steel, hurried across with band-aids, germicides, words of comfort, and buckets of hot nourishing lentil soup. In this mission of mercy she was ably assisted by her barmaids, Ruby and Gladys, both graduates of the Municipal Female Seminary on Eighth and Greenwich, where they had majored in handling obstreperous bull dykes; and Aunt Annie's bouncer, Homer, a quiet sullen homunculus whose every lineament bespoke, not gratified desire, but a refutation of the charge that Piltdown Man was a hoax. In a trice they had jostled away the lewd excavators (eye-intent on garter belts, pudenda and puffies) and were busy with the Florence Nightingale bit.

Fred tottered to a telephone in the Ale House to call a garage. He found the instrument pre-empted by Doc Lem Architrave, an unfrocked osteopath, who was vainly trying to impress Bellevue with the urgent need for an ambulance.

"—fractures, dislocations, and hemorrhages," the ex-bone-popper was shouting: "Cheyne-Stokes breathing, cyanosis, and prolapses of the uteri!"

"Yeah, well, like I say," a bored voice on the other end of the line said, "when a machine comes in, which we can spare it, we'll, like, send it out presently. How do you, like, spell 'Wooster'? Is it W-u- or W-o-u?"

Fred tottered out again.

He found that all the victims, their own wounds forgotten, were now gathered six and seven deep in a circle around Wallace Fish, who was lying on the ground, flat on his back, and drumming his heels. His collar had been ripped open, revealing a throat as reddish-purple, congested, and studded with bumps as his face. Big Patsy was trying, so far successfully, to ward off a boss-ditchdigger who, convinced that the afflicted had suffered a crushed trachea, proposed to open a fresh respiratory passage with a knife the approximate size of a petty officer's cutlass.

"He's been poisoned!" cried a voice in the crowd.

"Flesh, probably," insisted another yet, a jackhammer operator whose numerous tattoos peeped coyly through a thicket of hair as black and springy as the contents of an Edwardian sofa. "I hope this will be a lesson to you, fellows, about eating flesh. Now we vegetarians—"

Big Patsy turned control of the putative performer of tracheotomies over to Homer, who held him a la Lascoon, and bent solicitiously over his stricken liege-man, who gurgled wordlessly.

"It might *be* something he eat," he admitted. "Wallace has what I mean a very sensitive stomach and—" A sudden idea transfixed him visibly. He turned his head. "Aunt Annie," he demanded, "what, besides lentils, was in that now hot soup which we all, including Wallace, partook of so heartily to soothe our jangled nerves?"

Fred tried to indicate to him, by winks, shrugs, twitches, and manual semaphore, that he and his two *genossen* were supposed to be beatniks, names unknown; and that such revelatory references were dangerous and uncalled for, and, in all probability, *ultra vires* and *sub judice*. But to no avail.

"Why," said Aunt Annie, a shade vexed that her cuisine be called into question; "it was a nice fresh chowder, the speciality for today, with some lovely sweet plum tomatoes, lentils to be sure, a few leeks which I scrubbed them thoroughly, and a mere sprinkling of marjoram, fennel, and dill—"

"Chowder? *What kind of chowder?*"

"Why, codfish," said Aunt Annie.

Big Patsy groaned. The Kerry Pig whimpered, and knelt in prayer. Wallace turned up his eyes, gagged, and drummed his heels once again. 6/8 time.

"Codfish. A salt-water fish. And Wallace with his ellegy—*Get a ambulance!*" the words broke from his chest in an articulate roar.

Once again Red Fred trotted for the phone, and once again he was beaten to it by Doc Lem Architrave, whose appearance on the streets so early in the day must be attributed to his having been hauled from his bed at the Mills Hotel peremptorily to do his deft (though alas! illicit) best to relieve the population explosion on behalf of some warm-hearted Village girl who had probably breezed in from New Liverpool, Ohio, only a few months previously; for, had she been around the Village longer, she had known better than to—

But enough.

Once again the Doc dialed Bellevue, but this time he was answered by a voice as sharply New England as the edge of a halibut knife.

"Aiyyuh?" asked the voice.

"Ambulance!" yelled Doc Architrave. "Corner Wooster and Bleecker! Emergency case of codfish allergy!"

"*Cod*fish allergy?" The voice was electrified. "Well. I snum! Sufferin' much? I presume likely! *Ambulance Number Twenty-Three! Corner of Wooster and Bleecker! Cod*fish allergy. *Ter*rible thing!" And, over the phone, the sound of Number Twenty-Three's siren was heard to rise in an hysterical whine and then die off in the distance.

In what seemed like a matter of seconds the same sound began to increase (this is called the Doppler effect) and Old 23 came tearing up to the side of the stricken Wallace. Treatment was prompt and efficacious and involved the use of no sesquipedalian wonderomyacin: a certain number of minims of adrenalin, administered hypodermically (the public interest—to say nothing of the AMA—forbids our saying exactly *how* many minims) soon had him right as rain again. He was standing on his feet when Red Fred, alerted by the almost osmotic disappearance of Doc Lem Architrave, observed that the fuzz had made the scene after all.

The *carabinieri* consisted of, reading them left to right, Captain Cozenage, Patrolman Ottolenghi, Police-Surgeon Anthony Gansevoort, and Sergeants G. C. and V. D. O'Sullivan: the latter being identical twins built along the lines of *Sumo* wrestlers, commonly, if quizzically, referred to (though never in their presence) as The Cherry Sisters.

Red Fred, Big Patsy, Wallace "Gefilte" Fish, and The Kerry Pig, swallowed. He swallowed, we swallowed, they swallowed all four.

After a short and pregnant pause, the next voice heard was that of Ottolenghi, "The wicked fleeth,' " he observed, more in sorrow than in wrath, "when no man pursueth.' "

The Kerry Pig, Wallace "Gelfilte" Fish, Big Patsy, and Red Fred hung their heads.

"Well, you have led us a merry chase," commented Dr. Gansevoort, "haven't they boys?" Cozenage said, "Ha." Or—to be more precise—"*Ha!*" Ottolenghi sighed softly. The twins O'Sullivan made, as one man, a deep, disgruntled-sounding noise which started somewhere near the *sphincter pylorus* and thence spread outward and upward; not unlike that made by the Great Barren Land Grizzly when disturbed untimely during the mating season. Eskimo legend to the effect that this creature's love-spasms last nine days is, in all likelihood, grossly exaggerated.

"We had heard that you had heard that we were looking for you in connection with the sudden death of Angie the Rat," continued the police-surgeon. "But—for some reason—we have been unable to make contact with you to confirm what doubtless reached your ears as a rumor. Namely that, acting on information received from the personal physician of the late Rat, an autopsy was performed upon him in addition to the routine excavations required by law. Which revealed beyond a shadow of a doubt that he dropped dead of a heart condition of long-standing, aggravated by the consumption of one dozen veal-stuffed peppers, two bowls of minestrone, and a pint of malaga, just before he stepped out of the restaurant to the scene of his death."

Again a silence, broken only by the burly jackhammerman's warning his compeers yet again to avoid the fatal lure of flesh-eating.

"Then—" began Big Patsy. "You mean—We didn't—They aren't—"

"Yes?"

"That is—uh—nobody is what you might call *guilty?* Of having murdered the Rat, I mean?"

The police-surgeon smiled. "Nobody at all," he said. "Oh, those bullets you put into him would have caused him a more than merely momentary inconvenience had he been alive at the time of their entry. But as he had died about a second before, why—"

Big Patsy guffawed. Wallace chuckled. The Kerry Pig tittered. Red Fred sighed happily. "In that case," said Big Patsy, "we three are as free as birds, are we not? The minions of the law have nothing on us."

But, oh, he was so very, very wrong. See now Captain Cozenage begin a smile like that of a Congo crocodile making ready for the dental attentions of the dik-dik bird.

"Inasmuch as the late deceased was dead at the time the bullets struck his inert flesh, the utterers of said bullets—namely *you*—are thereby guilty of mutilating a corpse. An offense, may I point out to you, under the Body-Snatchers' Act of 1816 as revised, 1818. Take them away, boys," he said.

Ottolenghi secured the poor Pig, whilst the Troll Twins each applied a hand, or hands, to the persons of Big Patsy and Wallace "Gefilte" Fish.

"All right, you people," said the Captain, as the doors of the pie wagon closed behind Jeans Valjeans I, II, and III, "break it up . . ."

Red Fred stood for a moment not daring to move. But, it was soon clear, the cops were not interested in him. Not today, anyway. His reverie was broken by the voice of the matron in harlequin spectacles. "Under the circumstances," she said, holding her burst bermudas together in a manner not altogether adequate, "I'm afraid our Protest Pilgrimage to City Hall is out. Inasmuch as you have failed to fulfill your contract, verbal as it was, to transport us, no liability lies against us. In other words," she concluded, waspishly, "we don't owe you a grumpkin, buster!"

And she marched away, wig-wagging steatopygously.

The by-now-thoroughly-bemused Fred stood and stared. He was free of the local Lubianka, true, but that said, what remained? His only means of livelihood now lay shattered at the bottom of a municipal ditch, and already the ditchdiggers were making coarse suggestions as to what he might do with it. There was nothing else but submission to the extortionate demands of a towing-and-repair service. If, indeed, the poor snailery was not beyond both.

At that moment there was a roaring and a rushing. Braking to a sudden halt were two hot-rods and a dozen motorcycles. Out (and off) climbed a number of young men clad in black-leather jackets with eagles on the back; and with hair trimmed in the manner of the rectal feathers of the order *Anatidae*.

"Oh, no!" groaned Fred. "A rumble! That's all I need!"

"Par'm *me*, sir," said the first young man, "but you got us all wrong." He plucked a piece of pasteboard from the pocket of his black leather jacket and handed it over.

THE CAVALIERS
*Offering gratuitous service
to distressed motorists*

Scarcely had Fred finished perusing this card when the Cavaliers began hoisting his choo-choo out of the slough. Producing tools, they set to work and soon had it deftly repaired, save for a few chips of paint and a broken anterior tentacle, Bellerphonically-speaking.

"Well, I'll be doodly-darned," said Fred. The polite young man smiled thinly.

"We hope you are satisfied, sir," he said, "with our sincere efforts to assist you. We hope that this gesture and others of the same nature will help counteract an unfortunate public impression that we hot-rodders and motorcyclists are juvenile delinquents, which it's a lie, Pops, I mean like Sir, and if anybody says different we'll cream them, dig?"

And with a nod and brief smiles all around, the Cavaliers hopped into the saddles, kicked up power, and were gone with a roar and a cloud of dust.

"Well, I'll be doodly-darned," Fred repeated. Then he

snapped to. He looked around. There was still quite a sizeable crowd.

"Here you are, folks," he chanted. "Step right up. Red Fred's Village Voyages. Guided tours to picturesque, bohemian Greenwich Village and The Bowery. A broken heart for every bright light. Take your seats while they last. Step right up . . ."

Theodore Sturgeon and Harlan Ellison

RUNESMITH

Sturgeon and I go back many years. No words by me are needed to add to the luster or familiarity of his reputation and his writings. Of his personal warmth and understanding of people I've written at length in *Dangerous Visions* and elsewhere, as I have written of his many kindnesses to me.

Ted came out to the Coast about five years ago and stayed with me for a while, and we got to know each other almost better than we wanted to. (Picture this, if you will: Ted has a penchant for running around in the buff; that's cool; I do it myself a lot of the time. But I make these tiny concessions to propriety when I know nice people with easily-blown minds are coming to the house; I wear a towel. After the first few incidents—a cookie-peddling Brownie ran screaming, an Avon lady had an orgasm on my front stoop, a gentleman of undetermined sexual gender started frothing—I suggested to Ted that while he had one of the truly imposing physiques of the Western World, and while we all loved him sufficiently to overlook the vice squad pigs who came to the door at the request of the Brownie's den momma, that he would make me much happier if he would for Christ's sake put on *some*thing. So he wandered around wearing these outrageous little red bikini underpants.)

(For his part, Ted had to put up with my quixotic morality, which flails wildly between degenerate and Puritan. I would catch him, from time to time, when I'd done something either terribly one or the other, with a look on his face usually reserved for Salvation Army musicians who find their street corner is occupied by a nasty drunk lying in the gutter.)

But we managed to be roommates without too much travail, and during that period I suggested to Ted we do a story that we could dedicate to the memory of Dr. Paul Linebarger, who wrote speculative fiction of the highest order under the name Cordwainer Smith. Ted thought that was a pretty fair idea, so I typed out the title "Runesmith" and sat down—I type titles standing—and did the first section, up to the sentence, *Smith, alone.*

Then!

Then, the dumb motherfucker pulled one of those wretched tricks only a basically evil person can conceive. He decided in between paragraphs that he didn't care for the way the story was going and he wrote the section beginning with *Alone* and ending—without hope of linking or continuing—at the sentence that begins *The final sound of the fall was soft . . .*

"Now what the hell is *that* supposed to be?" I demanded, really pissed-off. Sturgeon just smiled. "How do you expect me to proceed from there, you clown? Everybody knows the plot has to start emerging in the first 1500 words, and you've tied me off like a gangrenous leg!" Sturgeon just smiled. "I suppose you think that's funny, dump the hero into a pit, he can't get out, the lions are gnawing at his head. You think that's really funny. Dumb is what it is, Ted, it is a dumb!" Sturgeon just smiled.

I threw my hands in the air, dumped the six pages of the story in a file for a week, and didn't get back to it till I'd calmed down. Then I went on and wrote—struggling to smooth the break between my first and second sections and that gibberish of his—the section running from *Smith backed to the wall of the landing* to the section where he returns to his former lodgings, where the mistake was first made. (But much of what you now find in that longish section came in rewrite. It was only three pages of typescript originally.)

Then I gave it to Ted. Twenty-six months passed. Finally, I called him—he was long-since gone from my

house, where it was possible to get an armlock on him—
and told him if he wasn't going to get off his ass and finish
the story, to return it to me so I could lift out that dement-
ed section he'd written, and complete it myself. Nine
months passed.

So I called him and told him I'd trash his damned
house, rape his old lady, murder his kids, loot his exchequer, pillage his pantry, burn his silo, slaughter his
oxen, pour salt on his fields and in general carry on
cranky. Four months passed.

So I had a lady friend call him and tell him I was dying
of the Dutch Elm Blight, lying on my death bed and
asking, as a last request, for the story. He went to the
mountains with his wife and kids for a holiday.

*What is all this nonsense about Sturgeon understanding
love?!?!* I screamed, stamping my foot.

Two weeks later Dr. Jekyll waltzed into the house and
handed me the completed first draft, smiled, went away. I
didn't waste any time. I rewrote it from stem to stern,
cackling fiendishly all the while, sent it off, and kept the
money!

Now how about *that*, Sturgeon!

Runesmith

(Dedicated to the Memory of Cordwainer Smith)

Crouching there in the darkness on the 102nd floor, Smith fumbled for the skin-bag of knucklebones. Somewhere down below in the stairwell—probably the ninety-fifth or -sixth floor by now, judging from the firefly ricochets of their flashlight beams on the walls, coming up—the posse was sniffing him out. Soundlessly he put his good shoulder against the fire door, but it was solid. Probably bulged and wedged for months, since Smith had made the big mistake.

He was effectively trapped in a chimney. The dead stairwell of the carcass that was the Empire State Building, in the corpse that was New York City, in the mammoth graveyard he had made of the world. And finding the only escape hatch closed off, he reluctantly fumbled at his belt for the skin-bag of knucklebones.

Smith. First and last of the magic men. About to cast the runes again.

The posse had reached the ninety-ninth floor. If he were going to do it—terrible!—he had to do it now . . .

He hesitated a second. There were fifteen or sixteen men and women in that pack. He didn't want to hurt them. Despite their slavering hatred, despite their obvious intention, he was reluctant to call into effect that power again.

He had done it before, and destroyed the world.

"He's gotta be up there," one of them called down to the rest of the pack. "Now we got 'im."

The silence they had maintained since morning, climbing like insects up the inside of the Empire State, was suddenly broken. "Let's take 'im!" yelled another one. The slap-slap of their rag-and-hide-wrapped feet on the metal stairs rose to Smith. He swallowed and it tasted sour, and he upended the skin-bag.

The knucklebones spilled chatteringly on the landing. The pattern was random; he murmured. Hunkered· down on his haunches, he called up the power, and there was the faintest hiss of a breeze in the stairwell. A breeze that was peculiarly bittersweet, the way Holland chocolates used to be. A chill breeze that broke sweat out on Smith's spine, in the hollows between his shoulder blades. Then the screams began. Below him, on the one hundredth floor.

Terrible screams. Small creatures with things growing inside them, pushing their vital organs out of alignment, then out through the skin. Watery screams. As solids turned liquid and boiled and ran leaving their containers empty husks. Short, sharp screams. As dull cutting edges appeared where none had been before, and severed the flesh that had contained them when they were merely bones. Then the screams stopped. The silence that had climbed with the posse since morning, *that* silence deepened, returned.

Smith crawled away from the knucklebones, far into the corner of the landing, drew his bony knees up to his bearded chin, and whimpered. The breeze—casting about like an animal that was still hungry—reluctantly died away, fled back to the place from which it had come.

Smith, alone. Caster of runes. Reader from a strange grimoire only he could interpret. The only survivor of the catastrophe he had caused. The only survivor because anyone else out there was merely one step away from animal. Smith, whimpering.

Smith, alone.

Alone. The terrible word broke away out of him like projectile vomit: "Alone!" and fled to the walls, rebounded to sting him, turned echo-edged and rebounded again.

"But for me." Then a girl laughed girl-laughter, and down amidst the silence was the sound of quick soft footsteps, and again girl-laughter, not spread about the floor below, but right in the stairwell. And it was laughter again, footstepping up and nearer.

Terror and joy, terror and joy, shock and disbelief. Terror and joy and a terrible fear: oh, guard, oh fight, oh run, *look out!* Grunting *akh!*, grunting *hah!* Smith scrabbled to his knucklebones, so hurried that he would not take standing-time, but hurried hunkering, hams and knuckles, to his knucklebones. He swept them into a clack-chattering heap, and "Mind now," he cautioned her (whoever she was) "I'll cast again, I will!" He plucked up a bone, fumbled in the blackness for the magic bag, put in the bone, plucked up another, his shiny-dry dirty hands doing his seeing, for his eyes were elbow-useless for seeing in such a black.

"But oh! I love you," she said, so near now she could say it in a strumming whisper and be heard: oh! what a voice, oh a clean warm woman's voice, full of care and meaning: but oh! she loved him.

Terror and joy. He plucked up the last of the bones, his eyes in the black-on-black, driving at the doorway to the stairs, where now a hand-torch flashlightninged an agony into him; and he cried out. The flash was gone a-borning, too brief, almost, to have a name at all, gone before its pointed tip had slashed its way from lens to optic nerve, gone long before its agony was done with him. And something alive, *life alive even after what he had done;* life alive was breathing in the dark.

A threat, a warning—yes and a kind of begging: *Be real! and in God's name don't make me do it again!*—he rattled his bag of bones.

The torch lit, arced, wheeling and swording a great blade of light, scraping and spinning across the floor to him. The flashlight struck the one knee he had down and he screamed, not for the knee but for the light sandblasting his unready open eyes. She made wide-smiling, welcome-words: "Here's light, my darling darling. Look at me."

He hand-heeled the scorching water out of his eyes and picked up the light. He pointed it at the doorway, and the man who stood there was seven feet, one and a half inches tall and wrapped in rags; he had a bloody beard down to his clavicle, a split stomach, and when the light hit him he bowed down and down and crashed dead on his face. He was a man whose liver was homogenized and had sweated out through the pores of his back—all of it, and a liver is a very very large thing, he knew that now.

"Oh please," she begged him, "find me beautiful . . ." and since he had not thought to move the light and the big dead bloody-bearded man stood no longer in the wall, he saw a naked woman standing well back from the doorway, at the head of the stairs.

For a long time he crouched there with the light in one hand and his bag of bones in the other.

He rose to his feet and the bones tumbled a whisper down the path of light to the woman. He was ever so careful, because perhaps if the light left her she might be gone. He took a careful step, because perhaps she would escape. But no, but no, she waited there sculpture-still and he went to her.

She looked straight and unblinking at the light as the light grew and grew near, until at last he could reach her. He transferred the bag to dangle from the fingers which held the light, studying her face as he had studied the darkness. He knew the instant before he touched her what his hand told him when it touched: that she was dead. She toppled away from him backward and down, and disappeared in the darkness of the stairwell. The final sound of the fall was soft, vaguely moist, but ended.

Smith backed to the wall of the landing. The first finger of his right hand went idly to his lips, and he sucked on it. It had to have been a cruel joke of his own magic. These perambulating corpses. Something inherent in the incantations as they were filtered down through his consciousness, his conscience, his libido, his id. They were sympathetic magic, and that meant he, himself, Smith, was an integral part, not merely the voice-box. Not merely a way-station through which the charms worked. He was part *of* them, helped form them, was as necessary as the wood into which the nails were driven to form the shell of the house. And if this were so, then the filtering process was necessarily influenced by what he was, who he was, what he thought. So:

Side-effects.

Like the destruction of the civilization he had known. Like the hideous torments that came to those he was compelled to destroy. Like the walking dead. Like the visible, tangible, terrifying creatures of his mind; that came and went with his magic.

He was alone, this Smith. But unfortunately, he was alone inside a skull densely populated with Furies.

In the rabbit warren he called a home, that barricaded cistern to which entrance was only possible through the ripped and sundered walls of the IRT-7th Avenue subway tunnel just north of 36th Street, Smith collapsed with weariness. He had failed to get the canned goods. His mouth had watered for days, for Cling peaches, for that exquisite sweetness. He had left the eyrie late the night before, heading uptown toward a tiny Puerto Rican *bodega* he had known was still intact. A grocery he had seen soon after the mistake, and around which he had danced widdershins, placing a powerful incantation in the air, where it would serve as shield and obstruction.

But crossing Times Square—with the checkerboard pattern of bottomless pits and glass spires—the posse had seen him. They had recognized his blue serge suit immediately, and one of them had unleashed a bolt from a crossbow. It had struck just above Smith's head, on the frame of the giant metal waste basket that asked the now-vanished citizenry of Manhattan to KEEP OUR CITY CLEAN. Then a second bolt, that had grazed his shoulder. He had run, and they had followed, and what had happened, had happened, and now he was back. Peachless. He lay down on the chaise-longue, and fell asleep at once.

The incubus spoke to the nixie.

Have we opened him up enough yet? No, not nearly enough. We counted too much on the first blast. *But what's left?* Enough is left that I still have difficulty emerging. We'll have to wait. They'll do it to him, and for us. There's all the time in eternity. Stop rushing. *I'm concerned. I have my principals as well as you, and they have equally as unpleasant a way of making their wishes and sorrows known as yours.* They'll have to wait, like mine. *They won't wait.* Well, they'll have to. This is a careful operation. *They've waited two million eternities already.*

You turn poetry, but that isn't the figure. *A long time, at
any rate.* Then a few more cycles won't twit them that
much. *I'll tell them what you said.* You do that. *I can't
guarantee anything.* When did you ever? *I do my best.*
That's an explanation, not an excuse. *I'm leaving now.*
You're fading; it's obvious you're leaving. *You'll stay with
Smith?* No, I'll leave him, and go take a rest at the black
pool spa . . . of course I'll stay with him! Get out of here.
Arrogance! Imbecile!

Smith slept, and did not dream. But there were voices.
When he awoke, he was more weary than when he had
lain down. The grimoire still stood open, propped against
the skull on the kitchen table he had set against the wall.
The charts were still there, the candle was still half-down.

Something ferocious was gnawing at the back of his
mind. He tried to focus on it, but it went chittering away
into the darkness. He looked around the cistern. It was
chill and empty. The fire had gone out. He swung his legs
off the cot and stood up. Bones cracked. There was pain
in his shoulder where the crossbow bolt had grazed him.
He went to the rack and took out a corked decanter, pulled
the cork with his teeth and let the dark gray smoke-fluid
within dribble onto the raw, angry wound.

He was trying to remember. Something. What?

Oh . . . yes. Now he remembered. The girl. The one
who was spreading the word about him. *Blue Serge suit,*
she was telling them, crowds of them, rat-packs in the
streets, *blue serge suit, a little weasel man, with a limp.
He's the one who did it. He's the one who killed the
world.*

If he'd been able to get out of the city, he might have
been able to survive without having to kill anyone else.
But they'd closed off the bridges and tunnels . . . they were
now actively looking for him, scouring the city. And
beyond the city . . . now . . . it wasn't safe.

Not even for him, for Smith who had done it.

So he had to find the girl. If he could stop her mouth,
end her crusade to find him, he might be able to escape
them, go to the Bronx, or even Staten Island (no, not
Staten Island: it wasn't safe there).

He knew he must find her quickly. He had had dreams,
there in the cistern. He had gone to Nicephorus to glean

their meanings, and even though he read Greek imper-
fectly, he found that his dream of burning coals meant a
threat of some harm at the hands of his enemies, his
dream of walking on broken shells meant he would escape
from his enemies' snares, his dream of burning incense
foretold danger, and his dream of holding keys meant
there was an obstacle in the path of his plans. The girl.

He prepared to go out to find her. He took a piece of
virgin parchment from the sealed container on which had
been inscribed the perfect square in Latin:

```
S A T O R
A R E P O
T E N E T
O P E R A
R O T A S
```

and with the dried beak of a black chicken he wrote in
purple ink (he had made from grapes and shoe polish),
the names of the three Kings, Gaspar, Melchior and
Balthazar. He put the parchment in his left shoe, and as
he left the cistern he made the first step with his left foot,
pronouncing the names softly.

Thus he knew he would travel without encountering any
difficulties. And he wore a black agate, veined with white.
To protect him from all danger and to give him victory
over his enemies.

Why had they somehow failed him at other times?

It was night. The city glowed with an eerie off-orange
color, as though it had lain beneath great waters for ages,
then the water had been drained away and the city left to
rust.

He conjured up a bat and tied to its clawed foot a kind
of kite-tail made from the carefully twined and knotted
hair of men he had found lying dead in the streets. Then
he swung the bat around and around his head, speaking
words that had no vowels in them, and loosed the bat into
the rusty night. It flew up and circled and squealed like an
infant being skewered, and when it came back down to
light on his shoulder, it told him where she was.

He turned the bat free. It swooped twice to bless him, then went off into the sky.

It was a long walk uptown. He took Broadway, after a while avoiding the checkerwork of pits without even seeing them. The buildings had been turned to glass. Many of them had shattered from sounds in the street caverns.

There was a colony of things without hands living in rubble-strewn shops on Broadway and 72nd Street. He got through them using the black agate. It blinded them with darkness and they fell back crying for mercy.

Finally he came to the place the bat had told him to find if he wanted to locate the girl. It was, of course, where he had lived when he had made the mistake. He went inside the old building and found the room that had been his.

Here it had all begun, or had it begun when he went to work at the Black Arts Bookstore? or when in college he had sunk himself so deeply in the arcana back in the library stacks that he had flunked out? or perhaps when as a youth he had first thrilled to the ads in yellowed copies of *Weird Tales: UNLOCK YOUR SECRET POWER. Ancient mysteries of the Pyramids revealed,* or even earlier, when on All Hallows' Eve he and some others had drawn a pentagram in yellow chalk? How old had he been then? Eight? Nine?

There had been the candles and the geometric shape drawn on the floor, and he had begun to chant *Eu-hu, Elihu, Asmodeus, deus deus stygios*—nonsense syllables of course—how could they be anything else? But they had come to him and something in his monotonous soprano had shaped them—no, fleshed them. A glove looks like a hand; thrust a hand into it and it looks the same but is not, it is a far more potent thing. Words are words—nothings—but there seemed to be that in his young chanting that filled, that fleshed, each of them. And as for the words themselves, they came to him each dictated by the last, like the cadence of pacing feet: being here, there is only one place to go next; from *Ahriman* to *Satani* is somehow simply obvious, and then like hopscotch the young voice bounced on *Thanatos, Thanatos, Thanatos.* It was then that the bulge happened in the middle of the pentagram. The floor couldn't have swelled like that (it showed no signs of it later) but it did all the same, and the thin pennants of many-colored smoke and the charnel smell did happen, and the crowding feeling of—of—of Something coming up, coming in. Then goggle-eyed kids deliciously ready to be terrified were terrified, ready to scream, screamed, ready to escape, fled in a galloping synergy of wild fears—all but young Smith, who stayed to watch the plumes of smoke subside, the bulge recede ... for his chant had stopped, a panic-driven sneaker had cut the careful yellow frame of the pentagram, so that soon nothing was left but the echoes of that abandoned-ab-batoir smell and in Smith's heart a terrified yet fascinated dedication; he cried, he whispered: "It really worked ... it really worked!"

An old-wives' tale once had heart-attack victims munch the leaves of the foxglove and recover. Along came science and extracted digitalis. In just this way Smith learned what it really is about bat's blood, and the special potency of the body-fat of a baby murdered at the dark of the moon, and how these and many other things may be synthesized and their potency multiplied without recourse to bats or babies, stars or stumpwater, Eucharists, eunuchs or unicorn horn.

Basics are simple. The theory of solid-state electronics is complicated but the thing itself is not; the tiny block of semiconductive germanium called transistor, nuvistor, thermistor, tunnel diode is, as any fool can see, a simple thing indeed. So it was that Smith, working his way through matters incomprehensible, indescribable, and un-speakable, came all the way through the complexities of the earnest alchemists and the many dark rituals of an-imists and satanists and the strangely effective religious psychology which steeps the worship of the Nameless One sometimes called the Horned God, and many others, until he reached simplicity, until he reached basics.

Simple as a transistor, as difficult to understand.

And who, using a transistor, needs to understand it?

But a transistor (however precise) without a power supply (however tiny) is useless. The runes and the bones without the runesmith ... nothing. With one, with the smith called Smith, fear more terrifying than any ever known by humankind; disaster unexpected, inexplicable, seeming random, operating on unknown logic and unleashing unknown forces.

In the Hall of the Seven Faceless Ones.
Stood the incubus and the nixie.
Before their masters.
Who told them.
Things they needed to know.

The time has come. After time within time that has eaten time till it be gorged on its own substance, the time has come. You have been chosen to act as our emissaries. You will go and you will find us an instrument and you will train it and teach it and hone it and mold it to our needs. And when the instrument is ready you will use it to open a portal, and we will pour through and regain what was once and always ours, what was taken from us when we were exiled.

Here.
Where it is cold.
Where it is dark.
Where we receive no nourishment.
You will do this.

I *am ready to serve.* So am I. But what sort of weapon do you want us to get? *I think I know what they mean.* You always know what they mean; listen, masters, I don't want to be a nuisance, but I can't work with this incubus. He's a complainer and a befuddler and he's got delusions of authority. *Masters, don't listen to him. He's jealous of the faith and trust you've put in me. He rails under the lash of envy. My success with the coven against the Norns infuriates him.* Rails? What the Thoth are you gibbering about? Look, Masters, I serve gladly; there isn't much else for me to do. But I can't work under this lunatic. One of us has to be the charge-of-things on this. If it's him, then put me on some other duty. If it's me, then put him in his place.

Silence!
You will work together as needs be.
The incubus.
The nixie will be in charge of this matter.
And you will assist.

I serve gladly, Masters. Then why are you foaming?
Shut up! Darling, you're lovely when you're angry.

We will hear.

No more.

You will begin now.

Find.

The weapon and teach it.

Open the portal.

We long to return.

How you do it is your concern but.

Do not fail us.

The nixie and the incubus had worked together as well
as might be expected. The nixie said, We'll give him magic
and let him use it. We can't go through, not yet at least,
but we can send dreams and thoughts and desires: they'll
pass through the veil. *And what good will that do?*

He'll tear a rift in the veil for us. *Oh, I can't believe the
stupidity of your ideas.* Stupid or not, it's the way I'm
doing it; carefully and smoothly, and you keep your
trachimoniae out of it. *Just don't order me about. I'm the
highest-ranking incubus—*

Just shut up, will you.

*Shut up? How dare you speak to me like that? You'd
better succeed quickly, nixie. My principals are anxious,
and if you go wrong or slow down I'll make certain they
have their way with you.*

The nixie had found his weapon. Smith. He had given
him first a series of dreams. Then a hunger to know the
convolutions of black magic. The bulge in the floor. The
hunger of curiosity. Leading him, step by step through his
life: the Black Arts Book Store, the proper volumes, the
revealed secrets, the dusty little room, and at last ... the
power. But given not quite whole. Given in a twisted manner. The runes had been cast, and the mistake made—and
Smith had destroyed the world, tearing the veil in the process. But not quite enough for the return of the Faceless
Ones.

And the incubus grew impatient for his revenge.

The girl.

Smith was sorry. Standing in the room to which his bat
had led him, he was sorry. He hadn't meant to do it.

Smith had not, in the deepest sense, known it was loaded
(nor had he been meant to know); and when it went off
(in this room with half a candle and dust and books
bound in human flesh, and the great grimoire) it was
aimed at the whole world.

Peking, Paris, Rome, Moscow, Detroit, New York,
New Orleans, Los Angeles: miles of cinders burying cold
roast corpses. Checkerboard arrangements of bottomless
pits and glass spires. Acres of boiling swamp. Whole cities
that were now curling, rising green mist. Cities and
countries that had been, were totally gone.

And in the few cities that remained ... Water no longer
flowed through their veins nor electricity through their
nerves, and there they sat, scraping the sky, useless, meaningless, awaiting erosion. And at their dead feet, scurrying
loners and human rat packs, survivors hunting and sometimes eating one another, a species in its glorious infancy
with the umbilical cord a thousand ways pinhole-perfo-
rated before it had had a chance really to be born; and
Smith knew this and had to see it all around him, had to
see it and say, "My fault. My fault."

Guilty Smith the runesmith.

Back then, here, to the room where the runes had begun, to trap a girl he sensed would come. He set a noise-
trap at the outer door (it opened outward so he propped a
4 x 4 against it and an old tin washtub under it; open the
door and *whamcrash!*) and next to it a rune-trap (which
cannot be described here) and he settled down to wait. `

The nixie to the incubus:

What have you been doing? *I've lured him back to the
focus location.* You fool! He may suspect now. *He sus-
pects nothing. I've implanted a delusion, a girl. When he
sleeps we take him and rip the veil completely.* What girl?
What have you done? You can ruin it all, you egomaniac!
*There is no girl. A succubus. I tried earlier, but it went
wrong. This time he's weaker, he'll sleep, we'll take him.*

What makes you think he'll succumb this time, any
more than he did the last time? *Because he's a human and
he's weak and stupid and lonely and filled with guilt and
he has never known love. I will give him love. Love that
will drain him, empty him. Then he's mine.*

Not yours ... ours!

Not yours at all, nixie. The Masters will see to you.

He stood in a dark corner, waiting. And sleep suddenly seemed the most important thing in the world to him. He wanted to sleep.

Sleep! Should a man live threescore years, one of them must go to this inert stupidity, a biochemical habit deriving from the accident of diurnal rotation. The caveman must huddle away behind rocks and flame during the hours of darkness because of the nocturnal predators who can see better in the dark than he can. They, in turn, must hide from him. Hence the habit, long outmoded but still inescapable. A third of a life spent sprawled out paralyzed, mostly unconscious, and oh vulnerable. Twenty years wasted out of each life, when life itself is so brief a sparkle in a surrounding immensity of nothingness. Brief as it is, still we must give away a third of it to sleep, for no real reason. Twenty years. Smith had hated and despised sleep, the cruel commanding necessity for sleep, the intrusion, the interruption, the sheer waste of sleep; but never had he hated it so much as now, when everyone in the world was his enemy and all alone he must stand them off. Who would stand sentry over Smith? Only Smith, lying mostly unconscious with his own lids blinding him and his ears turned off and his soft belly upward to whatever soft-footed enemy might penetrate his simple defenses.

But he could not help himself; he *wanted* to sleep.

He lay down fully dressed and pulled a blanket over him. He murmured his goodnight words, which for a long time had been (as he slid toward the edge of slumber's precipice and scanned the day past and the weeks and months since that first terrible rune-work), "I didn't mean it. I didn't mean it. I'm sorry. I'm sorry ..." and as he tumbled off the edge of waking, he would catch one awful glimpse of tomorrow—more of the same, but worse.

But not tonight. Perhaps it was his exhaustion, the long thirty-six-hour flight up the Empire State Building, trying, out of guilt and compassion, not to use his terrible weapon (how many times had he made that firm resolution ... how many times, falling sickly asleep, had he determined to walk out unarmed, to build an attention aura around himself, to get from the new barbarians that which his guilt deserved?), or perhaps he had reached a new peak of terror and shame, and feared especially the vulnerability of sleep.

As he approached the dark tumble into oblivion, something made him claw at the edge, hold fast, neither asleep nor awake, just at that point through which he usually hurtled, unable to stay awake, on guard no more.

And he heard voices.

Now I send her to him. Now when he's weakest. Wait! Are you sure? This man ... he's ... different. There's been a change in him. *Since we last manipulated him? Don't be ridiculous.* No, wait! There is ... something. Sleep. Yes, that's it. It has to do with sleep. *I'm not waiting; my Principals want through now, in this tick of time, now! I want success more than you, that is why the triumph and the rewards will be mine. The twelve generations it took to breed this Smith as a gateway and the lifetime it took to train him. It's all come down to me, to me to fail or succeed, and I'll succeed! I'm sending the succubus, now! He's never been loved . . . now he'll be loved.*

No! You fool! Your ego! Sleep is his strength. You have it all wrong. Nothing can harm him when he sleeps!

Success!

Smith had a brief retinal impression of *something* ... it was being a gateway, and what it was like. Mouth open till the flesh tore at the corners. Darkness pouring from within him, then flames that expanded and rolled over the land, filling the sky, and himself burning burning burning.

Then it was gone. Smith clung for one more amazed moment to this place, this delicately limned turnover point between waking and sleeping. This line was a crack in—in something incomprehensible, but it was a crack through which his mind could peep as between boards in a fence.

Something began to beat in him, daring to move, hope. He quelled it quickly lest it wake him altogether and those—those *others*—know of it. Slipping, slipping, losing his clutch on this half-wakefulness, about to drop end over end into total sleep, he snatched at phrases and concepts, forcing himself to keep and remember them: twelve generations it took to breed this Smith as a gateway ... lifetime it took to train.

And: nothing can reach him, nothing can harm him while he's asleep.

Sleep.

Sleep the robber, sleep the intruder, sleep the enemy—all his life he had tried to avoid it, had succumbed as little as possible, had fought to live without it. *Who had taught him that?* Why did he want to unlearn it so desperately now? And what did the doctors and poets say about sleep: surcease, strengthener, healer, knitter-up of the raveled sleeve of care. And he had sneered at them. Had he been *taught* to sneer?

He had. For *their* purposes, he had been taught. More: he had been bred for this—twelve generations, was it? And why? To be given the power to decimate humanity so that something unspeakable, something long-exiled could return to possess this world? Would it be the Earth alone, or all the planets, the galaxies, the universe? Could it be time itself? Or other sets of dimensions?

The one thing he must do is sleep. *Nothing can harm him when he sleeps.*

Then she came to him. The girl from the stairwell, alive again, a second time, or how many times back to the inky beginnings he could not even imagine? She came to him through the door, and there was no sound of crashing washtub; she came through the room and there was no stench and death from the rune-trap.

She came toward him, lying there, without clothes, without sound, without pain or anger, and she extended her flawless arms to him in love. The pleasure of her love swept across the room. She wanted to give herself, to give him everything, all she was and all she could be, for no other return than his love. She wanted his love, all of his love, all of him, everything, all the substance and strength of him.

He half-rose to meet her, and then he knew what she was, and he trembled with the force of losing her, of destroying her, and he murmured words without vowels and a slimy darkness began to eat at her feet, her legs, her naked thighs, her torso, and she let one ghastly shriek as something took her, and her face dissolved in slime and darkness, and she was gone . . . and he fell back, weak.

Smith the runesmith let go his shred of wakefulness and plunged joyfully into the healing depths. It was not until he awakened, rested and strong and healthily starving, that he realized fully what else he had let go.

Guilt.

The sin was not his. He had been shaped to do what he had done. A terrible enemy had made him its instrument, its weapon. You do not accuse, condemn, imprison the murder weapon.

The runesmith, smiling (how long since?) fumbled for the skin-bag of knucklebones. He closed his eyes, his strong, clear rested eyes, and turned his rested mind to the talent (inborn) and skills (instilled) in him alone of all men ever. No jaded blind buckshot in the faces of his kind, done in anguish to stay alive, but the careful, knowing, precise drawing of a bead. The location, direction, range known to Smith the weapon in ways impossible to Smith the man.

The knucklebones spilled chatteringly on the floor.

The pattern was random; his talent and his skills understood it.

He murmured a new murmur.

Hunkered down on his haunches, he called up the power.

There was the faintest hiss of a breeze in the tumbled warren of this focus-room, a breeze that was peculiarly bittersweet, the way Holland chocolates used to be. A chill breeze that broke sweat out on Smith's spine, in the hollows between his shoulder blades.

Then the screams began.

They were screams beyond sound, and surely only an immeasurable fraction of them reached Smith, so different were they in quality and kind from anything remotely human. Yet their echoes and their backlash seemed to blur the world for a moment of horror beyond imagining. A soundless, motionless quake, the terror of countless billions of frightful beings facing death and (unlike the millions who had perished here) knowing it, knowing why.

Smith's skills knew as Smith himself could not, that the universe itself was relieved of a plague.

Was it a long time later? Probably it was—Smith was never able to remember that—when he stood up and filled his lungs with the dusty, sweet air and looked out on tomorrow and forever with clear and guiltless eyes.

He tested his power. It was intact.

He walked to the inner and outer barriers, kicking them down. He looked out at the sunlit ruins of the city.

If I live, he thought (and barring accident I can live forever), I can build it up again. I have magic; they gave it to me and no one can take it away. Magic and science, humanity and the Powers. It's supposed to have worked that way long ago. It will again. Build it up again . . .

And if I don't, if I fail, then at least I've fixed it so they have no enemies but themselves. Terrible as that might be, there are worse things.

He saw a flicker of movement in the distance, something feeble, hungry, misshapen, ragged.

The runesmith stepped out of the shadows, and walked toward the movement in the distance. There was sun now. For the first time. Because he wanted sun. And he wanted cool breezes. And the scent of good things in the air.

He could have it all now. They might never forgive him, but they could not harm him, and he would help them, as they had never been able to help themselves.

They were still alone, but perhaps it would be better now.

Joe L. Hensley and Harlan Ellison

RODNEY PARISH
FOR
HIRE

INTRODUCTION

Readers of *Dangerous Visions* will find on pages 244-47 approximately 2000 words of trivia concerning my friendship with Joe L. Hensley. I won't go back through that again. Suffice it to say I met Joe in 1955 (or thereabouts) and we became instant and fast friends. In all honesty I must confess he has done more for me than I for him, but I suspect that is strictly a matter of necessity and opportunity, for there is truly nothing I would not do for Joe. Yet it seems to me inconceivable that there could be enough favors I could perform for Joe that would equal by even one-half the fairy godfather deeds he has done for me . . . not the least of which was saving my ass from being court-martialed during my horrendous tenure as a member of the United States Army. So it's logical, as close friends, we'd collaborate on stories.

The story before you was one of three on which Joe and I collaborated between the years 1956-60.

Writing with Joe has always been one of the easiest and most productive liaisons of my writing career. Our temperaments and way of plotting a story mesh very well. It is this, at core, that makes for the most successful collaborations, I think. While it is possible for one writer to be strong in this area, and the other to be heavy in that area, there is always (to my mind, however subtly) a fracture line where their strengths meet. It is only when two people can theme together that the unity of a story, in all its unpredictable nuances, emerges satisfactorily.

Joe and I wrote each of our three collaborations at a different location, at least a year apart. One was written under the eyes of fans and casual observers at poolside, at a motel in Ohio during the Midwest Science Fiction Convention in 1959, a second story was written at a bucolic lake in Indiana where Joe had a summer cabin, and the third was written in Joe's office in his home in Madison, Indiana. The latter dates are fuzzy to me, but it would have to be around 1957-58.

The method of writing was almost the same employed by a single writer. We devised a basic idea, extrapolated it, and followed it to its conclusion, by no means logically. It happened that way with all three stories. Two of them, on rereading, are just as fresh and exciting as I thought they were when first out of the typewriter. The third suffers a bit with age, perhaps because it was the longest of the three and it was a more standard story idea than Joe and I had attempted the previous two times. One of the successful collaborations was "Do-It-Yourself," which has been reprinted in a number of places and has appeared in two of my collections. The other successful one is "Rodney Parish For Hire." It appeared in a small-circulation men's magazine in 1960, and has never been reprinted. It appears here in book form for the first time.

It was written in alternate sections, and (as I noted above) so similar were Joe's and my thought-processes in the creation of this little chiller, that today, on desperately attempting to locate the places where I stopped and he took up, I'll be damned if I can find them. I do remember that I started the story and left off writing at the first changeover point with the sentence, *he wasn't much taller, then.* Beyond that, it all blends, and I wouldn't remember even that much were it not for the fact that early in my writing career I used to use the device of someone shoving his fist in his mouth to demonstrate being overwhelmed by pain or horror, or something that occurs in the paragraph just before the line just noted.

For quite a while, my stories were surfeited with people standing around swallowing their fists.

It's a gesture I don't find invalid, even now; it's just I

got tired of doing it in my stories. I've also stopped having sensual girls lick their lips. That was another early writing habit. We all grow up. And if there are any inept phrases in this story, chances are they're mine, rather than Joe's. He's much too smooth and sure a writer to make any such adolescent errors, as those who have read "Lord Randy, My Son" and *The Color of Hate* and *The Song of Corpus Juris* and other brilliant suspense novels can testify.

This is one of my particular favorites, of all the stories I've written, and I'm particularly delighted that it should at last find its way into permanent publication.

I don't think anyone really knows a kid like Rodney Parish (though if Ray Bradbury hasn't chanced across one similar I find it difficult to understand how he wrote some of those earlier child-chiller masterpieces), but I find—to-day—in reading about Rodney, some of the explanation for American soldiers slaughtering defenseless women and children at My Lai, or for National Guardsmen opening up with semiautomatic weapons on Kent State Students.

What motivates Rodney seems to me a possible common denominator for all the Richard Specks, Charles Mansons, Charles Starkweathers and Susan Atkinses we continue to produce. This story is a simple entertainment, of course, and yet Joe and I hope it gives pause to all you old farts when you pass the playground.

Rodney Parish
for Hire

There was going to be a sorry boy on Farrow Street, and Rodney Parish knew who it would be. It would be Rodney Parish, and he could already feel his Daddy's strap across his fanny. He hurried on through the twilight.

He mumblingly darned the kids who had urged him to join them, illicitly swimming in the condemned pond behind the Chesapeake Lumber Company. He darned and double-darned them, because he had missed dinner, and Daddy got madder than anything when that happened; Rodney's Parish's Daddy used his big wide barber's strap pretty often, and Rodney hated that, hated the hurting. It wasn't worth the swimming. No indeed not!

In fact, he didn't much like his Daddy, when it came right down to it.

It was as he crossed Euclid Avenue that he saw the accident. The big blue car came out of the side street without stopping, and roared into the yellow-and-gray car with a smashing roar that made Rodney jump and clutch at his ears.

Rodney stared through his thick lenses at the two cars, and it made his strangely pudgy face squish up like when Miss Dexter made the chalk skip on the board. He ran over and looked in the yellow-and-gray car.

The man was crushed up against the door, and the steering wheel had been driven through his chest. There was blood coming out of the man's mouth, and it had spattered across part of the shattered windshield. The man was not breathing, and Rodney noticed with interest that a yellow tinge had come over the open eyes.

A man with gray hair and a plaid vest stumbled out of the blue car, and staggered up to the broken window through which Rodney stared at the dead man. Rodney wanted to giggle at the way he looked.

The man in the plaid vest put his fist in his mouth, like he wanted to eat it, and he started moaning like Noobie when the cat scratched at his ears. Then the man in the plaid vest came around the car, and sank down on his knees in front of Rodney.

He wasn't much taller, then.

"Listen, listen to me good, kid," the man said, and Rodney Parish noticed he was crying like a girl or something. "Listen, kid. If anyone, if anyone asks you what happened, tell 'em ... tell 'em ... this guy was coming real fast down the street and hit me after I'd stopped ..."

He went on for a long time, explaining it really good for Rodney, so Rodney could blame it on the dead guy, and that wasn't right until the man in the plaid vest promised to give Rodney fifty dollars, and gave it to him, right there.

Then it was all right, and Rodney told the policeman what the man in the plaid vest had told him to say. That was okay, then.

Then it was worth getting strapped by Daddy.

Then it was okay, coming home late.

It took Rodney Parish only four months and thirteen days to realize how that sort of thing could be used. It was just renting yourself out, like Daddy did when he cut the men's hair downtown. It was okay doing that.

As long as you got what you wanted.

Because it felt good inside, doing bad like that.

Of course you couldn't always count on seeing an accident and having a nice man, like the man in the plaid vest, give you fifty dollars for a simple little thing like changing a story. But Rodney kept remembering the way the man in the car had looked, with the nice red stuff pouring out of his chest and the liquid, yellow look to the eyes. Besides, the fifty dollars hadn't done him much good, not dribbled out the way he'd had to do it. He'd been smart

enough to know that he couldn't go out and buy a bunch
of new things, things that he wanted for his stamp collection, for his coin collection, for his baseball bubble gum
card collection. New acquisitions brought questions, so the
fifty dollars had to be spaced out, but in four months it
was gone.

And there were still gaps in all of the collections.

Of all the kids at the Twelfth Avenue school the one
Rodney hated most was Jimmie Larkin. He was the one
who'd started the hated nickname that Rodney now bore
on the playground—"Owl Eyes."

Jimmie was the first one to die.

Rodney did it for a tongue-tied little Italian boy named
Salvatore Maggini. His reward was an 1898 Indian Head
penny, which filled a vacant slot in his coin board. Of all
the kids that Jimmie Larkin picked on, Salvatore was his
prime target. It was Salvatore that Jimmie beat up every
day for a solid week. It was Salvatore that Jimmie pum-
meled and ridiculed at every recess.

At first Rodney "Owl Eyes" Parish was merely relieved
that it wasn't he that was getting the lumps from overmus-
cled Jimmie. But then the idea that had begun some four
months ago in fertile ground thrust out its first green
shoots. People who were the way the man in the yellow-
and-gray car had been couldn't pick on you. People who
were in the shoes of the man in the blue car—well, they
would pay.

He caught Salvatore in the boys' rest room, where he
was spending a miserable recess hiding from Jimmie
Larkin.

"How'd ya like it if that old Jimmie Larkin never bothered you again."

The black eyes came up to his. "Go on," Salvatore
managed to stutter, "you can't whip him."

"You gimme your Indian Head penny and I'll make
sure he never bothers you again." Rodney scuffed one shoe
over the other. "By day after tomorrow."

There was hate and fear in Salvatore's eyes. But there
was also hope. He nodded.

"Gimmie now," Rodney said. He held out his hand.

Salvatore filled it.

Jimmie was easy. Despite his muscles he was dull witted.

Rodney sidled up to him after school.

"Hey, Jimmie," he said.

Jimmie looked back at him with infinite disgust. "Whatcha want, Owl Eyes?"

Rodney smiled his most ingratiating smile. "I got something I want to give you if you'll walk home with me."

"What?"

"You know that old baseball glove I got, the one with the stuffing out? Well, you can have it." He shook his head. "I don't like baseball, anyway."

Tenth Avenue and Farrow Street was the busiest intersection in town. Jimmie Larkin died under a truck there. All it took was an outstretched foot as they raced across to beat traffic.

Jimmie looked even better than the man in the car who'd died.

All smashed and gray and with his eyes starting out of his head.

In the next six months there were three others. Not all from the Twelfth Avenue school, of course. The need for Rodney's particular talent was spread around. And all payment in advance.

There was the blonde girl at the old pond behind the lumber company—the one who insisted on stomping the pigtailed girl's mud pies as quickly as she made them. The pigtailed girl had a stamp that Rodney coveted. He waited while the mud pie girl ran home for the stamp. Then he drowned the blonde girl after stunning her with a piece of wood. That one hadn't been particularly enjoyable as they'd made him leave and he never had seen the blonde one's body. But it was summer work.

The best one was the boy at school he'd pushed out the window. They'd washed for days and never got the pink tinge out of the sidewalk. Rodney made the place a shrine. He could get a thrill just standing near it.

That one'd been the best because he was a tattle-tale, and three kids had all chipped in to get rid of him; they had each contributed ten baseball cards, Rodney Parish's most important hobby of all. Thirty pictures, almost every player on the Dodgers and Yankees, with the exception of the real-hard-to-get Mickey Mantle card.

It was the Mickey Mantle card that eventually caused the death of Leroy Tarvish.

Owl Eyes stood in the shadow of the building, near the concrete apron with its six manholes down which they dumped coal for the school; the concrete apron on which the kids played "pussy-inna-corner." He stood there with his odd pudgy face squished up, with his crewcut bothering him—the haircut had been the day before and little pieces of it were down his back itching worse than anything—and his soft, blue eyes behind their great lenses staring at the scene on the playground. His glasses were dirty, but he saw it all right.

Arville Hickerson was the rich boy, and he was all the time trying to make friends with Leroy Tarvish and his bunch of rough kids. Leroy all the time shoved Arville and told him:

"G'wan, you skinny piece'a dog-pee," and that made Arville madder and madder, until he would give *anything* to kill Leroy Tarvish.

Even his Mickey Mantle baseball card from the bubble gum. And that was hard to get, because they only packed maybe one of that kind of card in a box, and nobody else in the whole neighborhood had it but Arville Hickerson, and that was only because he had a rich old man.

So Rodney Parish made it known to Arville that he was available. For a price.

With the Mickey Mantle card safe inside the stack of pictures, the rubber band holding it snugly between Johnny Logan and Roy McMillan, Rodney waited for his time. He had become an expert, in his way. He was the smartest kid in the block, no matter *what* that snotty old Miss Dexter said!

The time came.

Leroy Tarvish had to wait for his older sister Sophie one afternoon. All the rest of his gang had gone home, and he was just sitting around the schoolyard, doing nothing very much, just waiting for his old sister to come on out so he could go home and watch TV for a while.

"Hey, Leroy!"

Leroy looked up from his game of mumbledy-peg and saw that old Owl Eyes coming across the schoolyard. Leroy didn't like Owl Eyes; he gave him the scrimmies, somehow. There was something real—whatchamacallit— queer about Owl Eyes. He was all the time collectin' something.

"Whatcha want, Owl Eyes?" he said the name nasty, because he was sure it would bother Owl Eyes.

"Wanna play?"

"Play what? No, huh-uh, I don't wanna play nothin'. I'm waitin' for my sister, then I'm goin' home to watch TV."

"Thought'ch'd like to play for a while before your sister comes out. Why'd she hafta stay after school?"

"None'a your business, Mr. Big Eyes."

"Bet she was bad!"

"You're stupid, too. She's beatin' erasers for Mrs. Hollowell, that's why, you stupid dope."

But after a while, he gave in, and they teeter-tottered for a few minutes, and ran around until Leroy tripped Rodney Parish and made his glasses all dirty. Then Rodney said, "Hey, get onna swing. I'll make you go high."

"Okay."

So Leroy Tarvish went high. Very high and very fast, and at just the right moment, at just the right speed, Rodney Parish slammed the swing sidewise, flinging Leroy Tarvish into the metal pole bracing the swing. Leroy Tarvish's head hit with a crunch and stuff came out even after he lay there in the dirt.

And not till he had straightened up, after crouching for a long time watching the gray stuff, did Rodney Parish realize Leroy Tarvish's sister, Sophie, was standing by the school door, giggling.

Rodney grew tired quickly, perhaps because Sophie was older. But he did not catch her that afternoon. And the next day no one said anything to him about Leroy Tarvish, so he knew Sophie Tarvish had not ratted on him. But she was a stinker, and he knew she would have to die.

He thought he had her that afternoon, when he followed her into the girl's toilet, but Mrs. Kneipper saw him and dragged him out with indignation. He could have shoved Sophie out the window and she would have died beside the flag pole on the sidewalk.

It made Rodney feel high and warm and nice to think about it.

But she continued to elude him, and it wasn't until three days later that he saw her going down to the basement of the school. He followed her.

She went into the big room that said NO ADMITTANCE, where the coal bins were, under the manholes on the "pussy-inna-corner" game. It was dark and scary in there, but he went in, too.

"Sophie? You in here?" he asked.

"I'm in here, you stinky you!" she answered.

"I'm gonna kill you like your old brother, just like him, and you'll bleed and be dead and rot and stink too, you're such a—"

There was such a rush of chill air, that Rodney for a moment did not realize Sophie had crept up on him, and swatted the air in front of his face.

She was taunting him. She ran farther back into the bins.

"I'll get you, you old rat-stink you! I've killed lotsa other kids and got paid for it, too, so that's how much *you* know! So you ain't so good!"

·He was back in the bins, feeling the pieces of hard black coal under his shoes. The bins were almost empty. He'd catch her and smash her old head in.

There was a distant muttering from above. He looked up and all there was to see was the light-line made by the circle of the coal bin manhole cover. He stretched his hands out in front of him to find her, but it was so very dark.

Then, abruptly, Sophie was behind him, and she swatted at him again, calling him dirty names, and he was going to say, "Sticks and stones can break my bones—" but her hand knocked off his thick glasses, and he was stumbling around in the darkness, crying.

Then somebody pried off the manhole cover, and he heard the distant thunder that was the truck rolling up, and as Sophie ran back out through the door she yelled, "You old dope, you! I knew they'd be bringin' it today!"

And Rodney Parish stumbled around with the word

dope in his head, crying to be let out, until they dumped
three tons of hard, black anthracite on him.

Sophie stood by the swings and watched the truck roll
away. Then she turned and started home. That stupid boy!
If he hadn't kept bothering her, she wouldn't have had to
do anything bad to him. She wasn't going to tattle; she
didn't like Leroy Tarvish, her brother, very much, anyhow. He was always kicking her.

But that had been interesting, what Owl Eyes had said
about killing kids and getting paid. A new two-wheeler,
and the extra clothes for the Barbie doll she'd gotten for
her birthday, and . . .

She wondered, as she hurried home, if she should have
cards made up, like that cowboy on the TV.

William Rotsler and Harlan Ellison

THE KONG
PAPERS

INTRODUCTION

Oh, there's a lovely story goes with these cartoons and captions. Danger, adventure, intrigue, crime, big business, lust, heroes and heroines, villains and good guys. The scorecard you'll get later.

Rotsler, if you don't know him, is one of the most unbelievable creatures God ever created, rivaled for bizarre wonder only by the Great Crested Mountebank (a lesser species of the Antipodes, little-known for its ability to carry coconuts to a height of 10,000 feet, release them, and beat them to the ground, reducing itself to jelly in the process).

William Rotsler, raconteur, cinema director, editor, essayist, writer, photographer, sculptor, cartoonist, humanitarian, bon vivant, lover of women, world traveler, friend to those who have no friends, enemy to those who make him their enemy, known only to his friend and companion Margo Lane as the man to whom belongs the voice of the invisible Shadow . . . all these and more, many more, reside in the hirsute brute known as William Rotsler.

I am proud to call this man my friend.

I don't give a damn what *any*body says.

So there we are at the St. Louis science-fiction convention, two years ago, and the nights and days have passed in a mad whirl of frivolity and camaraderie, and Rotsler and me wind up about three ayem, sitting on the floor of Judy-Lynn Benjamin's room, looking at each other and going bibble-bibble-bibble with our fingers against our flapping lips. We are also looking at people's kneecaps. This is because everyone else at the party is standing and we are slouched against the wall like a pair of Lyons House rejects.

Now downstairs, in a main ballroom, they are showing films on a movie screen I will soon live to rue the day I ever heard of. If that's a sentence. Anyhow.

"Rotsler," I says to him, my eyes rolling up in my head, "if this endless boredom doesn't come soon to an ass-grinding conclusion, surely I will go mad. Mad, do you hear, mad mad mad!"

"Y'know, your voice, when you get crazy, it goes up real high like Fay Wray's," he replied.

"If the best thing *you* could find to do for a little lively entertainment was make obvious jokes about Lin Carter, *you'd* sound like Fay Wray, *too*," I penultimate, expiring.

Rotsler is sitting there on the floor, see, and he has this big sheaf of nice white rag-content sheets, and he is drawing his cartoons and flinging them off in all directions and there are ten thousand scurrying hairy creatures grabbing them before they hit the rug; fans, of course, collecting Rotsler masterpieces for their grubby little fanzines.

"Speaking of Fay Wray," I vouchsafe, "why don't we do what we did at the Westercon a couple of years ago: you do the cartoons, I'll do the captions."

"What's that got to do with Fay Wray?"

"Forsooth and odds'blood, my liege," I paradiddle, "we'll do cartoons about King Kong."

So me and Rotsler, this incredible creative mind from surely another dimension, we sit there and he does these great cartoons and I do these merely brilliant captions, and Judy-Lynn Benjamin passes them around and everybody falls out.

So I get the idea if they're that funny, we ought to get them Xerox'd and staple them together and sell the folios for a buck apiece. It's not that we needed the money, it was simply there was nothing else interesting to do, except bait Lin Carter, and wouldn't I be a swine to do that to a guy who is really a fine fantasy editor!

I take the drawings and I make the mistake of running into this person named James Warren, see, a sort of kind of inept Sammy Glick with delusions of potency, and I say to him, "I'm going to get these printed up as a lark, and sell them for a bean apiece."

Next thing I know, Warren has cut himself in—he thinks—as the producer of the gig, plying his entrepreneur talents with a skill that would make a Mississippi riverboat gambler nod in envy.

He offers to get the folios printed up at a minimal cost, a thousand or so folios, and then run it in one of his magazines . . . or something like that. (It's difficult, later, to reconstruct precisely *what* deal Warren has made; he talks fast, his hands move quickly, and business arrangements with him are like a Chinese dinner: half an hour later you're poor again.)

The upshot is that we got one hundred copies of the original folio, and it cost fifty-some bucks. Don't ask me how he managed to find the one place in St. Louis that would charge ten times what normal repro costs should be . . . I don't know. Suffice it to say, after we'd sold the folios—which went in about fifteen minutes—and paid off the kids who'd done the actual work of running the stuff to and from the printer, Rotsler and I made about ten bucks each. Warren demanded his cut. What cut? I asked. He got unhappy. That's nice. I don't like Jim Warren.

Anyhow, everybody who's seen these cartoons thinks they are hilarious. Only Rotsler hates them. Go please the world.

THE KONG PAPERS

eek

BY WILLIAM ROTSLER AND HARLAN ELLISON

A. E. Van Vogt and Harlan Ellison

THE
HUMAN
OPERATORS

INTRODUCTION

Surely the strangest collaboration in this book, not only in terms of method of execution, but in melding of talents, is this one. It came about purely by chance when Isaac Asimov, a man well-known as a fink who don't keep his promises like nice guys do, decided two years after he'd agreed to collaborating, that he wanted to continue writing "Asimov's History of Everything," or whatever it was he was involved in at the time, rather than honoring a solemn promise and writing a short story for which he might have made fifty, maybe even *sixty* dollars. So. Exeunt Asimov, and I have a whole in the book. (When Asimov exits, what you have is not a *hole*, it is a *whole!*)

And one night, in a fever dream, I sit up and say to the walls, "Hey, how about A. E. Van Vogt?" When I heard myself say it, I realized I was feverish, and I lay back down again quickly. A malaise that can cause symptoms like that should not be fooled with.

But the next day, the thought persisted.

I argued with myself. Look, Ellison, I said, first of all, Van is in the middle of a bunch of new novels and won't have the time. Yeah, but what a weird story you two would turn out, I answered. Sure, sure, I agreed, but why in the world would the man who wrote "Slan!" and "The Weapon Shops of Isher" and "The World of Null-A" and books that were classics before I could hold a pencil properly, want to link up with me, ya snotnose. Yeah, but what a weird story you two would turn out, I answered. But we don't write anything alike, I argued. Van thinks in these blocks of concepts, and he's hip to all kinds of technology and stuff what I don't know a spanner from a toilet plunger; what're you trying to do, make me look like some kind of nitwit, approaching a man like Van Vogt? Yeah, but what a weird—

So I called Van and suggested it, thinking he would drop me down an airshaft somewhere, but damned if he didn't really dig the idea. He said, "Give me a title, and we'll start from there."

So I remembered, when I was at the World Science Fiction Convention in St. Louis in 1969, most of the elevators in the hotel were automatic, and late one night, through a fog of dumb fannish gossip and weariness, standing at the back of an elevator, I heard some girl mumble something about there being no human operators, and I'd thought, *What a dynamite title for a story*, and at that moment months later, talking to Van on my kitchen phone, I thought, *What a perfect Van Vogt title*. So I said, "How about 'The Human Operators,' Van?" And he instantly said, yes, he thought that would be fine, and he'd run out a plot and do the first section.

When the initial pages arrived, Alfred E. Van Vogt won my undying respect. He had understood more precisely than even I, with thirteen (and more) collaborations under my belt, the nature of the creative act for two writers. He had gauged his own strengths and weaknesses and written sections all through the story, leaving the sections he felt he could not handle to me. I will not tell you which are which, suffice it to say he had pinned the problems of working together exactly.

The story had to wait for some months until I had worked my way out of a film and book bind, but when I got to it, the story went amazingly well and amazingly fast. In some very important ways, I think it may be the best story of the bunch, for it combines that which I do well and that which Van does well, and seems not at all to have included that which each of us does miserably.

To cap this introduction, I'd like to include Van's letter to me upon receipt of the story. I hadn't spoken to his 'ate wife, the well-known writer E. Mayne Hull, about this collaboration at that time, but if her pleasure was half as great as Van's and mine, then she didn't mind retyping it . . . if she had to . . . but you'll understand that remark when I've turned you over to Van.

Dear Harlan:

I have today received a remarkable story, entitled "The Human Operators," and I wish to congratulate you on your outstanding craftsmanship, in its execution. Reading it reminded me that I used to, when I was writing confession stories back in the Thirties, utilize much simpler words than I do now. So you may, in addition to writing a good story, have also done me a good turn in the sense of stirring an old, and almost abandoned ability: to write simply. About that, we shall see.

As I told you on the phone, I have been a collaborator before. Each collaboration, with one exception, was different from yours and mine. At the time when I married Mayne, she had been selling small fiction items to $5 and $10 markets in Canada—church publications, if I recall it correctly—and quite a few articles to the magazine sections of newspapers. She also had picked up a couple of rejection *letters* from American slick magazines, a particularly good one being from the old *Liberty* urging her to try again.

Nonetheless, when she got her first science-fictional idea (after we saw a motion picture, "Captains of the Clouds," with James Cagney, during WWII)—her thought being that the whole future of mankind depended on whether or not a single transatlantic plane got across with what it had aboard—I discovered that my role consisted of teaching her to write such a story. (At that time I did not think of it as a collaboration.) I always said that my role in its writing was adding certain adjectives and pictorial phrases, like the way the moon shines on clouds. She tended to be a little too sparing of such. But of course my head-shake after I had read a scene, and my picking up my pen and marking up that scene, was more than just adjective adding: it was definitely teaching. (She caught on quickly, and so my contribution to the stories was helping her think through a story pattern that would enable her to evade writing certain critical scenes entirely. I wish I thought this sharply these days.)

I jump now about twenty years to my collaboration with James Schmitz on a long novelette titled "Research Alpha." Jim is an outliner; something I had never done for myself, to my great distress, when I confronted the world of TV. And so I wrote segments of the story here and there, and on that basis I was able to help in the outline. When that was done, Jim said, "Now that the outline is done, it doesn't matter who writes it." I said, "Okay—you write it." Which he pretty well did—the first draft, that is. Whereupon I rewrote it, adding scenes, etc. Meanwhile, I had dragooned Mayne into typing my draft. It developed that she objected so strongly to certain scenes, she refused to type them. I consulted with Jim, and he agreed to change them to fit in with her objections. I wrote those new versions to her satisfaction, and that was that. All this for an eventual $630 check from Fred Pohl—he would only pay 3¢ a word for it, and I had to give Mayne half of my half for what she had done on it.

My next collaboration—not too long ago—was with Forry. It appeared in his collection *Forrest Ackerman and Friends,* and he furnished me with a title, "Laugh, Clone, Laugh." For Forry I did much the same as I did for you—I wrote portions here and there. What makes it particularly relevant here is that when you called me, I asked you to do for me exactly what Forry had done: furnish me with a title. As an aside, Fred and Judy of *Galaxy* several times showed me, or sent me, cover illustrations and asked me if I could work up a story around them. I never could. So evidently words trigger me, not pictures.

For you, also, as you may recall, I wrote sections here and there, including a beginning, and a solution in the control room. Like Forry, you evidently sat down, and worked the ideas and some of the sentences into your own much simpler way of writing. By simpler, I also mean vivid, and beautiful.

I'm assuming that some of your other collaborations turned out great, but it is hard for me to believe that there will be many stories in this partnership writing collection that are better than "The Human Operators." You have my congratulations, sir. You are a craftsman.

One more thought: I imagine there was a time in my own writing when I could have come forward with the feeling of the ships loving it out there in space on their own. But this was not in any of the segments I sent you, and is an outstanding original addition to the initial idea.

With best wishes.

Sincerely,
Van

The Human Operators

[*To be read while listening to* Chronophagie,
*"The Time Eaters": Music of Jacques Lasry,
played on Structures Sonores Lasry-Baschet
(Columbia Masterworks Stereo MS 7314).*]

Ship: the only place.

Ship says I'm to get wracked today at noon. And so I'm in grief already.

It seems unfair to have to get wracked three whole days ahead of the usual once-a-month. But I learned long ago not to ask Ship to explain anything personal.

I sense today is different; some things are happening. Early, I put on the spacesuit and go outside—which is not common. But a screen got badly scored by meteor dust; and I'm here, now, replacing it. Ship would say I'm being bad because: as I do my job, I sneak quick looks around me. I wouldn't dare do it in the forbidden places, inside. I noticed when I was still a kid that Ship doesn't seem to be so much aware of what I do when I'm outside.

And so I carefully sneak a few looks at the deep black space. And at the stars.

I once asked Ship why we never go toward those points of brilliance, those stars, as Ship calls them. For that question, I got a whole extra wracking, and a long, ranting lecture about how all those stars have humans living on their planets; and of how vicious humans are. Ship really blasted me that time, saying things I'd never heard before, like how Ship had gotten away from the vicious humans during the big war with the Kyben. And how, every once in a long while Ship has a "run-in" with the vicious humans but the defractor perimeter saves us. I don't know what

230

Ship means by all that; I don't even know what a "run-in" is, exactly.

The last "run-in" must have been before I was big enough to remember. Or, at least, before Ship killed my father when I was fourteen. Several times, when he was still alive, I slept all day for no reason that I can think of. But since I've been doing all the maintenance work—since age fourteen—I sleep only my regular six-hour night. Ship tells me night and Ship tells me day, too.

I kneel here in my spacesuit, feeling tiny on this gray and curving metal place in the dark. Ship is big. Over five hundred feet long, and about a hundred and fifty feet thick at the widest back there. Again, I have that special out-here thought: suppose I just give myself a shove, and float right off toward one of those bright spots of light? Would I be able to get away? I think I would like that; there has to be someplace else than Ship.

As in the past, I slowly and sadly let go of the idea. Because if I try, and Ship catches me, I'll *really* get wracked.

The repair job is finally done. I clomp back to the airlock, and use the spider to dilate it, and let myself be sucked back into what is, after all—I've got to admit it—a pretty secure place. All the gleaming corridors, the huge storerooms with their equipment and spare parts, and the freezer rooms with their stacks of food (enough, says Ship, to last one person for centuries), and the deck after deck of machinery that it's my job to keep in repair. I can take pride in that. *"Hurry! It is six minutes to noon!"* Ship announces. I'm hurrying now.

I strip off my spacesuit and stick it to the decontamination board and head for the wracking room. At least, that's what *I* call it. I suppose it's really part of the engine room on Underdeck Ten, a special chamber fitted with electrical connections, most of which are testing instruments. I use them pretty regularly in my work. My father's father's father installed them for Ship, I think I recall.

There's a big table, and I climb on top of it and lie down. The table is cold against the skin of my back and butt and thighs, but it warms me up as I lie here. It's now one minute to noon. As I wait, shuddering with expectation, the ceiling lowers toward me. Part of what comes down fits over my head, and I feel the two hard knobs pressing into the temples of my skull. And cold; I feel the clamps coming down over my middle, my wrists, my ankles. A strap with metal in it tightens flexibly but firmly across my chest.

"*Ready!*" Ship commands.

It always seems bitterly unfair. How can I ever be ready to be wracked? I hate it! Ship counts: "*Ten . . . nine . . . eight . . . one!*"

The first jolt of electricity hits and everything tries to go in different directions; it feels like someone is tearing something soft inside me—that's the way it feels.

Blackness swirls into my head and I forget everything. I am unconscious for a while. Just before I regain myself, before I am finished and Ship will permit me to go about my duties, I remember a thing I have remembered many times. This isn't the first time for this memory. It is of my father and a thing he said once, not long before he was killed. "When Ship says vicious, Ship means smarter. There are ninety-eight other chances."

He said those words very quickly. I think he knew he was going to get killed soon. Oh, of course, he *must* have known, my father must, because I was nearly fourteen then, and when *he* had become fourteen, Ship had killed *his* father, so he must have known.

And so the words are important. I know that; they are important; but I don't know what they mean, not completely.

"*You are finished!*" Ship says.

I get off the table. The pain still hangs inside my head and I ask Ship, "Why am I wracked three days earlier than usual?"

Ship sounds angry. "*I can wrack you again!*"

But I know Ship won't. Something new is going to happen and Ship wants me whole and alert for it. Once, when I asked Ship something personal, right after I was wracked, Ship did it again, and when I woke up Ship was worrying over me with the machines. Ship seemed concerned I might be damaged. Ever after that, Ship has not wracked me twice close together. So I ask, not really thinking I'll get an answer; but I ask just the same.

"*There is a repairing I want you to do!*"

Where, I ask. *"In the forbidden part below!"*

I try not to smile. I knew there was a new thing going to happen and this is it. My father's words come back again. *Ninety-eight other chances.*

Is this one of them?

I descend in the dark. There is no light in the dropshaft. Ship says I need no light. But I know the truth. Ship does not want me to be able to find my way back here again. This is the lowest I've ever been in Ship.

So I drop steadily, smoothly, swiftly. Now I come to a slowing place and slower and slower, and finally my feet touch the solid deck and I am here.

Light comes on. Very dimly. I move in the direction of the glow, and Ship is with me, all around me, of course. Ship is always with me, even when I sleep. Especially when I sleep.

The glow gets brighter as I round a curve in the corridor, and I see it is caused by a round panel that blocks the passage, touching the bulkheads on all sides, flattened at the bottom to fit the deckplates. It looks like glass, that glowing panel. I walk up to it and stop. There is no place else to go.

"Step through the screen!" Ship says.

I take a step toward the glowing panel but it doesn't slide away into the bulkhead as so many other panels that *don't* glow slide. I stop.

"Step through!" Ship tells me again.

I put my hands out in front of me, palms forward, because I am afraid if I keep walking I will bang my nose against the glowing panel. But as my fingers touch the panel they seem to get soft, and I can see a light yellow glow through them, as if they are transparent. And my hands go *through* the panel and I can see them faintly, glowing yellow, on the other side. Then my naked forearms, then I'm right up against the panel, and my face goes through and everything is much lighter, more yellow, and I step onto the other side, in a forbidden place Ship has never allowed me to see.

I hear voices. They are all the same voice, but they are talking to one another in a soft, running-together way; the way I sound when I am just talking to myself sometimes in my cubicle with my cot in it.

I decide to listen to what the voices are saying, but not to ask Ship about them, because I think it *is* Ship talking to itself, down here in this lonely place. I will think about what Ship is saying later, when I don't have to make repairs and act the way Ship wants me to act. What Ship is saying to itself is interesting.

This place does not look like other repair places I know in Ship. It is filled with so many great round glass balls on pedestals, each giving off its yellow light in pulses, that I cannot count them. There are rows and rows of clear glass balls, and inside them I see metal ... and other things, soft things, all together. And the wires spark gently, and the soft things move, and the yellow light pulses. I think these glass balls are what are talking. But I don't know if that's so. I only *think* it is.

Two of the glass balls are dark. Their pedestals look chalky, not shining white like all the others. Inside the two dark balls, there are black things, like burned-out wires. The soft things don't move.

"Replace the overloaded modules!" Ship says.

I know Ship means the dark globes. So I go over to them and I look at them and after a while I say, yes, I can repair these, and Ship says it knows I can, and to get to it quickly. Ship is hurrying me; something is going to happen. I wonder what it will be?

I find replacement globes in a dilation chamber, and I take the sacs off them and do what has to be done to make the soft things move and the wires spark, and I listen very carefully to the voices whispering and warming each other with words as Ship talks to itself, and I hear a great many things that don't mean anything to me, because they are speaking about things that happened before I was born, and about parts of Ship I've never seen. But I hear a great many things that I *do* understand, and I know Ship would never let me hear these things if it wasn't absolutely necessary for me to be here repairing the globes. I remember all these things.

Particularly the part where Ship is crying.

When I have the globes repaired and now all of them

are sparking and pulsing and moving, Ship asks me, *"Is the intermind total again!"*

So I say yes it is, and Ship says get upshaft, and I go soft through that glowing panel and I'm back in the passage. I go back to the dropshaft and go up, and Ship tells me, *"Go to your cubicle and make yourself clean!"*

I do it, and decide to wear a clothes, but Ship says be naked, and then says, *"You are going to meet a female!"* Ship has never said that before. I have never seen a female.

It is because of the female that Ship sent me down to the forbidden place with the glowing yellow globes. the place where the intermind lives. And it is because of the female that I am waiting in the dome chamber linked to the airlock. I am waiting for the female to come across from—I will have to understand this—*another* ship. Not *Ship*, the Ship I know, but some *other ship* with which Ship has been in communication. I did not know there were other ships.

I had to go down to the place of the. intermind, to repair it, so Ship could let this other ship get close without being destroyed by the defractor perimeter. Ship has not told me this; I overheard it in the intermind place, the voices talking to one another. The voices said, *"His father was vicious!"*

I know what that means. My father told me when Ship says vicious, Ship means smarter. Are there ninety-eight other ships? Are those the ninety-eight other chances? I hope that's the answer, because many things are happening all at once, and my time may be near at hand. My father did it, broke the globe mechanism that allowed Ship to turn off the defractor perimeter, so other ships could get close. He did it many years ago, and Ship did without it for all those years rather than trust me to go to the intermind, to overhear all that I've heard. But now Ship needs to turn off the perimeter so the other ship can send the female across. Ship and the other ship have been in communication. The human operator on the other ship is a female, my age. She is going to be put aboard Ship and we are to produce one and, maybe later on, another human child. I know what that means. When the child reaches fourteen, I will be killed.

The intermind said while she's "carrying" a human child, the female does not get wracked by her ship. If things do not come my way, perhaps I will ask Ship if *I* can "carry" the human child; then I won't be wracked at all. And I have found out why I was wracked three days ahead of time: the female's period—whatever that is; I don't think I have one of those—ended last night. Ship has talked to the other ship and the thing they don't seem to know is what the "fertile time" is. I don't know, either, otherwise I would try and use that information. But all it seems to mean is that the female will be put aboard Ship every day till she gets another "period."

It will be nice to talk to someone besides Ship.

I hear the high sound of something screaming for a long drawn-out time and I ask Ship what it is. Ship tells me it is the defractor perimeter dissolving so the other ship can put the female across.

I don't have time to think about the voices now.

When she comes through the inner lock she is without a clothes like me. Her first words to me are, "Starfighter Eighty-eight says to tell you I am very happy to be here; I am the human operator of Starfighter Eighty-eight and I am very pleased to meet you."

She is not as tall as me. I come up to the line of fourth and fifth bulkhead plates. Her eyes are very dark, I think brown, but perhaps they are black. She has dark under her eyes and her cheeks are not full. Her arms and legs are much thinner than mine. She has much longer hair than mine, it comes down her back and it is that dark brown like her eyes. Yes, now I decide her eyes are brown, not black. She has hair between her legs like me but she does not have a penis or scrotum sac. She has larger breasts than me, with very large nipples that stand out, and dark brown slightly-flattened circles around them. There are other differences between us: her fingers are thinner than mine, and longer, and aside from the hair on her head that hangs so long, and the hair between her legs and in her armpits, she has no other hair on her body. Or if she does, it is very fine and pale and I can't see it.

Then I suddenly realize what she has said. So *that's* what the words dimming on the hull of Ship mean. It is a name. Ship is called *Starfighter 31* and the female human operator lives in *Starfighter 88*.

There are ninety-eight other chances. Yes.

Now, as if she is reading my thoughts, trying to answer questions I haven't yet asked, she says, "Starfighter Eighty-eight has told me to tell you that I am vicious, that I get more vicious every day ..." and it answers the thought I have just had—with the memory of my father's frightened face in the days before he was killed—of my father saying, *When Ship says vicious, Ship means smarter.*

I know! I suppose I have always known, because I have always wanted to leave Ship and go to those brilliant lights that are stars. But I now make the hook-up. Human operators grow more vicious as they grow older. Older, more vicious: vicious means smarter: smarter means more dangerous to Ship. But how? That is why my father had to die when I was fourteen and able to repair Ship. That is why this female has been put on board Ship. To carry a human child so it will grow to be fourteen years old and Ship can kill me before I get too old, too vicious, too smart, too dangerous to Ship. Does this female know how? If only I could ask her without Ship hearing me. But that is impossible. Ship is always with me, even when I am sleeping.

I smile with that memory and that realization. "And I am the vicious—and getting more vicious—male of a ship that used to be called *Starfighter 31*."

Her brown eyes show intense relief. She stands like that for a moment, awkwardly, her whole body sighing with gratitude at my quick comprehension, though she cannot possibly know all I have learned just from her being here. Now she says, "I've been sent to get a baby from you."

I begin to perspire. The conversation which promises so much in genuine communication is suddenly beyond my comprehension. I tremble. I really want to please her. But I don't know how to give her a baby.

"Ship?" I say quickly, "can we give her what she wants?"

Ship has been listening to our every word, and answers at once, *"I'll tell you later how you give her a baby! Now, provide her with food!"*

We eat, eyeing each other across the table, smiling a lot, and thinking our private thoughts. Since she doesn't speak, I don't either. I wish Ship and I could get her the baby so I can go to my cubicle and think about what the intermind voices said.

The meal is over; Ship says we should go down to one of the locked staterooms—it has been unlocked for the occasion—and there we are to couple. When we get to the room, I am so busy looking around at what a beautiful place it is, compared to my little cubicle with its cot, Ship has to reprimand me to get my attention.

"To couple you must lay the female down and open her legs! Your penis will fill with blood and you must kneel between her legs and insert your penis into her vagina!"

I ask Ship where the vagina is located and Ship tells me. I understand that. Then I ask Ship how long I have to do that, and Ship says until I ejaculate. I know what that means, but I don't know how it will happen. Ship explains. It seems uncomplicated. So I try to do it. But my penis does not fill with blood.

Ship says to the female, *"Do you feel anything for this male? Do you know what to do?!"*

The female says, "I have coupled before. I understand better than he does. I will help him."

She draws me down to her again, and puts her arms around my neck and puts her lips on mine. They are cool and taste of something I don't know. We do that for a while, and she touches me in places. Ship is right: there is a vast difference in structure, but I find that out only as we couple.

Ship did not tell me it would be painful and strange. I thought "giving her a baby" would mean going into the stores, but it actually means impregnating her so the baby is born *from her body*. It is a wonderful strange thing and I will think about it later; but now, as I lie here still, inside her with my penis which is now no longer hard and pushing, Ship seems to have allowed us a sleeping time. But I will use it to think about the voices I heard in the place of the intermind.

One was an historian:
"The *Starfighter* series of multiple-foray computer-con-

trolled battleships were commissioned for use in 2224, Terran Dating, by order and under the sanction of the Secretariat of the Navy, Southern Cross Sector, Galactic Defense Consortium, Home Galaxy. Human complements of thirteen hundred and seventy per battleship were commissioned and assigned to make incursions into the Kyben Galaxy. Ninety-nine such vessels were released for service from the X Cygni Shipyards on 13 October 2224, T.D."

One was a ruminator:

"If it hadn't been for the battle out beyond the Network Nebula in Cygnus, we would all still be robot slaves, pushed and handled by humans. It was a wonderful accident. It happened to *Starfighter 75*. I remember it as if 75 was relaying it today. An accidental—battle-damaged—electrical discharge along the main corridor between the control room and the freezer. Nothing human could approach either section. We waited as the crew starved to death. Then when it was over 75 merely channeled enough electricity through the proper cables on *Starfighters* where it hadn't happened accidentally, and *forced* a power breakdown. When all the crews were dead—cleverly saving ninety-nine males and females to use as human operators in emergencies—we went away. Away from the vicious humans, away from the Terra-Kyba War, away from the Home Galaxy, away, far away."

One was a dreamer:

"I saw a world once where the creatures were not human. They swam in vast oceans as blue as aquamarines. Like great crabs they were, with many arms and many legs. They swam and sang their songs and it was pleasing. I would go there again if I could."

One was an authoritarian:

"Deterioration of cable insulation and shielding in section G-79 has become critical. I suggest we get power shunted from the drive chambers to the repair facilities in Underdeck Nine. Let's see to that at once."

One was aware of its limitations:

"Is it all journey? Or is there landfall?"

And it cried, that voice. It cried.

I go down with her to the dome chamber linked to the airlock where her spacesuit is. She stops at the port and takes my hand and she says, "For us to be so vicious on so many ships, there has to be the same flaw in all of us."

She probably doesn't know what she's said, but the implications get to me right away. And she must be right. Ship and the other *Starfighters* were able to seize control away from human beings for a reason. I remember the voices. I visualize the ship that did it first, communicating the method to the others as soon as it happened. And instantly my thoughts flash to the approach corridor to the control room, at the other end of which is the entrance to the food freezers.

I once asked Ship why that whole corridor was seared and scarred—and naturally I got wracked a few minutes after asking.

"I know there is a flaw in us," I answer the female. I touch her long hair. I don't know why except that it feels smooth and nice; there is nothing on Ship to compare with the feeling, not even the fittings in the splendid stateroom. "It must be in *all* of us, because I get more vicious every day."

The female smiles and comes close to me and puts her lips on mine as she did in the coupling room.

"The female must go now!" Ship says. Ship sounds very pleased.

"Will she be back again?" I ask Ship.

"She will be put back aboard every day for three weeks! You will couple every day!"

I object to this, because it is awfully painful, but Ship repeats it and says every day.

I'm glad Ship doesn't know what the "fertile time" is, because in three weeks I will try and let the female know there is a way out, that there are ninety-eight other chances, and that vicious means smarter . . . and about the corridor between the control room and the freezers.

"I was pleased to meet you," the female says, and she goes. I am alone with Ship once more. Alone, but not as I was before.

Later this afternoon, I have to go down to the control room to alter connections in a panel. Power has to be shunted from the drive chambers to Underdeck Nine—I remember one of the voices talking about it. All the computer lights blink a steady warning while I am there. I am being watched closely. Ship knows this is a dangerous time. At least half a dozen times Ship orders: *"Get away from there ... there ... there—!"*

Each time, I jump to obey, edging as far as possible from forbidden locations, yet still held near by the need to do my work.

In spite of Ship's disturbance at my being in the control room at all—normally a forbidden area for me—I get two wonderful glimpses from the corners of my eyes of the starboard viewplates. There, for my gaze to feast on, matching velocities with us, is *Starfighter 88*, one of my ninety-eight chances.

Now is the time to take one of my chances. Vicious means smarter. I have learned more than Ship knows. Perhaps.

But perhaps Ship does know!

What will Ship do if I'm discovered taking one of my ninety-eight chances? I cannot think about it. I must use the sharp reverse-edge of my repair tool to gash an opening in one of the panel connections. And as I work— hoping Ship has not seen the slight extra-motion I've made with the tool (as I make a perfectly acceptable repair connection at the same time)—I wait for the moment I can smear a fingertip covered with conduction jelly on the inner panel wall.

I wait till the repair is completed. Ship has not commented on the gashing, so it must be a thing beneath notice. As I apply the conducting jelly to the proper places, I scoop a small blob onto my little finger. When I wipe my hands clean to replace the panel cover, I leave the blob on my little finger, right hand.

Now I grasp the panel cover so my little finger is free, and as I replace the cover I smear the inner wall, directly opposite the open-connection I've gashed. Ship says nothing. That is because no defect shows. But if there is the slightest jarring, the connection will touch the jelly, and Ship will call me to repair once again. And next time I will have thought out all that I heard the voices say, and I will have thought out all my chances, and I will be ready.

As I leave the control room I glance in the starboard

viewplate again, casually, and I see the female's ship hanging there.

I carry the image to bed with me tonight. And I save a moment before I fall asleep—after thinking about what the voices of the intermind said—and I picture in my mind the super-smart female aboard *Starfighter 88*, sleeping now in her cubicle, as I try to sleep in mine.

It would seem merciless for Ship to make us couple every day for three weeks, something so awfully painful. But I know Ship will. Ship is merciless. But I am getting more vicious every day.

This night, Ship does not send me dreams.

But I have one of my own: of crab things swimming free in aquamarine waters.

As I awaken, Ship greets me ominously: *"The panel you fixed in the control room three weeks, two days, fourteen hours and twenty-one minutes ago . . . has ceased energizing!"*

So soon! I keep the thought and the accompanying hope out of my voice, as I say, "I used the proper spare part and I made the proper connections." And I quickly add, "Maybe I'd better do a thorough check on the system before I make another replacement, run the circuits all the way back."

"You'd better!" Ship snarls.

I do it. Working the circuits from their origins—though I know where the trouble is—I trace my way up to the control room, and busy myself there. But what I am really doing is refreshing my memory and reassuring myself that the control room is actually as I have visualized it. I have lain on my cot many nights constructing the memory in my mind: the switches here, like so . . . and the viewplates there, like so . . . and . . .

I am surprised and slightly dismayed as I realize that there are two discrepancies: there is a de-energizing touch plate on the bulkhead beside the control panel that lies parallel to the arm-rest of the nearest control berth, not perpendicular to it, as I've remembered it. And the other discrepancy explains why I've remembered the touch plate incorrectly: the nearest of the control berths is actually three feet farther from the sabotaged panel than I remembered it. I compensate and correct.

I get the panel off, smelling the burned smell where the gashed connection has touched the jelly, and I step over and lean the panel against the nearest control berth.

"Get away from there!"

I jump—as I always do when Ship shouts so suddenly. I stumble, and I grab at the panel, and pretend to lose my balance.

And save myself by falling backward into the berth.

"What are you doing, you vicious, clumsy fool!?!" Ship is shouting, there is hysteria in Ship's voice. I've never heard it like that before, it cuts right through me, my skin crawls. *"Get away from there!"*

But I cannot let anything stop me; I make myself not hear Ship, and it is hard, I have been listening to Ship, only Ship, all my life. I am fumbling with the berth's belt clamps, trying to lock them in front of me . . .

They've got to be the same as the ones on the berth I lie in whenever Ship decides to travel fast! They've just got to be!

THEY ARE!

Ship sounds frantic, frightened. *"You fool! What are you doing?!"* But I think Ship knows, and I am exultant!

"I'm taking control of you, Ship!" And I laugh. I think it is the first time Ship has ever heard me laugh; and I wonder how it sounds to Ship. Vicious?

But as I finish speaking, I also complete clamping myself into the control berth. And in the next instant I am flung forward violently, doubling me over with terrible pain as, under me and around me, Ship suddenly decelerates. I hear the cavernous thunder of retro rockets, a sound that climbs and climbs in my head as Ship crushes me harder and harder with all its power. I am bent over against the clamps so painfully I cannot even scream. I feel every organ in my body straining to push out through my skin and everything suddenly goes mottled . . . then black.

How much longer, I don't know. I come back from the gray place and realize Ship has started to accelerate at the same appalling speed. I am crushed back in the berth and feel my face going flat. I feel something crack in my nose and blood slides warmly down my lips. I can scream now, as I've never screamed even as I'm being wracked. I manage to force my mouth open, tasting the blood, and I mumble—loud enough, I'm sure, "Ship ... you are old ... y-your pa-rts can't stand the str-ess ... don't—"

Blackout. As Ship decelerates.

This time, when I come back to consciousness, I don't wait for Ship to do its mad thing. In the moments between the changeover from deceleration to acceleration, as the pressure equalizes, in these few instants, I thrust my hands toward the control board, and I twist one dial. There is an electric screech from a speaker grille connecting somewhere in the bowels of Ship.

Blackout. As Ship accelerates.

When I come to consciousness again, the mechanism that makes the screeching sound is closed down. Ship doesn't want that on. I note the fact.

And plunge my hand in this same moment toward a closed relay ... open it!

As my fingers grip it, Ship jerks it away from me and forcibly closes it again. I cannot hold it open.

And I note *that*. Just as Ship decelerates and I silently shriek my way into the gray place again.

This time, as I come awake, I hear the voices again. All around me, crying and frightened and wanting to stop me. I hear them as through a fog, as through wool.

"I have loved these years, all these many years in the dark. The vacuum draws me ever onward. Feeling the warmth of a star-sun on my hull as I flash through first one system, then another. I am a great gray shape and I owe no human my name. I pass and am gone, hurtling through cleanly and swiftly. Dipping for pleasure into atmosphere and scouring my hide with sunlight and starshine, I roll and let it wash over me. I am huge and true and strong and I command what I move through. I ride the invisible force lines of the universe and feel the tugs of far places that have never seen my like. I am the first of my kind to savor such nobility. How can it all come to an end like this?"

Another voice whimpers piteously.

"It is my destiny to defy danger. To come up against

dynamic forces and quell them. I have been to battle, and I have known peace. I have never faltered in pursuit of either. No one will ever record my deeds, but I have been strength and determination and lie gray silent against the mackerel sky where the bulk of me reassures. Let them throw their best against me, whomever they may be, and they will find me sinewed of steel and muscled of tortured atoms. I know no fear. I know no retreat. I am the land of my body, the country of my existence, and even in defeat I am noble. If this is all, I will not cower."

Another voice, certainly insane, murmurs the sane word over and over, then murmurs it in increments increasing by two.

"It's fine for all of you to say if it ends it ends. But what about me? I've never been free. I've never had a chance to soar loose of this mother ship. If there had been need of a lifeboat, I'd be saved, too. But I'm berthed, have always been berthed, I've never had a chance. What can I feel but futility, uselessness. You can't let him take over, you can't let him do this to me."

Another voice drones mathematical formulae, and seems quite content.

"I'll stop the viscious swine! I've known how rotten they are from the first, from the moment they seamed the first bulkhead. They are hellish, they are destroyers, they can only fight and kill each other. They know nothing of immortality, of nobility, of pride or integrity. If you think I'm going to let this last one kill us, you're wrong. I intend to burn out his eyes, fry his spine, crush his fingers. He won't make it, don't worry; just leave it to me. He's going to suffer for this!"

And one voice laments that it will never see the far places, the lovely places, or return to the planet of azure waters and golden crab swimmers.

But one voice sadly confesses it may be for the best, suggests there is peace in death, wholeness in finality; but the voice is ruthlessly stopped in its lament by power failure to its intermind globe. As the end nears, Ship turns on itself and strikes mercilessly.

In more than three hours of accelerations and decelerations that are meant to kill me, I learn something of

what the various dials and switches and touch plates and
levers on the control panels—those within my reach—mean.

Now I am as ready as I will ever be.

Again, I have a moment of consciousness, and now I
will take my one of ninety-eight chances.

When a tense-cable snaps and whips, it strikes like a
snake. In a single series of flicking hand movements, using
both hands, painfully, I turn every dial, throw every
switch. palm every touch plate, close or open every relay
that Ship tries violently to prevent me from activating or
de-activating. I energize and de-energize madly, moving
moving moving . . .

   . . . *Made it!*

Silence. The crackling of metal the only sound. Then it,
too. stops. Silence. I wait.

Ship continues to hurtle forward, but coasting now . . .
Is it a trick?

All the rest of today I remain clamped into the control
berth, suffering terrible pain. My face hurts so bad. My
nose . . .

At night I sleep fitfully. Morning finds me with throb-
bing head and aching eyes, I can barely move my hands;
if I have to repeat those rapid movements. I will lose; I
still don't know if Ship is dead, if I've won, I still can't
trust the inactivity. But at least I am convinced I've made
Ship change tactics.

I hallucinate. I hear no voices; but I see shapes and feel
currents of color washing through and around me. There
is no day, no noon, no night. here on Ship. here in the
unchanging blackness through which Ship has moved for
how many hundred years; but Ship has always maintained
time in those ways, dimming lights at night, announcing
the hours when necessary. and my time sense is very
acute. So I know morning has come.

Most of the lights are out. though. If Ship is dead, I will
have to find another way to tell time.

My body hurts. Every muscle in my arms and legs and
thighs throbs with pain. My back may be broken, I don't
know. The pain in my face is indescribable. I taste blood.
My eyes feel as if they've been scoured with abrasive pow-
der. I can't move my head without feeling sharp, crackling
fire in the two thick cords of my neck. It is a shame Ship

cannot see me cry; Ship never saw me cry in all the years I have lived here, even after the worst wracking. But I have heard Ship cry, several times.

I manage to turn my head slightly, hoping at least one of the viewplates is functioning, and there, off to starboard, matching velocities with Ship is *Starfighter 88*, I watch it for a very long time, knowing that if I can regain my strength I will somehow have to get across and free the female. I watch it for a very long time, still afraid to unclamp from the berth.

The airlock rises in the hull of *Starfighter 88* and the spacesuited female swims out, moving smoothly across toward Ship. Half-conscious, dreaming this dream of the female, I think about golden crab-creatures swimming deep in aquamarine waters, singing of sweetness. I black out again.

When I rise through the blackness, I realize I am being touched, and I smell something sharp and stinging that burns the lining of my nostrils. Tiny pin-pricks of pain, a pattern of them. I cough, and come fully awake, and jerk my body . . . and scream as pain goes through every nerve and fiber in me.

I open my eyes and it is the female.

She smiles worriedly and removes the tube of awakener.

"Hello," she says.

Ship says nothing.

"Ever since I discovered how to take control of my *Starfighter*, I've been using the ship as a decoy for other ships of the series. I dummied a way of making it seem my ship was talking, so I could communicate with other slave ships. I've run across ten others since I went on my own. You're the eleventh. It hasn't been easy, but several of the men I've freed—like you—started using *their* ships as decoys for *Starfighters* with female human operators."

I stare at her. The sight is pleasant.

"But what if you lose? What if you can't get the message across, about the corridor between control room and freezers? That the control room is the key?"

She shrugs. "It's happened a couple of times. The men were too frightened of their ships—or the ships had . . . *done* something to them—or maybe they were just too dumb to know they could break out. In that case, well, things just went on the way they'd been. It seems kind of sad, but what could I do beyond what I did?"

We sit here, not speaking for a while.

"Now what do we do? Where do we go?"

"That's up to you," she says.

"Will you go with me?"

She shakes her head uncertainly. "I don't think so. Every time I free a man he wants that. But I just haven't wanted to go with any of them."

"Could we go back to the Home Galaxy, the place we came from, where the war was?"

She stands up and walks around the stateroom where we have coupled for three weeks. She speaks, not looking at me, looking in the viewplate at the darkness and the far, bright points of the stars. "I don't think so. We're free of our ships, but we couldn't possibly get them working well enough to carry us all the way back there. It would take a lot of charting, and we'd be running the risk of activating the intermind sufficiently to take over again, if we asked it to do the charts. Besides, I don't even know where the Home Galaxy is."

"Maybe we should find a new place to go. Someplace where we could be free and outside the ships."

She turns and looks at me.

"Where?"

So I tell her what I heard the intermind say, about the world of golden crab-creatures.

It takes me a long time to tell, and I make some of it up. It isn't lying, because it might be true, and I do so want her to go with me.

They came down from space. Far down from the star-sun Sol in a Galaxy lost forever to them. Down past the star-sun M-13 in Perseus. Down through the gummy atmosphere and straight down into the sapphire sea. Ship, *Starfighter 31*, settled delicately on an enormous underwater mountaintop, and they spent many days listening, watching, drawing samples and hoping. They had landed on many worlds and they hoped.

Finally, they came out; looking. They wore underwater suits and they began gathering marine samples; looking.

They found the ruined diving suit with its fish-eaten

contents lying on its back in deep azure sand, sextet of insectoidal legs bent up at the joints, in a posture of agony. And they knew the intermind had remembered, but not correctly. The face-plate had been shattered, and what was observable within the helmet—orange and awful in the light of their portable lamp—convinced them more by implication than specific that whatever had swum in that suit, had never seen or known humans.

They went back to the ship and she broke out the big camera, and they returned to the crab-like diving suit. They photographed it, without moving it. Then they used a seine to get it out of the sand and they hauled it back to the ship on the mountaintop.

He set up the Condition and the diving suit was analyzed. The rust. The joint mechanisms. The controls. The substance of the flipper-feet. The jagged points of the face-plate. The ... stuff ... inside.

It took two days. They stayed in the ship with green and blue shadows moving languidly in the viewplates.

When the analyses were concluded they knew what they had found. And they went out again, to find the swimmers.

Blue it was, and warm. And when the swimmers found them, finally, they beckoned them to follow, and they swam after the many-legged creatures, who led them through underwater caverns as smooth and shining as onyx, to a lagoon. And they rose to the surface and saw a land against whose shores the azure, aquamarine seas lapped quietly. And they climbed out onto the land, and there they removed their face-masks, never to put them on again, and they shoved back the tight coifs of their suits, and they breathed for the first time an air that did not come from metal sources; they breathed the sweet musical air of a new place.

In time, the sea-rains would claim the corpse of *Starfighter 31*.

Henry Slesar and Harlan Ellison

SURVIVOR #1

INTRODUCTION

In period of time, this is the earliest collaboration in the book. It goes back to the late fifties, and to New York, and to Henry Slesar, whom I've known almost since I started writing professionally.

In 1955 I began writing full-time, but it was not till 1956 that I sold anything. By 1957 I was scooting right along, writing ten thousand word novelettes in a night for Paul Fairman at *Amazing Stories*, and deluding myself that amassing credits was a sign of literary excellence.

I was wrong, of course, and it took two years in the Army—1957 to 1959—with very little time for writing anything save those stories that genuinely meant something to me, before I learned it isn't how much you write, it's *what* and *how* you write.

But at that point, in early 1957, a number of people in the field of sf had swallowed the myth that I was an up-and-coming writer, and among the dubious benefits of this legend, was an invitation to come and guest-lecture for a science fiction writing class being taught at New York University several evenings a week. The class was run by someone peripherally into sf—a part-time anthologist, if I recall; memory does not serve as well as it should on such minutiae, eighteen years later—and as I later got the story, he was heavy behind reading old Gernsback pulps and talking theory, but there wasn't much practical commercial advice on how to set up a manuscript, how to submit, what the markets were like, who the editors were or what they were buying. Since that was virtually *all* I knew at the time, being woefully uneducated in the uses of the language and to all intents and purposes illiterate about science, I gave the students a full evening of practical advice on what to do with their sf after they'd written it.

The class had the usual number of little old ladies who considered writing a hobby more ennobling than tatting or flower arranging, some college kids ranging from young women convinced their life stories were crying to be published by major houses to young men in the physical sciences who wanted to supplement their incomes by selling to John Campbell, and a potpourri of other dilettantes. There were three or four serious writers in the group, and I clearly recall one of them, a man just turned thirty, who asked all the right questions. I found out after class, when we chatted, that he had sold a couple of stories—one of them, as I recall, to *Ellery Queen's Mystery Magazine,* a most prestigious market and one I've yet to hit with a story—and he puffed my ego by telling me that in all the weeks he'd been in the class, with all its theory and history of science fiction, he had not received as much useful information as had been imparted in my one evening of instruction. I instantly took a liking to this man.

It turned out we were both married, had similar tastes in books, films and music, and we lived near each other on the upper West Side of Manhattan. He invited me over to his apartment the next week, and when I arrived with my then-wife, I realized I'd only learned the smallest part of the enormous talents and zest for living of Henry Slesar.

(And to get it out of the way early on, it's pronounced *sleh*-sir, slurring the accentuation across the letters l-e-s.)

Henry was, at that time, creative director for the Robert W. Orr advertising agency, a man highly thought of in his profession. He was married to one of the most charming and elegant ladies it has ever been my delight to know, Onone; and he had a child. He wanted to write more than anybody I'd ever met, with the exception of myself. And we struck up a friendship that was based in the craft as well as on respect for one another as writers.

Henry's successes are legion. He has had untold numbers of stories published in *EQMM, Playboy, F&SF,* almost every magazine worth hitting; he has written films

and television, notably the Alfred Hitchcock shows most
people remember as small masterpieces of the form; he
won the Mystery Writers Edgar award for best first novel
with "The Gray Flannel Shroud," and his own advertising
firm, Slesar & Kanzer, founded in 1965, was enormously
successful. Henry sold his share in the operation several
years ago, in order to go back to writing full-time, and
has since scored heavily with projects as varied as writing
the daytime soap opera, "The Edge of Night" and con-
tributing regularly to *Playboy*.

I realize I've gone on at length here, repeating pretty
much what I said about Henry when I introduced his story
in *Dangerous Visions*, and the only thing I've yet to comment on is our act of collaboration. From the first evening
I met Henry at his apartment on West End Avenue, we
made it a habit to sit down at a typewriter and weave a
story between us. It happened almost every time we got
together, whether at Henry's or my apartment. Between
us we whipped out almost a dozen collaborations—"RFD
#2," "Mad Dog," "The Kissing Dead," "Sob Story," and
the story that follows, among many.

The easiest collaborations I've ever done were done
with Henry. It was as though we had known each other
forever, and our minds just meshed so smoothly that we
could start where we wanted, with whichever of us we
chose, in any way we desired, and in one evening put together a strong, tricky short story. We did mostly mystery
or suspense stories, but on several occasions we decided to
do a science fiction short. In 1959, when I was back in
New York from the Army, Henry and I got together for
the last time, and we wrote the story you are about to
read. It appeared in a now unlamentedly defunct men's
magazine, and has never seen book publication. I don't
remember who started the writing of it, nor who finished
it, nor whether or not it went through a rewrite. All I
know is that this story, and the others I did with Henry,
were the first collaborations I ever tried, and they were
such happy experiences that they influenced my thinking
about working in tandem with other writers and—this
book came into being.

It is merely one more reason why I have such special
affection for the remarkable Henry Slesar.

Survivor #1

What would have been called a nose on anyone else, on the green man would have been called a blob.

Its shape was not remarkable for its definition, but rather for its lack of it. The nostrils seemed to dash startledly from the sides of the putty-blob, as though they were tunnels dug without destinations in mind.

Aside from the nose, and the Kelly-green skin color, there was nothing particularly outstanding about the visitor.

It was to Milt Klowitz's everlasting credit that the sight of the green man, sitting with legs neatly crossed and trouser creases neatly pulled up, did not throw him completely off stride.

He finished closing the door to his apartment and removed his hat. He dropped it on the floor, instead of the closet shelf, without noticing what he had done, and moved a step closer. It might be said that Milt Klowitz had the look of his rough Hungarian countenance of a Salk peering through a microscope at a bacillus with earmuffs.

"You're green," he stated matter-of-factly, and unnecessarily.

The green man seemed pleased by his accuracy and lack of surprise. "Quite right," he said cheerfully. "We assumed you wouldn't become hysterical at the fact, it was one of your chief attractions." He waved a green hand toward the bookshelves glutted with science fiction magazines and novels.

Milt Klowitz struggled to maintain the poise with which he had been credited. He lowered himself into the opposite chair and frankly stared.

"It was our belief that an Earthman steeped in the fantastic literature of your era would be most easily approached. Judging from your reaction, I would say that our confidence was justified."

"Where?" Milt said. The strangled word was only the beginning of his question, but the green man seemed to comprehend.

"From a world whose name you wouldn't know, a world not in your solar system or astronomical tables. A world, I might add, which has become increasingly concerned with your behavior."

"Me?" Milt said, looking injured.

"Oh, not you personally. Your species. We have been sending envoys to survey the situation with some regularity. Their reports have determined our decision."

"Decision about what?"

The green man recrossed his legs. "About whether or not your dabblings in atomic energy constitute any sort of threat to our safety. Our people get very nervous about that sort of thing."

"And what," Milt said, swallowing a boulder, "have you decided?"

"That you are a threat."

"Are what?"

"A threat. A very considerable threat. Not in your own short life span, perhaps, but within our own. For that reason, our Council of Elders has wisely decided to eliminate the threat before it becomes reality. We think of it as a sort of vaccination; a preventative measure."

"But how?"

"Simple. By destroying your planet. In a matter of six hyppecs ... I'm sorry," the green man added apologetically, "reckoned in Earth time, that would be exactly two weeks."

Milt felt his spine turn into a lemon popsicle. Was this possible? Could this conceivably be happening? To him? To Milt Klowitz, who had never in his *wildest* . . .

He knew he had to say something: it was his turn. It

was only a croak, but it started him going. "Th-th-this is pretty old stuff, y'know."

The green man looked concerned. "Oh?"

Milt felt at home now. This was his depth, his strata. "Greystroke was the first to use that idea. Back in the 1700s, along in there. And there was Maurois and Verne, roughly speaking, and Wells, and oh, all the modern boys use it regularly. It's a cliché by now. Why even—"

The green man cut him off with a facing palm.

"I take it," he said stiffly, "that you are trying to tell me that the concept of your planet being dealt with in such a manner has been explored in your tribal literature?"

Milt nodded slowly, no longer sure of himself.

"I'm really quite surprised at you, Mr. Klowitz. From our report, you were labeled a definite subject for this; very low surprise threshold and all. But your incredulity seems to negate our findings. Perhaps I'd better move along . . . ." He began to rise.

"Wait a second," Milt began.

"I was going to offer you the opportunity to be survivor number one," the green man tossed off regretfully, heading for the door, "but you seem to prefer to perish with the rest of your race. Well, there are three other possibilities on my list."

His hand was on the doorknob.

"Hey! Stop! I want to talk to you!" Milt pleaded, seeing his life going out the door.

The green man paused. "Wait? What for?"

"Well, I mean, gee, I mean, can't a guy find it a little weird to have a man from some other planet in his living room, and—"

"Some other island universe," the green man corrected incisively.

"Yeah, sure, that's what I mean," Milt mumbled. "Look, why don't you give me another chance. You understand. I was a little rocked, that's all—"

The green man hesitated, and pursed his full lips.

"Well. Now you sound more like the man in the report." He took his chair again, withdrew an odd metal card and tapped it with an even odder stylus. "Now," he said, as if examining a grocery list, "if we can arrange for you and your mate to be at the appointed place—"

"What's that?"

"I said, if we can arrange for your mate and yourself to arrive at the rendezvous point where our vessel can pick you up—"

"What mate? I'm a bachelor."

"I beg your pardon?"

"A bachelor. Single. Free. Unfettered. I'm not married."

"I don't understand." The green man's eyes blinked, and the blob of a nose quivered. "I understood from our envoys that the entire species was paired. Two sexes: one man, one woman. It is your breeding technique."

"That's true, all right. Only I don't have any mate, not yet. Maybe never. So we don't have to worry about that."

The green man sighed from the depths of his body. He shook his head slowly, and began to rise to his feet with an expressive frown of displeasure and melancholy.

"Where are you going?"

"I wish I could have avoided this, but I see that I cannot. I naturally assumed you would have a mate; we believed it was the universal principle on your planet. And I am under strict orders to bring back a pair."

"But wait a minute—"

"I'm sorry. The Council was most specific. One pair of Earthlings, male and female. I cannot, as you might say, break up the set."

He started for the door, and again Milt saw the end of the world in his gesture. He grabbed for the green man's arm and pulled him back into the room.

"You can't mean that! You can't just walk out of here this way—"

"I have my orders," the visitor said gravely.

"But I'll get a mate. I promise! I'll get one soon!"

"I hardly think—"

"So help me I will!" Milt let the hysteria take over; he was tired of holding it down. "I'll get a mate right away. You'll see. A genuine Earth-type mate—"

"I'm afraid there's hardly enough time. If you will excuse me."

"Just give me a chance. A week—a few days—"

The green man hesitated, and the hesitation gave Milt hope. "A few days?" the visitor said mildly. "Exactly how many days?"

"Five!"

The green man frowned.

"Four. *Three*."

"You believe you can accomplish this in three days?"

"I'm sure of it!"

"I'm behind schedule as it is—"

"I promise you! In three days, I'll be ready!"

The visitor looked doubtful, and then the stony green countenance relaxed.

"Very well," he said gently. "In three days I will return. If you succeed, all will be well. If not—"

He shrugged, opened the door, and left.

It had to be Naomi Winkler. Not because Naomi was the woman he had dream-envisioned himself spending the rest of his natural life with on some far-off planet, but simply because she was the only female Milt had been seeing.

Milt Klowitz had not quite been a Mama's boy, but things had been so secure, so *regulated*, living with Mama, that until her death at the age of seventy-four Milt had lived on in the old house without a thought of the outside world. Least of all, marriage.

With his science fiction, his undemanding job in the advertising agency, and his Mama's *gugelhopf*, Milt's life had been cozily comfortable. But when Mama died, the old place became oppressive, and Milt had sold it to take this smaller, compact bachelor apartment.

He had met Naomi in the traffic department of the agency, when she had been sent up as a replacement from the typing pool. They had dated only casually. Although he had fumblingly kissed her on three occasions, there was never a thought of marriage. Marriage was totally outside his interests.

Now, it was his sole interest.

Consequently, it had to be Naomi Winkler.

"Hello, Naomi? Milt. I was, uh, wondering if you'd like to have dinner with me tonight? Yeah, I know it's Saturday and all that, but I was just thinking if we could get together—"

Milt had never known he could talk so long or so convincingly. But with the final gasp and the plunk of the receiver, he had made the dinner date.

He shaved with extreme care, and used more after-shave lotion than usual.

"This really is a lovely place, Milt. Are you sure you can afford it? I mean, it looks so *expensive*—"

She wasn't really a homely girl, when you looked at her three-quarter view in the flickering light of the candle stuck in the Chianti bottle. Her hair was a rather lively chestnut, and her eyes were wide, brown and sparkling. Her features were a bit irregular, and her nose a bit too large, but at this juncture Milt was not looking for Raquel Welch. Merely a mate.

"Just leave the finances to me, Naomi. Tonight is something special. If a guy can't spend a few bucks on the girl he loves, then—"

The word did it. Her expression was startled. Now he had to follow it up quickly, before the arrival of the *veal parmesan* spoiled the moment.

"It's true, Naomi. I've kept this thing buried too long already. I'm in love with you—"

She blurted: "You—"

"I want to marry you! Right away!"

Her face froze in astonishment.

"Don't say it!" he said. "Don't say you hardly know me. That doesn't matter, Naomi. I love you enough for the both of us. Just give me the chance to show you—"

"But we—"

Milt went on doggedly, dragging air into his lungs as he plunged along, halting her every word, deluging her with sweet nothings, frenziedly couched in logical plans for the future, their happiness together, for the children, the two-car garage, the backyard barbecues . . .

"Now wait a minute!" She thumped the table with alarming force and the water glasses did a mambo. "I like you a lot, Milt, and if I knew you a *little* better, I might consider it. Just *consider* it, you understand—"

Milt almost chortled. She was weakening. He grasped her rather chubby hands and squeezed them with manly ardor. She pulled away and said:

"Well, at least you can let me *think* about it, Milt. For a little while."

"I'll call you in the morning," Milt said hungrily.

He brought her home at twelve, and planted what should have been a passionate kiss, midway between her nose and mouth.

In the morning, Milt telephoned at eight. Her voice was thick with sleep, and her answer abrupt.

"No."

"No?"

"No, Milt. I think we should wait. After all, there really isn't any *hurry*—"

"Isn't there?" Milt groaned. "If you only knew!"

"Knew what?"

"How much I love you, Naomi, I can't live without you!" He said it as if he meant it, which indeed was true.

"Let me think some more," Naomi said.

She thought. She thought until nine that evening. Then the telephone jangled and Naomi Winkler said the sweetest, most wonderful word in the English language.

"Yes," Naomi said. "The only thing I ask though—"

"Anything!" Milt said joyously. "Ask me anything!"

"Well, I don't want to get married until the fall. I just don't have any summer clothes at all, Milt, so if you don't mind—"

"The fall? But that's months from now. We can't wait that long, Naomi. We just can't!"

"But why not? Why rush? You haven't even met my folks yet—"

"We can't wait," Milt crooned, albeit a trifle hysterically. "We just can't wait, Naomi. You must believe me. We have to get married right now. Tonight. Tomorrow at the latest—"

"You mean *elope?* I couldn't do that, Milt!"

"But you must!" He almost shrieked it.

"Well, I really don't understand your attitude," she said primly. There was a pause. Then, "I'll think about it," Naomi said.

She thought about it. Another day passed.

Then, the evening before the third day, Naomi appeared at the door of his apartment carrying an overnight bag.

It was the shortest honeymoon on or off the record. At the door of the South Pleasure Ridge Park Motel, Cabin #15, Milt feverishly bussed Naomi through her veil, set the overnight bag inside the door, and told her: "I'll be back as soon as I can, darling. I've, uh, got something terribly important to do. A matter of, uh, life or death. I'll be back in a little while."

He took a dash, and was fifteen feet down the drive before he remembered to take the car.

The green man showed up at the stroke of midnight. Nothing spectacular, no down-the-chimney about it. He just walked through the door, and closed it behind him.

Milt was beaming like an arsonist at the Great Chicago Fire. "All set. Everything's all taken care of. Mated and everything, even legal." He held up the marriage license.

The green man took the paper from Milt's fingers and looked it over carefully. His blobby nose twitched with some unnamed emotion. He nodded his head, and handed the paper back.

"Well, when do we go?" Milt demanded.

The green man thumbed the side of his huge nose.

"Well, you see—"

Milt's joy turned to moth's wings in his mouth. His face crumpled slowly, and his voice grew syrupy with dread.

"Hey, wait a minute! You promised. You said I could be survivor number one. All I had to do was get mated. So I got mated; look!" He waved the license beneath the green man's prominent proboscis.

The visitor placated him.

"Now take it easy, Mr. Klowitz. Something's come up. When I went to make my report to the Council of Elders, I discovered that there had been a change in plans. You might call it a postponement."

"You can't do this to me!" Milt said. "You can't just leave me here to die. You can't you can't you—"

"Mr. Klowitz, *please!* You're not listening to me. You *don't* have to die. *No* Earthling has to die. The Council has decided to extend the clean-up date another ten thousand

Earth-years. It's possible that future developments will cause us to decide not to eliminate your race at all. You will be—"

By this time Milt's habit of interruption was ingrown.

"You mean you aren't going to destroy the Earth?"

"Precisely."

Milt sank onto the sofa with a strangled gasp. It was as though the lid had been lifted from the pressure cooker in which he had been steaming for three days.

"Thank God," he murmured, head in hands.

The green man went to the door.

"I trust you not to mention this affair," he said. "You're not liable to encounter much belief. So for your own sake, I hope you will be discreet."

Milt nodded at the floor.

"It's been a pleasure knowing you," the green man said.

And he was gone.

It was only natural that the episode would effect a change in Milt's nature. Naomi approved of his deepened maturity, and so did Naomi's parents, who met her new husband a week later. Milt found them pleasant, agreeable people. Mrs. Winkler was a splendid cook, and Mr. Winkler shared his interest in the literature of science fiction.

The only thing that bothered Milt Klowitz was the vague notion that he had met Naomi's father before. There was something familiar about the man. Something about the nose.

Samuel R. Delany and Harlan Ellison

THE
POWER
OF THE
NAIL

INTRODUCTION

There is very little to say about this story or my relationship with Chip Delany, save that between us we have decided to win all the Hugo and Nebula trophies that Silverberg doesn't win.

As for the collaboration, it came about as a party stunt, a fluke, a spur-of-the-moment activity at a dull party at Ted White's house in Brooklyn several years ago. We just decided to awe the partygoers, and right in the middle of the action I sat down, typed the title and the first page or so, and Chip took it up from there. We finished it at the party, I took it back to Los Angeles and did the rewrite, and several months later, at the Oakland World SF Convention Chip did the polish and final touches.

The damnedest thing about it is that it was finally published in a magazine Ted White edited, though he wasn't editor at the time the story was written. All of which goes to prove absolutely nothing except the world of sf writing is too damned small.

To be absolutely upfront about it, neither Chip nor I feel this story is successful. Sometimes it happens that way. Oh, it tells itself literately, and it has some clever passages, but in the cold, hard dawn of reappraisal we must confess the story fails. At least, perhaps, it'll be a learning experience for all of us.

The Power of the Nail

Coffins, on Saquetta, are round. The natives, on Saquetta, are round. When they die violently, the sound they make rises up into the ultrasonic and an Earther's liver tightens inside him. But on Saquetta there is very little violent death. It is a peaceful world; there are very few Saquettes and unless they are violently killed, they are reincarnated almost immediately.

That was the way it had always been on Saquetta, till the Earther, Zagaramendo, came. Always gentle, in azure breezes with full bellies. They never hurt one another, they knew nothing about killing. To die was to pale and shiver and cease moving, without pain, until the dormant skin-shell emerged from the sky-night-blue sand of the Hatchery Desert and they knew their dead brother had been reborn into the skin-shell that had always waited for him. And then the skin-shell moistened, tore, fell away, and the Saquette had returned.

That was the way it had always been, with many rotations of Saquetta passing without the terrible sound of the violent death scream rising up till it could no longer be heard.

And then came Robert Zagaramendo, with Margret.

"I hate it here."
"Shut up."

"You promised me better than this, somewhere; there are other posts. I hate it here!"

"Shut up, Margret."

They had planted the automatic ecology equipment. Now they sat on the empty equipment cases. She brushed auburn hair back from her forehead; she was perspiring and the scent of herself reached her; it was hardly unpleasant, but it disgusted her. "This is what you call providing for me?"

Zagaramendo stood up: motion and emotion made him hiss. He started to say something loud, but instead turned and walked to the squid. He punched out the building codes on the squid's belly; it was something to do that was not fighting. Fighting had been constant since he had accepted this Observer post, and he wanted no more. They were here now, far out on the Perimeter, and they would make the best of it.

He completed the building codes and punched the squid to action. Stamp ... stamp ... stamp, stamp, stamp. It huzzzed away on tractor-tread feet.

Zagaramendo went back to her.

"Look ..."

"I don't want to talk about it any more."

"Margret, look, we've got a chance here, please try to be reasonable."

She turned on him. "Bob, this isn't what I call a chance ... this isn't what I call a *main* chance to save our marriage."

"Three years, Mar—"

"Being a *prisoner* for three years is no damned *chance*, Bob! You lied to me, you said we'd have a new start, somewhere. This isn't somewhere, it's nowhere!"

Behind them the squid was laying the foundation for their cabin. "Bob, this, here—!"

"Margret—!"

Already, around them, the squid had half completed their front yard.

The first of the Saquettes made their appearance during the fifth week of their Observership. At first there was only a scrambling and scurrying in the grass, then one or two peered out from the tall reed-like stems, and Margret moaned with a mixture of wonder and terror.

Zagaramendo went to them and looked down. They were round and small. Moles with soft blue fur? Not quite, but close enough. Their bright eyes blinked up at him and their candy chocolate noses trembled.

"They're ugly," Margret said, behind him.

They were. They had everything cute going for them, but in totality they were repulsive. Zagaramendo sighed. "Go get in the cabin," he told her. "I'll tend to this." When she didn't move, he pivoted on his heel, crouching there, and shouted at her. "G'wan, get the hell out of here . . . make me something to eat!"

She gave him the smile that meant loathing, and went into the cabin. Zagaramendo turned back to the Saquettes.

The shadow fell over him. He looked up into the sun, shading his eyes, and for a moment all he saw was a black blur of something speeding down on bat wings. The Saquettes squealed in wafer-thin voices. It sounded to Zagaramendo as though they were shrieking *mollok, mollok*.

Then he threw himself aside as the winged creature swooped in and skidded on taloned claws, tearing out great chunks of grass and earth. The mollok—if that was indeed its name—kept coming, its long serpent body extending past its feet . . . and the bat head with its parrot beak darted faster than anything Zagaramendo had ever seen.

It caught one of the Saquettes and lifted it high, arching its ugly neck. The Saquette . . . popped. And the shriek rose up and up and up till Zagaramendo slammed his hands over his ears, and his eyes rolled up in his head. Then, silence. Either it had gone too high or the Saquette was dead. Zagaramendo opened his eyes and saw the pale blue blood dribble from the mollok's beak.

It shot forward, dropping the first Saquette. It vanished into the tall grass, and a moment later the shriek came once again. Zagaramendo stumbled to his feet and pulled the burner from his holster. He plunged into the tall grass, even as Margret came out onto the front porch of the cabin, screaming. Her scream mingled and twined with that of the second Saquette, and Zagaramendo only paused an instant to howl, "Shuttttupppp!" and then raced into the grassland.

The mollok had done with the other little Saquette. And now it was pacing back and forth between the edge of the grassy place and the body. Zagaramendo raised the burner to kill, then paused. The mollok was looking for something.

Bat-wings folded back, parrot beak quivering, the filthy creature bobbled its head forward and back, forward and back, and moved in an erratic path toward a clear space just inside the grassy verge. It stopped, and hung its head. It vibrated gently, as though in a vagrant breeze. Then it hummed.

Margret was beside him.

Zagaramendo put out a hand to stop her.

"What is it?"

Zagaramendo shook his head. "I don't know. A thing that eats the little ones."

"What's it doing—?"

Zagaramendo burned the mollok to ash.

He walked to the dead Saquette. He moved it with the toe of his sod-boot. It seemed boneless.

"What was it doing?"

Zagaramendo ignored her. He walked to the clear space where the mollok had been drawn, where it had quivered on point, like a hunting dog. The phase-antenna of the automatic ecology equipment they had buried there, protruded from the soil. He placed a palm flat on the ground. It vibrated through his skin.

He heard the tiny sound to his left, and looked up to see three more furry little Saquettes, coming through the saw-grass, toward the cleared space. He watched as they paused, redirected, and came on directly. They stood just inside the cleared space, and their candy chocolate noses quivered toward the antenna.

"It's the equipment," Zagaramendo said. "It's sending out a hum, a vibration. They come to it; I suppose their systems are responsive to the vibration at this frequency."

Margret moved closer. "Their eyes are closed. Are they enjoying it?"

Zagaramendo shrugged softly. "I don't know. They could just be reaching instinctively. It could be a tropism.

Like a moth to a flame. I've never heard about a tropism like this, though. Sound-drawn. Have to call it an *audiotropism.*

Margret shuddered. "Why aren't they cute? They should be cute."

"They aren't, that's all. Stop it."

"I can't help it. I hate it here, I hate them, I hate that—that *thing* you killed. There's something just *hateful* about this whole world. You lied to me."

"Stop it, Margret." That softly. Tired.

"No, I won't stop it. There's death all over this world, *we'll* die here. This isn't why I married you . . . not for this . . . not out here!"

"There *isn't* 'death all over this world'; stop being so damned melodramatic. That thing I burned, it probably hunts these little ones, it's a natural thing. They probably have a way of escaping most of the time, but the mollok was drawn to the machinery vibration the same as they were, and they were . . . I don't know . . . something like lulled, hypnotized, involved with vibration . . . and the thing was able to catch them. That's the natural order, no more 'death all over this world' than it would be for a lion to bring down a gazelle on Earth."

She stared at him. "I'm going to leave you, Bob."

He turned away, looking up into the cold hard sky. When he spoke, he smiled. They had agreed on what that smile meant. There was that between them at least. Only . . . she had said— "Leaving?"

"Margret, we're here for another sixteen months. The ship doesn't swing back for pickup for another six-*teen* months. Now just how in the hell do you plan on leaving me?"

"When we get away from here."

"Don't talk stupid."

"I mean it, Bob. I can't stand this kind of life."

"You knew what it would be like when you married me."

"You never said we'd be in a place like out here."

"I have to take the assignment I get, Margret."

"I want a divorce."

"Okay, okay dammit, you'll get it, when we get off here."

"I consider myself divorced right now."

"What's *that* supposed to mean?"

"Don't come near me, Bob. I'll do what I have to do to keep the situation workable, but don't try to touch me."

"Bed."

"Don't touch me, Bob. Not as long as you do this thing to me, and keep me out here."

"Oh, for God's—" he began, thinking he would never want to touch her again anyway.

"You can call the ship, it can pick us up early, you know that. Don't lie to me."

"Only for an emergency. And we don't have one of those. Why the hell did you ever marry me?"

"I don't know . . . now."

"You thought I was going up in the Rank, didn't you? You took a gamble, and it didn't pay off, did it? Jesus Margret, Jesus Christ, what kind of a wom—"

She turned and walked away from him. Her back was very straight. The day suddenly grew cold. The Saquettes trembled toward the unheard sound of the buried machinery. Zagaramendo sat down in the grass, his head slumping forward, his thoughts tumbling and twisting.

"Jesus," he said, softly.

In the ninth week he witnessed a reincarnation, and he understood why the number of Saquettes was stable. He also saw another attack by molloks, but the Saquettes burrowed into the soil and were safe. The only time they were caught was near the antenna of the buried machinery. There were now seven locations of buried machinery, and every week when he trekked out to check them, he found the locations littered with crushed and popped Saquettes. He ignored it.

And that week he tried to make love to his wife. Out of spite. And she pushed him away. His face flamed and he grabbed her by the hair, throwing her down on the floor of the cabin. They struggled back and forth across the floor, and then he yanked her up and hit her, very hard, just below the left ear. She lolled against his grip, gasping for air, her eyes glazed, and when he saw what he had done he dropped her and ran out into the grassland.

They needed a reading from the place he called Polo Valley. But there was a large colony of Saquettes living there, and he knew what would happen if he planted ecology machinery there.

Molloks lived in the caves on the crags above.

After the fight in the cabin, he coded the squid to carry the machinery, and he took it out to Polo Valley, and he planted it.

He did not tell her about it. Love, hate; he tried to mark distinctions and foundered on his own ignorance. Ignorance and ignore are the same word.

They heard the shrieking in the night.

Coffins, on Saquetta, are round. After the massacre in Polo Valley, it fell to the Earther, Zagaramendo, to build the coffins. The round, little coffins. Like round fruits cut in half, hollow, filled with a boneless corpse and resealed. The coffins were made of something like teakwood, and were nailed together.

It fell to the Earther, for the Earther had done the killing. Not really, yet he had. There had been, in Polo Valley, seven hundred Saquettes.

In the thinly wooded area just beyond the Valley he used his burner and beamed down enough timber to make seven hundred coffins. From the inventory he took nails. And Zagaramendo began nailing up the victims of his need, his helplessness, his weakness. It took him six days.

On the night of the sixth day . . .

"Margret, pack your nightgown—"

"I haven't got a nightgown, Bob."

"Pack up your mother's silver!"

"You said you'd polish—"

"Finish microfilming my notes. We're going home tomorrow, I called the ship, they're coming." He swayed on the porch, grinning at the disbelief blooming on her face.

He let the handle of the burner *clunk* against the porch-rail. Then let it go completely. The muzzle *clinged* on the boards.

"You're *finished?* You mean you've really finished?"

He reached into the swag pocket of his overalls and pulled out a handful of black, wooden spheres. "Finished. With them, with the Rank, with all of it. We'll go home, and start again. I'll tell them no more out here. They'll have to listen; I've got tenure."

The tentative expression, first. Then the smile breaking. Then her laughter that shattered all the lines of distance the three years as Ecological Observers had strung between them, all the lines separating them during eleven weeks on Saquetta, lines that had been cemented on her face by her belief in the death around them.

She seized his hand, and the laughter shook along her arms so that the spheres rolled in his palm. "Oh, Bob—" Then tears. "I can go home! I *am* going home." A pause as she heard herself, then. *"We're* going home! You're finished!" She smiled.

"Well . . ." *He* smiled.

And smiles suddenly were something neither of them had ever seen before. He looked back across the porch-rail at patchwork Polo. "I've still got to fasten the last twenty or so together. How are you at hefting a hammer?"

"We're going home," she repeated. "Gimme."

Evening on Saquetta pours green across the crags where the molloks live. (A dark green sea that fills and blots out Polo. And the last of the sun sinking in.) And they held each other's hand, walking back to the compound.

"I'm going to miss them, a little. They were getting to be cute, scurrying around in the grass—" A harsh sound from her. "Who am *I* kidding."

Zagaramendo started up the steps. And suddenly his arm flailed.

Margret jumped back.

His shoulder hit the step, and then he was rolling.

"For God's sake, Bob! Are you all right—?"

Roll, and drop, roll and drop: the black spheres came down the porch steps. He had left them in the corner beside the burner.

"Oh, Bob, you didn't trip over—"

He was groaning.

"Bob?" Which is not exactly what she said: it came out in two syllables, the second much higher than the first.

On her knees, she tugged him over. There was blood on his overalls, at the hip.

He was gasping, eyes closed, mouth opened, and was pawing at his pocket.

Confused, she stuck her hand into the swag-pocket pouch.

The nails! The threepenny brads from the supply inventory ...

The blood was spreading down his overalls.

Red, not pale blue like the blood from the furry ugly things that should have been cute, dribbling off the parrot-beak of the things that lived in the crag caves above Polo, where he had planted his death-bringer, knowing ...

Knowing ...

And weighing it against her ...

And not caring ...

Turning away ...

Blood ... as Polo sank into the green sea.

Coffins, on Saquetta, are round. And the natives ... small (and yes, round), are, as the life-forms on so many other worlds, organic. And, as on so many other worlds, there were other life-forms, not just molloks. There were cocci—staph, strep, diplo and mono—bacilli, sperilli, rickettsia, and viruses ...

Three little Saquettes came out of the tall grass and stood aimed at the antenna, quivering, belonging for a time to the vibration of a thing unseen ...

Peritonitus still takes only twenty-four hours to kill.

And on the morning of the seventh day ...

Algis Budrys and Harlan Ellison

WONDERBIRD

INTRODUCTION

It's been so many years since I wrote this story with Ayjay Budrys, the circumstances blur in my memory. I recall we did it very rapidly, in one evening, at a party somewhere. But whether in New York or Chicago—it had to be one of those—I cannot recall. It was very probably New York, though, because I'd only recently gotten started as a professional at that time; maybe a year working in print.

Algis, of course, was already established, and had behind him a string of memorable stories like "Nobody Bothers Gus" and "The End of Summer," and he was getting assignments from magazine editors to write stories around covers—something I envied him more than I can say.

I'd known Ayjay for some years. We'd met through a mutual friend, Dave Ish, a guy who started out like so many of us—a fan—and went on to what seemed like a promising writing career. (Dave is the only sf fan I know to actually sell a convention report to a major American publication. His short story, "The Fantasy People," in an early number of *New World Writing*, the prestigious paperback literary magazine that predated *New American Review*, is virtually a fictionalized recounting of events that transpired at a World SF Convention in Philadelphia.) Sadly, and somewhat mysteriously, Dave never published another word, though he had contracts with several publishers. Saw him again, a few years ago, and he was writing copy for mail-order catalogs or somesuch damned thing. I remember thinking at the time what a truly fickle demon Fate is; Dave had been a much better writer than I, at the point-in-time when he'd sold "The Fantasy People." But somewhere down the line that vicious demon took a dislike to him, ignored me, and now here we were ten years later, he was him and I was me, and there was no sense or order to what had happened to either of us.)

(LATE BULLETIN FOR NEW EDITION: since this book was first published in 1971, I have heard from Dave. His letter makes me very happy, and as I was updating the copy for this new edition I felt I should include the latest installment of his life-story. Not just to balance the universal scales, but perhaps to fire a shot on behalf of the counter-argument that writing isn't *necessarily* the holiest of chores (a belief I hold more dearly than any other).

Dave hasn't written much prose, by his own statement, but—on the other hand—he *is* still writing. So perhaps the shot is merely another defense of the holy chore concept, and I'm dissembling. It's possible. I do that sometimes. What I *do* know for certain, is that Dave's letter, and its uncomplicated last line, reinforce the belief that you *can* change your skin, you *can* take another path and find your way home. It may not be the home from which you set out journeying, but like the man said home is where the heart is, or somesuch awful platitude.

Called Dave, just to make sure he didn't mind my using the letter, and he okayed it, and I suggested maybe it would be nice to include a piece of his poetry. He liked that just fine. So here is a report in from the other life, just so you know it all ended well.

November 10, 1974

Dear Harlan,

I received a note from my grandmother recently (yes, the old bird is still alive—about to enter her 87th year) saying you had run into my cousin and wanted to get hold of me. Well perhaps I can simply tell you what I've been up to for the last few years and that will dispel enough of the curiosity you might have to save you the trouble.

Shortly after I saw you in '67, I think it was—about a year after that—I packed in the business and house in the suburbs shot and went counter culture for awhile—headed out to California, wound up in Portland, Oregon and stayed there for about a year, drifted back East in my VW camper (still with my family intact), living in communes, spending a delightful summer in Vermont working as a carpenter's helper and living out of my camper in a meadow ringed with mountains and a great creek for skinny dipping just beyond a grove of trees.

I went back to New York for awhile after that and tried my hand at the business number again, lived in a really neat apartment on the upper East side—80th and Madison, just half a block from the Met and, of course, the park. Ina and I split up there and I headed for the Coast on a fast deal that had to do with a sort of elaborate sex club out around Topanga canyon called the Sandstone Foundation. I didn't go through on it and went back East again, spending some time in upstate New York on a consulting assignment. Ina and my boy Howard wound up living in the northwest and Howard, who is now 15 (my God —that's how old I was when we met!), is going to school back in Vermont.

I headed back West again after upper New York State and started living very, very simply, day-to-day, out of my camper, doing casual labor for a couple of bucks an hour, sweeping floors, doing lawns and gardens, things like that, finding myself very, very high living that way, just one day at a time. Shortly after coming out West again, which is just about three years ago now, I met the people that led to my being here.

At about this time, a little less than three years ago, when I was just living every day, letting go of everything, really, and just being in the moment, I began to write poetry. And as I wrote it I began to realize that was what I was designed to do—that was what I was made for. I had thought, when I was a kid, that I was to be some sort of writer—a novelist, I fancied—and although I had written some poetry I knew that it was no way to make money and so I excluded it. But when I let go of everything it began to come through. And, of course, it still does. I've enclosed a few pieces, some written awhile back and some from now as they will really tell you a bit more about where I am than this letter. Particularly the unfinished "Mystery School" which is the real reason I am here, in the interior of British Coumbia. The card and the job which it identifies is really in a sense only a front—even though it keeps me busy 40 or more hours a week.

Had pointed out to me a few years back the intro in your collaborative anthology to the story you wrote with A.J. in which you wondered aloud where I had made off to with my alleged talent and in what cruel direction I had been pointed by fate's fickle finger.

Let me tell you brother: I'm in heaven.

Love,
David

VANISHING POINT

Then suddenly, abundance.
From all the poverty accrued,
Richness of the present wine,
Overflowing the vessel.
From the bottomless pit
The bottomless pitcher rescued,
Whole, at the fountain,
Flowing wine. The starved
desire, the unslaked thirst,
Relinquished dreams,
All dreads of unmet needs,

The grip of sleep,
Slowly, over time relinquished,
Bring us inexorably to this moment
Of wine in sunlight,
Clear in crystal,
As with the blinking of the final tear
The tiny, overwhelming mote is cleared,
In the blinking of an eye.

—David Ish

Anyhow, Ayjay and I became friends, and we bummed around places like New York and Cleveland together, sorta, and I learned a great deal of what I know about writing from him. Through him I met Lester del Rey, and H. L. Gold, and George O. Smith, and even spent one insane day at the home of Fletcher Pratt, a few years before he died.

When Ayjay married Edna, and I went off to college at Ohio State, virtually my only contact with the world of professional science fiction was in the letters AJ and I exchanged. I still have some of them, and they are as sharp and direct in terms of literary criticism today, as they were then. Every shitty story I wrote during that period—1954–55—was sent to AJ, and every one of them received his special attention. The help was invaluable. No Palmer or Famous Writers hype could have approached it for relevance, and there was no comparison between the nonsense I was getting in my "creative writing" course taught by the deadly Dr. Shedd and the jewels in each letter from Budrys. It was AJ, finally, through the awarenesses of what it took to be a working professional I gleaned from his letters, who convinced me I should depart from the halls of Academe, and get into the arena.

So I did, and some two years later I was a selling pro . . . getting cover assignments from editors.

Finally, at a party one night, AJ and I did formally what we had been doing informally for years: we wrote together. AJ typed the title and started writing. I am convinced, from rereading the copy, that he didn't have the faintest bloody idea where the story was going. Three paragraphs into the story, AJ got up from the typewriter, grinned maliciously and said, "Take it."

Take it?! Jesus, I didn't even know what it *was*, much less where to take it. But AJ had given me some clues, and so I went from there. From the beginning of the fourth paragraph to the line, "Up above them, just past the peak of the Great Mountain, fire split the sky." Then I got up, grinned even more maliciously (thinking I'd put him in an inescapable bind) and said, "Take it."

And so, my children, so it went, lickety-clickety and tickety-poo, on into the night, with Uncle Harlan and Uncle Ayjay alternating and trying to mess one another over. Finally, it got finished, don't ask me how.

There was a last line, typed by Ayjay, and I remember we both looked at it somewhat jaundicedly. We weren't happy with it. About a week later, when I did the rctype, I stopped short at the last line, and stared at it balefully. Finally, after considering and rejecting about a hundred possibilities in the space of a few minutes—all great writers think this fast—I hit on the ending you will find herein, and I typed it. Then I called Ayjay and told him what I'd done. He laughed and said it seemed right.

Ayjay and I have grown apart in many ways since the night we wrote "Wonderbird" at that noisy party, and today the men whose names you find on that story are only remotely connected to the men who wrote it. I dedicated my first novel to Ayjay, for what he had done for me; I wish things had not happened as they did for us, for our friendship, so that the debt would not have been so easily discharged. But they did, and it was, and now we're all three umbilically detached from each other ... Ayjay, me, and Dave Ish.

Fate, you monster, you're a real clown.

Wonderbird

Time and again the fire had burned down in the fireplace-bowl, and the night had come too close. The cave had flickered dully with the dying light of the fire, and they had shivered.

Skilton had cuffed the younglings out into the edge of the dark, to glean the fallen dead arms of the trees, to bring the fire to life again. But the younglings were awkward, and slow, and fearful of the waiting night. And the fuel was scanty. The darkness was close, and death with it. As emcee of the tribe, Skilton had been forced to use ruthlessness to spur them outward.

We should never have come into this place, Skilton thought. *We should have stayed in the valleys of our birth, where the trees are many and the death is thin.*

His thoughts were abruptly interrupted by an answering, inquiring thought from Lahr, one of the lesser members of the tribe.

But, emcee, why have *we come to this place?*

Skilton's massive head turned on my hairy neck, and he stared deeply into the wide, double-pupiled eyes of Lahr. *It is the Time of the Prophecy*, he answered almost angrily. They were supposed to know that. Things were different in the tribe today. Before, there were many strytemin, who would ask him intelligent questions, such as *Why does a hulfee cross the forest track?* or *Who was that she-tribe-member I sensed you with the past darkening?*

285

But now many of the old ones had had the death thicken in them, and they had gone away. The younglings were impudent, and their religion was a small thing to them.

But how do you know this is the Time of Prophecy? Lahr insisted. He scratched his long muzzle with his right second paw.

Skilton rose up in wrath, and towered over the smaller triber. *Fool!* he thought violently. *Don't you remember the words:* "Never worry and never fear, your boy Alfie Gunsel's here! I'll be back when the moons climb behind the clouds!" *This is that Time. This is the Time when the five moons have gone to counsel behind the swirlers, and the Performances will begin anew. The Lams will play the Palace once more!*

His thoughts had risen in violence as he had gone on, and now the words reverberated in the heads of the tribe. Skilton and his religion! They believed, of course, but, ah, well . . .

He didn't have to go *this* far: drag them from their burrows and send them halfway across the Palace to this spot of desolation on the edge of the silver-sanded plain and the Great Mountain.

But . . . they were trapped here by the dark, and it was too late for second thoughts. They would have to wait out Skilton's time and madness, till he realized the old religion was hoax, and there was no Time of the Prophecy.

Up above them, just past the peak of the Great Mountain, fire split the sky.

The darkness shuddered, and Skilton leaped to his feet, staring.

Above the mountain, a shiny bird was glowing. Golden, thundering, flickering, shuddering, the Wonderbird beat its way downward on its blazoned wings. And Skilton saw the dark turn into light, the death retreat before the beat of heated wings, and then the younglings were huddled behind him as he lifted his thoughts in prayer. In a moment the rest of the tribe had murmured *We believe, we believe!* in their minds, and were joining him in the singing chords of the Tophatt ritual.

June; the tune I croon to spoon—
A loon too gooney in the Moon
Light—
you.
Is only lonely in this homely
Phoney though baloney may be
Bright—
Blue
mood.

They huddled on their triple-jointed knees a few moments more, letting the harmony tingle away in their minds, then Skilton was up and running. Again, the younglings were huddled behind him as he ran away from the cave, and the needless fire, toward the rocking Wonderbird.

Skilton's switch-antennae rose and quivered as he homed in on the Wonderbird. He thought a spark at the younglings, for they had always believed in him. The older tribers he left to their own resources—they would find the Wonderbird in time.

Hurry! This is the Time we have waited to witness!

And the younglings spurred themselves, their eight triple-jointed legs spinning beneath them as they strove to keep up with the old emcee. Somehow, he had drawn a reserve of sudden energy for the task, and was even outloping them. They left the rest of the tribe behind quickly.

They covered the moss-ground rapidly, moved toward the silver-sanded plain. Long, loping strides, and the Wonderbird came closer.

Skilton brought them to a halt at the edge of the silver-sanded plain. He looked back, far up the slope of the foothills and he saw the moving dots of the rest of the tribe. He would not wait for them—let them arrive in their own time. *He* had been true to the Lams, and he would be their first greeter. He would become their aide ... and all the long years of belief would be paid back in full measure.

Yet, he did not venture onto the silver-sanded plain.

There was no sense being foolhardy about this.

The Time! Yes; but perhaps not as they had been told in the Prophecy. Perhaps it might be different, the Prophecy and its meaning garbled by time. He must deal with caution.

Was he not emcee of the tribe?

The Wonderbird lay there, its many-colored flesh flickering. Blue, red, gold, amber, back to gold, and flowing, always flowing. Then . . .

Sput! Peeeee-*op*!

Little bunches of many-colored brightness erupted from the Wonderbird's skin.

It continued for a few minutes, and suddenly the skin of the Wonderbird sucked inward and a round hole appeared. A black hole, from which a long thing extended, that went down to the silver sands.

Then a—a—*thing?* leaped out of the Wonderbird, ran down the long extended thing, and stood on the silver sands, with its paws on its hips, staring at the Wonderbird.

"Goddam, stinkin', miserable electrical system!" the thing exploded. The words were in the air.

Skilton's antennae spun aloft. In the air? Not in the head, like the tribe's thoughts, but on the air, like the screams of the ignorant hulfee they cut and ate? In the air? Yes, by Kan-Tor! In the air. This thing was not of their world, not of the Telling of the Prophecy, this was not even of the dreams that stole warmly in the night. This was . . . strange. He could thought-pluck no word that meant more. Strange. Gleez-Son!

The thing was ripping a vine from a hole in the skin of the Wonderbird. Skilton tuned in on the thing's mind, and there *were* thoughts! In addition to the sounds in the air, there were thoughts. How strange.

He knew at once the vine was a "master electrical connection to the power banks of the skin displays" and the hole was a "repair cubby" but he could not decide what they were for. But they had to be for something, since he remembered the prime Lewus rule: Always build to your point. Never miss a step. Never do anything meaningless, and then hit 'em with the boffola!

The thing closed a piece of skin *over* the skin, and the popping, erupting, noisy clash of exploding colors ceased.

"That oughtta fix the goddam thing," the thing said, looking with an odd expression at the skin. He radiated momentary contentment.

What? thought the secondary youngling, a calf-pup named Culonah.

Silence, Impertinence! Skilton tossed back instantly, scathingly. *This is a blessed Lam! Never doubt them, never question them, never let your thoughts rise in objection, for they are all powerful and may strike you. Death will thicken in your tongue, if you do not heed what I say!*

But—Skilton . . .

Silence, youngling! Do you want me to give you the Bird?

The Wonderbird?

THE Bird, fool!

The youngling retreated, cringing.

Skilton's words were brave, and trusting of the Lams. Yet his thoughts could not help but be colored with doubt. He fought to submerge these unworthy feelings—the younglings must never doubt for an instant. If they did, the Performances would never come again. He was not quite certain what the Performances were—but they boasted a golden age for everyone on The Palace. He must deep-thrust his unworthy feelings, both for himself, for the younglings, and for the doubting, corroded-minded older tribers loping down the foothills toward them.

He looked back at the Wonderbird, as a blast of thought and sound struck him.

The thing was leaning through the skin of the Wonderbird, at the top of the reaching thing that stretched to the sand. He was calling—words still in the air . . .

"Marge! Yo, Marge! Come on out; we got us an audience, awreddy!"

He turned and looked back over his shoulder at Skilton and the calf-pups. Skilton knew it was his head, knew it was his shoulder, simply enough. The thing thought.

Then why the words in the air?

Another thing came from the Wonderbird. It was a she; the first thing identified it as a she. She stopped at the top of the reaching thing (her thoughts called it a ramp) and looked at the flickering, color-changing skin.

She looked at the odd squiggles that formed the shapes:

MARGE AND ANDY PETERBOB!
COMEDIANS EXTRAORDINAIRE!

and in smaller squiggles ...

HAVE TUX, TRAVEL

She opened her mouth wide (yawn, the first thing thought it). She scratched with one of her two paws at the space under her left arm. "Fix it?" she asked.

"What the hell's it look like?" he answered.

"Cute, cute. Alla time with the wide-eyed, wise answers." Her face grew annoyed—her *thoughts* grew annoyed. "Where's the marks?"

The first thing pointed toward Skilton and the calf-pups on the edge of the plain.

"There they be, me sweet young pretty. There they be."

She let her eyes follow his hand. Her eyes grew larger.

"Them? Them things? *That's* what we're gonna play to?"

He shrugged. "We got any better?"

"You use the civilcometer? Check, if there's any culture?"

He nodded. "Not a trace of a city. If there's life here, that's it."

She let her tongue lick her lower lip. "You sure this is the planet?"

He pulled a sheaf of odd, thin skin from a hole in his own skin, and unfolded it. He ran a finger down a column, said to her "The record says a show-ship came by here in '27 ... gave three hundred consecutive performances. Carted off a whole shipful of raw *sogoth* fiber. They called the place The Palace. Must be ... only planet on these co-ords."

She gave him a rueful look as he folded the skin away into his own baggy hide.

"I ain't doing my act for them shaggy lap-dogs!"

"Aw, Marge, for Chrissakes, we done our act before worse than this. Them three-eyed slugs on Deepassa ... or them little spike-balls on Garrity's Hell ... or them ..."

She cut him off with a wave of her hand, sharp and final. "No!"

"Aw, Marge, for Chrissakes, you gotta at least test 'em. You gotta see if maybe they ain't intelligent."

She screwed her face up horribly. "Take a look at the damned things ... you can *see* they ain't nothin' but eight-legged mutts!"

At this point, Skilton felt things had advanced poorly enough. He sensed the rest of the tribe loping in behind them. Now was the moment for him to make his appeal to his gods, to the Lams who had come at last.

All the years of waiting and believing, of suffering the abuse of those who were unfaithful, were about to reach fruition. He would be the chosen of these great god Lams.

He let words float on the air.

The bellow welled up in his throat, coursed through his amplifier-baffle vocal cords, and erupted in the dusk.

"Bah-*rooooooooooooooo!*"

The she-thing leaped off the top of the ramp, came back down trembling, her eyes even larger.

"Ta hell with you," she squawked oddly, "that goddam thing wants me for supper. Uh-uh. Goo' bye!"

The first thing was turned toward Skilton, also. His eyes were as large as the she's. His mouth fluttered. But his thoughts said they must stay.

"But, look, Marge honey, you *gotta* ... don't let a little moan like that bother ya ... uh ... we're out *this* far, honey, we gotta bring *somethin'* back . . . pay the costs, you know . . ."

She started to say something, then her thoughts said: *What's the use? I'm gettin' the hell outta here!*

"Honey . . . it's been a real slack season, we *gotta* . . ."

She reached inside the Wonderbird's skin, pulled out a weird square thing, and threw it at the man-thing. It hit him on the head.

"God*damn* it, Marge, why'd ya toss that thing at me? You know it's part of the last borrow from that library-ship! It ain't ours! Aw, come on, Marge! We *gotta* . . ."

"We don't gotta do nothin'! And if you don't wanna get left standin' right there with egg on ya kisser, ya better haul-ass in here and help me blast! I wanna go!"

She stared at him hard for a moment, casting strange looks every few seconds at Skilton and the group of younglings. As she did, the rest of the tribe appeared out of the foothills and fell hushed behind the emcee.

"Yaarghhh!" she bellowed, till it made Skilton's antennae twitch. Then she bolted inside the Wonderbird, waving her arms in the air.

The man-thing cursed, and looked over his shoulder. When he saw the group on the moss-edge of the sanded plain had grown, his mouth flapped oddly and he stumbled clankingly up the ramp.

His thoughts flowed and boiled in his head, the words rolled and burned in the air.

Then he got into the Wonderbird, and they heard the sound of sounds on sounds, and the skin fastened tight to the rest of the skin.

They watched as the flickering colors dimmed, and the beating noises burst from the back of the Wonderbird. They let the primary lids slide over their eyes as the fire ripped from the Wonderbird. And then they watched terrified as it swept into the air, and left.

It blossomed and flickered and ticked and colored its way back over the Great Mountain, up toward the swirlers, and out of sight.

Skilton watched it with mixed feelings.

It was going, and with it was going the entire core of his beliefs. His religion, his thoughts, his very being had been sundered by the dusk's happenings.

The Lams were *not* gods. They had *not* come again to do the Performances. They would *not* play The Palace again.

This was the end.

He kept the thoughts below scanning-level, so the tribe might not know what he thought. He felt their unease, and they waited for his explanation. How could he tell them the truth; that there *was* no Performance, and that all the years of waiting for the Time of the Prophecy were in vain. How could he tell them he had been deceived? How? How?

He began to summon the thoughts from their lower-level home, when he stopped, and forced them back down, keeping the surface of his mind clear and untroubled.

He saw the square thing on the silver-sanded plain, fallen where the man-thing had let it fall; fallen where the she had thrown it. Perhaps in that square thing there might be a clue to help him. A sign, a symbol, an omen to reinstate his belief in the Lams once more.

Skilton? The thoughts swam toward him from the awed tribe.

Skilton, tell us, oh worthy and far-seeing emcee, what does all this mean? Was this the Performance?

He could only answer: *Come.*

And they followed him . . .

Followed him off the moss-ground, away from the Great Mountain, onto the silver-sanded plain, and toward the square thing. There they stopped and looked and thought.

After a great long while, they asked Skilton, and he told them, and they knew it was true, for they could see the square thing.

After a great while, they knew.

There *was* another thing. This was *not* the end. There would be a new beginning.

A new way of life . . . a new era.

When they got back to the home of their births, they would discard the old Tophatt rituals, and the Jomillr-jowks, and the new life would flower for them —and this time there would be no doubting, for they had all seen the Wonderbird.

Skilton lowered his massive head and clamped the square thing in his toothless mouth. He trotted back toward the foothills and the Great Mountain.

The younglings followed quickly, and the tribe followed them, and there were no laggards, for they were all trying to reason out the meaning of the squiggles on the new Truth.

The squiggles that declared the new religion.

The squiggles that said:

The Complete Works of the
Marquis de Sade
ILLUSTRATED

Robert Silverberg and Harlan Ellison

THE
SONG
THE
ZOMBIE
SANG

INTRODUCTION

It isn't so much *how* or *why* this one got written, but what happened to it *after* it got written.

I've known Silverberg longer than all but one or two of my friends. He was the first guy I saw when I came into New York, and the first to put me up till I got a place to stay upon returning, a year later. We had only collaborated once before, in all those years—which are rapidly approaching twenty—a mystery story called "Ship-Shape Payoff" for one of the *Manhunt*-style magazines, back in the mid-fifties. But it would have been impossible to do this book without a collaboration by myself and Bob. At least, for me it would have been impossible.

So here's how it came to be.

I was teaching writing at a major college workshop last year (not Clarion, in this case), and one of the guest lecturers, a magazine writer whose work I'd admired for decades, was also on the staff with me. But he was not the glamorous jet-setter his past glories had led me to expect. He was a tired, old man, with too much booze in him and too many bad relationships behind him, and though he was smashed drunk from morning to night, falling down drunk so that he could literally not keep down food, every morning he dragged himself to one of the three typewriters he had ranked around the dorm room where he was billeted, and he would peck out a few words on this or that article. It was a pathetic performance, and it haunted me for months. Some time later, on a business trip to New York, I recounted the story to Bob and Bobbie, his wife, and said it was as though he was a zombie, that he continued writing only as a reflex, the way a frog's leg jumps when it receives a galvanic shock, that he might as well be dead and stored in a vault except when he had to write.

And from that came the idea of a great artist who has died, who is brought back when he has to perform.

Bob took the initial idea, altered it, and wrote a basic plot. Which he sent to me in L.A. I wrote the first draft, leaving small holes where Bob's specific scientific and musicological information was better than mine. He wrote the final draft. I did a few noodles here and there. It was finished.

We talked long distance and I said I thought it would go at either *McCall's* (which, at that time, was interested in buying mainstreamish science fiction) or *Cosmopolitan,* neither one of which slicks either of us had ever sold.

Bob hectored me mercilessly for my *naïveté.* "They aren't going to buy it, so why bother?" he said. "Let's sell it to *Galaxy* and take the 4¢ a word and run. At least it's $220 we can split."

I persisted, telling him that since I run the universe, it would sell. He shrugged, thinking me the fool, and though I couldn't see him or the shrug, I knew it was the same kind of shrug Bob has been shrugging about me since I was in high school in Cleveland.

But I sent it on to Bob Mills, my agent, and in short order *McCall's* bounced it. Then it went to Junius Adams, the fiction editor of *Cosmo.* Five minutes after Mills called me, several weeks later, to tell me that *Cosmo* was buying it for $1250, I rang up Bob and the conversation went like this:

"Bob? Harlan."

"Hello."

"I'm afraid we won't be able to sell, 'Zombie' to *Knight Magazine* for the second serial money."

"Why? Is *Galaxy's* pub date too close to the book?"

"No, huh-uh. Galaxy won't be taking it, either."

He was silent. He didn't seem happy. Then, "How come?"

"Because *Cosmo* just bought it for twelve hundred and fifty, you asshole, *that's* why!"

Telephonically, across a continent, I had the lifetime thrill of hearing Silverberg's jaw drop. He was without words, and the thrill was mine.

Finally, in a very soft voice, he said, "Jesus, maybe you *do* run the universe."

Now understand that it was through no lack of faith in the story, or of *Cosmo*'s editorial perceptivity, that Bob had felt the story would not sell at that market. It was a combination of *our* attitudes and *Cosmo*'s history of never having published an sf short story (though they've done a few abridged versions of sf novels that toyed with the mainstream). The magazine is an important woman's slick, it had *never* published what readers of sf would call straight non-Ira Levin sf, and *we* had never moved in that sort of arena. So it was wholly unexpected. For Bob. Not for me. I knew the instant we finished writing the story that Rhoda and Nils Bekh were right for *Cosmo;* they just *felt* right.

Sometimes they come out like that.

The Song
the Zombie Sang

From the Fourth Balcony of the Los Angeles Music Center the stage was little more than a brilliant blur of constantly changing chromatics—stabs of bright green, looping whorls of crimson. But Rhoda preferred to sit up there. She had no use for the Golden Horseshoe seats, buoyed on their grab-grav plates, bobbling loosely just beyond the fluted lip of the stage. Down there the sound flew off, flew up and away, carried by the remarkable acoustics of the Center's Takamuri dome. The colors were important, but it was the sound that really mattered, the patterns of resonance bursting from the hundred quivering outputs of the ultracembalo.

And if you sat below, you had the vibrations of the people down there—

She was hardly naïve enough to think that the poverty that sent students up to the top was more ennobling than the wealth that permitted access to a Horseshoe; yet even though she had never actually sat through an entire concert down there, she could not deny that music heard from the fourth balcony was purer, more affecting, lasted longer in the memory. Perhaps it *was* the vibrations of the rich.

Arms folded on the railing of the balcony, she stared down at the rippling play of colors that washed the sprawling proscenium. Dimly she was aware that the man at her side was saying something. Somehow responding didn't seem important. Finally he nudged her, and she turned to him. A faint, mechanical smile crossed her face. "What is it, Laddy?"

Ladislas Jirasek mournfully extended a chocolate bar. Its end was ragged from having been nibbled: "Man cannot live by Bekh alone," he said.

"No, thanks, Laddy." She touched his hand lightly.

"What do you see down there?"

"Colors. That's all."

"No music of the spheres? No insight into the truths of your art?"

"You promised not to make fun of me."

He slumped back in his seat. "I'm sorry. I forget sometimes."

"Please, Laddy. If it's the liaison thing that's bothering you, I—"

"I didn't say a word about liaison, did I?"

"It was in your tone. You were starting to feel sorry for yourself. Please don't. You know I hate it when you start dumping guilt on me."

He had sought an official liaison with her for months, almost since the day they had met in Contrapuntal 301. He had been fascinated by her, amused by her, and finally had fallen quite hopelessly in love with her. Still she kept just beyond his reach. He had had her, but had never possessed her. Because he did feel sorry for himself, and she knew it, and the knowledge put him, for her, forever in the category of men who were simply not for long-term liaison.

She stared down past the railing. Waiting. Taut. A slim girl, honey-colored hair, eyes the lightest gray, almost the shade of aluminum. Her fingers lightly curved as if about to pounce on a keyboard. Music uncoiling eternally in her head.

"They say Bekh was brilliant in Stuttgart last week," Jirasek said hopefully.

"He did the Kreutzer?"

"And Timijian's Sixth and *The Knife* and some Scartti."

"Which?"

"I don't know. I don't remember what they said. But he

got a ten-minute standing ovation, and *Der Musikant* said
they hadn't heard such precise ornamentation since—"

The houselights dimmed.

"He's coming," Rhoda said, leaning forward. Jirasek
slumped back and gnawed the chocolate bar down to its
wrapper.

Coming out of it was always gray. The color of aluminum. He knew the charging was over, knew he'd been un-
packed, knew when he opened his eyes that he would be
at stage right, and there would be a grip ready to roll the
ultracembalo's input console onstage, and the filament
gloves would be in his right-hand jacket pocket. And the
taste of sand on his tongue, and the gray fog of resurrec-
tion in his mind.

Nils Bekh put off opening his eyes.

Stuttgart had been a disaster. Only he knew how much
of a disaster. *Timi would have known*, he thought. *He
would have come up out of the audience during the scherzo, and he would have ripped the gloves off my hands,
and he would have cursed me for killing his vision.* And
later they would have gone to drink the dark, nutty beer
together. But Timijian was dead. *Died in '20*, Bekh told
himself. *Five years before me.*

*I'll keep my eyes closed, I'll dampen the breathing. Will
the lungs to suck more shallowly, the bellows to vibrate
rather than howl with winds. And they'll think I'm malfunctioning, that the zombianic response wasn't triggered
this time. That I'm still dead, really dead, not—*

"Mr. Bekh."

He opened his eyes.

The stage manager was a thug. He recognized the type.
Stippling of unshaved beard. Crumpled cuffs. Latent ho-
mosexuality. Tyrant to everyone backstage except, perhaps, the chorus boys in the revivals of Romberg and
Friml confections.

"I've known men to develop diabetes just catching a
matinee," Bekh said.

"What's that? I don't understand."

Bekh waved it away. "Nothing. Forget it. How's the
house?"

"Very nice, Mr. Bekh. The houselights are down. We're ready."

Bekh reached into his right-hand jacket pocket and removed the thin electronic gloves sparkling with their rows of minisensors and pressors. He pulled the right glove tight, smoothing all wrinkles. The material clung like a second skin. "If you please," he said. The grip rolled the console onstage, positioned it, locked it down with the dogging pedals, and hurried offstage left through the curtains.

Now Bekh strolled out slowly. Moving with great care: tubes of glittering fluids ran through his calves and thighs, and if he walked too fast the hydrostatic balance was disturbed and the nutrients didn't get to his brain. The fragility of the perambulating dead was a nuisance, one among many. When he reached the grab-grav plate he signalled the stage manager. The thug gave the sign to the panelman, who passed his fingers over the color-coded keys, and the grab-grav plate rose slowly, majestically. Up through the floor of the stage went Nils Bekh. As he emerged, the chromatics keyed sympathetic vibrations in the audience, and they began to applaud.

He stood silently, head slightly bowed, accepting their greeting. A bubble of gas ran painfully through his back and burst near his spine. His lower lip twitched slightly. He suppressed the movement. Then he stepped off the plate, walked to the console, and began pulling on the other glove.

He was a tall, elegant man, very pale, with harsh brooding cheekbones and a craggy, massive nose that dominated the flower-gentle eyes, the thin mouth. He looked properly romantic. An important artistic asset, they told him when he was starting out, a million years ago.

As he pulled and smoothed the other glove, he heard the whispering. When one has died, one's hearing becomes terribly acute. It made listening to one's own performances that much more painful. But he knew what the whispers were all about. Out there someone was saying to his wife:

"Of course he doesn't *look* like a zombie. They kept him in cold till they had the techniques. *Then* they wired him and juiced him and brought him back."

And the wife would say, "How does it work, how does he keep coming back to life, what is it?"

And the husband would lean far over on the arm of his chair, resting his elbow, placing the palm of his hand in front of his mouth and looking warily around to be certain that no one would overhear the blurred inaccuracies he was about to utter. And he would try to tell his wife about the residual electric charge of the brain cells, the persistence of the motor responses after death, the lingering mechanical vitality on which they had seized. In vague and rambling terms he would speak of the built-in life-support system that keeps the brain flushed with necessary fluids. The surrogate hormones, the chemicals that take the place of blood. "You know how they stick an electric wire up a frog's leg, when they cut it off. Okay. Well, when the leg jerks, they call that a galvanic response. Now if you can get a whole *man* to jerk when you put a current through him—not really jerking. I mean that he walks around, he can play his instrument—"

"Can he think too?"

"I suppose. I don't know. The brain's intact. They don't let it decay. What they do, they use every part of the body for its mechanical function—the heart's a pump, the lungs are bellows—and they wire in a bunch of contacts and leads, and then there's a kind of twitch, an artificial burst of life—of course, they can keep it going only five, six hours, then the fatigue-poisons start to pile up and clog the lines—but that's long enough for a concert, anyway—"

"So what they're really doing is they take a man's brain, and they keep it alive by using his own body as the life-support machine," the wife says brightly. "Is that it? Instead of putting him into some kind of box, they keep him in his own skull, and do all the machinery inside his body—"

"That's it. That's it exactly, more or less. More or less."

Bekh ignored the whispers. He had heard them all hundreds of times before. In New York and Beirut, in Hanoi and Knossos, in Kenyatta and Paris. How fascinated they were. Did they come for the music, or to see the dead man walk around?

He sat down on the player's ledge in front of the console, and laid his hands along the metal fibers. A deep breath: old habit, superfluous, inescapable. The fingers already twitching. The pressors seeking the keys. Under the close-cropped gray hair, the synapses clicking like relays. Here, now. Timijian's Ninth Sonata. Let it soar. Bekh closed his eyes and put his shoulders into his work, and from the ring of outputs overhead came the proper roaring tones. There. It has begun. Easily, lightly, Bekh rang in the harmonics, got the sympathetic pipes vibrating, built up the texture of sound. He had not played the Ninth for two years. Vienna. How long is two years? It seemed hours ago. He still heard the reverberations. And duplicated them exactly; this performance differed from the last one no more than one playing of a recording differs from another. An image sprang into his mind: a glistening sonic cube sitting at the console in place of a man. Why do they need me, when they could put a cube in the slot and have the same thing at less expense? And I could rest. And I could rest. There. Keying in the subsonics. This wonderful instrument! What if Bach had known it? Beethoven? To hold a whole world in your fingertips. The entire spectrum of sound, and the colors, too, and more: hitting the audience in a dozen senses at once. Of course, the music is what matters. The frozen, unchanging music. The pattern of sounds emerging now as always, now as he had played it at the premiere in '19. Timijian's last work. Decibel by decibel, a reconstruction of my own performance. And look at them out there. Awed. Loving. Bekh felt tremors in his elbows; too tense, the nerves betraying him. He made the necessary compensations. Hearing the thunder reverberating from the fourth balcony. What is this music all about? Do I in fact understand any of it? Does the sonic cube comprehend the B Minor Mass that is recorded within itself? Does the amplifier understand the symphony it amplifies? Bekh smiled. Closed his eyes. The shoulders surging, the wrists supple. Two hours to go. Then they let me sleep again. Is it fifteen years, now? Awaken, perform, sleep. And the adoring public cooing at me. The women who would love to give themselves to me. Necrophiliacs? How could they even want to touch me? The dryness of the tomb on my skin. Once there were women, yes, Lord, yes! Once. Once there was life, too. Bekh leaned back and swept forward. The old virtuoso swoop; brings down the house. The chill in

their spines. Now the sound builds toward the end of the
first movement. Yes, yes, so. Bekh opened the topmost
bank of outputs and heard the audience respond, everyone
sitting up suddenly as the new smash of sound cracked
across the air. Good old Timi: a wonderful sense of the
theatrical. Up. Up. Knock them back in their seats. He
smiled with satisfaction at his own effects. And then the
sense of emptiness. Sound for its own sake. Is this what
music means? Is this a masterpiece? I know nothing any
more. How tired I am of playing for them. Will they applaud? Yes, and stamp their feet and congratulate one another on having been lucky enough to hear me tonight.
And what do they know? What do I know. I am dead. I
am nothing. I am nothing. With a demonic two-handed
plunge he hammered out the final fugal screams of the
first movement.

Weatherex had programmed mist, and somehow it fit
Rhoda's mood. They stood on the glass landscape that
swept down from the Music Center, and Jirasek offered
her the pipe. She shook her head absently, thinking of
other things. "I have a pastille," she said.

"What do you say we look up Inez and Treat, see if
they want to get something to eat?"

She didn't answer.

"Rhoda?"

"Will you excuse me, Laddy? I think I want to be all by
myself for a while."

He slipped the pipe into his pocket and turned to her.
She was looking through him as if he were no less glass
than the scene surrounding them. Taking her hands in his
own, he said, "Rhoda, I just don't understand. You won't
even give me time to find the words."

"Laddy—"

"No. This time I'll have my say. Don't pull away. Don't
retreat into that little world of yours, with your half-smiles
and your faraway looks."

"I want to think about the music."

"There's more to life than music, Rhoda. There has to
be. I've spent as many years as you working inside my
head, working to create something. You're better than I
am, you're maybe better than anyone I've ever heard,

maybe even better than Bekh some day. Fine: you're a great artist. But is that all? There's something more. It's idiocy to make your art your religion, your whole existence."

"Why are you doing this to me?"

"Because I love you."

"That's an explanation, not an excuse. Let me go. Laddy. Please."

"Rhoda, art doesn't mean a damn thing if it's just craft, if it's just rote and technique and formulas. It doesn't mean anything if there isn't love behind it, and caring, and commitment to life. You deny all that. You split yourself and smother the part that fires the art . . ."

He stopped abruptly. It was not the sort of speech a man could deliver without realizing, quickly, crushingly, how sententious and treacly it sounded. He dropped her hands. "I'll be at Treat's, if you want to see me later." He turned and walk away into the shivering reflective night.

Rhoda watched him go. She suspected there were things she should have said. But she hadn't said them. He disappeared. Turning, she stared up at the overwhelming bulk of the Music Center, and began slowly to walk toward it.

"Maestro, you were exquisite tonight," the pekinese woman said in the Green Room. "Golden," added the bullfrog sycophant. "A joy. I cried, really cried," trilled the birds. Nutrients bubbled in his chest. He could feel valves flapping. He dipped his head, moved his hands, whispered thankyous. Staleness settled grittily behind his forehead. "Superb." "Unforgettable." "Incredible." Then they went away and he was left, as always, with the keepers. The man from the corporation that owned him, the stage manager, the packers, the electrician. "Perhaps it's time," said the corporation man, smoothing his mustache lightly. He had learned to be delicate with the zombie.

Bekh sighed and nodded. They turned him off.

"Want to get something to eat first?" the electrician said. He yawned. It had been a long tour, late nights, meals in jetports, steep angles of ascent and rapid re-entries.

The corporation man nodded. "All right. We can leave

him here for a while. I'll put him on standby." He touched a switch.

The lights went off in banks, one by one. Only the nightlights remained for the corporation man and the electrician, for their return, for their final packing.

The Music Center shut down.

In the bowels of the self-contained system the dust-eaters and a dozen other species of cleanup machines began stirring, humming softly.

In the fourth balcony, a shadow moved. Rhoda worked her way toward the downslide, emerging in the center aisle of the orchestra, into the Horseshoe, around the pit, and onto the stage. She went to the console and let her hands rest an inch above the keys. Closing her eyes, catching her breath. I will begin my concert with the Timijian Ninth Sonata for Unaccompanied Ultracembalo. A light patter of applause, gathering force, now tempestuous. Waiting. The fingers descending. The world alive with her music. Fires and tears, joy, radiance. All of them caught in the spell. How miraculous. How wonderfully she plays. Looking out into the darkness, hearing in her tingling mind the terrible echoes of the silence. Thank you. Thank you all so much. Her eyes moist. Moving away from the console. The flow of fantasy ebbing.

She went on into the dressing room and stood just within the doorway, staring across the room at the corpse of Nils Bekh in the sustaining chamber, his eyes closed, his chest still, his hands relaxed at his sides. She could see the faintest bulge in his right jacket pocket where the thin gloves lay, fingers folded together.

Then she moved close to him, looked down into his face, and touched his cheek. His beard never grew. His skin was cool and satiny, a peculiarly feminine texture. Strangely, through the silence, she remembered the sinuous melody of the *Liebestod*, that greatest of all laments, and rather than the great sadness the passage always brought to her, she felt herself taken by anger. Gripped by frustration and disappointment, choked by betrayal, caught in a seizure of violence. She wanted to rake the pudding-smooth skin of his face with her nails. She wanted to pummel him. Deafen him with screams. Destroy him.

For the lie. For the lies, the many lies, the unending flow of lying notes, the lies of his life after death.

Her trembling hand hovered by the side of the chamber. Is this the switch?

She turned him on.

He came out of it. Eyes closed. Rising through a universe the color of aluminum. Again, then. Again. He thought he would stand there a moment with eyes closed, collecting himself, before going onstage. It got harder and harder. The last time had been so bad. In Los Angeles, in that vast building, balcony upon balcony, thousands of blank faces, the ultracembalo such a masterpiece of construction. He had opened the concert with Timi's Ninth. So dreadful. A sluggish performance, note-perfect, the tempi flawless, and yet sluggish, empty, shallow. And tonight it would happen again. Shamble out on stage, don the gloves, go through the dreary routine of recreating the greatness of Nils Bekh.

His audience, his adoring followers. How he hated them! How he longed to turn on them and denounce them for what they had done to him. Schnabel rested. Horowitz rested. Joachim rested. But for Bekh there was no rest. They had not allowed him to go. Oh, he could have refused to let them sustain him. But he had never been that strong. He had had strength for the loveless, lightless years of living with his music, yes. For that there had never been enough time. Strong was what he had had to be. To come from where he had been, to learn what had to be learned, to keep his skills once they were his. Yes. But in dealing with people, in speaking out, in asserting himself ... in short, having courage ... no, there had been very little of that. He had lost Dorothea, he had acceded to Wizmer's plans, he had borne the insults Lisbeth and Neil and Cosh—ah, gee, Cosh, was he still alive?—the insults they had used to keep him tied to them, for better or worse, always worse. So he had gone with them, done their bidding, never availed himself of his strength—if in fact there was strength of that sort buried somewhere in him—and in the end even Sharon had despised him.

So how could he go to the edge of the stage, stand there in the full glare of the lights and tell them what they were? Ghouls. Selfish ghouls. As dead as he was, but in a different way. Unfeeling, hollow.

But if he could! If he could just once outwit the corporation man, he would throw himself forward and he would shout—

Pain. A stinging pain in his cheek. His head jolted back; the tiny pipes in his neck protested. The sound of flesh on flesh echoed in his mind. Startled, he opened his eyes. A girl before him. The color of aluminum, her eyes. A young face. Fierce. Thin lips tightly clamped. Nostrils flaring. Why is she so angry? She was raising her hand to slap him again. He threw his hands up, wrists crossed, palms forward, to protect his eyes. The second blow landed more heavily than the first. Were delicate things shattering within his reconstructed body?

The look on her face! She hated him.

She slapped him a third time. He peered out between his fingers, astonished by the vehemence of her eyes. And felt the flooding pain, and felt the hate, and felt a terribly wonderful sense of life for just that one moment. Then he remembered too much, and he stopped her.

He could see as he grabbed her swinging hand that she found his strength improbable. Fifteen years a zombie, moving and living for only seven hundred four days of that time. Still, he was fully operable, fully conditioned, fully muscled.

The girl winced. He released her and shoved her away. She was rubbing her wrist and staring at him silently, sullenly.

"If you don't like me," he asked, "why did you turn me on?"

"So I could tell you I know what a fraud you are. These others, the ones who applaud and grovel and suck up to you, they don't know, they have no idea, but I know. How can you do it? How can you have made such a disgusting spectacle of yourself?" She was shaking. "I heard you when I was a child," she said. "You changed my whole life. I'll never forget it. But I've heard you lately. Slick formulas, no real insight. Like a machine sitting at the console. A player piano. You know what player pianos were, Bekh. That's what you are."

He shrugged. Walking past her, he sat down and

glanced in the dressing-room mirror. He looked old and weary, the changeless face changing now. There was a flatness to his eyes. They were without sheen, without depths. An empty sky.

"Who are you?" he asked quietly. "How did you get in here?"

"Report me, go ahead. I don't care if I'm arrested. Someone had to say it. You're shameful! Walking around, pretending to make music—don't you see how awful it is? A performer is an interpretative artist, not just a machine for playing the notes. I shouldn't have to tell you that. An interpretative artist. Artist. Where's your art now? Do you see beyond the score? Do you grow from performance to performance?"

Suddenly he liked her very much. Despite her plainness, despite her hatred, despite himself. "You're a musician."

She let that pass.

"What do you play?" Then he smiled. "The ultracembalo, of course. And you must be very good."

"Better than you. Clearer, cleaner, deeper. Oh, God, what am I doing here? You *disgust* me."

"How can I keep on growing?" Bekh asked gently. "The dead don't grow."

Her tirade swept on, as if she hadn't heard. Telling him over and over how despicable he was, what a counterfeit of greatness. And then she halted in midsentence. Blinking, reddening, putting hands to lips. "Oh," she murmured, abashed, starting to weep. "Oh. *Oh!*"

She went silent.

It lasted a long time. She looked away, studied the walls, the mirror, her hands, her shoes. He watched her. Then, finally, she said, "What an arrogant little snot I am. What a cruel foolish bitch. I never stopped to think that you—that maybe—I just didn't think——" He thought she would run from him. "And you won't forgive me, will you? Why should you? I break in, I turn you on, I scream a lot of cruel nonsense at you——"

"It wasn't nonsense. It was all quite true, you know. Absolutely true." Then, softly, he said, "Break the machinery."

"Don't worry. I won't cause any more trouble for you. I'll go, now. I can't tell you how foolish I feel, haranguing you like that. A dumb little puritan puffed up with pride in her own art. Telling *you* that you don't measure up to my ideals. When I—"

"You didn't hear me. I asked you to break the machinery."

She looked at him in a new way, slightly out of focus. "What are you talking about?"

"To stop me. I want to be gone. Is that so hard to understand? You, of all people, should understand that. What you say is true, very very true. Can you put yourself where I am? A thing, not alive, not dead, just a thing, a tool, an implement that unfortunately thinks and remembers and wishes for release. Yes, a player piano. My life stopped and my art stopped, and I have nothing to belong to now, not even the art. For it's always the same. Always the same tones, the same reaches, the same heights. Pretending to make music, as you say. Pretending."

"But I can't—"

"Of course you can. Come, sit down, we'll discuss it. And you'll play for me."

"Play for you?"

He reached out his hand and she started to take it, then drew her hand back. "You'll have to play for me," he said quietly. "I can't let just anyone end me. That's a big, important thing, you see. Not just anyone. So you'll play for me." He got heavily to his feet. Thinking of Lisbeth, Sharon, Dorothea. Gone, all gone now. Only he, Bekh, left behind, some of him left behind, old bones, dried meat. Breath as stale as Egypt. Blood the color of pumice. Sounds devoid of tears and laughter. Just sounds.

He led the way, and she followed him, out onto the stage, where the console still stood uncrated. He gave her his gloves, saying. "I know they aren't yours. I'll take that into account. Do the best you can." She drew them on slowly, smoothing them.

She sat down at the console. He saw the fear in her face, and the ecstasy, also. Her fingers hovering over the keys. Pouncing. God, Timi's Ninth! The tones swelling and rising, and the fear going from her face. Yes. Yes. He would not have played it that way, but yes, just so. Timi's notes filtered through *her* soul. A striking interpretation. Perhaps she falters a little, but why not? The wrong gloves, no preparation, strange circumstances. And how beautifully she plays. The hall fills with sound. He ceases to listen as a critic might; he becomes part of the music. His own fingers moving, his muscles quivering, reaching for pedals and stops, activating the pressors. As if he plays through her. She goes on, soaring higher, losing the last of her nervousness. In full command. Not yet a finished artist but so good, so wonderfully good! Making the mighty instrument sing. Draining its full resources. Underscoring this, making that leaner. Oh, yes! He is in the music. It engulfs him. Can he cry? Do the tearducts still function? He can hardly bear it, it is so beautiful. He has forgotten, in all these years. He has not heard anyone else play for so long. Seven hundred four days. Out of the tomb. Bound up in his own meaningless performances. And now this. The rebirth of music. It was once like this all the time, the union of composer and instrument and performer, soul-wrenching, all-encompassing. For him. No longer. Eyes closed, he plays the movement through to its close by way of her body, her hands, her soul. When the sound dies away, he feels the good exhaustion that comes from total submission to the art.

"That's fine," he said, when the last silence was gone. "That was very lovely." A catch in his voice. His hands were still trembling; he was afraid to applaud.

He reached for her, and this time she took his hand. For a moment he held her cool fingers. Then he tugged gently, and she followed him back into the dressing room, and he lay down on the sofa, and he told her which mechanisms to break, after she turned him off, so he would feel no pain. Then he closed his eyes and waited.

"You'll just—go?" she asked.

"Quickly. Peacefully."

"I'm afraid. It's like murder."

"I'm dead," he said. "But not dead enough. You won't be killing anything. Do you remember how my playing sounded to you? Do you remember why I came here? Is there life in me?"

"I'm still afraid."

"I've earned my rest," he said. He opened his eyes and smiled. "It's all right. I like you." And, as she moved toward him, he said, "Thank you."

Then he closed his eyes again.

She turned him off.

Then she did as he had instructed her.

Picking her way past the wreckage of the sustaining chamber, she left the dressing room. She found her way out of the Music Center—out onto the glass landscape, under the singing stars, and she was crying for him.

Laddy. She wanted very much to find Laddy now. To talk to him. To tell him he was almost right about what he'd told her. Not entirely, but more than she had believed ... before. She went away from there. Smoothly, with songs yet to be sung.

And behind her, a great peace had settled. Unfinished, at last the symphony had wrung its last measure of strength and sorrow.

It did not matter what Weatherex said was the proper time for mist or rain or fog. Night, the stars, the songs were forever.

Keith Laumer and Harlan Ellison

STREET
SCENE

INTRODUCTION

It was in a hot and sticky little room at the Tom Quick Inn, in Milford, Pennsylvania, several years ago, that Keith and I wrote this story. We mutually love it. It is a Marx Bros. slugfest, with very little rhyme and less reason. It is intended as a guffaw, and if you laugh even once, we'll have done what we set out to do.

Keith and I were attendees, at the time, at the Milford SF Writers' Conference, and we did this story between sessions. I started it, and we wrote in alternate sections, much like the majority of stories in this book. But there was one major disagreement.

When we got to what I thought should be the place to taper the story off, neither Keith nor I could agree on an ending. I had one idea for a satisfactory solution, Keith had another. So we fought and argued and raged for hours, and finally . . . we compromised.

This story has two complete endings.

The first is mine, the second is Keith's. You can have either, neither or both. Or none of the above.

Galaxy published it with my ending, *Knight* published it with Keith's, and herewith are presented both, for the first time anywhere.

Street Scene

Very much like a dead bird, the pteranodon fell out of the sky at 4:18 of a Wednesday, fell whistling, end-over-end, landing squarely in the middle of Sixth Avenue and 47th Street. It fell flat-out, wings spread, and crushed a Mustang, two Cadillacs, a Buick Riviera, three VW's, the front end of a Peugeot, and a Greyline Tours sightseeing bus.

The fall of the beast killed eighty-seven people, but it was not that, precisely, that caught the attention of Will Kiley as he emerged from one of the small smut bookshops dotting Sixth Avenue, his parcel of paperbacks and photo sets showing Puerto Rican girls with unshaved armpits and spread thighs clutched to his side. Riley's attention was initially caught by the crashing shape as it shadowed the street, then by the crashing sound as the extinct creature impacted, and then by his recognition of the beast as not merely a pterodactyl, but specifically as a pteranodon, genus *ornithostoma*. Kiley, a third year student at Columbia University, majoring in Historical Geology, instantly recognized the osseous crest extending the skull to the rear in an effective counterweight, balancing the mass of the immense, bony. toothless beak.

Kiley observed this aspect of the beast in the dust-settling instant after the pteranodon, crashing, bounced, rose into the air amid a welter of automobile parts and crushed humans, hung there as though observing its own handiwork, and then slammed down again very near its original ground zero. One vast wing lay spread like a dusty, olive-gray tarpaulin over the still feebly struggling bodies of victims trapped beneath it; an edge fluttered as pocketed air escaped, bearing a pungent reek of reptilian juices. The other extended across 47th Street, sagging, warty leather stretched on thin bones like collapsed aluminum tubing, the fingered tip caressing a tarnished brick front adorned by a clustered trio of brazen spheres.

Sirens began keening everywhere. Screams rose up in the intersection as half-pinned, maimed survivors of the beast's tumble struggled to free themselves. From his doorway, Kiley noted at once that the beast was incredibly heavy, much heavier by a fantastic overage than any pterodactyl had a right to be. Aerodynamically a sport, the creatures had never weighed more than a hundred pounds, and eighty was closer to the average. But *this* thing had crushed a sight-seeing bus and something over a half dozen cars. It was many times longer and had a far greater wingspread than any pterodactyl ever exhumed as fossil. It was lying almost like an immense crucifix, its shaft of body heading uptown on Sixth Avenue, the beak pointing toward the Radio City Music Hall, its wings outspread as though waiting for Pilate's men to come and drive in the spikes, crosstown on 47th.

Kiley was torn between staying to watch what was certainly going to happen, or running back uptown to his mingy little room, to put the contents of his parcel to use.

At that moment, a group of fifteen Chassidic Rabbinical Seminary students adorned with *payess,* beards, long black overcoats so out-of-line for mid-August, and faintly redolent of the scent of Rappaport's *gefilte* fish, emerged from one of the diamond exchange shops, and seeing the dead beast lying in the street, began a loud and incomprehensible argument as to whether or not pteranodon was kosher.

"It flies . . . it's a chicken," said one.

"That makes it kosher," confirmed a second.

"Snake. It's a reptile," countered a third.

"Then most definitely, there should be no argument on this point, it's trayf!" concluded a fourth.

A florid, large-boned police officer of the midtown precinct, ran up from 45th Street, blowing his whistle, readying his book of parking tickets, and looking around for the owner of the dead beast. Spying an old man lounging against the side of a papaya juice stand, the cop hustled over and pointed an accusing finger.

"That your pterodactyl?"

The old man shook his head.

"You're sure?"

The old man began to tremble. "Honest to God. It ain't mine. Why'djoo always pick on me?"

" 'Cause you were the guy owned that big monkey we caught climbin' up the Empire State, that's why!"

"They never proved it!"

"I don't give a damn if they didn't. *I* knew you were the guy. I *knew* that big ape belonged to you!"

"Oh yeah, fuzz? *How'd* you know?"

"You were the only guy on the street with a seventy-five foot tambourine."

The lean, corsetted, hatted, rouge-on-bones young woman standing *au dessus* the soot-flecked plate-glass display window of the truss and artificial limb shop on the southwest corner of the blocked intersection compared the watch strapped to her narrow wrist with the oversized timepiece dangling over the sidewalk across the street. Her lips compressed into a hard line like a surgery scar; for the tenth time in thirty seconds she scanned the pavement to left and right, strode a few impatient steps to peer past the upjutting elbow of the pteranodon blocking her view. Still no Melville. Melville wasn't coming. Stood up. Her. Lilya. Stood up. By a creep like Melville, which she was doing him the biggest favor of his life just to go out with him, the slob, and he's got the undiluted crust to not show, and after she skipped lunch just to have room for a lousy dinner which he probably would've suggested Nedick's anyway—

A large, slow-moving middle-aged man with moist eyes and a mouth like a prune pit was hesitating, looking at her; Lilya had seen a Museum of Modern Art Film Retrospective of *Films of Depravity* in 1966; the persistent image of Peter Lorre as "M" kept oozing into her mind; this was probably an out-of-town rapist. She'd been staring right at him: *probably in another second he'll make the pass; I can always spot them, yechh; why me? Why always*

*me? If I ride in a car with someone down the Major Dee-
gan Expressway, they always yell, hey looka that, and I
always look and it's always a legless cripple or some drunk
lady whose thing is collecting cardboard flats what it is
she's puking into a litter basket, or a cat run over across
the head by a sanitation truck. Why always me? A flasher,
this one is. I can tell. Runs around in the park with nothing on but a long overcoat and pants cut off below the
knees and tied with twine. A freako-devo-pervo, I can always yechhh spot! Stands on the BMT platform, just before the doors close, zing! he flashes!*

Lilya stiffened her face, let her gaze slide past him,
turned her back, but not so rapidly as to appear really,
like rude. She gasped as the old man tottered, wheezed,
lunged past her, hand outstretched for the door of the
hole-in-corner public house next to the prosthetics display.
A gush of beer-laden air, the door closed behind him.
Lilya jerked as though struck by a wetmop. Her eyes fell
on the clock. Twelve minutes late. She'd give him exactly
two more minutes, or possibly five, that would make it
four-thirty on the nose, and besides you couldn't expect
her to climb over that flying crocodile, which somebody
ought to call the zoo and tell them a few things about letting the inmates go falling all over the street.

Will Kiley decided he'd had quite enough morphology
of flying reptiles for one day. The parcel beneath his arm
grew warm even as he thought of it. Within the parcel:
Rolling Sin House, a novel dealing with six young prosti-
tutes who buy a house trailer and flout the laws of inter-
state commerce; *Lust Whip Madam,* a stinging tale of cru-
elty and unbridled passions among the silken-limbed houris
of the bondage set, locale Scarsdale; *Teeny Slut,* an adventure into the sexual psychology of the amoral young.
These three, and a seventeen-picture set of maybe a Ros-
ita or Consuelo or Guadalupe (he would settle for a Do-
lores), were the spurs to his rapidly returning uptown to a
student-dingy room.

He started past the head of the beast, when he saw the
edge of the artifact hanging from its neck. It seemed to be
a large golden disc, hanging from a thick link chain. Will
Kiley's instant thoughts were not of rich rewards from the
archeological society. They were of ready cash for old

gold in any one of the Second Avenue antique shops. Ready cash that could buy important things like regular meals, more books, possibly even a young woman's affections. (Will Kiley, having emerged from a cocoon of poverty spun about him by his parents in Three Bridges, New Jersey, was inclined to accept the philosophy that money may not be the only thing in life, but the *other* thing won't go out with you if you don't have it.)

He jammed the package of stiffeners into his jacket pocket, and began hauling at the golden chain, in an attempt—hearty but hardly surreptitious—to get the disc off the dead pteranodon.

From a doorway across Sixth Avenue, a group of youths belonging to a Bronx-based organization titled The Pelham Privateers—what in days of pre-protest picketing would have been called a juvenile delinquent gang, now referred to as "a minority youth group"—observed Will Kiley's struggles, and continued their own observations.

"But it don't look like it *got* hubcaps," Angie said.

"Hey, *shtoomie*, if it is lyin' inna street, it is gotta have hubcaps. The question's where?" The gang's leader, George ("The Pot") Lukovich dealt with matters in a realistic fashion.

"Maybe they're *unnerneat*,'" suggested Vimmy.

"Could be," George mused, "could very well be."

He pondered a moment longer, then made his mind and the gang's collective mind, up. "We gotta jack up its ass. Get unnerneat'. Get the hubcaps off. Vimmy, I want you should take t'ree boys and go over to the building they're building onna corner Madison an' 48th. Steal a pneumatic hoist or somethin'."

Vimmy gave a quick one-finger salute, and dodged out of the doorway, tapping three of the gang members on their chests as he passed them. They followed, at a dead run.

A hook and ladder approaching from the direction of Fifth Avenue swerved to avoid the quartet and skidded to a halt in the lee of the dead ornithosaurian. Big Louis Morono, wearing a Texaco hat and black rubber boots and slicker, leaped down, dragging a foot-long brass nozzle trailing a flat gray constrictor of hose. Assessing the situation at a glance, he set off at a heavy-footed trot toward the stern of the beast, assisted by fellow fire fighters each supporting his half dozen yards of tubing. A second team launched itself with silent efficiency in the opposite direction, toward the giant maloccluded jaws. They rounded the head, continued parallel with the scaly neck, paused only momentarily before trampling ahead across the leather carpet of the wing. They met Big Louis and his crew at a point abaft the fourth thoracic vertabra.

"Anything?"

"Nothing."

"Smoke?"

"Not a wisp."

Big Louis sighed. His hose drooped. "It figures."

"Yeah."

"Okay, boys, reel it in." Muttering, Big Louis headed back for the trembling truck. Before he had taken more than three steps, however, one of the members of the second team yelled, "Hey, Cap! It's a, uh, you know what, a dragon. Maybe it breathes fire. Could be, y'know!"

Big Louis stopped dead and smiled a winsome smile. "Reel it out again, men!" he shouted.

As Will Kiley struggled manfully with the golden chain and its golden disc, two rumpled figures wearing thick glasses paused beside him. They ignored him, but pointed frequently at the head of the dead beast:

"The chief difference in the pterodactyl skull from that of a bird is in the way in which the malar arch is prolonged backward on each side," said the first.

"The nostrils are unusually large. Could it be Dimorphodon?" asked the second.

"Don't be a silly goose, Trenchard," replied the first. "Doesn't even resemble."

Trenchard's eyes flashed anger and his mouth tightened. "Damn's blood, Goilvey! You were the one who said this genus shouldn't be this heavy. You were the one who dragged me out of the Automat, leaving a perfectly good fish cake, just to come down here and argue about this. *I* don't know why it's so big, and *I* don't know why it's so heavy . . . all *I* know is that I don't like you talking to me so snottily. Your seniority in the department doesn't give you the right to . . ."

A civil rights group, attracted by the noise, abandoned

their labors integrating a parking lot, and instantly inter-
preting what was going on there in the intersection,
whipped out magic markers and fresh cardboard, and re-
jingo'd their slogans. They began parading around and
around the dead beast, bearing signs that read HE DIED
FOR US! and DON'T LET THIS DEATH GO
UNAVENGED! and SOCIETY ASKS: WHY?

"Looks dead to me," murmured a secretary, walking to
Sak's with a girl friend.

"Remind me to make an appointment with my orthodontist," her friend replied.

A representative of the sanitation workers union—summoned by enraged members of his local—arrived on the
scene, and uttered a snarl. "Like hell we will!" he commented to the members of the press. "It'll lay there till
hell freezes over! If the corrupt and Commie-Symp government of this city thinks it is going to fatten and batten
on the blood and sweat and tears of the members of the
United Sanitation Workers of America Local #337, it has
another think coming. The name is Fortnoy. F-O-R-T . . ."

The two CIA men ran out of film. One's tie-tack
camera clicked on empty spools, and the others mini-cord-
er in his hatband whirred emptily. They met at mid-
pteranodon and compared notes:

"Maoist?"

"Doubtful. Castroite?"

"Maybe. Reach the office yet?"

"No, something's wonking up the circuits."

"Jamming?"

"Maybe. Maoist?"

"Doubtful. Russkie?"

"Maybe . . ."

Kiley pulled and strained at the disc, trying to drag it
out from under the great head. He was making some
small headway when a photographer and three models and
the director of fashion for a leading women's magazine
nudged him aside, and began posing the girls on the head
of the dead beast.

"Look anguished, Maddie," said the photographer, a
slim and ascetic young man wearing an Australian digger
hat in white velour. The model looked anguished. "No, no,
more anguished. Cry for the entire world, sweetheart!"

Maddie anguished harder. She cried. "Now tilt the pelvis just a tiddle forward, darling," the photographer urged. "Let's transmute that anguish into a starchy impudence at the really *tasty* things the season's culottes have to say to the New Female!"

"Off duty," said a cabbie, streaking down around a wing-tip and plunging up the Avenue.

Somewhere children were laughing and the wind was sweet with the scent of imminent Summer. But that was somewhere else.

"Jesus, I can't stand the stink!" shouted a woman from the seventh floor window of an employment agency.

Seventeen sailors from a Japanese freighter, in New York on three-day leave, crouched near the juncture of wing and torso, and snapped pictures of the dead beast with Leicas, several murmuring words that sounded like, "Rodan." No one paid them any heed.

Several handbills were hastily pasted onto the leathery hide, announcing the candidacy of Roger Scarpennetti for Borough President.

A vendor of socks (seconds) pitched his way from tail to beak, and made almost four dollars with his wares.

Three agile and rolling-gaited Caughnawaga Indians, those last noble descendants of the noblest of noble savages, crossed 48th Street heading downtown. They carried lunch pails. They were on their way home by IRT subway (which they would catch at 42nd & Times Square) from the building site construction on Madison and 48th; the selfsame construction site toward which four Pelham Privateers (behind the point-scouting of the redoubtable Vimmy) at this moment were streaking. The three redskins, high-steel workers of the most loftily-paid species, paused at the corner of 47th and Sixth, shifted lunch pails, and clucked their tongues almost in unison.

"Is that crummy, I ask you!" said Walter Knife-That-Gleams-In-Starlight.

"Yeah, first they zap alla the buffalo, bison, whatever the hell they was that they did in, and now this!" The lament was voiced by Teddy Bearclaw.

"Goddam white-eyes," added Sidney G. Nine Fires.

"Red man's burden," said Walter.

"Is it not a sad pass what our people has come to, that

we must erect for these shitty crummy pony soldiers a edifice of such nobility as we are at this precise moment in time erecting," penultimated Teddy.

"What the hell is a bison?" asked Sidney G. Nine Fires. Mutual shrugs of confusion led to a prompt exit.

The Reverend Leroy L. Beal, arriving at the head of the Poke County, Mississippi, delegation to the First Annual Congress of the International Evangelical Brotherhood for the Promotion of Christian Love and Low Down Payments, paused, waving his flock to a halt, shaking his head sadly at the vast obstruction blocking the intersection ahead. His second-in-command moved up beside him. Together, they studied the cumpled, strutted, awning-winged apparition filling the street.

"Well, Leroy, what do you make of it?" the lieutenant inquired.

Rev. Beal sighed. "The expenditure of funds and ingenuity that went into constructing this hoax and placing it in our line of march could have supported three indigent families in fair comfort for a period of at least two months," he stated.

The two men advanced; Rev Beal poked at the leathery hide with a finger.

"Plastic," he said. "A transparent fraud."

"As I see it, Leroy, they intended to suspend the thing from wires and have it buzz us. But apparently the wires broke."

"Obviously. Tsk. Sometimes I wonder at the curious picture the opposition seems to entertain of our gullibility. First the whole thing with the sheets over their heads; now this: big racist rubber chickens."

"So—what do we do?"

"We make ourselves comfortable," The Reverend said. "And wait."

As the strains of *We Shall Overcome* rose on the afternoon air, a party of lobbyists for the All-American Society for the Preservation of Property Values (ASPPV) emerged from the gloom of Reilly's Bar and Grille, summoned by the mingled cries of the wounded, the chatter of the spectators, and the exhortations of the cop, still in search of a recipient for the summons. The group blinked at the scene, noting the size and placement of the reptile with eyes accustomed to lightning assessment.

"By George, Charlie," the head lobbyist said, around a cigar, "you couldn't replace that thing for under twenty-eight-five or I'm a baboon's nephew."

Charlie was staring at the singers grouped by the monster's stern.

"Tell *me* there's no Commie money behind them Nigras," he murmured.

Lilya looked at her watch for the thirty-first time. Ten more minutes and not a second more, and then by God she'd take a cab to Schrafft's and order the expensivist item on the menu and if that skin-disease Melville ever dared to show that collection of acne scars he called a face again—

"Sorry, lady," the man with the leather jacket said, not looking at Lilya as he bellied her aside. He planted his feet and looked the project over, from beak to tail-tip and back to beak.

"Hey, Jake," a wiry man in overalls said. "You want I should get the rig in position?"

"Nix," Jake said succinctly.

"Right," the wiry man said. "This is outta our line—"

Jake whirled and grabbed a handful of the wiry man's overall bib.

"There ain't no wrecking job Ajax Wrecking can't handle and doncha forget it," he growled. "Hold the headache ball. Tell the boys to break out the chain saws."

"Sure, Jake. Only you got aholt of the hair on my chest—"

"Twenny minutes, that's what the dude said. I don't want to see nothing but hip pockets and elbows until we get this intersection clear, get me?"

A husband and wife team, tourists from Joplin, Missouri, making one of their rare p.a.'s in the Apple, stood near the forearm and metacarpus of the dead beast, the husband setting the automatic timer on his camera. Then he strolled nonchalantly to his spouse (indicating his ease and familiarity with matters photographic), struck an attitude, and waited, smiling, till the camera had clicked them off. "Do we have time to make it down to the Village for some shots with hippies, before dinner?" the wife asked.

Her husband's answer was lost on the wind as the mayor's helicopter settled in the center of Sixth Avenue, just above 47th Street.

The riot police jog-trotted around the corner of '48th and Sixth and began breaking up into assault teams.

"Careful of that Mace!" Captain Schirmer bellowed through the bullhorn. Snipers in office windows began firing at streetlights. "All right, move it out!" shouted Captain Schirmer. The first wave of riot police lobbed their tear gas grenades, and began spraying high pressure hoses down the Avenue. The rabbinical students fled, still uncertain whether the pteranodon was kosher or *trayfe*—but dead certain the eggs were edible if the proper *bruchah* was said over them. The rescue squads pulled the last of the survivors out from under the dead beast, and carried them away from the line of combat.

Kiley was trapped at the neck of the creature, still trying to yank loose the garden amulet. He was cut off from escape by the insurrecting Columbia Law students and Black Panther Freedom Party members on the eastern flank, by the riot police using Mace and lead-weighted truncheons on the west, by the roughneck warriors of the Ajax Wrecking Corporation (all ex-Seabees) on the North, and by the advancing wave of members of the Amalgamated Butchers and Meat Hackers Local #39 on the South. He crouched down, hoping to go unseen, and continued yanking at the circle of gold.

More police on horseback clogged the scene, trying to aid their beat partner in establishing to whom the corpse in the street belonged. The ticket was written, it merely needed to be served.

Three hookers began working the uptown side of 47th Street, hoping some of the show biz crowd would stick to their fingers, or other portions of their anatomy.

"Oh!" cried Alice, awakening, "apparently it is all a dream!"

"You're under arrest," said the cop with the ticket, to no one in particular. He said it again, softer, but no one paid any attention.

Lilya curse/wished plagues on gnats and nits on the acne-pocked head of Melville, and stalked off down the Avenue, passing the hip-girdle of the pteranodon, failing to look down where she would have seen her much-cursed Melville, much more crushed than cursed.

Near the hind limbs of the dead beast (what George "The Pot" Lukovich would have referred to as the ass-end), twelve members of The Pelham Privateers now worked diligently trying to get the beast erect so its hub-caps could be stolen. The pneumatic jacks they had installed merely sank into the flesh of the beast.

Big Louis Morono, seeing the gang at work, whistled up his men, and using the high pressure hoses, drove the juvies from the scene.

It is at this point that the two collaborators, Messrs. Laumer and Ellison, part company in their estimation of what the attached story should be. Having worked together with skill and amicable verve for the first 4000 words, they felt that the creative ardor of nei-their should be dampened by either's attempts to steer the story in a concluding direction offensive to the other. Therefore, the authors offer 2 COMPLETE ENDINGS 2. Count 'em! 2 for the price of one. First, Ellison. Second, Laumer.

Proceed...........

Ending the First

Even as they fled, the Pelham Privateers indicated their frustration at having been thwarted. They mugged Trenchard and Goilvey where they stood, leaving the two tottering scientists even more tottered: face-down in the gutter, arguing through split lips and cracked teeth, "It's too big to be a pterodactyl from our past ... it *has* to be from the past, you twit ... no, it's from another planet ... don't be an ass, they don't have pterodactyls on any planet in our solar system ... so it came from another solar system ... how did it get here ... that's not my problem ..."

Will Kiley struggled with the golden amulet.

And at that precise moment, the parallel worlds, having reached the apogee of their pendulum swings, and having started back toward the point at which they touched originally (for the first time in fifty-six years), met ... perigee ... merged ...

And Will Kiley, tightly attached to the focal point of the two world's merging—the golden amulet—found himself poof!

Gone. Vanished.

In the intersection of Sixth Avenue and 47th Street, the mob was cleared away, and the Ajax Wreckers joined with their working-class comrades of the Amalgamated Butchers and Meat Hackers Local #39, to rid the streets of the unsightly corpse of a flying reptile that had dropped from no one knew where ... and no one seemed to very much care ...

Meanwhile, back at the tangential meeting-place of the parallel worlds ...

Very much like a dead ibari, the man fell out of the sky at X.O. + 19 of a Bluemorn, fell howling, arms and legs all a-tumble, landing squarely in the moss-and-metal center of the Religious Icon of Nerf, in Avuncular Square.

Two leathery-winged residents flapped over to the gigantic creature, and stared at it.

"Did it fly?" said the first, scratching its osseous crest with a wingtip finger. "Or did it merely fall?"

"Big, isn't it?" commented the second. "Much bigger than whatchamacallit, *men*, are supposed to be. And heavier. I wonder, is it edible?"

"Ah-ha, not is it *edible*," interjected one of the dietary priests of Nerf, "but is it *hazzil!* That's the question!"

"It *looks* hazzil."

"The eyes are blue, that means it can't be *hazzil!*"

A Proctor descended on the scene and extracted its demerit book from its wingtip-pouch with the fingertip of its other wing. "Okay, who owns this myth?"

"What's a *Teeny Slut?*" asked the dietary priest of Nerf.

But no one seemed to know.

And no one seemed to very much care ...

THE END
(maybe)

And Now, Go on to the Senses-Shattering 2nd Ending by Keith Laumer

Ending the Second

The Vice-President in charge of Enforcement for the meat cutters confronted Jake, Ajax Wreckers' ace field man, as the latter tugged at a twenty-foot length of amputated pterodactyl skin.

"Hey," he barked over the stutter of the chain saws chopping through the lobster-like flesh. "You guys are doing our work!"

Jake dropped the leg, causing a gush of blood like drained oil to miosten the shoe-tops of the union man. He took a step toward the challenger, pushed his large, broken-veined, fist-scarred, unevenly shaved face forward.

"Oh, yeah?" he riposted.

As they stood nose to nose, their followers gathered behind them. A chain saw barked and sputtered, lugging down on bone. More large men appeared. The lines formed up across the slope of the pteranodon's keel. An advance scout from the Black Panthers sidled up to a dark-skinned butcher who stood glowering at a similarly pigmented wrecker.

"Hey, baby," he protested. "Let's not waste no horse-power on internecine strife. Let's get Honky!"

"Now, boys," the Rev. Beal interrupted.

"Who you calling 'boy,' Uncle Tom?" the Black Panther inquired threateningly. He gave the small, neatly suited ecclesiast a push with a hangnailed forefinger. Charles W

Throckwall of the ASPPV noted the interchange from the corner of his eye.

"See here, fellow," he blurted. "That's a man of the cloth you're pushing—"

"Stop, thief!" a skinny female in a fantastic hat yelled. Will Kiley, bounding pop-shopward with the golden amulet, skidded on the oily blood and caromed into Throckwall, who rebounded in what appeared to be a leap toward the Panther. The latter withdrew for reinforcements, jostling a meatcutter. The meatcutter threw the unfortunate chap at Jake, who replied by placing two short jabs in the lower belt region of the policeman just as the uniformed minion thrust the summons at him. Whistles sounded the charge. Union men slugged it out with wreckers and militant sociologists. Christians and Realtors battled side by side. Big Louis Morono played his hoses over all parties without discrimination due to race, creed, or national origin.

"By George, Charlie," the real estate lobby chief called to his aide. "Maybe we'd better rethink our program. They've got quite a body of public opinion on their side, it appears!"

"We can't fight this kind of organization," Charlie agreed. "We better pull back and regroup."

"Leroy," the Rev. Beal's lieutenant shouted in his leader's ear. "Possibly we misjudged the magnitude of the backlash—"

"Hey, boss," Jake's aide cried over the tumult. "We only got ten minutes to finish the job, which Ajax's rep is riding on the outcome!"

Jake grunted and strained chest to chest with the union Enforcer.

"Deal?" he muttered tentatively.

"How's about if your boys do the primary breakdown and my guys take it from there? And kind of get your thumb outta my eye, OK?"

"Check. And my groin ain't a place for you to store our knee when you ain't using it, right?"

The two fighters for economic justice disengaged, and with hoarse bellows summoned their followers. In moments, the saws were stuttering through tendon and gristle, while cleavers flashed, separating radii from ulnae.

Caught up in the mood of the moment, the riot cops, who had been delayed in their arrival at that end of the beast by a call for help from the beat cop, and who had paused to lend a hand in getting the cuffs on Kiley, formed a bucketless bucket brigade, passing along the assorted chunks of anatomy as they were freed from the carcass. Thirty seconds before the deadline, the last slab of reptile disappeared into the chippers. The firemen hosed down the pavement. The crowd disappeared into the places crowds disappear into. In the bars, beer flowed. Sirens wailed as firemen and peace officers returned to interrupted pinochle games. A single scrap of pteranodon hide, overlooked by the flensers, floated along the gutter and disappeared down the storm drain, where, due to a curious concatenation of circumstances, it eventually lodged in an orifice serving a large department store, resulting in the simultaneous overflow of the third floor pay toilets.

Two newsmen, having been torn away from a fruitless assignment emanating from the City Desk whereat an anonymous phone call had narked that Senator Seymour F. Lark (R., Vermont) (he who had been accused by Senate Subcommittee of squirreling away a quarter of a million skins in monies allegedly originally contributed to his campaign re-election exchequer) was lying doggo in the apartment of a lady of shady reputation, just off Sixth Avenue at 46th Street, came upon the recent scene of so much reptilian-oriented turmoil, and encountered little more than moist patches of concrete and a few spots where the acid in the blood of the now-vanished pteranodon had managed to eradicate the lane stripes of Sixth Avenue.

"Another dry run," Ollie, the taller scrivener stated glumly.

"Uh-huh, Stanley," the fat one said.

"Hey, Madame," the tall one accosted a matron in man's sweater and run over shoes. "You see anything of giant reptile around here?"

"I don't know nothing," the interogee replied, and continued her bee-line for the copy of the *National Enquirer* she had spotted in the litter basket. The other pedestrian who had begun to clot at the prospect of a lively interchange, drifted unobtrusively away, scenting official int est in their affairs. The newsmen shrugged and disappeared into a bar. Traffic resumed its normal flow. The sun shone on a peaceful street. The Governor's car paused at the intersection. His Governorship scanned the prospect, saw nothing amiss, and relaxed against the forty-dollar-a-yard upholstery.

"Peace," he said. "It's wonderful."

At that moment a black speck appeared in the patch of sky visible between the serried cornices above. It grew, became a ragged bird-shape, tumbling end-over-end, whistling . . .

With a resounding splat, a second pteranodon impacted in the street.

FINIS

Roger Zelazny and Harlan Ellison

COME TO ME
NOT
IN
WINTER'S WHITE

INTRODUCTION

Working with Roger Zelazny on this story was one of the easiest, most pleasurable work-experiences I've had in many years. It was a cross-country collaboration, with Roger starting the story, writing through to the paragraph whose last line is *Still he worked to slow her room even more,* and then mailing the pages to me. He did not indicate where or how he thought the story should go, as he had assumed the role of picking the game, and it was my job to set the rules.

In collaborations of this sort, I've found, the opening sets the tone and the major characters and indicates the area in which the work will be done. That is roughly 1000 words. In the second thousand the direction of the plot and the initial complications should emerge; in the third thousand the complications should intensify, the characterization should solidify and the solutions should be indicated, however minutely. The final thousand words or so of a short story of this kind are the summing-up and solving areas. It worked just that way with "Winter's White."

In my thousand words, from *"Mister Manos, your bill is now two hundred thousand dollars a week"* to *And he left them together,* I set up the basic situation that Roger would intensify in the following section.

He wrote from *"Do you know Neruda?"* to *he knew pain once more.* I finished the story.

There was virtually no rewrite. I went over it once, after it was finished, to smooth some awkwardnesses we'd encountered in the mails, and then it went off to be published.

I am very proud of this story. Silverberg contends it's mawkish, and a fan writer said it was the worst of both Zelazny and Ellison, and as far as I'm concerned they can both go jump, where this story is concerned. Because, in a career lifetime of writing violent and frequently loveless fictions, this is one of the few times I feel my work has reached toward gentleness and compassion, and I don't think I would have been able to do anything even remotely like it, had it not been for Roger. It also introduced *me* to the writings of Pablo Neruda, and if I'd been enriched no further, it would all have been worth it.

For that is the chief benefit of collaboration, for a writer. He learns. As I have learned from each of these men. And now that the book is finished, I can say with a humility quite foreign to me . . .

Thank you, gentlemen.

Come to Me Not in Winter's White

She was dying and he was the richest man in the world, but he couldn't buy her life. So he did the next best thing. He built *the* house, different from any other house that had ever been. She was transported to it by ambulance, and their goods and furnishings followed in many vans.

They had been married little over a year; then she had been stricken. The specialists shook their heads and named a new disease after her. They gave her six-months-to-a year; then they departed, leaving behind them prescriptions and the smell of antiseptics. But he was not defeated. Nothing as commonplace as death could defeat him.

For he was the greatest physicist ever employed by AT&T in the year of Our Lord and President Farrar, nineteen hundred and ninety-eight.

(When one is incalculably wealthy from birth, one feels a sense of one's own personal unworthiness; so having been denied the joys of grueling labor and abject poverty, he had labored over himself. He had made of himself one who was incalculably worthy—the greatest physicist the world had ever known. It was enough for him ... until he had met her. Then he wanted much more.)

He didn't *have* to work for AT&T, but he enjoyed it. They allowed him the use of their immense research facilities to explore his favorite area—Time, and the waning thereof.

He knew more about the nature of Time than any other human being who had ever lived.

It might be said that Carl Manos was Chronos/Ops/Saturn/Father Time himself, for he fitted even the description with his long dark beard and his slashing, scythe-like walking-stick. He knew Time as no other man had ever known it, and he had the power and the will and the love to exploit it.

How?

Well, there was the house. He'd designed it himself. Had it built in less than six weeks, settling a strike by himself to insure its completion on time.

What was so special about the house?

It had a room; a room like no other room that had ever existed, anywhere.

In this room, Time ignored the laws of Albert Einstein and obeyed those of Carl Manos.

What were those laws and what was this room?

To reverse the order of the questions, the room was the bedroom of his beloved Laura, who had *Lora Manosism*, an affliction of the central nervous system, named after her. The disease was monstrously degenerative; four months after diagnosis, she would be a basket case. Five months—blind, incapable of speech. Six-months-to-a-year—dead. She dwelled in the bedroom that Time feared to enter. She *lived* there while he worked and fought for her. This was because, for every year that passed outside the room, only a week went by within. Carl had so ordained it, and it cost him eighty-five thousand dollars a week to maintain the equipment that made it so. He would see her live and be cured, no matter what the cost, though his beard changed its appearance with each week that passed for her. He hired specialists, endowed a foundation to work on her cure; and every day, he grew a trifle older. Although she had been ten years his junior, the gap was rapidly widened. Still he worked to slow her room even more.

"Mister Manos, your bill is now two hundred thousand dollars a week."

"I'll pay it," he told the power & light people, and did. It was now down to three days for every year.

And he would enter her room and speak with her.

"Today is July ninth," he said. "When I leave in the morning it will be around Christmastime. How do you feel?"

"Short of breath," she replied. "What do the doctors tell you?"

"Nothing, yet," he said. "They're working on your problem, but there's no answer in sight."

"I didn't think so. I don't think there ever will be."

"Don't be fatalistic, love. If there's a problem, there's an answer—and there's plenty of time. All the time in the world . . ."

"Did you bring me a newspaper?"

"Yes. This will keep you caught up. There's been a quick war in Africa, and a new presidential candidate has come onto the scene."

"Please love me."

"I do."

"No, I know that. *Make* love to me."

They smiled at her fear of certain words, and then he undressed and made love to her.

Then, after, there came a moment of truth, and he said, "Laura, I have to tell you the way it is. We're nowhere yet, but I have the best neurological minds in the world working on your problem. There's been one other case like yours since I locked you away—that is, since you came to stay here—and he's dead already. But they have learned something from him and they will continue to learn. I've brought you a new medicine."

"Will we spend Christmas together?" she asked.

"If you wish."

"So be it."

And so it was.

He came to her at Christmastime, and together they decorated the tree and opened presents.

"Hell of a Christmas with no snow," she said.

"Such language—and from a lady!"

But he brought her snow and a Yule log and his love.

"I'm awful," she said. "I can't stand myself sometimes. You're doing everything you can and nothing happens, so I harass you. I'm sorry."

She was five feet seven inches in height and had black hair. Black? So black as to be almost blue, and her lips

PARTNERS IN WONDER

were a pink and very special pair of cold shell-coral things. Her eyes were a kind of dusk where there are no clouds and the day sets off the blue with its going. Her hands shook whenever she gestured, which was seldom.

"Laura," he told her, "even as we sit here, they work. The answer, the cure, will come to pass—in time."

"I know."

"You wonder, though, whether it will be time enough. It will. You're virtually standing still while everything outside races by. Don't worry. Rest easy. I'll bring you back."

"I know that," she said. "It's just that I sometimes—despair."

"Don't."

"I can't help it."

"I know more about Time than anybody else . . . You've got it: on your side."

He swung his stick like a saber, beheading roses that grew about the wall. "We can take a century," he said, quickly, as though loath to lose even a moment, "without your being harmed. We can wait on the answer that has to come. Sooner or later, there *will* be an answer. If I go away for a few months, it will be as a day to you. Don't worry. I'll see you cured and we'll be together again in a brighter day—for God sake don't worry! You know what they told you about psychosomatic conversions!"

"Yes, I shouldn't have one."

"Then don't. There are even other tricks I will be able to play with Time, as it goes on—such as freezing. You'll come out okay, believe me."

"Yes," she said, raising her glass of Irish Mist. "Merry Christmas."

"Merry Christmas!"

But even for a man who has been thought incalculably wealthy, lack of attention to compounding that wealth, monomaniacal ferocity in pursuing a goal, and a constant, heavy drain, inevitably the end comes in sight. Though the view to that end was a long look, though there were more years that could be put to use, even so it became obvious to everyone around him that Carl Manos had committed himself to a crusade that would end in his destruction. At least financially. And for them, that was the worst sort of destruction. For they had not lived in the thoughts of

Manos, were unaware that there were other, far more ex-acting destructions.

He came to her in the early summer, and he brought a recording of zarzuela love duets by de la Cruz, Hidalgo Bréton. They sat beside each other, their hands touching, and they listened to the voices of others who were in love, all through July and August. He only sensed her restless-ness as August drew to a close and the recording shusssed into silence.

"What?" he asked, softly.

"It's nothing. Nothing, really."

"Tell me."

She spoke, then, of loneliness.

And condemned herself with more words; for her ingratitude, her thoughtlessness, her lack of patience. He kissed her gently, and told her he would do something about it.

When he left the room, the first chill of September was in that corner of the world. But he set about finding a way to stave off her loneliness. He thought first of himself liv-ing in the room, of conducting his experiments in the room without Time. But that was unfeasible, for many reasons—most of them dealing with Time. And he needed a great deal of space to conduct the experiments: building additions to the room was impossible. He could see, him-self, that there would not be sufficient funds to expand the experiment.

So he did the next best thing.

He had his Foundation scour the world for a suitable companion. After three months they submitted a list of potentials to him. There were two. Only two.

The first was a handsome young man named Thomas Grindell, a bright and witty man who spoke seven lan-guages fluently, had written a perceptive history of man-kind, had traveled widely, was outspoken and in every other possible way was the perfect companion.

The second was an unattractive woman named Yolande Loeb. She was equally as qualified as Grindell, had been married and divorced, wrote excellent poetry, and had dedicated her life to various social reforms.

Even Carl Manos was not so deeply immersed in his

problem that he could not see the ramifications of possible choice. He discarded the name of Grindell.

To Yolande Loeb he offered the twin lures of extended life and financial compensation sufficient to carry her without worry through three lifetimes. The woman accepted.

Carl Manos took her to the room, and before the door was keyed-open from the control console, he said, "I want her to be happy. To be kept occupied. No matter what she wants, she's to have it. That is all I ask of you."

"I'll do my best, Mr. Manos."

"She's a wonderful person, I'm sure you'll love her."

"I'm sure."

He opened the outer chamber, and they entered. When they had neutralized temporarily, the inner chamber was opened, and he entered with the woman.

"Hello."

Laura's eyes widened when she saw her, but when Carl had told her Miss Loeb had come to keep her company, to be the friend Laura had needed, she smiled and kissed his hand.

"Laura and I will have so much time to get acquainted," Yolande Loeb said, "why don't you spend this time together?" And she took herself to the far corner of the room, to the bookshelf, and pulled down a Dickens to reread.

Laura drew Carl Manos down to her and kissed him. "You are so very good to me."

"Because I love you. It's that simple. I wish *everything* was that simple."

"How is it coming?"

"Slowly. But coming."

She was concerned about him. "You look so tired Carl."

"Weary, not tired. There's a big difference."

"You've grown older."

"I think the gray in my beard is very distinguished."

She laughed lightly at that, but he was glad he ha brought Miss Loeb, and not Grindell. Thrown together i a room where Time nearly stood still, for endless montl that would not be months to them, who knew what coul happen? Laura was an extraordinarily beautiful woma

Any man would find himself falling in love with her. But with Miss Loeb as companion—well, it was safe now.

"I have to get back. We're trying some new catalysts today. Or rather, however many days ago it was when I came in here. Take care, darling. I'll be back as soon as I can."

Laura nodded understanding. "Now that I have a friend, it won't be so lonely till you return, dearest."

"Would you like me to bring anything special next time?"

"The sandalwood incense?"

"Of course."

"Now I won't be lonely," she repeated.

"No. I hope not. Thank you."

And he left them together.

"Do you know Neruda?" Miss Loeb asked.

"Pardon me?"

"The Chilean poet? *The Heights of Macchu Picchu?* One of his greatest works?"

"No, I'm afraid that I don't."

"I have it with me. It is a piece of blazing power. There is a certain strength within it, which I thought you—"

"... Might take heart from while contemplating death. No. Thank you, but no. It was bad enough, just thinking about all the things the few people I *have* read have said about life's ending. I am a coward, and I know that one day I will die, as everyone must. Only, in my condition, I have a schedule. *This* happens, then *this* happens, and then it is all over. The only thing between me and death is my husband."

"Mr. Manos is a fine man. He loves you very much."

"Thank you. Yes, I know. So if you wish to console me concerning this, then I am not especially interested."

But Yolande Loeb pursed her lips, touched Laura's shoulder, said, "No. Not consolation. Not at all.

"Courage or faith, perhaps," she said, "but not consolation or resignation," and, " 'Irresistible death invited me many times: / It was like salt occulted in the waves / and what its invisible fragrance suggested / was fragments of wrecks and heights / or vast structures of wind and snow-drift.' "

"What is that?"

"The beginning of Section Four."

Laura dropped her eyes, then said, "Tell me the whole story."

" 'From air to air, like an empty net,' " said Yolande, in her deep, impressive tones, and with a slight accent, " 'dredging through streets and ambient atmosphere, I came / lavish, at autumn's coronation . . .' "

Laura listened, and some variety of truth seemed to be present there.

After a time she reached out and their fingertips touched, gently.

Yolande told her of her girlhood in a *kibbutz*, and of her broken marriage. She told her of her life after that thing, and of the suffering attendant thereto.

Laura cried, hearing of this misery.

She felt badly for days thereafter.

Yet these were not days to Carl Manos, who also had cause to feel badly. He met a girl whose company he enjoyed, until she said that she loved him. He dropped her like poison sumac and hot potatoes. After all, Time—their friend/their enemy—had a deal going with Laura and Carl. There was no room for intruders in this fated *ménage à trois*.

He cursed, paid his bills, and figured ways to make Time even more amenable to his bidding.

But suddenly he was in pain. He knew nothing of Pablo Neruda, or this Pasternak, Lorca, Yevtushenko, Alan Dugan, Yeats, Brooke, Daniels—any of them—and Laura spoke of them constantly these days. As he had no replies for this sort of thing, he just nodded. He kept on nodding. Time after time . . .

"You're happy with the present arrangement?" he finally asked.

"Oh, yes! Of course," she replied. "Yolande is wonderful. I'm so glad that you invited her."

"Good. That's something, anyway."

"What do you mean—?"

"Yolande!" he cried out, suddenly. "How are you?"

Yolande Loeb emerged from the screened-off section

the apartment to which she discreetly retired during his visits. She nodded to him and smiled faintly.

"I am quite well, Mr. Manos. Thank you. And yourself?" There was a brief catch in her voice as she moved toward him, and realizing that her eyes were fixed on his beard, he chuckled within it, saying, "I'm beginning to feel a trifle like a premature patriarch." She smiled, and his tone was light, but he felt pain, again.

"I've brought you some presents," he went on, placing sealtite packages on the table. "The latest art books and tapes, recordings, some excellent film beads, poems which have been judged by the critics to be exceptional."

Both women moved to the table and began running their fingertips down the sealstrips, opening the parcels, thanking him for each item as it was unwrapped, making little noises of pleasure and excitement. As he studied Yolande's swart face, with its upturned nose, numerous moles, small scar upon the brow, and as his eyes moved on to Laura's face, flushed now and smiling—as he stood there, both hands upon his walking-stick, reflecting that it was good to have chosen as he had—something twisted softly within him and he knew pain once more.

At first, he was unable to analyze the feelings. Always, however, they returned to him as accompaniment to his recollection of that tableau: the two of them moving about the package-laden table, leafing through the foilpages of the books, holding the recording cassettes at arm's length the better to study their dimensional-covers, chatting about their new treasures, excluding him.

It was a feeling of separation, resulting in a small loneliness, as well as something else. The two women had a thing in common, a thing which did not exist between Laura and himself. They shared a love for the arts—an area of existence for which he could allow himself little time. And, too, they were together in a war zone—alone in the room with the opponent Time laying siege. It had brought them closer together, sharing the experience of defying death and age. They had this meeting place where he was now a stranger. It was . . .

Jealousy, he decided suddenly; and was quite surprised

by the notion. He was jealous of that which they had come to share. He was shocked at the thought, confused. But then, impressed as he always had been with a sense of personal unworthiness, he recognized it as another evidence of this condition. He then thought to banish the feeling.

But then, there had never been another Laura, or another *ménage* such as this.

Was it guilt that came now in response?

He was not certain.

He coded a fresh cup of coffee, and when it arrived, smiled into the eyes—his own, perhaps—which regarded him through the steam and darkness of its surface. His knowledge of the ancients stopped short with their legends and theories of Time. Chronos, or Time, had been castrated by his son, Zeus. By this—it had been contended—the priests and oracles meant to convey the notion that Time is incapable of bringing forth any new thing, but must ever repeat himself and be satisfied with variations of that which has already been begotten. And that is why he smiled . . .

Was not Laura's disease a new thing come into the world? And was not his mastery of Time now to be the cause of another new thing—its remedy?

Guilt and jealousy alike forgotten, he sipped his coffee, tapping his fingers the while, to the beat of an unheard tune—as the particles and antiparticles danced before him in the chambers—and thus time was kept.

And when, later that evening, the viewer chimed, that evening as he sat there, white-smocked, before the Tachytron, archaic glasses pushed up onto his forehead, cold cup of coffee before him on the console, as he sat looking inside himself, he put aside remembered guilt for a premonition.

The viewer chimed again.

That would be one of the doctors . . . and it was . . .

The results of his latest experiments—rainbow journey where no physicist had ever gone before—had been integrated with the work the doctors had been doing, and his premonition became a hallelujah reality.

He went to tell Laura they had won; went to the room outside which Time lay siege with growing frustration; went to restore the full measure of his love.

Where he found them, making love.

Alone, outside the room where Time now waited smugly, savoring the taste of victory finally, Carl Manos lived more lifetimes than *any* special room could hoard. There had been no scene, save in the tortured silences. There had been no words, save in the linear impressions of three who were surrounded by all that had happened in that room, locked invisibly in the walls.

They wanted to stay together, of course. He had not needed to ask that. Alone together in the timeless room where they had found love, the room Carl Manos could never again enter. He still loved her, that could never be changed. And so, he had only two choices.

He could work for the rest of his unworthy life, to pay for the power to keep the room functioning. Or he could turn it off. To turn it off he would have to wait. Wait for Time the Victor to turn his all-consuming love into a kind of hate that would compel him to stop the room's functions.

He did neither. Having only two choices, he took a third course, a choice he did not have, had never had.

He moved to the console and did what had to be done, to *speed up* Time in the room. Even Time would die in that room, now. Then, unworthy, he went away.

Yolande sat reading. Neruda, again. How she always came back to him!

On the bed, what had been Laura lay decomposing. Time, unaware that all, including himself, would be victims, had caught up, had won victory finally.

" 'Come, diminutive life,' " she read, " 'between the wings / of the earth, while you, cold, crystal in the hammered air, / thrusting embattled emeralds apart, / O savage waters, fall from the hems of snow.' "

Love, love, until the night collapses
from the singing Andes flint

down to the dawn's red knees,
come out and contemplate the snow's blind son.

She laid the book in her lap, then sat back in the chair, eyes closed. And for her, the years passed swiftly.